Praise for

Tan Lines

"A really great beach read. I loved it!"

—Jackie Collins

"A Jacqueline Susann–style thriller by way of Candace Bushnell, Salem's scorching debut...throbs with intensity, spiked with erotic detail."

—*Publishers Weekly*

"Summer's hot read will be this sexed-up novel... Smut from the gut." —Cindy Adams, *New York Post*

"Nothing less than the beach read of the summer, perhaps the decade." · —Michelle Buonfiglio, MyLifetime.com

"WARNING: J. J. Salem's *Tan Lines* burns on every page. With a scorching mix of scandal, sex, and murder, this deliciously bitchy beach read really brings the heat." —Lisa Jackson, #1 *New York Times* bestselling author of *Fatal Burn* and *Shiver*

"Even Jacqueline Susann would be shocked! Incendiary and captivating, J. J. Salem has found a literary voice that is one part *Valley of the Dolls*, one part *Sex and the City*, and one part pure grit. *Tan Lines* engages you with complex issues of femininity, sex, and control embodied by three strong female characters who ultimately yearn for freedom."

—Barbara Seaman, author of
Lovely Me: The Life of Jacqueline Susann

"Sexy beach trash of the highest order." —*Elle* (UK)

Tan Lines

J. J. SALEM

St. Martin's Paperbacks

This is a work of fiction. All of the characters, organizations, and events portrayed in this novel are either products of the author's imagination or are used fictitiously.

TAN LINES

Copyright © 2008 by J. J. Salem.
Excerpt from *The Strip* copyright © 2009 by J. J. Salem.

Cover photograph © Shirley Green

For information address St. Martin's Press, 175 Fifth Avenue, New York, NY 10010.

Library of Congress Catalog Card Number: 2008012871

ISBN: 0-312-55675-6
EAN: 978-0-312-55675-4

Printed in the United States of America

St. Martin's Press hardcover edition / July 2008
St. Martin's Paperbacks edition / May 2009

St. Martin's Paperbacks are published by St. Martin's Press, 175 Fifth Avenue, New York, NY 10010.

10 9 8 7 6 5 4 3 2 1

For Rona Jaffe, Harold Robbins,
Sidney Sheldon, and Jacqueline Susann,
with the hope that all of them are smiling down...

Acknowledgments

First and foremost, special thanks to my agent, Kimberly Whalen of Trident Media Group, the gorgeous she-devil in Chanel who signed me on a two-page premise for this book and championed it from outline to proposal to final manuscript.

Enormous thanks to Jennifer Weis, my brilliant editor, who set me free to craft the novel I've always wanted to write and then offered a penetrating insight that pushed me harder and made the book stronger.

True appreciation for Jackie Collins, my idol extraordinaire, who graciously nudged me in the direction of my new publishing home at St. Martin's Press.

Huge gratitude to the amazing team at SMP—Sally Richardson, Matthew Shear, Jennifer Enderlin, John Murphy, Steve Troha, John Karle, Lisa Senz, Jianna Schroeder, Christina Harcar, Michael Storrings, and quite frankly, *everyone* at the house—not only for the incredible support but for making me feel like a real novelist at last.

Major thanks to my UK publisher, Macmillan, particularly Rebecca Saunders, Stephanie Sweeney, and Emma Giacon (and all those who dished *Tan Lines* at the watercooler). The enthusiasm from "across the pond" has been the stuff of daydreams.

My most sincere thanks to Merrill McKewen for the introduction to Audrey and Phillip Davis, who generously opened up their Hamptons home and their Hamptons lives to give this starry-eyed writer an unforgettable immersion that has been woven into these pages.

A fond shout-out to my number one writing war buddy, Stephanie Bond, who never lost her cheerleader pep for this project and who literally shoved me into the path of the agent who made everything happen.

And finally, my deepest love to Jim and Donna Salem, great parents, and even better, great friends . . .

Prologue

Page Six sizzled with hot items about a grisly murder, a premature birth, and a public meltdown.

Faye Hudson of North Bay Lane in East Hampton devoured the main gossip headlines, amazed that all of them involved the three girls who signed last year's summer share lease on the very property she called home nine months of the year.

Liza Pike, Kellyanne Downey, and Billie Shelton.

Faye rarely remembered the young singles who made their invasion of the Hamptons a summer ritual, hitting the streets and beaches like locusts on crops. Year after year, a new set would come and go. The names and faces were sketchy, as the previous season's residents often blurred into the next. Usually, they were just cash to her, a way to finance her decadent summers in the south of France. But this last group had been different. Sin by sin, their sordid lives were played out in the traditional columns and online gossip sites. Scandal. It seemed to be the new generation's proof of life.

Tossing the *New York Post* aside, Faye pushed through the French doors and stepped out onto the balcony. She would read the rest later. The sun shone a bright, mellow glow, every Hollywood lighting director's dream. Eastern Long Island was magical that way.

The clatter of men at work boomed louder and louder from the living room. They were replacing the hardwood floors, stripping the walls, carting away the furniture. Thank God. She could not look at those ghastly bloodstains one more day.

But it would take more than an extreme home makeover to get the place in proper shape for the rental season. Once upon a time, her house had been Pottery Barn perfect. Now she wondered if anyone would show an interest in occupying it this year, even at a drastically cut rate.

These days, her home radiated a certain Amityville quality. People cruised by slowly in their cars, windows down, fingers pointing, no doubt re-creating the brutal scene in their voyeuristic minds. Fifteen stab wounds. And they said she had put up a ferocious fight.

Faye banished the image from her mind as a slight mist began to form in her eyes. The newspaper beckoned. She stepped back inside to consume all the details. It was a heady realization to vividly recall the way those girls had been in the beginning, before everything had gone so wrong. No one ever could have imagined that it would all come down to this.

Suddenly, last summer . . .

Billie

|

There are eight thousand nerve endings in the clitoris, and this son of a bitch couldn't find any of them. Billie Shelton had definitely picked the wrong guy tonight.

It was almost over. She could tell by the rapid breathing and the slight body shudder. Anyone who thought nineteen-year-old boys possessed serious stamina should be introduced to Robbie Shamblin.

"Oh, fuck!"

Billie rolled her eyes. Is that what this was? At least he had the optimism of youth.

Robbie shot a look at the computer monitor, where two cheap blondes with implants and multiple body piercings were getting it on. "Shit, that was awesome." He jumped up and carelessly flung his condom to the floor. Then he sat down and started up a street racing game on Xbox 360.

Billie had been with her share of lame assholes, but this guy was a shoo-in to make her greatest hits list. "Well, I guess we're done here."

Robbie glanced back at her for a fraction of a second, causing his digital Shelby GT500 to skid onto the make-believe sidewalk. "Motherfucker!" He focused on the screen for several long, obsessed seconds. Finally, he spoke. "I could eat you out, if you want. But most girls say I suck at that."

Billie began to search for her clothes. She'd gone for the lean, funny guy on the main stage, the one who'd brought down the house at the Comic Strip. Big mistake.

And right now the choice was slowly killing her. To think she'd opted for this idiot over the hot marine. God, what a waste. The military man would've fucked her all night. And he wouldn't have needed to diddle around with his computer to get hard, either.

That insult bugged her more than the bad sex. Jesus Christ. She was Billie Fucking Shelton, a goddamn indie rock star. But that wasn't enough anymore. Not in the age of Internet porn. Guys had become desensitized by streaming smut on demand. Women today had to compete with super-sluts like Jenna Jameson. And for what? Fifteen minutes of awkward groping followed by a jizz spill? Men were lazy shits.

Billie sat on the edge of the futon and slipped on her shoes. From the TV, engines roared. From the computer, XXX whores moaned. Whatever. Chalk it up to another lost night. It wasn't the first. It wouldn't be the last.

"You heading out?" Robbie asked without so much as a look in her direction.

"Yeah."

"Do me a favor. Knock on the door across the hall and tell my roommate he can come back in."

Billie laughed. At least this loser could make her

do that much. "I haven't heard that kind of shit since college. Is this your apartment or your dorm room?"

"Huh?"

"Forget it," Billie said. Starting out, she went straight for the stairwell, then doubled back to grant Robbie his little favor. Hell, maybe she'd get lucky and end up doing herself one instead. After all, the last place she wanted to go was home. It was still too early. She was still too horny.

A hot guy answered the door. Better face than Robbie's. Better body, too. In the background, another man with a nasty bruise under his eye smoked a joint. He looked like a young Al Pacino from the first *Godfather*.

Without exactly being invited, Billie walked inside. "Your roommate doesn't know how to fuck . . ."

When the telephone blasted her awake hours later, Billie groped for it, if only to stop the shrill ringing from its relentless attack on her brain. "Hello?"

"You sound like shit." It was Amy Dando, her manager.

"I feel like shit. Call me later. I need to sleep."

"There is no later," Amy barked. "We're supposed to be in Todd Bana's office at eleven."

Billie groaned, craning her neck to get a look at the alarm clock. It was almost ten. "I can't. I'm all fucked out. Reschedule."

"No way."

"Come on. Today's not the day. Trust me."

"This is bullshit, Billie. You *need* this meeting. Todd is close to dropping your ass altogether. Just get in the goddamn shower. I'm coming over there." And then Amy hung up.

Billie was dripping wet and staring at herself under the harsh bathroom light when she heard Amy let herself inside her apartment. "I'm up," Billie called out. The reflection in the mirror had startled her. She looked shockingly bad.

Amy appeared in the doorway, very glamour-puss in a jewel-tone satin/chiffon number, a bulky Christian Dior ID bracelet blinging on her slim wrist. "If I had to guess right now, I'd swear you were thirty-eight."

"Fuck you." Billie puckered her lips, dramatically emphasizing her cheekbones. "I don't look that old." She peered closer. "But maybe I should get some injections. You know, Botox. And maybe laser resurfacing for the sun damage. I hear Dr. Parikh at the Tribeca Skin Center is a miracle worker."

"Maybe you should just get some sleep and stop drinking and smoking so much."

Billie rolled her eyes. "Why don't you save the speech and just leave the pamphlet on the coffee table?"

Amy opened up her snakeskin Gucci bag and pulled out a makeup case. "I've got my tools. I'll do what I can. But that hair is your problem."

Billie gave her an up-and-down glance. "You must've seen *Nick* last night."

Amy's face revealed nothing, which revealed a lot. "Why do you say that?"

"Because you always dress extra pretty the day after." Billie started to giggle. "So . . . did he use the strap-on?"

Amy had it bad for a twenty-two-year-old named Nicole. In lesbian culture, Nicole was what they called a *boi*—young, masculine, and ready to party. She worked as a Federal Express courier, took testosterone supplements, and recently spent $7,500 on surgery to remove her breasts.

Billie couldn't keep up. The dyke world was so much more than bad haircuts and box-shaped asses these days. Nicole dressed in NBA jerseys, oversize jeans, and baseball caps flipped to the back, while insisting that everyone call her Nick. And here stood Amy, ridiculously girly and runway stylish, every straight man's fantasy lesbian.

"Your situation with Nicole is so fucked up," Billie said. "Don't ever try to talk about my life."

"Nick," Amy corrected. "And FYI—as your manager, it's my job to talk about your life, especially when it interferes with your work." She sighed and began using a small white sponge to apply foundation to Billie's face. "In a perfect world, this would be a shade lighter."

Billie grinned. "I bet you used to say that to all the girls."

Amy cracked a smile. "It *was* a great way to meet women."

A few years ago, Amy had spent her days as a makeup artist, working the Chanel counter at Bergdorf Goodman on Fifth Avenue. By night, she hit the Manhattan bar scene, trolling for musicians who just might be eager enough to sign a management contract with a novice. Billie was the first to take the leap. Every good firm in the city had already turned her down flat, and Amy was promising to manage Billie's career away from after-midnight acoustic sets in crappy bars.

"So how did you meet this freak anyway?" Billie asked.

"Craigslist," Amy said. "And Nick's not a freak. She's just different."

Billie couldn't believe that classy Amy frequented the online meat market. "*Craigslist?* Seriously?"

"I think her headline read, BOI SEEKS GIRL." Sifting through the makeup bag, Amy smiled at the thought. "There was a photo." She shrugged. "What can I say? I was hooked."

"I don't get it. She had her tits removed, she dresses like a guy, and she uses a strap-on. Why not save yourself the trouble and just find a man?"

"It's not the same," Amy insisted, making two quick sweeps over Billie's eyelids.

"I guess everybody's got their kinks."

"Your skin looks awful," Amy said. "You should go in for one of those lunch-hour chemical peels. I'll set up something with my dermatologist." Amy glanced around the bathroom. "I don't see any skincare products. What are you using these days?"

"Hot white cum," Billie said, trying to keep a straight face but losing the fight. "You should try it sometime."

Amy's mouth tightened. "You've been blessed with beauty and talent, Billie. But you have to nurture those gifts. Otherwise, you'll fuck it all away." As she made her speech, she carefully lined Billie's eyes and lips. "Your hair's a mess, your skin's a wreck, and your body's seen better days." She reached for the underside of Billie's upper arm. "Look at that jiggle. When's the last time you saw the inside of a gym?"

Billie's first internal impulse was to lash out, but something deep inside told her to resist. Amy dished out the tough love for good reasons. At the end of the day, Billie Shelton was a corporation, and Amy Dando owned 20 percent of it. The relationship between artist and manager was intense. It ranked up there with husband, boyfriend, and parents, none of which Billie had presently. Amy was the only person in Billie's life truly looking out for her best interests.

"I've been working," Billie murmured, finally.

"On what?" Amy demanded. "You haven't done any shows. You haven't written any new music."

"I've got some great songs in my head. I just have to get them down on paper."

Amy dipped a skinny brush into a gloss pot and began to paint Billie's lips. "You make me crazy. If you had the killer drive of a Madonna, there's no telling where you'd be today."

"What about my third CD? I worked my ass off to finish it, and Todd's been sitting on those tracks for months."

"The label wants a hit single," Amy said matter-of-factly. "Can you blame them?"

"There were at least—"

"Billie, that album was shit, and you know it. I don't think you spent one sober moment in the studio. Now shut up, so I can finish."

Billie stole a glance in the mirror. Amy was applying an explosive Mardi Gras red, making her lips pop with inevitable sin. They were Billie's best feature. Especially her lower lip. It was naturally, impossibly, decadently plump, with a deep gully carved down the center.

Men loved her mouth. Sometimes she could hear the horny gears churning in their stupid heads as they wondered what it would feel like to have her lips wrapped around their cocks. Onstage she took full advantage of this, practically fellating the microphone. Her fans went wild for it every time. *Christ.* The fucking fans. They conjured up alternate feelings of gratitude and rage.

Billie had left Dartmouth with a degree in government and a six-song demo recorded in the bathroom of her college apartment. The last thing she wanted to do was enroll in law school or work for some tight-ass politician. So she moved to New York and began making the rounds with her music.

In the beginning, she was a walking cliché. Girl with guitar. A Michelle Branch wannabe. A poor man's Jewel. All the rejection had been slow murder on her soul. And she made quite a spectacle of herself at management firms and record labels, telling bitchy receptionists to fuck off and refusing to leave until someone who made decisions turned up to give her a chance.

Luckily, she found Amy before causing this scene at Olympic Records. BMG Entertainment had just acquired it, and the buzz on its founder, Todd Bana, was deafening. He'd gone from producing concerts on his college campus to launching his own independent label with an all-girl punk band called Menstrual Cramps. The group had gone on to sell over a million copies of their first release, *That Time of the Month.* Now Todd was a multimillionaire and the president of a major label. And the bastard wasn't even thirty yet.

The first meeting Amy set up for Billie had been with Todd. He signed her right away, even though he thought her demo was weak. He told her to write songs that would grab listeners by the throat and squeeze hard. She dug deep, and the result was *Dick Magnet,* a crude collection of sexually charged anti-love songs that spoke to men and women of her generation. The breakout track was "Make Me Laugh and Make Me Come and I'll Fucking Marry You." College radio went ballistic. Rock critics went apeshit.

They said that she had more to say than Sheryl Crow, that her vocal chops outranked Alanis Morissette.

Sales were so-so. The CD got halfway to gold, about a quarter of a million copies. But her first tour did boffo business. She sold out small venues and wowed the fans. Word of mouth began to build that Billie Shelton could deliver a live show that kicked ass. A fifteen-date trek became thirty, then sixty. Ultimately, she stayed on the road for more than a year. It was exhilarating. It was exhausting, too.

Touring life could be a real bitch. It was boring, monotonous, and lonely. Musicians put up with so much shit just for that ninety-minute orgiastic rush of performing before a crowd. And it was easy to be seduced into the never-ending rock-and-roll cycle. Getting drunk, getting laid, getting to the next gig.

Billie turned the old double standard upside down. Male rockers who banged every groupie in sight were studs. Well, what was she supposed to do after a show—sit around doing a BLESS THIS HOME cross-stitch? Fuck that. She had groupies, too. College guys. They were young, they were hot, and they made up for a lot of lost time.

In high school, Billie had been the depressed ugly girl with bad skin. Mommy died of ovarian cancer. Daddy killed himself over the loss. She got shipped off to live with a bitchy aunt. But a few years later, Billie blossomed. The acne went away. Once awkward features chiseled into exotic good looks. A new confidence to explore her artistic side materialized. It sounded like a bad Lifetime movie, but it was her fucking life story.

Before the whole rock chick thing, she'd only slept with two guys in her entire life. Now she couldn't even begin to count how many men there'd been. On-line message boards crackled with I-Fucked-Billie-Shelton stories. Of course, most of them were far from the truth. "She gave me a blow job after her show in Birmingham!" But she'd never once set foot in Alabama.

Billie hated the hypocrisy. The way people worried about a woman who went out there and fucked like a man. Nobody speculated that Adam Levine of Maroon 5 had been molested by his Uncle Charlie. A guy who enjoyed sex and balled his way across the country was a cocksman, but a woman who did the same had to be damaged goods, acting out some past violation. What bullshit.

Still, the dick parade was growing tiresome. For every mind-blowing session that made her toes curl (a rugby player from Trinity College came to mind), there were always several encounters that did nothing at all for her. Like last night's interlude with Robbie, the comedian. Maybe one day he'd figure out that his funniest joke was dangling between his legs.

When would the boy train stop and let her off? All the college dudes. And other musicians. Oh, God, the musicians. Even if they were twenty years older, they were still boys. Where were the real men? Not listening to her music and showing up at her concerts. That's for goddamn sure.

Billie's core base of support skewed younger—primarily eighteen- to twenty-four-year-old males, but some females, too. And here she was inching closer and closer to twenty-nine. The thought was sickening. Her true die-hard fanboys called themselves Billie Goats. They waged online wars to see who could build the most lavish Internet shrine dedicated to the worship of Billie Shelton. Depending on the day, this could make her feel grateful, dismayed, or just creeped out.

It didn't help that her first album had been so fucking awesome. *Dick Magnet* was widely regarded as a masterpiece. And nobody let her forget it, least of all the Billie Goats. They wanted another one just like the first.

Pussy Power sure as hell wasn't. That had been her follow-up, or, as the industry commonly referred to it, her sophomore slump. Sales on the set dropped 30 percent from her debut. It contained no buzz tracks, either. The only silver lining was the concert revenue for her second tour. That remained strong. But it was the old music that triggered passionate crowd responses. The new songs just didn't excite them.

Billie could see the writing on the wall, and it terrified her. She didn't want to be one of those new artists whose best work was already behind them. Maybe that's why she'd stayed drunk throughout the recording of her third CD. After all, alcohol dulled fear. And if worse came to worst, it was something to blame failure on, too.

Suddenly, Amy broke her free of the reverie, guiding Billie's head to face the mirror directly. "See . . . you're almost pretty again."

Billie stared at her own image as if at an X-ray. "Almost" was right. A journalist had once described her ripely round yet sharply angular face as an aesthetic wonder. But none of that seemed to be working for Billie now. Had the slow rot from years of raunchy living suddenly become visible?

Amy reached for the blow-dryer and began fluffing out Billie's long black hair.

"Make me an appointment with that dermatologist

you were talking about," Billie shouted above the hot air flow. "And a good hairstylist. I want a personal trainer, too. I need to put this package back together."

Amy nodded blankly to the beat of each request.

Billie eyed the pack of Marlboro Lights near the sink. Oh, God, how she wanted one. And in all honesty, she deserved it. Usually, a cigarette was in her mouth before she opened her eyes in the morning. Amy had screwed up her routine today, so one smoke right now would still be cutting back.

Amy shut off the dryer. All of a sudden, she seemed pissed off. "You know, I shouldn't have to do this, Billie. I've got other clients. Having to wipe your ass all the time is getting old."

Billie lit up, dragging deep. Right away she felt better. She didn't understand why Amy was talking shit. "Yeah? Well, get over it. I'm your biggest act."

"Not anymore." The comeuppance in Amy's tone was bracing. "Internal Bleeding is."

For a second, Billie just looked at her. "Those losers you found at that bar mitzvah?"

Amy nodded. "One of their songs just got tapped for the next Ben Stiller movie. And they're going to be opening for the Killers. A lot of press is coming their way, too. There's a *Blender* interview scheduled for later today."

Each bit of news hit Billie like a punch in the gut. One of *her* songs should be in a movie. Why hadn't Amy landed *her* a gig as an opener for a major act? And speaking of *Blender*, *she* should not only be featured in the magazine, but on the fucking cover. This made Billie wonder if Amy was doing enough for her. Maybe she needed to start thinking about a new manager.

"I know what's going through your head," Amy said. "You're wondering why all of this isn't happening for your career."

Billie stared, taking another drag on her cigarette before answering. "Yeah, that thought crossed my mind."

"It's because these guys actually give a fuck. And they work their asses off."

Billie stomped out of the bathroom and began pillaging through her closet, searching for something to wear, practically setting herself on fire with her own cigarette in the process. She chose a schoolgirl's uniform skirt and a distressed T-shirt emblazoned with Minnie Mouse grabbing her crotch and flipping her middle finger.

Amy turned up in the doorway of the cluttered bedroom. "I'm sorry, but that's the truth."

Billie turned on her hotly. "You know what the real truth is? I signed up when you were just a lipstick girl. But you had some success with me and got inside the system. That's how you're making things happen for your new clients. Some fucking loyalty would be nice. I took a chance on you. Make something happen for me!"

"What do you think I'm trying to do? Without me, you would've slept through today's meeting or shown up looking like a road whore. By the way, take off that hideous shirt."

"I thought you didn't want to wipe my ass anymore. Now you're picking out my clothes."

Amy sighed, shutting her eyes for a moment. "Jesus, Billie, you're exhausting. Sometimes I wonder if it's worth it anymore. Are you happy with me? Do you want to end this?"

Billie experienced a minor sense of alarm.

"Maybe you should find a new manager."

Billie couldn't believe it. The bitch was looking for an out. And this scared the hell out of her. Shopping for new management when her career was in a slump could be risky. She might easily end up with someone lower on the food chain than Amy. "I can't believe you just said that. We fight all the time. Now all of a sudden you think I want to call it quits?"

Wearily, Amy leaned against the door. "I don't know what you want anymore. I just know that you're high maintenance and not worth the trouble. It's May, Billie, and you haven't earned a dime of new income this year. You made some nice money on your tours, but not enough to keep living the way you do."

"Am I broke?" Billie had no idea about her personal finances. She just relied on ATMs, charged up credit cards, and wrote out checks, assuming there would always be plenty of money to cover the damage.

"No, you're not broke," Amy said. "*Yet*. But you don't listen. I told you that Hamptons house was a bad idea. Keep spending fifty grand on a summer share, and you *will* be broke."

Billie had to admit the price tag on the East Hampton digs was high—$150,000 for the full season. Even split three ways, the figure stung. But Billie and two girlfriends, Liza Pike and Kellyanne Downey, would be living like stars in a spacious palace with ample privacy.

Liza had secured all the arrangements, obviously thinking money was no object. From her vantage point, why should it be? Her first book, *Whore*, had been a bestseller. It was basically a four-hundred-page bitch session about the way American culture sexualizes young women too soon. Billie never got through the first chapter. Beyond that, Liza wrote a syndicated newspaper column and appeared on an issues-oriented cable talk show every week. As for Kellyanne, she had no money worries, either. Some married real estate developer in Miami bankrolled her every move. So how could Billie poor-mouth and balk at her share of the summer house? After all, *she* was the fucking rock star.

The idea of spending an entire summer with the girls made her nervous, though. Back in college, this was a group that had forged a bond during a spring break trip to Cancún. To Billie's amazement, they still kept in touch. Once a year, they plotted a weekend getaway—shopping in Los Angeles, a spa retreat in Arizona. But a whole summer together?

Now Billie was smiling at Amy, hoping for an instant truce. In all honesty, she needed her. Amy didn't blow smoke up her ass. If something was fucked up, she said so. Billie could trust her. And Amy kept her eye on the big picture all the time. These were critical qualities in a good manager. "I know this summer share thing is a splurge—"

"*A splurge?*" Amy cut in. "Paying retail for a Gucci bag is a splurge. This is completely irresponsible."

"Even if you have a standing invitation to come any weekend you want?"

Amy didn't appear to be sold. "I hate the Hamptons."

"Why? It's beautiful—the sun, the beach, the fresh air. What are you going to do? Stay in the city all summer? Aren't you sick of the same crappy dyke bars night after night? I bet Nick would get really turned on by the sight of tan lines on you."

A faint smile found its way onto Amy's lips. "I'll think about it."

Billie gave her a look of contrition. "Are we cool now?"

"We're cool," Amy said. "But please change your shirt. I don't want Todd to mistake you for Courtney Love's little sister."

Todd Bana inhabited so much cocksure macho swagger that Billie swore she could hear his balls clang when he walked. It was uncanny how closely he resembled Scott Caan, the actor with the Hollywood pedigree. They shared the same good looks, muscled physique, and height challenges. Both men stood five foot five, providing they had on boots with a generous heel.

But Todd Bana would do nicely. He was just as hot as his more famous look-alike, if not more so. Even better, he was right in front of her, sitting behind his massive desk as if he ruled a small country.

Billie and Amy had been forced to cool their heels in his outer office for almost an hour. Had he really been busy? Or was it just a sick opportunity to make an artist sweat the outcome of her future?

She glanced over to see Todd's assistant—a sleek, efficient-looking fag in regulation Prada—discreetly off to the side, headset microphone in place, pen poised for quick note-taking.

Billie knew that she should be feeling anxious right now. Her career at Olympic could already be over. This meeting might just be the formal goodbye. But deep down, she sensed otherwise. Most companies were motherfuckers about such things. If they were dumping her, she'd likely read about it on the entertainment newswire, along with everybody else. Plus, Todd couldn't take his eyes off her mouth. Those famous Billie Shelton lips. She knew exactly what he wanted them to do.

"What do you feel like hearing first?" Todd asked. "The good news or the bad?"

Amy spoke up. "The bad. We assume it has something to do with your sitting on the third CD."

Todd propped up his feet. The soles of his expensive Italian shoes were unblemished, as if he'd just taken them out of the box. "Sitting on it implies that we're waiting on the right time for release. There is no right time to release absolute shit."

Billie stared at him impassively, even though she was seething inside. What a smug son of a bitch. She waited for Amy to rise to her defense. Playing bad cop was the manager's job at business meetings. But Amy just sat there like a dumb-ass while Todd went on.

"Instead of releasing Billie from the label, I'm willing to try something else." He zeroed in on her now. "I liked what you had to say with your first CD, but your second one was weak, and this third effort was a disaster. Maybe you've hit a dry well when it comes to writing your own songs. Nothing wrong with that. Happens to artists all the time."

Amy leaned forward, finally showing signs of life. "I think you're rushing to judgment, Todd. Billie's toured extensively. But she's had some time to recharge creatively. I think her next batch of—"

Todd cut her off. "Plenty of artists tour extensively. You record, you promote, and you hit the road. That's the gauntlet for everybody."

"Give Billie a chance to—"

"That's exactly what I'm doing," Todd snapped. "I'm giving Billie a chance that most labels wouldn't."

Then he threaded his fingers behind his head and smiled.

Billie noticed Todd's biceps straining the fabric of his shirt. As much as she hated him right now, she found him insanely sexy, too. "And what chance would that be?" she asked.

"To go back into the studio and record again," Todd explained. "But not on your own, this time. You'll just be a singer working with outside producers and writers on material that I preselect."

Billie shot a look to Amy, who didn't seem happy at all. But Billie wanted to hear more. Just showing up to sing? It sounded like a vacation. Writing and producing her own stuff had always been a real grind. Maybe Todd was right. What if creating the kind of music that made up *Dick Magnet* was all part of her past?

"I want to mainstream your image," Todd went on. "Glam you up a bit." He gave her a quick, assessing once-over. "You should lose at least ten pounds. Do something with your hair, too. The goal is to take things in more of a pop direction but still keep that rock edge. I just had a meeting with White Tiger. They've got three new songs that would be perfect for you. And they're interested in hooking up."

Billie just sat there, humiliated by the makeover bit, stunned by the proposal, but mostly shocked by the mention of White Tiger. They were a writing/production team that had generated radio hits for scores of bubblegum acts with factory-like regularity.

Amy lengthened her spine. "*White Tiger?* Todd, what the fuck are you thinking? They've worked with Hilary Duff and Britney Spears. You're talking to Billie Shelton."

"I know that," Todd said. "They worked on the last Hannah Montana record, too. That went platinum. Meanwhile, I can't scrape together gold adding up sales on all my Billie Shelton albums put together."

Amy shook her head. "I don't like this. The shift is too extreme. It alienates her fan base. And if it bombs, what then? She's back at zero. An alternative rocker who sold out."

Billie just sat there. What scared her more than the idea of failing at something big was the thought of just scraping along. She didn't owe the Billie Goats a goddamn thing. How could Amy sit there and worry about a fan base that didn't have the numbers to push her to gold? Fuck them! What was so wrong about going pop? Hell, she'd go polka if it meant a platinum record. Why should that fake punk bitch Avril Lavigne squeeze all the cash from those Hello Kitty purses?

Billie looked at Amy. Then she turned back to Todd. "I'm in." By peripheral glance, she could see the surprise on Amy's face.

"Good," Todd said, winking at her. "Because I'm going to make you the baddest bitch in pop music."

Billie smiled. She liked the sound of that. It might mean selling out. But it also meant trading up.

Todd swung his feet to the floor and rested his forearms on his desk, shifting to serious business mode. "Amy, we'll need to work out a new deal. I'll want a piece of the action on Billie's touring and merchandising to offset the investment in a launch like this."

Billie saw the immediate flush of anger hit Amy's cheeks. Traditionally, those pieces of the artist's pie were off limits. But the business was changing. Every possible revenue stream was up for grabs.

The Internet and the iPod revolution had turned the old music industry economic model upside down.

When Billie nodded her agreement, Amy stood abruptly. "Call me later, Todd," she said tightly. "We'll hammer out the details. I'm late for another meeting." And then she glared at Billie and walked out.

Todd gestured for his assistant to exit, then got up to shut the door behind him. He turned the lock. "I'm going to make you rich, Billie. Famous, too." His gaze never left her mouth as he unhooked his belt and started toward her. "I'm going to get your next single all over the radio. Do you want the cover of *Rolling Stone*?"

Billie moistened her lips with her tongue and nodded.

"I'll get you that, too." He stopped directly in front of her and dropped his pants. "So what are you going to do for me?"

Billie went to work, determined to suck Todd Bana until his eyeballs fell out if that's what it took to get the Olympic machine behind her. She thought about his platinum promises. She thought about the Hamptons getaway, too.

"Goddamn, you've got a hot mouth," Todd moaned.

Billie gazed up. The idea of this man becoming a beach boyfriend had a certain appeal. Todd could spend his weekdays making her a star and spend his weekends making her come. The fantasy was almost as delicious as he was. And she no longer had to wonder why Todd was such an overachiever. He was a short man with a big cock. Those kind of guys were unstoppable. They wanted to conquer *everything*.

Billie thought about Liza and Kellyanne, the way

they always laughed at her for attracting stoners and skater boys. But this time she might have a major music mogul on her arm. That easily trumped their men. Liza's husband was a fireman, and Kellyanne's benefactor was old enough to be her grandfather. Game over.

As she snaked her tongue up and down Todd's long and thick shaft, a certain feeling struck her. Even with Memorial Day still more than a week away, Billie knew that this would be the most unforgettable summer of her life.

"Come on, baby, show me how deep you can take it," Todd whispered thickly.

Billie laughed to herself. The bastard had no idea . . .

Liza

2

"It used to be that any girl in a horror movie caught sleeping around—or even losing her virginity to a guy she loved—was guaranteed a slashed throat," Liza Pike said.

Slyly, she checked her appearance on the monitor. The flirty, banana-print Chloe dress rocked; the freshly blown-out hair went on forever. She was a twenty-first-century fashionista feminist. Hated by the old guard, but loved by the new. *Feminism* had become a dirty word. Her goal: to make the next generation *own* the label. *Glamour* had recently voted her one of their Women of the Year. It was a step in the right direction.

"Classic misogyny," she went on. "The slut has served her purpose, so let's kill her. Now, thanks to movies like *Watch Her Bleed,* she just needs to be smart and accomplished to deserve an ugly death."

Tom Shapiro, host of CNBC's *The Roundtable,* raised his brow and gestured to Liza's on-air sparring partner, March Donaldson. *"Watch Her Bleed* just spent a second week at the top of the box office, March. Should we be concerned?"

March shook his head. "I don't see the big deal here. This is an R-rated thrills-and-chills popcorn flick. Besides, I get to see Jenny Barlow take a shower. You won't hear me complaining."

Liza pounced. "So you'll rail against Paris Hilton and *Sex and the City* reruns for being cultural poison, but garbage like *Watch Her Bleed* is okay?" She regarded him closely. "I'm impressed, March. For a man so young, you have the Republican double-talk down to a fine art."

He brushed off the political dig, flashing a smile that would make Tom Cruise insecure about his dental work. A halting arm went up. "There's a difference. When we've got middle school girls identifying themselves as Carries and Samanthas, society has a problem on its hands. But this is a movie for grown-ups. Relax. Have a Junior Mint."

Liza laughed at him. "Come on! Do you actually believe that this film is being marketed to adults? They're going after fourteen-year-old boys!"

March gave the host a deadpan look. "Tom, I think she's suggesting that I'm an adolescent."

Liza smiled. "If the shoe fits . . ."

A few crew members chuckled.

But March Donaldson was a good sport who knew how to laugh at himself. "Actually, my fiancée might say that it does."

Tom shifted his attention. "In all seriousness, Liza, you're deeply offended by this film, aren't you?"

She gave him a serious nod. "The women in this movie have one thing in common—they're assertive, opinionated, high achievers who, one by one, are stalked, terrorized, humiliated, and brutally murdered.

This reflects a trend of sexualized cruelty prevalent in mainstream pornography."

Wearily, March groaned in protest, then opened his mouth to speak.

But Liza thundered on. "And I'm not talking about the extreme material that exists on the fringe. I'm talking about the mainstream product that neighbors, bosses, husbands, and boyfriends are watching on DVD and the Internet. This movie is an extension of that. Tonally, it's the eroticization of pushing women to the edge. The larger question is why are men getting off on this?"

Tom Shapiro leaned forward. "I should tell our viewers that Harrison Beck, the writer and director of *Watch Her Bleed,* declined our request to be here."

"Lucky for him," March cracked.

"Oh, I don't think he's lucky at all," Liza said. "Any man who uses his creative gifts to display that much anger toward women must have a very small penis."

The crew exploded into guffaws.

Tom shrugged helplessly, as if to say, "I can't control what comes out of her mouth."

March tried to fight off laughter but lost the battle.

"That will have to be the last word for this week's Culture Wars segment," Tom said. "Liza, March—a spirited discussion as always." He turned slightly to address another camera. "Until next week, thank you for visiting *The Roundtable.*"

"And we're out!" the producer shouted.

"You just had to go for the crotch shot," March muttered under his breath.

Liza cut a glance to the blond, buff, tanned, and hazel-eyed Texan. She widened her thumb and index finger apart to measure about four inches. "And I'm probably being generous."

March shook his head. "Poor guy. He won't get a date all summer."

Liza smiled, knowing an insult like that would be played up and often in the press, extending the life of the debate, solidifying her position as the go-to It Girl for topical feminist spin.

The building blocks for a brilliant career were stacking up nicely. She had a bestselling book on her résumé with *Whore,* a weekly stint on *The Round-table,* a syndicated newspaper column, a regular blog on *The Huffington Post,* and a new deal in the works to join Sirius as a satellite radio talk-jock. Total media saturation. Politically, it was the only way to be heard in today's culture.

She rose and extended a hand to March. "Thanks. It's always a pleasure to wipe the floor with guys like you."

His shake was firm, his look flirtatious. "Well, one of these days you're going to have to let me be on top."

It drove Liza crazy that she found March Donaldson so attractive because she found conservatism so repulsive. March was a young Republican mover, the kind of man who grew up watching *Crossfire* and reading Peggy Noonan's *What I Saw at the Revolution.* He finished a law degree at the University of Texas, then joined George W. Bush's health-care policy pod in Washington. It didn't take long for his youth and sex appeal to generate fierce attention. The party needed some hot guy mediagenic bombast. Now he ran his own right-wing think tank, Our America, and played pundit hopscotch on network and cable news outlets.

She breezed past his double entendre. "Republicans are outnumbered five to one in the city. Manhattan dinner parties must be a real bitch for you."

March winked. "Not so much. Being on television gets me laid all the time. What can I say? I'm family values and rock and roll."

Liza wondered about his fiancée, Amaryllis Hartman. She worked in PR for fashion designer Stella McCartney and hailed from an impressive lineage of old money Connecticut Democrats. Beyond the obvious, what did a woman like that see in a man like March? His brand of contemporary narcissism hardly called for long-term commitment.

"Family values and rock and roll?" Tom Shapiro repeated this as he laughed. "If you ever run for office, use that for your campaign slogan. You'll own the young male swing vote."

Liza managed a wry smile. "Don't encourage him, Tom." She started out. "I'll see you next week."

"Hey, you up for a drink?" Tom called after her.

"Next time," Liza promised. "I'm heading back for a book party."

Tom pulled a disappointed face. He was astonishingly handsome—fine features, beautiful teeth, a smattering of sun freckles, slightly rumpled brown hair. With his easy speaking style and cool gesticulations, he gave off intellectual frat boy vibrations. The cable brass saw him as their great hope to attract young viewers, a demographic that got most of their news from Jon Stewart and Stephen Colbert.

But Tom Shapiro was the real thing, having endured a short tour of duty in the White House press corps. At daily briefings, he shrewdly hogged the mic with long what's-your-question questions. This ensured that the superimposed video ID would hit the screen and identify to 40 million people his name and affiliation. The exposure got him an agent, and a few months later, his own cable show.

As Liza picked up her pace, March fell into step beside her. "I'm guessing this book party isn't for Ann Coulter."

Liza grinned in spite of herself. She hated that cunt for the radical right. March knew it, too. "And they say you're not inclined to think big."

"Who says?"

She played coy. "No one in particular."

"Is Tucker Carlson bashing me again?"

Her smile was teasing.

"He says I'm more like a guy in a sports bar who won't shut up than a political analyst." One beat. "Dick. He's just jealous because I get more face time on TV."

Liza started to laugh and pushed open the exit door, bracing herself for the shock of going from meat locker air-conditioning to sticky summer heat.

A Town Car and driver were waiting, ready to whisk her from the Englewood Cliffs, New Jersey, studio back to New York.

"So, tell me, how does a feminist like you spend the summer?" March asked. "Will you slip into a swimsuit at some point, or does that represent man's evil plot to reduce you to a sexual object?"

"See? You *are* that guy in a sports bar."

March shrugged. "I've been called worse." He gestured for Liza's driver to remain seated and opened the rear passenger door.

"Believe it or not, I'm renting a house in the Hamptons for the season with a few girlfriends," she announced, slipping into the roomy cabin. "How's that for girly?"

March kept his hand on the door and leaned inside. "My fiancée's parents own a house in Watermill. I'll be there every weekend." He grinned, practically dripping with sexual heat.

With a pang of guilt, Liza thought of Justin. "Good. I'd love to watch my husband kick your ass in beach volleyball."

March rose up to his full height and gave her a cocky nod. "You're on." He shut the door, then just as quickly knocked on the tinted window.

Liza zipped it down.

"Don't get me wrong. I have great respect for firemen. But that pussy is going down."

She laughed as the driver coasted away, her body tingling with the animated energy that flirtation brings. And then came the shame. But Liza convinced herself that she harbored no desire for this to turn into something else. It was nothing more than the charming suggestion that, in another life, without her husband in the equation, without March's fiancée in the wings, they might have a fantastic time together. Her anxiety eased, Liza reached for her cellular to call Justin.

He picked up on the first ring. "Hey."

"How was your day?"

"Long and boring."

She breathed a quiet sigh. It was relief to her, misery to him. Justin was a truckee, a distinction that made him responsible for finding the fires and getting the survivors to safety. He worked Engine 40, Ladder 35 on Amsterdam and Sixty-sixth, a station house that had lost twelve men on September 11. "I'm on my way back," Liza announced. "The party starts at seven. If nothing else, the food will be good. Have you eaten?"

Justin hesitated. "What party?"

"Pila Anderson's book party. She gave me an advance quote for *Whore*. We've talked about this half a dozen times."

"I forgot," Justin said lamely. "Right now I'm heading to the gym with a buddy. Will you be pissed if I skip it?"

"I'm pissed that I even had to remind you," Liza spat. "Get your ass home, get a suit on, and get to the party. Details are on the fridge." She slammed the phone shut. "My fucking husband!"

The driver adjusted his rearview mirror, seeking eye contact, hoping for conversation.

But Liza didn't have the energy for chatter. She turned away, gazing blankly out the window in an effort to pinpoint the root cause of her annoyance. It couldn't be Justin exclusively. From time to time she had to get parental, all part of the currency of marrying a man-child.

Maybe it was her gnawing hunger. In the days that led up to a television appearance, she went on a punishing calorie restriction diet. Nothing but flaxseed, rice bran, brewer's yeast, sprouts, green tea, and sugar-free gum. This not only kept her model-thin but the preoccupation of always thinking about what she ate crowded out other worries. Of course, it didn't help that a strange ravenousness hit her after every taping of a show.

As she dug into her purse for a piece of Trident, she noticed the syringe. A wave of dread spread across her abdomen. Better to just do the deed fast before she had a chance to get anxious. She pulled up the skirt of her dress and jammed the needle into her hip.

It was a hormone cocktail—Perganol, Gonal-f,

and Lupron—designed to stimulate her ovaries to mature multiple eggs for freezing. This would be her second round at fifteen grand a pop. But it meant she could put off having a baby until forty. At twenty-nine, her eggs were still young, brilliant, and beautiful, not the old, dark, and grainy things they'd be if she waited.

At moments like this, she felt like a fraud, as if her public persona didn't represent a true ideology but a mercenary career move. Liza Pike, tough-talking feminist. Yeah, right. What would people think if they knew the real truth? That she had married a big, strong, stupid guy out of fear of being alone, that she starved herself even though she was already thin, that she had succumbed to baby panic propaganda and had thrown herself onto the guillotine of high-tech science.

Everything changed when the first plane hit the World Trade Center's north tower. Liza had been outside her TriBeCa apartment, close enough to feel the heat of the explosion on her face. From that moment on, nothing seemed the same. A garbage truck hitting a grate could scare the breath out of her lungs. For a long time she stopped taking elevators, refused to drive over the George Washington Bridge, and avoided the subway altogether. She also bypassed major airlines, thinking small carriers would be safer and likely under the radar of terrorists.

Relationships were altered, too. Tony Grant, a victims'-rights lawyer based in London, had been her boyfriend for two years. After a few days of consoling her about the attacks, he wanted to move on to other things—phone sex, politics, his tennis game, anything but her paralyzing fears. Playing the emotional caretaker was beyond him and, as the weeks went on, bad conversations got worse. She ended up dumping him the night he tried to argue that U.S. foreign policy had justifiably provoked the jihad.

For a few months, Liza did fine alone, but then CBS aired the six-month anniversary special with graphic new footage of the towers falling, images that simply reactivated her traumatic symptoms. Feeling vulnerable again, she reached out to Tony, though his weeklong visit failed to repair the relationship. There was nothing quite like those long, silent minutes—after disconnected sex and before sleep—to trigger deep reflections on how absolutely wrong Tony was for her. When he returned to London, Liza knew it was over for good, only to discover weeks later that she was pregnant.

Tony had announced over drinks on their first date that he didn't want children. The last thing she needed to hear was some crude offer to pick up the tab for an abortion, so she never told him. Liza volunteered at a Planned Parenthood location near her apartment, but it had recently been destroyed by arson. She went to another clinic but knew no one on staff. The nurse was aloof, helping to guide Liza's hips to the edge of the table but offering little else. The doctor never said a word. He just stepped into the room and roughly pushed in the speculum. She remembered the cramping, the painful tugging sensation, the daze of the relaxant. And then it was over.

Liza thought about her decision every day. She even noted the anniversary to herself, a morbid birthday for a baby never born. But she didn't regret it. There'd been so much she wanted to accomplish career-wise. And the idea of being linked to Tony Grant by way of a child seemed unbearably wrong. So Liza mourned, she gave her body time to heal, and then she swore off self-absorbed urban types by trespassing into bars where real men hung out.

It was time for an action-figure guy. After all, you couldn't find a toy based on a lawyer or a stockbroker. Liza wanted a cop, a cowboy, a fireman, someone who'd make love like an animal and lug a sofa bed up five flights of stairs without complaint.

When Liza saw Justin Beal for the first time at a casual bar near Ground Zero, he stood out like neon. Nicknames were big deals in firehouses, and all the men referred to Justin as Calvin Klein. Knocking back his beer in distressed jeans and a white tank, he did look more like a male model than a rescue worker.

But he was no high-maintenance pretty boy. There was hair on his chest. His hands were large and rough looking. And the corded musculature of his arms looked like the natural result of years of sports and physical work, not slavish dedication to a Bowflex machine. That night, he'd been the object of both ridicule and celebration for being cover boy of the new FDNY hunk calendar.

But Liza had managed to cause a minor commotion of her own. She knew how to take elements of elegance and mix them with nonchalance—a killer dress, wash-and-go hair, makeup so light you couldn't tell she was wearing any, and flats. This set her apart from the other huntresses who stalked the man jungle with their peekaboo cleavage and hooker heels.

Justin had responded to the novelty and approached her right away. She found him so desirable that the air seemed to leave the room. Shallow banter turned more shallow, and they ended up at her apartment. After the best sex of her life, he unloaded his survivor's guilt for breathing, eating, and fucking while the bodies of some of his firefighter brothers remained unaccounted for. Liza held him. For a first-night hookup, it was off the charts for intensity. Six weeks later, they were married. And more often than not, she still wondered why.

Zipping open her Celine clutch, Liza inspected her face. In the grind of the traffic halt, she carefully reapplied her Nars Hot Voodoo lipstick. *Shit.* They hadn't moved an inch in five minutes. Goddamn New Jersey. She huffed and shoved the tube back into her purse. More time to reflect on her darling husband.

Liza knew that saying those vows to Justin had been more of a response to circumstances than to love. The sky had already fallen once. She didn't want to be alone if it happened again. Plus, a new husband represented her post–September 11/post-Tony view on men: *simple guys only.* And that, Justin was. His interests were limited to work, sex, food, and the gym. Talk was scarce. He didn't read or keep up with the news enough to offer cognitive volley on anything.

But this gave Liza private space to think, a cerebral sanctuary all her own. She could do intellectual sparring at the office. At home, she thought she wanted something else—to feel safe and protected. Six years in, it wasn't working. But what else could she expect? The paradox of fearing loneliness and craving solitude was hardly the first building block for wedded bliss.

Liza had come to learn that simple men were just self-absorbed in their own way. Justin was no different. His needs were primitive, and they rarely involved her now. Even physically. In that first blush of togetherness, the sex had rocked her world. In fact, she could honestly admit that their relationship had been purely based on it. But now the act took on no greater or less a role than it would have with a Tony clone or some other man who in his lifetime had actually read a novel from beginning to end.

She tried not to think about Justin as a freeloader. The salary for a fireman would never catch up with the exalted status of being one. There were men at his firehouse—with children and stay-at-home wives—who were eligible for food stamps. But Justin was content. His ambition chromosome seemed to be missing. Even taking the exam to become an officer was beyond him. But he definitely lived better than his station buddies. After the wedding, he moved out of his dinky apartment in one of the outer boroughs and into the TriBeCa loft that she owned.

Liza felt like a bitch for thinking this way, but knowing that she could provide for herself financially conjured up a crazy lust to live off her husband. As if that could ever happen. The last wire transfer from her literary agency for a foreign sale of *Whore* was more than Justin's take-home pay for the year. And that money had been a surprise. Adding up American royalties, the contract with CNBC, the new Sirius deal, revenue from her Web site, newspaper syndicate income, and speaking fees, Liza easily brought in eighty dollars for every one that Justin earned.

Not that it bothered him. Why worry about how much money he made when he could just spend hers on expensive guy toys—the plasma TV, the top-of-the-line stereo equipment, the motorcycle. And it's not as if he even attempted to make up for his lack of income by overcompensating in other areas. Being

responsible for a single goddamn meal was too much
to expect.

Once, on his day off, with Liza on a schedule
gauntlet from hell, Justin had promised to take care
of dinner. She came home to find on the table a pot
of overcooked pasta and a room-temperature jar of
Prego. No wine, no salad, no bread. His excuse? "I
never cook. I didn't know." Yet the man had been eating his whole fucking life. Even worse, meals were
the social center of firehouse living. The men usually
took turns putting on feasts. He knew what to do. The
son of a bitch just didn't care enough to make the effort.

Moments like that were hardly a turn-on. Liza
never rejected Justin sexually, but then she didn't
exactly transmit seductive signals, either. They morph-
ed into—at best—a once-a-month couple. Sometimes
she regarded him as an overgrown boy with an unde-
served allowance. So she really had no desire to pay
the American Express bill and then suck his dick to
make him feel like a king.

Maybe Pila Anderson's book party would be a
shot in the arm. Her new tome was called *The Sex
Factor,* a manifesto on the epidemic of passion-
deprived marriages, complete with tips on reigniting
the erotic fire. But time apart could help ease Liza's
hostility, too. Liza was looking forward to weekends
in the Hamptons with the girls. Hearing about Billie's dead-end romances and Kellyanne's geriatric
sugar daddy just might make her stop and appreciate
what she had with Justin.

As often as that little voice told her to put an end to
their union, Liza ignored it, knowing instinctively
that seeing a fading tan line on her ring finger would

dial up feelings of failure and regret. She didn't want to be one of those starter-marriage women, the kind who emerge from what should be a lifetime commitment with all the emotional despair of a college party girl bidding adieu to a spring break fuck buddy.

The Town Car stopped in front of the Rem Koolhaas–designed Prada store in SoHo. Liza stepped out, feeling sexy in her towering Cesare Paciotti sandals. No wonder March Donaldson had followed her out of the studio like a stray dog.

She adored the sensation of knowing that she looked fabulous, a character trait which earned her the wrath of feminist colleagues. They labeled her a lightweight, argued that she was just in it for the media attention, and openly resented her rapid rise and high-profile position. Even among the intelligentsia set, it was still high school all over again. Three cheers for sisterhood.

Liza spotted Justin right away. It was amazing what a beautifully cut jacket and a great pair of shoes could do for a man with ramrod-straight posture. She felt the urge to just drag him home right then and there. Stopping a strutting waiter, she relieved him of his last champagne flute with a smile and drank deeply to prepare herself for the night. A gazillion familiar faces. The place was a total ratfuck.

A stressed publicist moved the mouthpiece of her headset out of the way and approached. "Are you from *The Apprentice*?"

Liza shook her head. "Sorry."

A copy of *The Sex Factor* got shoved into her hands anyway. "Hold this up when you pose with Pila." Then the flak grimaced, scanning the area for her reality-show PR prize.

Liza pressed onward, waving across the room to

one acquaintance, then another, finally closing in on Justin.

Her husband kissed her lightly on the lips and tasted of crab cakes. "You were right. The food's good."

Liza fidgeted with the hem on her short dress. Suddenly, she didn't want to be here. But she loved Justin for following her bitch rant orders to the letter. His reward would be an early exit and a smashing blow job the moment they got home. "Give me a minute to say a few hellos, and we're out of here."

Locating Pila among a crowd of well-wishers, she started over.

"Liza!" The shriek came from a rotund man in funny glasses. K.K. Vermorel. He was a freelance fashion stylist who recently outfitted Liza for a "New Manhattan Braintrust" pictorial in *Bazaar*. "You didn't tell me you were renting Faye Hudson's house for the season! You'll love it!" K.K. kissed her on both cheeks and gave her an approving once-over. Then he scoffed at the book in her hand as his gaze danced around the room. "You don't need that book, you lucky bitch. Where's that hunky husband of yours?"

Liza merely laughed. If he only knew. "Maybe I'll see you at some parties this summer. I'm thinking about hosting one with my friends."

"That sounds delicious," K.K. gushed. "And speaking of parties, I can't wait for Harrison Beck's Memorial Day bash. It's shaping up to be quite the event, what with all the success of *Watch Her Bleed*. Have you seen it? God, I had to look away. It was awful. Not the violence—that I could handle. Did you notice Jenny Barlow's breast implants? One is bigger than the other!"

Liza decided to let the subject pass. What could she possibly say to someone who left the multiplex with that mindless thought?

"Of course, you'll be there," K.K. went on.

"Actually, I didn't get an invitation."

K.K. swatted away this potential obstacle like a gnat. "You and your friends can be my plus one. A fat queen with a harem. It'll be a scream."

Liza instantly accepted. Today's taping of *The Roundtable* would air on Sunday. By Monday, Page Six would plant a snarky item about Liza's speculation on the size of Harrison Beck's dick. But instead of hiding out, she'd be drinking his Krug champagne with no remorse. That son of a bitch was about to find out that women were not just tits and ass.

Some girls have balls.

Kellyanne

3

The first time Kellyanne Downey kissed a woman, she was in college. A fraternity party at the University of Alabama. On a dare from a group of guys who were probably still masturbating to the memory today, she made out with a drunk cheerleader for the Crimson Tide.

Now it was happening again. No dare this time. Just some naughty encouragement from Jab, the sexy bartender at Silk Electric, a new Miami restaurant/bar/place-to-be-seen.

Midnight ticked past. It was Kellyanne's last shift. Beyoncé and Jay-Z had just left her a monster tip. The only other waitress still on duty, Pommie, had been flirting with her all night, shooting seductive glances across the crowded floor, instructing Jab to sneak them raspberry Bellinis in celebration of Kellyanne's final hours on the job.

Pommie was gorgeous—a tall, leggy Italian with dark olive skin and wild, jet black curls that cascaded down the small of her back. Her lips were full and pliant, her mouth exquisitely yielding.

Kellyanne felt a jolt in the stomach as Pommie's tongue swirled around her own. Their knees were touching. Oh, God, this is how she remembered it—the softness, the sweetness, the same rhythm. But when Pommie's hands began easing up her torso and toward her breasts, Kellyanne pulled back.

Pommie's dark eyes flashed with frustration.

"Shit, don't stop," Jab hissed. "I smuggled six drinks your way. At least let her suck some nip."

Pommie scowled at him. "You're a pig."

They were in a dimly lit corner near the bar. The three Bellinis had gone to Kellyanne's head. But she still knew the truth. Jab was a harmless straight guy obsessed with girl-on-girl action. The real pigs were in the last party holding up the restaurant's closing. "I better get back to my table." She started off.

Pommie reached for her arm. "Come home with me," she whispered.

"Now we're talking," Jab said.

Kellyanne shot a sharp glance in his direction. "How are those four Ketel Ones coming?"

All of a sudden, Jab got busy.

Pommie nuzzled closer. "Just one night—you'll never look back."

Kellyanne started to giggle. Maybe it was the alcohol. Maybe it was the fact that she was actually warming up to the idea. Sort of. "I can't . . . Pommie, this isn't me. Not really. I'm just goofing off. Don't read anything into it."

Pommie sighed in defeat. "I can't believe you're blowing *me* off, but you let that old man put his shriveled old dick—"

"Walter's a decent guy," Kellyanne cut in.

Pommie rolled her eyes. "Yeah, well, if it wasn't for that liver-spotted sugar daddy, you wouldn't be leaving."

"Bless your heart, you're going to miss me." Kellyanne thickened her already thick Southern drawl.

Pommie cracked a smile.

"It's just for the summer. I'll be back in the fall." Her voice was breathy, almost singsong.

"No, you won't," Pommie said. "You'll find a richer guy in the Hamptons and become a kept woman there."

"I'm not kept," Kellyanne insisted lightly. "I'm just not opposed to generosity, that's all." She grinned. "Anyway, you can visit. Most of the time my friends will be going back to the city during the week. You should fly out for a few days." She glanced over at the bar. "You, too, Jab."

"Is this Bellini talk?" Jab asked. "Because I'll definitely take you up on a free place to crash."

Kellyanne laughed. "Y'all should come together. We'd have a blast."

Pommie traded a high five with Jab. "You're on, bitch."

Jab gestured to Silk Electric's last remaining customers, a raucous group of four. "Are those assholes giving you any trouble? Because I'll happily whip out my special straw for these cocktails."

Kellyanne shook her head, laughing. Jab was famous for using his penis to stir the drinks of particularly rude patrons. "Keep it zipped. They're just a little loud. Nothing I can't handle." She took the tray and off she went, praying that this would be the last round. Maybe if she suggested the perfect strip club to keep the party going, they'd get the hell out.

"Hold on a minute, dude! All I'm saying is we could do better. We've got some hot girls lined up, but we could do better." The leader of the pack was talking—late thirties, buzz cut, about six foot four, dressed down in a T-shirt, board shorts, and flip-flops. "Take this chick." He robbed a Ketel One from Kellyanne's tray and raised the glass to salute her. "She's fucking beautiful. I mean, come on, dude! Nobody we signed up has anything on this girl."

Kellyanne pretended not to hear and simply distributed the drinks as each guy zeroed in on her with a laser intensity. "Can I put this on one check?" She knew how to ignore men even as she was talking to them. Always being the hottest girl—on campus, at the party, in the room—had taught her such skills.

The obnoxious one continued staring. Even behind the sunglasses at night, she could see his eyes swirling kaleidoscopically. Typical male reaction.

Kellyanne knew the drill. Since blossoming almost overnight at fifteen, guys would take one look at her and all brain activity would revert from their head to their crotch. She was a dewy drop of California nectar by way of the Deep South—an object study in blond superiority. People didn't bother talking about her beauty. Why struggle to articulate the obvious? It was like pointing out the sun.

She was tiny, just five foot one, but not built like a little girl. Kellyanne's body screamed, *And God Created Woman,* only in miniature—hips so slim and narrow that some internal organs appeared to be missing, breasts that were pert and shapely, and, despite her slight height, limbs that seemed long and languid. No matter the season, there was an impossible golden glow to her skin and hair, a perpetual just-walked-off-the-beach look. Exercise bored her to death. Luckily, she possessed a metabolism that didn't require it. Her secret was to just take vitamins and echinacea until her body rattled. That kept everything together.

It wasn't all perfection, though. Kellyanne's nails were hideous. From the age of eight, she'd been a chronic biter. And no amount of behavior modification sessions could roll back the nasty habit. Walter had spent a fortune on hypnosis therapy, and that'd been a bust, too. Even the foul-smelling lotions designed to make her fingers taste bad failed miserably. After chewing down the first nail, she stopped noticing the yucky flavor. The overall act was familiar routine now, almost pleasurable.

"So what did you do today, baby? How come you weren't at the Palms auditioning for my show?"

Kellyanne gave him a look she usually reserved for roadkill. She knew this type. In high school, he was the parking lot stoner, the kind of guy who spent his weekend hours earning money for pot at some loser job behind a Smoothie King counter. Now he had a lame gig in entertainment that pulled girls who would show him their boobs for as little pay as a free beer. And he thought he was a junior Hugh Hefner.

The asshole tilted up his shades to reveal bloodshot eyes. "I'm Brad Lucas, by the way. But call me Bonzi." Going clockwise around the table, he introduced his cronies. They all had grandiose, meaningless titles preceded by the qualifying classification of "assistant." They all had names, too.

But Kellyanne was barely listening. If somebody held her at gunpoint, then she might be able to recall that one of the idiots was Jeff. Maybe John. She couldn't be sure.

"So what's your name?" Bonzi asked.

She told him.

"*Kellyanne.*" There was a lewd timbre to his voice. "Sweet, Southern Kellyanne. That is *hot.*"

She sighed impatiently. "I'll be right back with your check."

"Hold on a minute!" Bonzi cried. "You never answered my question. How come you didn't audition for my show?"

"And what show is that?" Kellyanne asked. "*Girls Gone Wild South Beach*?"

Bonzi looked genuinely offended. "I don't produce shit like that. I'm in reality television. I've got a development deal at Fox. Ever watch *The Cul-de-Sac*?"

Kellyanne nodded vaguely. She remembered people at the restaurant talking about it. Some trash involving a group of sexy singles who move into a neighborhood to tempt the married residents.

"That was my show," Bonzi said proudly.

"Congratulations," Kellyanne sniffed. Please. As if the shit were *Masterpiece Theatre.*

"The bank already has," Bonzi shot back. "Congratulated me, that is. Last year it was Fox's second-highest rated show among the eighteen-to-forty-nines."

"I don't watch much TV."

"What are you doing for the next two weeks?" he asked.

"Actually, I'm leaving tomorrow for the whole summer."

Bonzi shrugged diffidently. "So delay that. I can put you up in a mansion on Star Island."

Kellyanne started to leave. "No thanks."

"At least let me tell you about my new show."

She glanced at her Cartier tank watch—a gift from
Walter—and saw Jab closing down the bar and
Pommie knocking back another Bellini. "Okay," she
relented. "Give me a thirty-second pitch. But then
you guys have to take off."

His face lit up, and he began speaking in a stream
of exclamations. "Okay! It's called *Soul Mates*. Fox
has us locked in this summer. *Everybody*'s gonna be
watching. No joke. This show is gonna be fucking
huge! At first, you think it's a rip-off of *The Bachelor*.
We've got thirty smoking fine girls going after this
one dude. And this guy's hot—former pro athlete,
did some modeling, now he makes seven figures running the family consulting business. I'm telling
you—this dude's the shit. There's not an ounce of
fag in me, and *I'd* fuck him." Bonzi laughed as his
posse practically convulsed under the table. He
turned back to Kellyanne. "You like Brad Pitt?"

A half-smile curled onto her lips and threatened
to stay there. "Who doesn't?"

"This man is like a Brad Pitt. No lie. His name's
Vlad Branigan. So my man Vlad has thirty beauty
queens on his jock. He's trying to decide which one
he digs the most. By the way, when you introduce
yourself, it'll be fucking over. He loves blondes.
He'll fall for you big time. I swear to that. But just
when he narrows it down and is about to choose between two of the original thirty, we've got a twist
that'll knock him on his ass." He paused for dramatic effect. "A blast from the past. The one that got
away. It took some serious background research to
find a guy this perfect with a lost love, but we did it.
Are you with me?"

Kellyanne nodded. His thirty seconds were up a

minute ago, but she actually found this doofus mildly entertaining.

"So Vlad's heart is fucking bleeding on camera. Does he go for his new soul mate or the soul mate from his past? But the gag is this—no matter which girl he chooses, dude goes home alone. The new girl and the old girl split a million bucks and leave his ass high and dry on national television!"

At first, Kellyanne just laughed. "You're joking, right?"

"No, I'm fucking serious!"

"But that's so mean," Kellyanne said.

"That's the point! People are sick of these fucking bachelor types having their pick of the litter like some Saudi prince. This dude will get humiliated. It'll be awesome!"

"If you say so." She started off again.

"Does that mean you're in?" Bonzi asked.

Kellyanne stopped and gave him a quizzical look. "In what?"

"The show," Bonzi said. "You'll be on it, right? He stood up and turned to his boys. "Can you believe I just told this bitch the big reveal? I'm fucking trashed, man. Which one of you has a clean copy of the boilerplate?"

One of the men dug through a worn leather satchel and pulled out a document at least one hundred pages thick.

Bonzi passed it to Kellyanne. "Sign this and you're on the show. It's usually not this easy, but I've got a feeling about you." He retrieved a silver case from his back pocket and handed over a business card.

She fingered the embossed lettering. BRAD "BONZI" LUCAS, THREE KEGS ENTERTAINMENT.

"Call my cell when you decide," he said. "But don't wait too long. I'll need an answer by noon to-morrow."

When Kellyanne walked through the door of her condo and saw Walter Isherwood passed out on the couch, she experienced a moment's pure dread. The last thing she ever wanted him to do was tell his wife that he wanted a divorce. Kellyanne saw him too much as it was.

Rushing over to nudge him awake, she halted all of a sudden, admiring the peaceful image of him sleeping. Even at sixty-four, he still possessed an undeniable appeal and virility. Walter had the sort of timeless charisma that made men like Jack Nicholson so sexy to younger women. He swam a mile every day and lifted weights three times a week, which made for a body more taut and firm than could be found on many men half his age.

A late-night infomercial for Proactiv Solution was blaring from the plasma television that floated on the wall like a prop from a sci-fi movie set.

Kellyanne dug out the remote control from underneath Walter's hip and zapped the power off, noticing the empty highballer on the Noguchi coffee table. He loved his Scotch. A little too much at times. Gently, she shook his shoulder. "Walter . . ."

He stirred slightly, slowly opened his eyes, and gave her a groggy smile. "What time is it?"

"It's almost two," she whispered. "What are you doing here?"

"You're not happy to see me?" There was an instant edge to his voice.

She kissed him. "Don't be stupid. I had no idea

you were coming tonight. You should've told me. I wouldn't have stayed behind to have a drink with Pommie and Jab."

He gestured to the bulging *Soul Mates* contract under her arm. "What's that?"

Kellyanne tossed the thick packet onto the Noguchi. It landed with an almighty thud. "It's too late to get into that. I'll tell you about it later. Shouldn't you be getting home? I can make some coffee."

"There's no rush. Connie's on a cruise with her sisters."

Connie was Walter's wife of thirty-two years. They had three children, each close in age to Kellyanne. For the past few years, she'd heard about all of them in bits and pieces. To deal with the guilt, she began to think of herself as some sort of family friend and inquired about them often. How was Connie's museum benefit? Did Allison get that promotion? Has Brock set a wedding date yet? And so on. Now she found herself genuinely curious about this cruise. "Where'd they go?"

"Alaska . . . Bermuda . . . who knows?" Walter's uncertainty on the subject matched his lack of interest. Slowly, he ran his hands down Kellyanne's slender arms, a faraway look of lust in his intelligent green eyes. "I took a Levitra a few hours ago . . ."

It was the same routine. He studied her as she went through the rituals of getting ready for bed. For Walter, this constituted foreplay. He watched her take a bath. He watched her shave her legs. He watched her pee. He watched her apply all the expensive La Prairie skincare products that his credit card paid for.

Walter always insisted that Kellyanne tell him everything about her day, too, and he was a good listener, even as his arousal heightened and he began to touch himself. On this night, she relayed stories about her near car accident on the way to Silk Electric, the three-hundred-dollar tip that Beyoncé and Jay-Z left behind, her silly makeout session with Pommie, and the standing offer from Brad "Bonzi" Lucas.

It'd been three or four hours since he popped the Levitra, but that little pill remained on call in the body for up to six. By the time they slid into bed, he was as rigid and randy as a soldier on weekend furlough. But his skills as a lover were average at best.

Walter loved going down on her but lacked the know-how. Forget the G-spot. He could never stimulate her clitoris properly, either. And he never applied pressure or used his fingers. He just lapped like a baby kitten taking in a saucer of milk. But Kellyanne writhed and moaned appropriately. No need to make him feel insecure at sixty-four.

Just one night—you'll never look back.

Pommie's bold assertion played back in Kellyanne's mind as she lay there, bored as hell and ready for sleep. Thank God she was going away for the summer. Of course, she owed that indulgence to the very man she wanted to get away from. When she told Walter about Liza's idea, he'd scratched out a fifty-thousand-dollar check the moment the details came through. He told her that she deserved a break and waxed lyrical about rendezvousing in New York a few times each month. Secretly, Kellyanne hoped that it'd be less than that.

Walter ran the Isherwood Group, a residential real estate development company. There were definite perks to being the president's girl on the side. For instance, he put her up in the Jade building, a forty-eight-story waterfront condominium property on

Brickell Bay. Her unit was a one bedroom/two bath with amazing views, a stainless-steel kitchen with built-in wine cooler and cappuccino maker, and an in-home touch-screen monitor in every room for security and personal services. The spoiling went on with a silver Mercedes SL600 Roadster, too. Kellyanne had to admit that the Isherwood Group was *very* good to her.

"You're nice and wet," Walter announced. "I think you're ready now." He turned Kellyanne onto her side, slid into her, and began pumping in his typical rhythm-challenged manner. When he came, there was a loud cry and a violent shudder. Levitra orgasms were deliciously forceful. They left Walter's face so hot and flushed that each time Kellyanne swore she might have to call 911.

He was still breathing hard when he reached into the nightstand drawer, pulled out two Wrist Rockets from the London-based erotica shop Coco de Mer, and passed them over with a dirty grin. "My favorite part." And then he settled back for the show.

Kellyanne slipped her hands through the straps and twisted the tips of the pink, bullet-shaped devices. The single-speed motors revved up. She rested one against her anus and positioned the other on her clitoris. It didn't take long for the vibrating power-tool toys to work their magic. Her satisfaction was quick and intense.

"You're beautiful when you come," Walter said, stroking the inside of her thigh.

Kellyanne smiled. "I thought I was beautiful when I slept."

"That, too." Sighing heavily, he rolled over to stare up at the vaulted ceiling.

She brushed a tendril of hair away from his eyes. "What's wrong?"

"You leave tomorrow, right?"

"I'm supposed to."

"We've got some problems with the Indian Creek project. I might not make it to New York as often as I thought this summer."

Kellyanne fought to conceal her relief. It was precisely what she'd wished for. The Indian Creek highrise was the most ambitious construction of Walter's career. Its Atlantic, intracoastal, and city views would be unparalleled. "Then I'll just come back home to see you," she said, practically holding her breath for his response.

"No . . ." he began softly.

Thank God!

"This is your time away with your girlfriends. I'll get there. It just won't be as often as I planned."

Kellyanne spooned into him and began playing with the light hairs on his chest. "Maybe the problems won't be as bad as you think. Besides, if anyone can set things right, you can." A few beats of silence passed. "You never said anything about the reality show. What do you think?"

Walter yawned. "I don't know. What does Adam say?"

Adam Griffie worked out of the William Morris Agency office on Miami Beach. Another mistress benefit. Walter had called in a favor to get Kellyanne representation. The idea had been to lift her acting career off the ground. But sometimes she wondered if it was all just a ruse to keep her distracted. So far, Adam had only served to get her one lousy commercial and a walk-on in some rap video for an artist she'd never heard of.

"I'm going to show him the contract tomorrow," Kellyanne said. "I never thought about a reality show before. It always seemed so stupid. But it'd give me some great exposure. Don't you think?"

Walter was silent.

Kellyanne glanced over to find him asleep. He didn't give a fuck about her career. And suddenly, it struck her. What career? It was more like a delusion than anything else. She'd been at this for eight years. Shit! That was almost an entire decade. And with nothing to show for it. Miami was her third crack at a new city, too.

The first campaign happened in Los Angeles. She was fresh out of college with a degree in theater. As if anyone in Hollywood cared. Most casting agents told Kellyanne she was *too* beautiful—appealing to men but threatening to women. Back then, the executives wanted the next Julia Roberts. Today they wanted the next Katherine Heigl.

A few times, she got lucky. A producer or director or actor with connections would take her out and make vague promises of helping her get work. Always code for "if you sleep with me." Often, she did. But only with the ones she found attractive. It sure beat the rejection battering ram at audition after audition. And it usually included a fabulous dinner and drinks. Still, whatever job materialized turned into nothing. Once she showed up for a two-line party scene, but the lead actress took one look at her and said, "I'm not sharing the screen with her. Fire that bitch." L.A. was hell. In fact, she got out just in time.

She moved to New York to try her luck there. Things were no better, though. People complained about her thick Southern accent. One casting director said, "If we ever decide to do a revival of *Hee-Haw,* we'll give you a call, honey." Bitchy queen.

Kellyanne ended up killing a few years with service-oriented jobs. Like being a greeter at Abercrombie & Fitch. All she had to do was wear bottom-skimming shorts with a tight tank top and flash a smile as people walked inside. She also waited tables at the Coffee Shop on Union Square, thinking it might bring her good karma. After all, Taye Diggs and Jennifer Esposito had once worked there doing the same thing. But nobody ever discovered her.

Except Walter. He sat in her section one morning and flirted outrageously. And it wasn't I'm-an-old-man-and-I'm-just-lonely flirting. It was clearly of the I'm-an-old-man-and-I-want-to-take-you-to-bed variety. She found his cockiness sexy. Plus, he seemed kind, handsome, and easy to talk to. The ultimate seduction was that he appeared genuinely interested in what she had to say. When he asked her back to his hotel, Kellyanne said yes right away. He was sweet, she was bored, and a night at the Four Seasons sounded better than the dump she shared with two sloppy roommates she could barely stand the sight of.

The sex left something to be desired, but he was gentle and tender, almost worshipful. All the kinkier stuff came later—the toys, the let-me-watch-you-pee bit, the dirty talk. But it was basically harmless. Whatever turned him on. There was no pain or humiliation involved.

Convincing her to move to Miami proved easy. Nothing was happening for her in New York, and she missed the sun and the water. So eight years after college, here she was, pushing thirty, schlepping expensive meals, and playing sex kitten to a man older than her father.

Walter had set things up in the way that only a shrewd bastard could. No assets were in her name. Not the condo, not the car. Her entire way of living was on loan. At the snap of his fingers, Kellyanne could be homeless and without transportation. That's why she insisted on working, even if it was just waiting tables at Silk Electric. Having her own source of cash made her feel more in control. And the staff camaraderie was good balm for her soul. Otherwise, she might just waste away hours until Walter decided to walk through the door.

Finally, Kellyanne drifted off to sleep, and the next morning, she woke up to find Walter still there, sipping coffee on the balcony. Her unit was on the forty-first floor, and the sensation of being up so high always made her stomach do somersaults.

"You better be careful," Kellyanne teased, kissing the back of his neck. "Spending the night, hanging around for breakfast. I just might start calling myself *Mrs.* Isherwood."

Walter smiled and took in the view—of her—as the breeze lifted Kellyanne's silk robe and exposed white lace briefs by La Perla, a pair that fit low enough to expose her tan line. He stared silently for a long time and then reached down to adjust himself.

"Did you take another—"

"Yes, I did," he cut in thickly. "It's been a half-hour already, so your breakfast should be ready anytime now."

Kellyanne refused to think of this as a scientific miracle. Those goddamn pills caused more problems than they solved. "I want Adam to look over that contract. Do you think he'll see me without an appointment?"

"Why wouldn't he?"

Kellyanne shrugged. "I don't know. Sometimes it takes him a week to return my calls. I'm not exactly a priority client."

Walter grimaced, reached for his cell phone, scrolled through his stored numbers, and made a selection. "Adam, Walter Isherwood . . . I'm fine, can't complain. Listen, Kellyanne wants to stop by this morning and get your advice on some reality show she's up for . . . I'd consider it a personal favor if you rescheduled that appointment and made time for her . . . Expect her in about an hour or two . . . Thanks, Adam."

Kellyanne shook her head. "I can't even get that man on the phone!"

"That should change," Walter said. "Remind him that he wants a good deal on one of the Indian Creek apartments."

Kellyanne giggled. "I can tell him that?"

"If you're not getting what you need, then absolutely," Walter said. "But I don't think you'll have a problem. Adam understands that one good turn deserves another." He loosened the tie on his robe and let it fall open, exposing another rigid hard-on. "Do you?"

Kellyanne reached for his hand, hoping to pull him inside.

Walter resisted. "Right here," he said. "On the balcony. Show Miami what you do best."

She grabbed a cushion from one of the chairs and threw it down to protect her knees.

* * *

Adam Griffie kept her waiting. Big shock. But he let go with an impressive stream of so-glad-to-see-you bullshit the moment his Eva Longoria–look-alike assistant ushered her inside his inner sanctum.

William Morris was the largest and oldest talent agency in the world with offices in Los Angeles, New York, London, and Nashville. That a branch had opened on Miami Beach was a major event. But not, so far, for Kellyanne. Maybe they handled so much Latin talent that they didn't know what to do with a blond girl from Tuscaloosa, Alabama.

Adam sat perched on the edge of his desk—impeccably groomed, well dressed, and very tan. Probably gay, too. Because he didn't seem even remotely affected by her beauty. Instead, he regarded her with something close to annoyance, as if she were yet another bimbo-with-a-dream that some rich bastard had twisted his arm into dealing with. "Walter tells me you're thinking about doing a reality show."

Kellyanne handed over the contract and told Adam about meeting Brad Lucas.

Her reluctant agent's head bobbed knowingly. "*Bonzi.* He's hit the ratings jackpot with his last few projects. Fox has him locked in to an exclusive deal."

"Do you think a show like this could help my career?"

Adam gave her a look that translated, "What career, bitch?" Then he began to casually thumb through the contract. "If the show takes off, you could end up with some celebrity magazine coverage, maybe get an offer from *Playboy.*"

"I've *had* an offer from *Playboy,*" Kellyanne shot back. "A long time ago. I'm not interested in that." She remembered how close she'd come to posing, though. It was during the L.A. years, and she'd called home to discuss the opportunity with her father, who owned a machine shop.

"Baby, I'd be a hypocritical son of a bitch if I told you not to do it. I've been getting that magazine for years, and those Playmates are somebody's daughters."

It was the closest thing she could expect for a parental endorsement. But she still said no.

"Put it this way, if the show's a hit—reality's tricky but Bonzi's on a hot streak—opportunities will surface," Adam said. "No doubt about that." He continued going through the contract.

"How does it look?" Kellyanne asked.

"Standard. They basically own you for up to a year after the show airs. Until then, any publicity or creative activity has to be approved in advance by the producers."

"But you're my agent. Can't you do better than that?"

Adam shook his head. "Reality's a different animal. Nobody negotiates. You don't want to sign— fine. In five minutes, they can find ten girls on the beach who will." With a shrug, he passed back the bundle of slave pages. "My advice—go for it. What do you have to lose?"

Quite a bit—her anonymity, the control of her image, and her dignity, for starters. She thought about Liza. Oh, God, she'd hate the idea. First, doing the show would mean missing the first few weeks of their vacation, leaving Liza alone to contend with Billie. And even worse, Liza believed reality television was rolling back the progress of the feminist movement.

Kellyanne experienced a pang of shame as she

realized that her own life was hardly a step forward for the cause. By signing this contract, she'd simply be trading Walter's rule of law for Bonzi's. Wasn't it time she started living life on her own terms?

But she found herself reaching for a pen and signing on the dotted line.

Billie

4

"I think it's a mistake," Liza said. "Kellyanne's going to regret this. *A reality dating series?* Come on! All the women on those shows are depicted as vulnerable, desperate, or manipulative. One look at the prince, and they're ready to slit their wrists if they don't get chosen. It's disgusting, misogynistic crap."

Billie downed the last of the Angelo Gaja and signaled the waiter for a second bottle. It might be rude to casually add another two hundred and fifty bucks to a bill she had no intention of paying, but if she had to sit here and listen to this shit, then at least she deserved the most expensive wine on the menu.

They were at Savanna's on Elm Street in Southampton. It'd been Liza's idea. And a fucked-up one at that. The restaurant sat right across from the train stop and, on Friday nights, every bitch and bastard migrating from Manhattan mobbed the place. At least the atmosphere was pleasant. Votive candles lined the windowsills and beautiful Grecian columns supported the structure. But the next time she walked through the door, Todd Bana better be her date, not Liza.

"You know what? I'm glad she's doing it," Billie said. "Maybe it'll lead to something. What do you want her to do? Suck that old fuck's cock for condo squatter's rights the rest of her life?"

Embarrassed, Liza glanced around to see if any other patrons had overheard. "*Billie*," she admonished in a low hiss. "This isn't a tour bus."

Billie rolled her eyes. She didn't care what people thought. "All I'm saying is at least she's doing *something*. Think about it. What has Kellyanne really accomplished in the last ten years?"

Liza was silent.

"Exactly. She's moved from city to city waiting tables, and now she's a private whore for some rich guy in Miami." Billie took a stab at her Chilean sea bass. "Oh, I forgot. She had a nonspeaking part in a tampon commercial and was bikini girl number six in a rap video." With a whoop-dee-doo twirl of her fork, Billie went on. "Shit, maybe the problem is that she doesn't have any talent. I've never seen her act. Have you?"

Liza lengthened her spine defensively. "Of course, she's talented. She has a degree in theater."

Billie cackled just as the waiter returned to go through the ceremony of opening the second bottle. As far as she was concerned, he couldn't pour it fast enough. The first gulp gave her the incentive to continue. "That doesn't mean anything. I have a degree in government, but I'm nobody's mayor. Personally, I think Kellyanne's lazy. She doesn't try that hard, and she's never taken any real acting classes that I know of. All she does is trade on her looks."

Liza mulled this over as she tore off a piece of fo-caccia bread, brought it to her lips, and then re-turned it to her plate.

Billie noted the sly maneuver. No wonder she was so skinny. The bitch didn't eat. She just pretended to.

"We shouldn't talk about her this way," Liza said. "It's not fair."

"Why not?" Billie countered. "Whenever the third Musketeer is out of the picture, the other two always talk about her like a dog. It's called friendship."

Liza laughed lightly. "Remind me to stick around all summer." Sipping her wine, she took in the dining room with a circular gaze. "I love to people watch. Don't you? Think of all the plots that are being hatched here tonight."

Billie glanced around and gave a little snort of derision. These status-seeking star fuckers didn't impress her. "Who cares? Anyway, I thought the Hamptons were supposed to be over. Aren't people moving up to Ulster County?"

Liza swirled her wine as if to dismiss the notion altogether. "A few. But it's not like there's a mass exodus. Besides, they've restricted the club scene somewhat. This place will never go out of style." With her fork, she played with the oven-roasted half chicken and moved around the sautéed spinach. But she never ate very much. All of a sudden, she gave Billie a studied once over. "You know, I just saw you about a week ago, and you didn't look this thin. Your hair looks great, too."

Billie finger-combed her shorter locks. Amy had booked her chair time with Paul Podlucky. The mas-ter hacked off four inches and gave her a new look with heavy bangs and face-framing layers, insisting that the style would play up her cheekbones. Then he put his color talents to work, taking her base hue a shade lighter and weaving in gold highlights.

But that was the easy secret to tell. Explaining the rapid weight loss? Not so much. Billie had considered a cleansing camp in the Adirondacks—several days of saltwater only, then a strict regimen of greens and supplements. By the end, a girl was supposed to be pounds thinner and positively glowing. It sounded too hard core, though.

Luckily, Todd Bana had turned her on to a better method. They'd been partying into the night. She was drunk. He was high. His coke supply was gone, and for a man fucked up and still going strong at two in the morning, this could be a mood killer. But Todd had a quick solution.

They ran across the street to an all-night doughnut shop. He touched his nose as he made eye contact with a black guy loitering near the counter. The man approached. A discreet exchange followed. And back they went.

At first, Billie wanted no part of it. Crystal meth? That drug was for freaks and fags. But then Todd gave it the Tony Robbins pitch.

"It's not just for trailer trash," he'd said, as if reading her mind. "In Hollywood, lots of executives are into it. A buddy in L.A. gave me a hit of his stash once. It's like fucking rocket fuel. Sex is *insane* on this shit. Oh, and talk about an awesome diet boost." He snapped his fingers. "Ten pounds in a week. Gone. Just that quick. You have to be careful, though. Only use it in moderation. Like any drug, I guess." He laughed. "Or else you could end up tricking for a street fix on your way to rehab."

Todd crushed the rock into powder. For his own

hit, he tapped some onto a tiny square of toilet paper and swallowed it, telling her that pro tweakers called this parachuting. For Billie, he did something even more wild. He loaded up a syringe with meth powder and water and shot the mixture straight up her ass. Users referred to this as a booty bump. And it was *fanfuckingtastic*.

But what Todd told her about sex on meth was a lie. Insane? Hardly. The experience went so far beyond that. Every touch . . . every sensation . . . every erogenous pulse was heightened to the *n*th degree. The euphoria stretched on and on. It was binge fucking. Completely mad. They did it for hours. The frightening thing was that Billie craved more than even a cranked-up Todd could humanly offer. She felt like taking on a football team. And given the chance, probably would have. It was no wonder so many crystal addicts ended up HIV-positive.

Even after the high, she still had killer energy. And no appetite. Billie didn't eat for four days. It was ridiculous. But in a good way. Coming off the bender, she looked almost svelte. So she begged Todd for another hit. Not because she needed it. Just to get rid of the remaining weight. One more booty bump.

Todd obliged her but didn't indulge himself. His next several days were slammed with business on the West Coast. The fever rush of her second dose worked the same voodoo as the first. *Var-o-o-o-o-o-o-m!* Todd did what he could to satisfy her and then told her to go fuck a doorknob if she had to.

Instead, Billie stayed up for hours and wrote songs. The inspiration was macrocosmic, like receiving an internal telegram from the fourth dimension. Creativity flowed. Her tunes wrote themselves. The process was sublime. She opened a window. The noise from the street below took on a natural rhythm. She wrote lyrics. She crafted melodies. It was sub-atomic harmony. And she couldn't wait to show them to Todd. As soon as he got back from Los Angeles. Once he heard Billie's new stuff, then he'd ditch that White Tiger idea. Outside writers and producers? Bullshit. After all, she was no studio puppet like Brit-ney. She was Billie Fucking Shelton!

The second time around also transformed her body. Oh, God, she looked fabulous. She was lean and cut. Losing more weight in her face enhanced her cheekbones. Now they were as sheer as a Mexi-can cliff.

A booking agent from Marilyn, Inc. stopped her on Park Avenue and wanted to know if she was al-ready a model or interested in becoming one. Billie accepted the card and promised to call and set up an appointment.

Todd loved the idea but told her to wait. Maybe when the new album was ready to drop. He said everything had to be planned with military precision, that launching her new image would be like going to war.

It was an interesting comparison. Billie just hoped that Todd had better strategic instincts than Cheney, Rumsfeld, and the other neocon assholes who'd managed to fuck up the Middle East.

"How did you lose the weight so fast?" Liza was asking.

Before Billie could toss out a lie, a dead-sexy man approached the table and smiled intimately at Liza. "And so the season begins."

Billie knew the accent. Definitely Texas. Obvi-ously, he'd worked hard to get rid of it, but a slight twang remained. She'd performed enough concerts in Austin to recognize it. His impossibly white teeth were glinting. And she was swooning. Literally. Like an eleven-year-old girl in the face of a Zac Efron sighting. She felt caught up in the tidal wave of his charisma. The way he filled out a simple pink Oxford and a pair of old jeans. It was sick.

Liza beamed back a knowing smile that telegraphed a certain smugness to the current population at Savanna's. *We have an inside joke. Aren't we clever?* She seemed almost lit from within.

None of this was lost on the woman accompanying the object of immediate lust. She lingered just a few steps behind—icy and perpetually pissed off— like the always-ignored wife of a rock star.

"Where's the husband I'm supposed to whip in beach volleyball?" he asked.

"Back in the city waiting for a fire to start," Liza replied. Then she gestured to Billie and made the necessary introductions. "March and I scream at each other once a week on *The Roundtable.*"

"You're Billie Shelton the singer, right?" he asked, his face bright, his tone hopeful. There was almost a fanboy quality to his expression.

Billie nodded.

"I love your stuff. I just downloaded some of my favorite tracks onto my iPhone."

Liza stared up at March in complete dismay. "*You* like Billie Shelton music?"

"What's wrong with that?" He glanced at Billie, then back to Liza.

Billie wanted an answer, too. Should it be such a fucking shock that someone appreciated her songs?

Liza seemed to pick up on the instant resentment. "Don't get me wrong, Billie. I'm only surprised because March here is a young Republican. I thought

Lee Greenwood might be more his speed." The smirk on her face was intended for him.

"Now why would you think that?" March wondered easily. "I don't assume that all feminists listen to Melissa Etheridge."

"What's your favorite song of Billie's?" Liza asked. There was a challenge in her tone, as if she half expected him to be unable to name one.

March winked at Billie. " 'Make Me Laugh and Make Me Come and I'll Fucking Marry You.' " He paused a beat. "That's a personal favorite." Suddenly, he reached back to clasp the forgotten girl's hand. "Forgive my rudeness." Then he proceeded to introduce as his fiancée a cold bitch named Amaryllis Hartman.

Billie hated her on principle. Because she had the impervious countenance of a girl who came from real money. Because her aloof, patrician blond beauty made for a legitimate comparison to Gwyneth Paltrow. And because March had asked her to marry him.

It surprised Billie that she was crushing so hard and so quickly. And over a man like March. God, he wasn't her type at all. Usually, she went for the guys who had a prison yard's worth of tattoos running down their arms and legs. Or a son of a bitch like Todd Bana—he was young and successful in a cutthroat industry, which required a certain amount of sleaze. Plus, he could advance her career. That made it love.

And here stood March Donaldson. A conservative Texas male. Jesus Christ, this didn't make any sense. They were polar opposites. He was a political animal. She was almost thirty and had never registered to vote. But he was without a doubt the hottest guy Billie had ever met. A stunning specimen of man.

She noticed Amaryllis discreetly pinch the palm of his hand with her perfectly manicured nails.

"We need to run," March said. "It's Amaryllis's birthday."

The luckiest whore in the room winced as he mentioned this. Probably because it only delayed their escape.

Billie merely stared back impassively.

Liza started in with predictable and meaningless best wishes.

"Her parents are hosting a party in the outdoor pavilion," March went on. "Come have a glass of champagne before you leave."

Amaryllis managed a tight, insincere smile. "It's just family and a few close friends." Her implicit message came through loud and clear: *In other words, not you two bitches.*

Liza watched them go.

Billie clocked her reaction. "Are you fucking him?"

Appalled, Liza drew back. "What? No!"

"But you want to," Billie accused.

Liza put on her best you-must-be-crazy face. "*March Donaldson?* Billie, the man stands for everything that I fight against. We've found a little corner of the earth where we can deal with each other. It may look a bit flirty, but it's completely harmless. So *no,* I don't want to."

Billie drank deeply of her wine. "Well, I do."

Liza's brow went up.

Billie grinned.

"Isn't he a little traditional for you? March actually goes to church." One beat. "And I'm pretty sure that he loves his mother."

"Okay, I have to admit—that's some scary shit."

Liza laughed.

"But he probably only goes to pray for his soul. I bet he's a secret party animal."

"Not like you're used to," Liza said. "He's a Texas fraternity boy. It's just beer kegs and yelling at the television during football games."

Billie didn't buy that. A gut feeling told her that March Donaldson was a closet freak. And her instincts were rarely wrong about such things.

"Anyway, he's engaged," Liza said dismissively. "But Amaryllis seems nice."

"A fiancée wouldn't stop a man like that. A wife wouldn't, either. And even from that brief exchange, we both know that Amaryllis is a cunt."

The waiter swooped in to take away their dinner plates and inquire about dessert.

Billie announced her intention to finish the wine.

Liza ordered coffee.

Billie noticed that Liza seemed relieved when they moved past the subject of March. She didn't quite believe her friend's denial. How could Liza be content with a man like Justin? Okay, physically, he was flawless. But Liza was such an intellectual creature. March's politics might take a hard turn to the right, but at least the man could think. When Justin wasn't pumping iron, he just sat around waiting for an alarm bell to ring.

There was real electricity between Liza and March. Billie was almost drunk, but she could still read a situation. It didn't matter, though. Not now. March was fair game. She'd given Liza every opportunity

to stake a claim of interest, even on a look-but-
don't-touch fantasy level. So Billie would just have
to take the woman at her word.

They lingered at the table, nibbling on the peanut
brittle teasers, talking about their first weekend in the
summer share. They intended to spend most of the
daylight hours working on their tans. With a two-
week head start, they just might be able to stand next
to Kellyanne without looking like a couple of ghosts.

Beyond that, the evenings were all planned out.
Reservations at Nick & Toni's for Saturday night.
Half a dozen cocktail parties on Sunday. Film director Harrison Beck's big Memorial Day bash in
Sagaponack on Monday. Too bad they had to be escorted there by K.K., the fat queen. Billie had seen
him on television leading a panel to dish red carpet
fashion after an awards show. Cartoon fags were so
annoying.

When the check arrived, Billie made no move to
contribute. It wasn't her idea to come here. Liza
didn't blanch, though. With tip, the bill had to be almost eight hundred dollars. But she just threw down
her American Express Black. Must be nice. Amy lec-
tured Billie regularly on cutting down her spending.
Meanwhile, Liza was making money in her sleep.
And for what—raising hell about some stupid slasher
movie? Some people had all the luck.

As they made their way out of Savanna's, Billie
announced, "I'm going to the ladies' room. Meet
you outside, okay?"

Liza seemed to think nothing of it and ventured on.

Billie fell back, waiting for her to exit, then made
a beeline for the pavilion. There was a tentlike structure. More Grecian columns. A beautiful garden. But
with balloons everywhere and a table chockablock

72   J. J. Salem

full of gifts, it looked as if Amaryllis was celebrating her sweet sixteen.

Suddenly, March appeared and offered a flute of champagne. "Where's Liza?"

Billie drank up and passed the empty glass back to him. "Waiting for me outside."

He took a step closer. "That's not very sociable."

"I can't stay, either. I just wanted to give you my number." She slipped a scrap of paper into his front pocket.

He smiled. "Is that the kind of information that could get me into trouble?"

Billie licked her lips. In her white jeans and black lace camisole top, she knew that she looked hot. "Use it. Find out for yourself."

March opened his mouth to speak.

But Billie was already gone.

From across the room, Amaryllis stood watching.

Billie matched her glare for glare. Then she silently mouthed the words, "Happy birthday, bitch," and walked out.

Liza

5

Liza had forecasted the sequence of events like a gifted palm reader. On Sunday, Thursday's taping of *The Roundtable* aired on CNBC. Now it was Monday, and her dig at Harrison Beck led the Page Six gossip parade in *The New York Post*.

Size Matters

Laughing about the size of a guy's . . . *ahem* . . . equipment is like Kryptonite to the male ego. Just ask that hunky morning news anchor whose wife was overheard complaining about his true measurement. Now **Harrison Beck**, director of the current blockbuster *Watch Her Bleed,* is seeing green. Fashionable feminist spin girl **Liza Pike** recently told TV viewers that the real issue behind the high female body count in his creepy and very violent new movie is the filmmaker's tiny tool. Any ex-lovers care to confirm or deny this?

"Liza Pike, you are a witchy, witchy woman," K.K. sang. "Did the Eagles write that song about you?"

They were crammed into the stylist's Porsche 911 Carrera 4 and cruising down Parsonage Lane in Sagaponack, on their way to Harrison Beck's Memorial Day bash.

"I can't believe I'm helping you crash this party! If only I'd known you were going to insult the host's dick on national television!" K.K. squealed gleefully, no doubt adoring the fact that just by showing up with Liza, he was tangentially linking himself to the mini-scandal.

"I don't see the big deal," Billie said, folded into the backseat and still hung over from the Saturday–Sunday party gauntlet. "If it's not true, all he has to do is pull down his pants and prove it."

Liza and K.K. laughed.

Before eighties excess set in, Sagaponack had been a forgotten little hamlet of the Hamptons, home to sweeping acres of potato fields. Parsonage Lane ran through the center of what were once large tracts of agricultural land. But you could only build so much in trendier East Hampton and Southampton. So multimillion-dollar homes were now lined up and down these fields like toy soldiers.

K.K. pulled up behind a gleaming BMW and shut off the engine.

Liza admired the sight of rolling farmland and, in the distance, gorgeous beachfront. "Does he own all of this?"

"Some of that land's reserved," K.K. said. "But Harrison's house sits on about seven acres. Not a bad spread."

Liza ran the calculations. Easily $8 million, if not

more. Impressive. And this property was acquired before his *Watch Her Bleed* windfall.

Liza, Billie, and K.K. tumbled out of the car and fell into step with a few others making their way up the path. Harrison Beck lived in a two-story English Country estate with an adjacent carriage house, both with wood-shingled roof and exterior. There was a sunken Har-Tru tennis court, too.

Familiar faces dotted the lawn and splashed in the pool. So far, it seemed like the same social animals attended the same parties. Forget fresh conversation until Labor Day. What did people in the Hamptons say to each other by the Fourth of July?

K.K. offered up both arms. "Shall we, ladies?"

Just as Liza moved to accept the gesture, her BlackBerry vibrated. Scooping it out of her Hermès bag, she read JUSTIN CALLING on the screen. "Give me one minute," she said, stepping off to the side.

"Hey, baby. I miss you." His tone was overly sweet.

Right away Liza sensed a hidden agenda. "Miss you, too." A rote response. But did she actually mean it? In all truth, the weekend had been a nonstop whirlwind, and Justin had scarcely entered her mind. Or maybe she'd deliberately put him out of it.

"You having a good time?" he asked. Too solicitous. Something had to be up.

"It's been fun. We're hitting our last party right now, and then I'll be home in time for dinner."

There was a pregnant pause.

"A buddy in Brooklyn called and needs some help with his car. We're gonna get a racquetball game in first and then take care of things in his garage. I'll probably be late getting back. Don't wait up, okay?"

"A husband who's really missing his wife wouldn't make plans like that."

"Come on, baby. He needs my help." Justin laughed a little. "Carl didn't marry a rich woman like I did. They can't afford to take the car to the shop."

The sound of his voice and the content of his answer made her smile. Maybe she did miss him. Liza thought back to the big romantic plans she had in store after dragging him home from Pila Anderson's book party. But Justin pleaded a stomach upset from the food and spent the rest of the night crashed in front of the plasma screen, watching *Braveheart* for the millionth time.

A few incidents like that had now hardened into a sinister trend. Sex had practically come to a full stop. At first, Liza thought it'd been her doing, but now she believed otherwise. Justin had the uncanny ability to be absent when a husband's ardor and affection would be expected. After a few nights apart. On a lazy weekend morning unburdened by work or appointments. He always had something to do, some other place to be.

Liza wondered if her success, ambition, and earning power were part of the reason. Did Justin feel emasculated? The boys at his station house teased him about the fact that she'd kept her maiden name. How much did that really bother him?

But the more she tried to figure Justin out, the more he perplexed her. It'd be strange if the money she made caused him to feel diminished in some way. Because he sure didn't have a problem spending it. And nothing seemed to truly reach him. She could pinpoint the most emotion he'd ever expressed. It happened during those first few nights together, when he openly mourned his fallen comrades from September 11.

Oh, God, what she wouldn't give for a little bit of feeling! Here she was flooding her body with hormones to ensure the chance of one day having his baby, yet he could never conjure up so much as, "How are you doing?" Justin just blindly marched on—casual, carefree, always up for a good time with the guys. Except for work, he lived like a college boy who never went to class. Only lately, like one who rarely seemed interested in sex.

Suddenly, a male hand gently covered Liza's eyes. "Boo!"

She pulled it away, spinning around to find Tom Shapiro.

Embarrassed to discover that she was on the phone, Tom mouthed an apology and started off.

Liza reached out for his hand to make him stay. "I guess I'll see you later then," she told Justin. "Love you."

"Me, too." And then he hung up.

Leaning in to kiss Tom, she let out a half-sigh, half-groan.

"Everything okay?"

"I'm fine. It's just my fucking husband." She waved for Billie and K.K. to go inside without her.

"What is it with women in New York?" Tom wondered. "It's either the fucking husband you married or the fucking husband you can't find."

Liza grinned. "I don't think that's unique to Manhattan. It's a fairly universal complaint."

"So what's the issue? I've watched enough *Dr. Phil* to offer something."

"We live totally separate lives," Liza said matter-of-factly.

"Don't change that," Tom advised. "As I understand, it's the only thing keeping most marriages alive today."

Liza laughed and took a step back to admire *The Roundtable* host in his striped Izod shirt, weathered khakis, and battered canvas boat shoes. "I didn't expect to find you in this crowd."

"Harrison must be feeling guilty for turning down the interview. His office FedExed an invitation." Tom gave her a pointed look. "You're the real surprise guest. It took some balls to show up here."

Liza curled her lips mischievously. "I'm not exactly a guest. I'm crashing."

"Let me upgrade that to balls of steel. It's no wonder you're pissed off at home. You don't need a husband. You need a wife."

"Please. Sometimes I feel like I have one. I make all the money, and I can't seem to get laid. This is supposed to be progress?"

Tom chuckled. "It's the alpha woman/beta male syndrome. I can actually help with this one."

Liza folded her arms and stared back expectantly. "I'm listening, Dr. Phil."

"You might need reassurance that you're still feminine."

Liza rolled her eyes. "I've got that part covered. I need reassurance that my husband still has a dick. But thanks for trying, Tom." She began walking toward the front entrance.

Tom picked up his stride to join her. "I should probably stick to politics."

"Probably," Liza agreed. "But actually, talking about this helped. I might write about it in my next column."

"Good idea. Let his firefighter buddies read about how he can't get it up. That'll make him horny."

"They don't read. Not past the sports section anyway." Reaching the precipice of the wide-open door, Liza hesitated.

"You can't turn back now. He's already seen you," Tom whispered, cutting his eyes to a man halfway up the staircase.

Harrison Beck stared down at the latest arrivals, a big Montecristo jutting out of his mouth like an exclamation point. Going bald but not trying to hide it, he had an aura that screamed volcanic confidence. He was a middle-aged, unpolished Jewish-Italian tough guy of average height, his body hairy, taut, and compact.

One look into his blue-gray eyes and Liza knew that he didn't sleep much, that his neurotic, hyper-achieving ways woke him up at three A.M. with night sweats, that his favorite pastime was riding in his Ferrari with a girlfriend born the year Internet service was invented.

The presence of Liza and Tom created a ripple of awareness in the big yet charming house—at least six thousand square feet and tastefully decorated, with large public rooms flowing easily into one another.

Harrison's guests knew she was the publicity-hungry feminist who engineered social takedowns dressed up in political drag. They knew he was the young and on-the-rise television host, rumored to be closeted but still frustratingly ambiguous about his sexual orientation.

Harrison locked a ray-gun gaze onto Liza and stepped down to the bottom of the stairs. "You've got a bad source of information." He was still chewing on the cigar that seemed to be smoking him. Then he unfastened his Gap jeans and pushed down his Burberry boxers, giving her the full monty.

Everybody in the immediate vicinity howled, causing a stampede from other areas of the house to see what was happening.

Harrison Beck was uncircumcised. And he had nothing to be ashamed about. Even without the benefit of an erection, no one could deny that the man was impressively hung.

Mortified, Liza just stood there on the French limestone floor. She was famous for always getting in the last word. Right now she was momentarily speechless. But then she regained her composure. "That's a neat trick. You unzip your pants and your brains fall out."

By this point, a standing-room-only crowd had gathered, so there was a bigger audience for Liza's punch line, which she'd actually pinched from a Jackie Collins rant about Hollywood men. Original or not, the laughter was deafening.

A flush of embarrassment started at Harrison's neck and spread all the way to his cheeks. Finally, he pulled up his jeans and gave her a conciliatory shake of the head. "Show's over!" he shouted to the masses. "Now everybody get drunk and forget this happened!"

Liza smiled. A man with a sense of humor about himself. No reason to vote him off the island . . . *yet.*

Harrison approached and boldly took her hand. "Walk with me." He started out in a rush, pulling her with him.

Liza turned back to see Tom staring at her in startled amusement. Billie and K.K. were nowhere in sight. She struggled to keep up as Harrison bounded down the porch and cut between the main house and the carriage house, heading directly into an expansive stretch of field. "Where are you taking me?"

"Someplace where there's no audience, no camera, and no microphone," Harrison growled good naturedly. "That probably scares the shit out of you."

Liza tottered behind him, feeling like a total spasmodic, her spike-heeled Manolos doing little to help her navigate the earth like a true farm girl. "Not really. The scariest place for me is any multiplex showing your crap movie."

Harrison laughed heartily. "The studio says it'll top a hundred million within twenty-one days."

"Congratulations. Knowing Hollywood, that means a sequel's in the works. How many ways will you hack women to death next time around?"

"You're wrong about my movie. You just don't get it."

Liza stopped dead in her tracks. "What's to get about tits, ass, and gore? Besides sick to my stomach."

"I don't hate women," Harrison said, finally taking the cigar out of his mouth. "You can spout off about me having a cocktail-wiener dick. I don't care about that. But don't lay this bullshit misogynist label on me. I'm on friendly terms with both of my ex-wives. I've got three daughters. I take good care of my mother—"

"Who are you trying to convince here?" Liza cut in. "Me or yourself?"

His face broke out into a maniacal smile, and he raised his hands, shaking them as if to strangle her. "Shit! You're impossible!"

"That doesn't answer my question."

Harrison walked away, then turned around and

pointed his finger at her. "You know what? You're a goddamn fraud."

Now Liza started after him, incensed with fury. "*I'm* a fraud?"

"There were great parts for women in my picture," Harrison said passionately. "It was a smart, literate script. Those characters were public intellectuals, politicians, heads of industry. I've heard you bitch about the lousy roles for actresses in film today. I do something that makes it better, and you're still busting my balls."

Liza laughed at him. "So *Watch Her Bleed* actually has a profeminist agenda? Oh, excuse me. I take everything back now."

"It's an homage to the slasher film," he began, employing a tone that implied teacher to dense pupil. "Remember those? *Halloween*, *Friday the 13th*, *Slumber Party Massacre*. The women in those movies were either getting caught naked in the woods with the high school quarterback or heading down into a dark basement in nothing but a short towel. *Watch Her Bleed* is—"

"Not much better and maybe even worse," Liza cut in savagely. "In your movie, the audience—mostly young males, mind you—*participates* with the psycho in voyeurism as he stalks these women. When he kills, they celebrate with him. Hooray! He chopped up the congresswoman fighting for equal pay in the workplace." She rolled her eyes. "So what's the message to an impressionable teenage mind? I'll tell you what it is. Women who achieve their goals and have strong opinions should be chainsawed. Welcome to high art, Harrison Beck style."

"That's your warped point of view!" Harrison thundered. "And it's bullshit! People like you can find a crazy angle in anything. You're just as bad as that dead asshole Jerry Falwell. He thought Tinky Winky was sending gay messages to three-year-olds. Your take on my movie is just as fucked up."

Liza wanted to scream. To be compared to that fascist pig was the ultimate abuse. "Hide behind your paint-by-numbers politics all you want. Hopefully, you and your therapist will figure out the real issue one day."

"Speaking of issues, what's yours?" Harrison asked, his tone ominous.

Liza didn't answer.

"You parade around like this tough feminist with all the answers, only you dress like a *Maxim* girl. And the first thing you do after Osama and his crew attack is run out and marry a fireman. Talk about mixed messages."

Liza stood stock still and silent—a resistance to her immediate impulse to yell, "Fuck you!" and run back toward the house. Suddenly, she felt self-conscious in her Chloe number, the short white sleeveless tunic with beaded fringe, wondering if she looked like a bimbo. God, he knew how to give as good as he got. First Jerry Falwell and now her clothes. And she didn't even want to factor the damage to her psyche for the crack about Justin. "Touché," she said quietly.

Harrison made a sudden retreat inward, focusing his gaze on the sprawling land. "You know what? I moved here as a teenager," he said wistfully. "About thirty years ago. The fields used to stretch all the way to the dunes. And when you stood along the shore, you could look out as far as the eye could see and only find four or five houses, six at the most. Now look."

"It's still beautiful," Liza murmured, knowing that the words rang hollow in the actual presence of overdevelopment.

Harrison sighed. "Yeah, I guess it is." He looked at her and smiled. "So are the gloves off now?"

She averted her eyes and pretended to take in the scenery. "For the moment, I guess."

"Have dinner with me tonight."

"I can't."

"Why?"

"I came here with friends."

"That's not a reason."

Liza faced him now. "Okay, how's this for a reason—I don't want to."

"Liar."

She gave him half a smile and started back toward the house.

"Can I tell you a secret?" Harrison shouted after her. "I got a hard-on when we were arguing! You know what that means, don't you? The sex would be great! And you've seen what I have to offer!"

Liza broke out into a run, moving fast to get away from him. Almost impossible in these fucking heels, but she gave it a go. She was laughing. She was blushing. Because she knew that the son of a bitch was right.

And it scared the hell out of her.

Billie

6

Exactly four days.

That's how long it took March Donaldson to call. The distraction saved Billie from a murder charge. She couldn't decide who she wanted to kill more— that son-of-a-bitch label president Todd Bana or her goddamn manager Amy Dando. Hell, it was a toss-up.

Todd landed on her shit list first. He'd just returned from Los Angeles, and getting in to see him took more trouble than it was worth. All because of Van, his fiercely protective assistant, who treated Billie like some cruise ship singer angling for audition time.

"Todd's in the office but unavailable at the moment." After three calls, Van was still blowing her off.

Billie went ballistic. "Listen, pretty boy, you may kiss his ass, but I actually do what you fantasize about—I suck his cock! Now get him on the goddamn phone!"

A minute later Todd picked up the line. "Billie, why are you terrorizing my assistant?"

"This is the third time I've called. Doesn't that bitchy fag know to put me through?"

"He's not supposed to. I'm swamped. It's the first day after a holiday weekend, and I'm just back from L.A. Give me a chance to dig out from under. I'll—"

"Take me to lunch," Billie insisted. "You have to eat, and I'm starving. There's something I'm dying to show you."

"I'm already booked."

"So cancel. A week ago, I was swallowing your cum. Now I can't get a lousy lunch?"

"Fuck!" Todd yelled, exasperated but still in good humor. "I've got a Mariah on my hands! A royal pain in the ass!"

Billie laughed as she thought about being compared to the superdiva.

"I'll have Van get us a table at Sixty-Six. Meet me there at one."

Billie walked in at one-thirty. Why should she bust her ass to show up on time when she was the fucking talent? Todd seemed pissed off, even as he chowed down on steamed lobster claws.

Billie ignored his mood and glanced around, taking in the sumptuous details of chef-entrepreneur Jean-Georges Vongerichten's Chinese-on-acid eatery. The Eames chairs. The Saarinen tables. The waitress flitting around in a Vivienne Tam–designed uniform. It was an explosion of modernism—frosted glass, steel mesh, resin—courtesy of architect Richard Meier. Too bad it'd soon bite the dust and reopen as a sushi-and-soba restaurant. She loved this place just as it was.

Billie dreamed of the day when she could afford to buy a massive apartment, gut it, and then hire a mastermind like Meier to reinvent *her* space. It could happen. All she needed was one big record. Everything else would fall into place—the tours, the merchandising, the endorsements.

Jessica Simpson popped into her mind. That screaming bitch rang the bell with her stupid reality series first, after which the music kicked back into gear, followed by the commercial offers. The ditz was a complete joke, but she was still worth mega-millions. If Kellyanne got lucky like that with *Soul Mates*, then Billie just might have to kill herself. Here she was, trying to do it the old-fashioned way—on sheer grit and talent—while someone less deserving could easily leapfrog ahead. All because of some cheesy reality show.

Billie slipped into the seat opposite Todd and grabbed a lobster claw that reeked of ginger. "Hey, thanks for waiting."

"You asked for this meeting, and I've been sitting here for thirty fucking minutes. What are you dying to show me?"

"Relax."

As if on cue, the waitress appeared.

Billie asked for fried crab, squab, and scallion pancakes. By the time it arrived, she might take half a bite of each. But so what? Olympic was paying. Glancing down, she took note of Todd's water. "You're not drinking?"

"I'm jet-lagged, and I'm jammed up with meetings. Need to keep my head clear." He checked his watch—a flashy Rolex. "I squeezed you in. Let's get on with this."

"As always, impatient and not enthusiastic enough. Do you approach everything the same way you give head?" Billie smirked.

Todd surrendered a reluctant grin. "Okay. You got me to smile."

"What's your problem?"

"Just a rough day." He rubbed his eyes. "So show me this big surprise."

Billie reached for a spiral notebook and slid it across the table. On the night she had written the new songs, her lyrics ended up all over the place—on cocktail napkins, paper towels, old receipts, utility bills, any scrap of paper she could get her hands on. But she had transcribed everything into the notebook—by her own hand—to prove to Todd that her creative block was a problem of the past.

"What's this?" He stared at the offering as if it were a mess on the side of the road.

Billie leaned in meaningfully. "Some new songs. I'm still working on the melodies, but the lyrics . . . shit, Todd, I feel like I've come up with . . . *Dick Magnet: The Sequel! This* should've been the follow-up to my first album."

Todd nodded vaguely, opened the notebook, and began flipping through the pages. He scanned the words with something close to boredom. At the end, he gave her an indifferent shrug. "I thought we agreed to use outside writers and producers."

"That was before!"

"Before what?"

"Before I got my muse back!"

Todd closed the cover and pushed her handwritten heart and soul back across the table. "I know what your muse is." His tone was cold. "I'm the guy who shot it up your ass. Remember?"

For a moment, Billie believed the scene was happening outside of her own body. It felt that horrible. "This has nothing to do with the meth! These are great songs!"

Todd shook his head. "They're shit, Billie."

"But you hardly—"

He held up a hand to stop her. "I saw enough. Now listen to me. The old Billie Shelton is over. She's finished. Do you have any idea how many CDs you sold last week?"

She stared back at him.

"Less than a hundred."

The news flattened her spirit.

"Whatever force existed for *Dick Magnet* worked in that moment. But you didn't keep it going. Or maybe it was never meant to continue. Who knows?"

"But when I tour—"

"By the end of your last tour, you were selling maybe sixty percent of the house. Amy would have trouble keeping you on the road in today's market. And whatever discipline you had is gone. You'd probably cancel shows at the last minute, like that train wreck Amy Winehouse. But at least she's got the popularity to back it up. You'd have to be paired with a hotter act or start booking clubs."

Billie fingered the notebook with longing. Maybe Todd was lying. He had to be. This was just a bullshit game to rattle her confidence. That way she'd say yes to all his new ideas, like some scared little girl. The music industry was so fucking sleazy. "You know what I feel like right now?" she launched in hotly. "I feel like I'm in the porn business, and you're some producer who's brainwashing me with doomsday career talk just so I'll sign on to do a gang bang."

Todd lifted his eyebrows and sipped his water. "That's quite an analogy."

Billie's fists hit the table. "Don't fucking patronize me!"

"I don't have a chance," Todd said with a calmness that infuriated her. "You're too busy patronizing yourself. Or going psycho." He shook his head and laughed a little. "What goes on in that mind of yours? Right now, White Tiger is the most sought after production team out there. They decide who they want to work with, and they want to work with you. It's just going to take a little time. We're waiting for their schedule to open up."

Billie looked at Todd. Really looked at him. And the sexy bastard held up under the scrutiny.

"I thought you were on board with this," he continued. "I thought you wanted a big radio hit."

All of a sudden, Billie's eyes welled up with tears. "I did . . . I do . . . It's just . . . I still think my songs are good."

"No one's telling you to stop writing."

She gently wiped her eyes with her fingers and wondered how fucked her makeup was. "Yeah, telling me they're shit is great encouragement. Thanks."

Todd gave her a half smile. "What can I say? I shoot straight. If you like writing songs, do it for yourself. Just don't expect me to let you record them. Not on my label anyway."

"You missed your calling," Billie said. "You should be doing motivational speeches."

This made him laugh. The expression on his handsome face was one of bemused affection. "Jesus, Billie, you're like a relic from the seventies. It's all sex, drugs, and rock and roll to you. Music used to be *it*.

But you can't think that way anymore. Not in today's culture. There's so much fucking noise. You've got cell phones, video games, DVDs, iPods, high-speed Internet, reality TV. Shit, the list goes on forever. It takes so much to break through all that and create any kind of impact. These days you need a radio hit, a L'Oréal commercial, and maybe a sex tape floating around to be considered a star."

"Are you suggesting that we set up a camera in your bedroom?"

Lasciviously, Todd flickered his tongue. "Nah. That shit's over. We partied. We swung from the chandelier. But we better keep it strictly business from now on. Things will be intense enough. Don't think I won't miss it, though. You've got a magic pussy." He laughed. "And unlike your lyrics, that's not the meth talking."

Billie couldn't believe it. He was flushing her songs down the crapper and breaking up with her, too. And lunch hadn't even been served yet. What a fucking prick!

"Be glad you're a dyke, Amy, because men are shit."

Billie was still in TriBeCa, stomping down Church Street and blabbing on her cell phone. She knew Liza lived nearby but couldn't remember where. Hell, forget it. Amy would just have to listen to her bitch. She raged on.

"I don't know what the fuck they want. I'm a great broad. I'm as wild as a horse's ass. I can hold my liquor. I can handle my drugs. Think about it. I'm full of hell and always ready for sex. Yet men consistently use me like a rest stop on their way to a *real* girlfriend. Did I tell you about March, that hot guy I met in the Hamptons over the weekend? He's engaged to some frigid thing named Amaryllis. One drink and I bet you have to hold that bitch's head over the toilet. Anyway, Todd's not a serious loss. I would've dumped him in the middle of a blow job for a chance at this March guy. But it still hurts that he unloaded me first."

"Billie, I can't do this right now," Amy said tightly.

"Do what?"

"Play therapist because you did some stupid shit like screw Todd Bana. I've got a million things to do."

"If I needed a therapist, do you really think I'd call you?"

"Then what do you want?"

"What I want is for you to act like the fucking manager I pay you to be and make that asshole take my new songs seriously!"

"Let me refresh your memory since it seems those drugs you handle so well have fried your brain. The last time I tried to act like your manager, we were sitting in Todd's office. That's when you ignored my objections and agreed to this style overhaul in the first place. I haven't even heard these songs yet. But what does it matter? You'll probably jump back into bed with him and say yes to recording a Christmas album with the Wiggles."

Billie pictured Amy in her cramped little office on Broadway, hunched over the shabby desk that was always adrift in CDs, paper, pictures, and music paraphernalia. "I can bring the songs to you now."

Amy sighed. "Just wait until I get back."

"From where?"

"I leave for Japan in the morning."

"What for?"

"One of my new acts is on her first promotional

tour. She's too young to handle Tokyo alone, her parents are idiots, and I don't trust the label rep."

Billie hated to hear about Amy's other clients. They always seemed to be getting deals and perks that eluded her. Olympic had never sent Billie Shelton overseas. "So you'll hold her hand across the fucking world, but you won't take a minute to look at my new songs?"

"I have to go. I'll call you when I get back."

Billie started to protest. But Amy had already hung up.

For a long moment she stood there in the middle of the sidewalk, the phone still in her hand, feeling as if everything was slipping away.

The ring startled her. At first, she assumed it was Amy calling back to say bring the songs over, but Billie didn't recognize the incoming number. "Hello?"

It was March Donaldson.

Most men punched the clock. They went down on a girl because it was the polite thing to do and usually guaranteed a blow job in return. But March ate Billie like she was his last meal on earth.

She lifted her hips to meet his mouth. She was sweating. She was clawing his back. She was crushing his skull with the pressure of her thighs.

Oh, God! It was the best ever.

He started slow, breathing hot breath onto her panties. Then he ironed out her labia with big, soft, lingering licks as she squirmed under his expert attention.

The man was a fucking Jedi master of the art. He knew how to circle up and around the clitoris and back again. He knew how to suck her magic button into his mouth and lick it at the same time.

But when he dove in face-first and nuzzled her with his nose, she wanted to have his baby. And by the time he did a simultaneous up-lick with his tongue and downward tug with his fingers, she was lost in a Richter-scale orgasm. Again. And again.

Even after March rolled over onto his back and lit up some hellacious smelling herb, Billie was still having little convulsions. "Well . . . that was certainly worth a ride on the Jitney."

He pinched the joint and puckered his lips, dragging slow and deep.

"You smoke that like a pro," Billie said.

He smiled. "It's not just rock stars and snowboarders who appreciate."

"So tell me. Are there more Republicans like you out there? I just might have to join the party."

March laughed.

They passed the joint back and forth.

Billie noticed that his upper lip was swollen. She started to giggle. "I can't believe it! You've got a fat lip from eating me out!"

"My tongue is numb, too," March said. "What can I say? I love my work."

She admired him. Sprawled across the white sheets. Naked, tan, and more gorgeous than any man had a right to be.

"Usually, I come while I'm doing it," he went on. "I don't even have to touch my cock. I just get so excited that I start shooting."

"So what happened?"

"I've already jacked off a few times today."

She gave him a curious look.

He shrugged. "I was bored. In the middle of my third round, I thought about you. That's when I decided to call."

"Perfect timing, too. I think you saved me from killing my manager."

"Glad to be of service." He finished the rest of the joint, smoking it down to his fingers.

Billie felt properly baked now. Oh, God, she was relaxed. "This is some really good shit."

"I've got a great dealer. He looks like a Wall Street guy—nice suits, expensive briefcase. People think he's a lobbyist when he shows up at my office."

"I'm jealous."

"I'll give you his number."

They stared at the ceiling in an easy silence that stretched on for a long time.

Finally, March broke it. "I hate all this propaganda about smoking pot's being a serious drug problem. The whole country's on drugs. Have you watched TV lately? Every other ad is for an antidepressant. Take Paxil: You'll have fun at the company picnic again! And now we're doing it to kids. Little Johnny's scared about the first day of school, so let's give him Prozac. What a scam. A little reefer now and then? There's nothing wrong with that. To me, it's a reward. Like a fancy after-work cocktail."

At first, Billie didn't know how to respond. It's not as if she ever watched *Hannity & Colmes*. Politics bored her. "You're right." Okay, not the most articulate thing to say, but what man didn't want to hear it?

March moistened his finger and reached down to trace the outline of her little flower tattoo. "That's sexy. Just above your pussy like that. Did it hurt?"

"Like hell."

He went sliding down to kiss it.

Bless Kellyanne for signing up to do that dumb-ass reality show. With her still in Miami and Liza back in Manhattan until Friday, Billie had the run of their

East Hampton rental. Ice queen Amaryllis had returned to the city, too, and even though March had
her parents' house all to himself, he didn't want to
risk the staff seeing him with another woman. So Billie's summer digs made the perfect spot for an adult
play date.

She stroked his hair. "You know, we can stay here
all week . . ."

"I wish."

Billie held her breath for the rest.

"We're due at a fund-raiser on the Upper East
Side tomorrow. I need to take off in the morning."

His choice of pronoun killed her a little bit.
"What about the next day?"

"I'll be in Washington." His fingers started to en-
circle her delicate tangle of pubic hair. "Will you
wax your bush for me?"

Billie felt a surge of delight. It meant that he
wanted to see her again.

"I like the Brazilian. It's just a narrow strip in
front. Smooth to the touch. Smooth to the taste."

She glanced down at him. "Is that what Amaryllis
does to hers?"

"Not quite. She went through laser removal. It's
completely bald down there. I prefer some hair. Not a
lot. Just a little. Go to J. Sisters. They do great work.
It's on West 57th."

"Instead of a landing strip, maybe I should ask
them to shape your initials."

March let out a soft moan. "That'd be hot."

"Consider it done," Billie said.

With a sudden and delicious roughness, March
turned Billie over onto her stomach. "I guess this
means you're my summer bitch." Three masturbation
sessions be damned. He slid into her from behind

with a velocity and hardness that knocked the breath from her body.

"I guess so," Billie whispered, realizing with a strange mix of lust, fear, and dread that, in the space of one afternoon, March Donaldson had become her most urgent reason for living.

Kellyanne

7

Signing that contract was a horrible mistake. Kelly-anne had set herself up as a willing prisoner in some tasteless mansion on Miami's Star Island. Now she desperately wished she could be anywhere else—back at her apartment waiting for Walter, on a plane heading to the Hamptons, even in a Humvee rattling down a booby-trapped road in Iraq.

Anywhere but here.

"I'm good television," real estate agent Dee Loner-gan announced for what must have been the millionth time in the span of a week. She smacked her lips, swiping on another coat of gloss as she faced the smudged and splattered mirror inside the filthy bath-room.

Kellyanne cut a polar glance at her.

"I'll probably get some endorsements after this," Dee went on, never taking her eyes off her own re-flection. She was pretty in that very standard, very forgettable way, the kind of girl who took first runner-up in the state beauty pageant and spent the rest of her life talking about how she should've won.

Suddenly, Kellyanne got elbowed by Bunny Corvette, a Hooters waitress rudely angling for more room to glob on her drugstore mascara. "Sorry." The apology barely made it past the girl's plump lips.

"No problem," Kellyanne sniffed. "I was sick of that rib anyway."

"Whatever," Bunny murmured under her breath. "You're just pissed because Vlad barely paid attention to you on the group date."

"Yes, it was *devastating.*" Kellyanne doused a cotton square with La Prairie Cellular Refining Lotion and applied it to her face and throat in quick circular sweeps.

Dee spoke up. "The show is called *Soul Mates,* not *Slut Search.* Vlad's not going to choose the girl with the stripper name who won't stop sticking her tongue down his throat."

Bunny glared at Dee. "And you think he's going to choose you—the house bitch?"

Dee continued perfecting her lips. "Let's just say that packing up your shit before the next key ceremony wouldn't be the worst use of your time."

Bunny just stood there, stunned and hurt, though her posture seemed to indicate that she was still ready for battle.

"You're going to take that?" Rhett taunted. He was just out of college and working as a *Soul Mates* story editor. One of his jobs was to follow behind the ubiquitous camera operators and look for situations to exploit into dramatic opportunities. "Yell at her! Throw something at her!"

Kellyanne groaned and gathered up her products,

slipping out just as the shrieking and clatter of flying makeup commenced.

She could hardly blame Rhett. The poor bastard was just a struggling writer desperate to get a foot in the door of the television business. But Brad "Bonzi" Lucas had slapped him with the meaningless title of story editor, a shrewd way to bypass the Writers Guild of America and enslave Rhett to a flat pay contract for what amounted to an eighty-hour workweek with no overtime, no meal periods, no health benefits, and no participation in residuals. The de facto salary turned out to be less than ten dollars per hour.

Kellyanne marched back into the master suite she shared with Dee and Bunny. During the first few days of shooting, there'd been two other roommates—a black girl named Starleana and a Japanese fitness model who called herself Asia. But Vlad Branigan—in the tradition of most white male reality stars searching for a lover on national television—had disposed of all the women of color in the first round of elimination.

A palpable sense of regret came over Kellyanne, and, as if weighed down by it, she sank onto the edge of the twin bed. What was she doing here? Why had she agreed to this? Oh, yeah, that's right. She was doing it all for her career.

In retrospect, she felt like a fool for thinking that a reality show would move her acting ambitions even one step forward. The world was littered with D-list losers who'd thought exactly the same thing.

Kellyanne tried to recall the exact selling points from Bonzi's booze-fueled marketing pitch. She should've known right away that *Soul Mates* would only be more garbage for TV's summer scrap heap.

Except for the final twist, the show was a complete rip-off of ABC's *The Bachelor.*

Kellyanne was among thirty girls who'd moved into the rented Star Island mansion and instantly been denied access to newspapers, television, radio, the Internet, and phone service. One girl had been caught using a smuggled Razr V3 and was quickly jettisoned from the show.

Beyond the half-hearted attempt at assembling a diverse cast—Starleana, Asia, one plus-size girl, and an Indian belly dancer—Bonzi and his coconspirators had chosen contestants whom they could easily mold into predetermined types.

Dee Lonergan was the Antagonizer, an ice queen quick on the draw, with such bold announcements as, "I'm not here to make friends" and "You think I'm a bitch now? You haven't seen anything yet."

Bunny Corvette was the Slut. And Kellyanne had been there when Rhett fed her the line, "I prefer sex on the first date. It's like test-driving a car. If I don't like the way it rides, then I move on to another vehicle."

There was also the Disney Princess, in this case Samantha, a sweet girl from Virginia who talked in unprompted bumper-sticker speak about "finding my Prince Charming" and "meeting the man of my dreams."

Kellyanne had been recruited as the Southern Bombshell and was frequently encouraged to play up her accent and drop cornpone regional expressions such as "ain't got enough sense to bell a cat." That was just one of the ridiculous sayings that Rhett had discovered from a half-assed online search. She refused to utter such nonsense, giving them a few y'alls but nothing more.

The program stuck to typical genre conventions. There was the meet-and-greet event, where all of the women paraded around Vlad Branigan, desperate to make an impression before the first selection ceremony, at which point he winnowed the pool to a field of twenty by presenting oversize heart-shaped keys as he offered these words: "I think you could be my soul mate. Tonight I offer this key to my heart."

There was also a series of formal dinners to ratchet up catty conflicts, a soundproof video chamber to record daily confessionals, group dates to prove Vlad Branigan's ability to attract a devoted harem, and every possible contrivance to get the women into bathing suits.

As for Vlad, he was hardly the second coming of Brad Pitt that Bonzi had promised. His hunk factor was quickly snuffed out by macho arrogance and a humorless, lunkhead personality. Every group date seemed to end in the hot tub with Vlad's directing the women to rotate positions so that he could sample them individually.

Kellyanne thought she would mercifully be denied a heart key after turning away to avoid Vlad's open-mouthed kiss in the Jacuzzi. But she was still here. Now he thought of her as a challenge. It'd come back to her through one of the production assistants—a smart girl who took a lot of shit from the other assholes on the crew—that Vlad had said, "The Alabama bitch is playing hard to get, but she'll be begging for my dick before this is over."

Kellyanne buried her face in her hands and fell backward onto the bed, feeling the full impact of all the regret, disappointment, and self-loathing that had been building throughout the week. There was a spiritual cost to signing that contract. And she was paying it right now.

Whenever she imagined the show's actually being broadcast, she experienced a suffocating sense of dread. Four letters summed up the feeling—WWLT . . . What Would Liza Think? Kellyanne knew that her opinionated friend would blast *Soul Mates* as another example of the reality TV factory stripping away women's intelligence and self-awareness to portray them as desperate sexual objects.

And she'd be right. Of course, Kellyanne had known this all along. The thought had even lanced her brain as she scratched her signature onto the contract. But a core need to have something significant of her own had propelled her forward. Oh, God, how pathetic. Her life was so empty that something like *Soul Mates* could come along and instantly qualify as significant.

She envied Liza and Billie. They had purpose. Liza's career was born out of passionate beliefs, and she'd become her own cottage industry, encompassing books, television appearances, blogging, and more. By comparison, Billie was a professional mess, but at least she possessed raw talent. It'd been harnessed before to spectacular results. No doubt it'd be harnessed again. And what did Kellyanne have? A horny old man financing her lavish lifestyle and an agent who regarded her career as an absolute joke.

"Kellyanne?"

She rose up with a start to see one of Bonzi's assistants—a guy they called Crabs for reasons she didn't want to know—standing in the doorway.

His gaze always lingered a few seconds too long.

It was creepy. "Bonzi wants to see you. He's in the main production trailer."

She nodded, deciding instantly to change out of her form-fitting tank and into a regular T-shirt. The less provocative, the better. Bonzi had taken every opportunity to hit on her during the past week, and she was in no mood for his bullshit right now.

Kellyanne started down the staircase, quietly amazed at how much damage could be done to a home in such a short time. She noticed scratches on the limestone floors and fireplace mantel, broken screen doors and skylights, large holes drilled into walls to accommodate cabling, and trash strewn about everywhere—cigarette butts, personal hygiene items, beer and liquor bottles. It looked like the aftermath of a raging college party. Some misguided fools had wanted the ego boost of seeing their home as a glorious set piece for a major television program. They'd rue the day.

The production trailers crowded the mansion's circular drive, causing fatal injury to once-immaculate landscaping. Bonzi's sanctuary was a gleaming silver Airstream that hummed nonstop. The rest of his staff settled for what looked like hobbled trailers from FEMA, the kind that had been issued to Hurricane Katrina victims. Prior to the trailer invasion, footage of Vlad Branigan driving up to the mansion in his black Spyker C8 Laviolette had already been shot.

Kellyanne rapped the trailer door with three fast knocks. And then she waited. She started to try one last time when the door swung open.

Bonzi stood there, looking disheveled in an oversize NFL jersey and baggy board shorts that stopped just past his knees. Why did he feel compelled to dress like a hip-hop wannabe? Impatiently, he motioned for Kellyanne to come inside as he screamed into his BlackBerry.

"That motherfucker pitched my idea! Dude, this sucks! I've got a call in to another network. He can't edit on location. He does it after wrap in L.A. We can beat him onto the air. I'd love to see that douche bag's face when he finds out I got a green light. Call me if you hear anything else. Later." He tapped his earpiece to disconnect. "Some cocksucker stole my idea for *America's Hottest Bartenders*."

Kellyanne gave him a bored look. "And it's so original to begin with." She glanced around at the guitars, heavy metal posters, and horror film memorabilia, wondering if Bonzi would ever grow up.

"I've got something to show you." His tone was ominous.

Kellyanne braced herself for a fast exit, thinking he might drop his pants and ask for a blow job, as he'd done once before.

But this time Bonzi stepped over to an impressive bank of Macintosh computers. "Do you know what *zsuj* is?"

Kellyanne just looked at him blankly. He pronounced it *zhoodge*. She'd never heard the word.

"It's all about the *zsuj* in soaps," Bonzi explained smugly. "You know, lots of romance, candlelight, love scenes. It's a concept to make people believe they're seeing more sex than they actually are. Smoke and mirrors, you know? At the end of the day, sex rules." He raised the bushy brows canopying over his bloodshot eyes.

"Is there a point here?" Kellyanne asked impatiently.

And then Bonzi maneuvered the cordless mouse to activate an application called Avid. After a series of clicks, a night vision image filled the twenty-inch monitor. And then the scene began to play.

It was Vlad Branigan, naked in bed with an unidentifiable blonde kneeling between his legs. Over the chickachika-pow-wow music playing in the background, there were exaggerated sound effects—moaning, slurping, gulping—all being utilized to drive home the fact that oral sex was being performed. In the next scene, Kellyanne, dressed in a camisole and panties, was seen exiting a room and wiping a white substance from the corner of her mouth as she moistened her lips with her tongue.

Instantly, a sick feeling came over her. "You son of a bitch!" she screamed. "This is bullshit! I was coming out of the bathroom that I share with the other girls! And I'd just finished brushing my teeth!"

Bonzi answered with a wicked laugh as he froze the image on the screen. "Isn't it funny how the night-vision camera makes toothpaste look like cum? And this is just a rough cut."

With a few more clicks of the mouse, another picture filled the monitor, this one of Kellyanne tipping back a glass of champagne. In the next scene, she was weaving through the bathroom doorway and retching into the commode. The vomiting went on and on.

"I looped the wettest barf sound over and over again," Bonzi said proudly. "People will think you were really hammered and puking up your guts."

Kellyanne could scarcely contain her anger. It was white-hot and rising. "You know that I got sick on the sushi that your caterer provided!"

Bonzi gave a diffident shrug. "Doesn't look that way to me. It's all in the editing, I guess."

"You can't do this," Kellyanne said. But her words

lacked conviction, because she knew that she was powerless.

"Read your contract. I can do whatever I want with this footage."

Kellyanne blinked back tears as she stared Bonzi down, her eyes burning with hatred. "Why are you doing this to me?"

"Because I can." He swiveled his chair to face her full on. "You've been a disappointment. Onscreen." He paused a beat. "And off." He raked her up and down with a crude glance. "Make me feel good, and I'll make you look good."

The mere thought disgusted her. "You're a pig."

He laughed at her. "What? You've got something against sucking a pig's dick? Since when?"

Kellyanne spun fast and started out.

Bonzi reached out to grab her wrist and squeezed hard.

Kellyanne wrestled free from his grasp, adrenaline pumping as a true, cold fear consumed her. Bonzi was a big man—tall, strong, and, judging from the empty Bud Light bottles cluttering the portable editing bay, more than a little drunk. If he forced himself on her, then she'd be no match for the bastard.

Ultimately, he waved her off with a bored gesture. "Get out. If your pussy was actually worth all this trouble, you'd be a real actress by now." He turned back to the monitor, dismissing her altogether.

Kellyanne just stood there as the impact of Bonzi's words sliced into her psyche. How had she gotten here? When would she stop living this dumb life? And why did every man—her married lover included—see fit to treat her like the cheapest slab of meat in the market?

This was the tipping point. She wanted out. Right now. No matter the consequences. "I quit."

Bonzi's face registered nothing. "Fine. I've still got enough footage to paint you as the show's resident cum Dumpster. And a drunk one at that." He smirked.

Even as she was seething inside, Kellyanne did her best nonchalant act. "I'll take national humiliation over sleeping with you any day."

He cocked his head to the side, as if pondering the wonderfully cruel outcome in store for her. "Remember this moment, bitch. You'll regret it."

Suddenly, it occurred to Kellyanne that she had a card to play. *Soul Mates* was one of those meta-reality shows built around the gimmick that the viewing audience is in on a secret but the cast is not. A Ketel One–soaked mind made for loose lips, and Bonzi had boasted about the show's big reveal on the night she met him at Silk Electric.

"You might regret it, too," Kellyanne shot back acidly. "Especially after I tell Vlad about the trick you have planned for him at the end of the show. I'm sure the other girls would like to know about it, too."

Bonzi gave her a smug grin. "I think they just want to be on television. And I know Vlad is just in it for the pussy. It doesn't matter how fake things are. Haven't you heard? Reality is the new substitute for truth."

For a moment, Kellyanne considered a shock and awe campaign of destruction. She had the reservoir of anger to do it. And the idea of smashing up Bonzi's editing bay filled her with a certain glee. But she knew the act would be futile. No doubt the footage was stored on some unseen server. Destroying his equipment would just enrage him more.

Wordlessly, she walked out, making a beeline for

the house and dashing upstairs, determined to gather up her things and leave. Before Kellyanne reached her room, a camera operator was rushing to capture her every move.

She worked fast, checking the contents of her Louis Vuitton beauty case and shoving whatever clothes she could locate into her matching keep-all.

It took no time for a gaggle of girls to form in the doorway, their faces a collage of confusion, concern, and relief.

Kellyanne ignored their questions, if only to deny Bonzi any additional footage that might be used to complete the bogus story arc he was creating.

She pushed past the throng, avoiding eye contact and jutting out her bags to force an open path.

"The girl's quitting because she knows that Vlad's not going to give her a key," Dee taunted. "I don't know how she got on the show, anyway. She must be the quota slot for Alabama white trash."

It took every cell in Kellyanne's body to fight against responding. She vaulted forward as if the bitch had never spoken.

"Did you hear what Dee just said?" Rhett asked, his voice soaked in desperation. This was a big reality-show moment. He needed a beginning, middle, and end. "Why are you leaving, Kellyanne? Is it something that Vlad did? Is it a personal crisis?"

She reached the bottom of the stairs and spun around to face him. "I need to make a call. Can I borrow your cell?"

Rhett hesitated, his expression pained. "I could get fired for that."

"I quit the goddamn show, Rhett. I just need to find someone to get me out of here," Kellyanne implored him.

Rhett shook his head. "I'm sorry."

"Whatever," Kellyanne spat. She stormed out, pushing open the front door, not bothering to close it behind her as she stalked down the drive.

It was time to get a fucking life.

Liza

8

"I don't believe in female sexuality as a zero-sum game," Liza said matter-of-factly. "This idea that you're either a *Girls Gone Wild* slut who will lift up your top for a free T-shirt or a puritan who vows virginity until marriage in exchange for a promise ring from Daddy is intellectually and emotionally dishonest."

"A classic liberal response," March Donaldson countered via satellite feed from Washington, DC. "How anyone can find fault with a teenage girl's choosing the path of abstinence is beyond me. I'm proud to see a new generation of young women embracing traditional values."

Liza shot a look at Tom Shapiro that told him she was about to annihilate her political foil. It would be another moment from *The Roundtable* destined to stir up the always intense blogosphere.

The fact that March was outside the studio sharpened Liza's instinct to not just maim but to completely destroy. "I don't think it's *traditional* for fathers to impose guilt and shame about sex onto their daughters. I think it's dysfunctional. And the double standard makes me sick. I don't hear about mothers asking their sons to remain pure until marriage."

"Maybe they should," March shot back.

Liza pounced on the lame retort. "Is that what *your* mother did?"

There was the slightest hesitation as March realized how badly he'd set himself up for the kill.

Tom shook his head ruefully.

Liza pressed on. "Are you still a virgin, March?"

"I'm taking the Fifth on that one." The Texas-born political stud flashed a sexy smile, living up to his media hype as the Matthew McConaughey of the Republican right. "I think Liza's main issue with this new modesty movement is that it's being led by young girls. I guess you could call them antirebels. But they're strong in their beliefs, and they face a great deal of social alienation in doing so. We should be applauding them."

Tom gestured to Liza. "You wrote a national best seller—*Whore*—which chronicled the flipside of this. Do you see young modesty as a true revolution?"

Liza tilted her head philosophically. "In some ways, yes. I believe there are girls who feel under attack by the oversexed media and overly permissive parents—particularly the mothers who are buying into the *Desperate Housewives* validation of being considered a MILF."

March comically feigned a malfunctioning ear-piece. "Excuse me, did she just say *MILF*? Are we on HBO?"

Tom laughed a little.

Liza merely grinned. "But there's a strong component to this trend's being driven by organized religion so, at the end of the day, I think it's more of a dangerous campaign that young girls are being duped into joining."

"*Dangerous*?" March shook his head incredulously. "Well, Liza is a liberal. If Christians are involved, then it must seem dangerous to her."

"The danger is in the dishonesty," Liza went on, refusing to be rattled. "As a society, we're very undisciplined when it comes to these issues. We're more likely to debate the extremes than wrestle with the complex middle ground. A girl who acts out every horny male's stripper fantasy isn't exercising her sexual power. She's being used. And a girl who takes a vow of chastity and accepts a promise ring from her father isn't choosing purity. She's being manipulated."

Tom's brow shot up provocatively. "You view it as manipulation?"

Liza nodded severely. "The conservative position is based on a rigid set of values that don't reflect current realities. Sure, a girl can promise to Daddy that she'll save herself for marriage. But then, virginity becomes a game of semantics. There's a high percentage of girls pledging abstinence but still engaging in oral and anal sex. I don't think getting by on a technicality is the point here. But it underscores the dishonesty and avoidance at work."

"March, we're out of time," Tom said. "But I'll let you have the last word."

"If Liza's saying that even the good girls are bad, then a lot has changed since I was in high school. Wish I could go back there now." He punctuated his remark with another disarming smile.

Tom shifted to address a different camera. "And that's it for this week's Culture Wars segment. I want to thank Liza Pike and March Donaldson, as well as my earlier guests, Senator Barbara Boxer and environmental activist Laurie David. Until next week, thank you for visiting *The Roundtable*."

"And we're out!" the producer shouted.

"Did you really have to bring my mother into this?" March asked good naturedly.

"She raised you," Liza answered lightly. "I figure she bears some responsibility."

March grinned. "Tom, I'm not even there, and I can still feel the chill. Who else can we get for this gig? I know. Call Rosie O'Donnell's people."

Tom laughed.

"I'm worse than *Rosie*?" Liza pretended to be shocked but in the end couldn't hold her laughter. "When are you coming back? I don't like playing in the sandbox alone."

March winked. "Just admit it. You miss me like crazy."

Liza rolled her eyes. "Spoken like a true narcissist."

"I'll be back in Long Island this weekend. I'm just here to scare up PAC money for my think tank. Oh, and you'll love this—I'm the luncheon keynote for the College Republicans Conference at the Hilton."

"An entire ballroom of the young and the ignorant. How frightening."

March smiled, his movie-star teeth gleaming on the monitor. "I'm slammed with fund-raising meetings for the rest of the day, so drink a few shots in my honor."

"Who says we're drinking?" Tom teased, sharing a knowing look with Liza.

"It was more of a suggestion," March said. "Liza

seems really uptight. Hey, instead of a couple of drinks, maybe she just needs a good—"

Suddenly, the satellite feed fizzled out.

Liza turned to Tom, a question in her eyes.

He put a finger to his earpiece. "Perry, we just lost March's signal." A few beats passed. Then an amused smile curled onto Tom's lips. "Apparently, it's nothing on our end. I think that was March's doing."

"Son of a bitch!" Liza spat. But even she had to concede that it was funny.

"You owe him big time for that one," Tom said, sliding out of his chair as a production assistant rushed over to first detach Liza's microphone, then Tom's. "Thanks, Corey." He looked at her and smiled. "You're great. Why don't you have your own show?"

"Every network turned down my pitch for the Feminazi Variety Hour."

Tom chuckled.

"I can't do what you do," Liza said. "I've been told that a little of me goes a long way on television. I'm more appealing when presented to the viewing public in smaller doses."

"Says who?"

"Agents and critics. And I'm giving you the most diplomatic version."

"Well, I've got two words for you—Nancy Grace."

Liza smirked. "But I can't cry at the drop of a dime. And I can't look in the camera and call viewers 'friend' with the same sincerity, either."

Tom laughed a little. "My interview with the deputy director of Homeland Security got canceled, so I'm finished here and heading into the city. Can I offer you a ride? The limo is fully stocked with liquor."

"Say no more. All I get is a lousy Town Car. And if I want a bar, then I better have some of those airline liquor bottles stashed in my purse."

"Well, I don't get the perks because I'm a man. It's because I'm an established CNBC *star*." He gave her an exaggerated haughty look.

"Yes, I know. I've seen the promotional ads wrapped around buses. I didn't think this was possible, but your teeth are actually whiter in person."

Tom gave her a true megawatt smile. "Let's get out of here. Traffic is going to be a bitch."

The black limousine stretched out as long as an oil spill.

While Tom busied himself as a cabin bartender, Liza obsessively checked her BlackBerry. Her addiction to the device was total. It vibrated on the nightstand when she tried to sleep. It beeped on the vanity when she took a shower. And just putting the fucking thing on silent mode for her segment on *The Roundtable* triggered a certain anxiety.

There were several missed calls—Kellyanne, Billie, her lecture agent, her literary agent, and her editor at New Woman Press. No doubt the last two wanted an answer to the same question: Where was the goddamn proposal for her second book?

She scanned through the recent e-mails, then read with interest a text message from Kellyanne sent mere minutes after her attempt to call.

```
I quit the reality show. LONG story. Arrive to-
night at JFK. Will ride the Jitney. Can't wait 2 c
u!!!
```

Tom proudly presented her with a crystal high-baller swirling to the rim with a potent-looking dark red concoction. "Pomegranate and Absolut. With a splash of lemon juice and simple syrup. Cheers." He clinked glasses and sipped greedily.

Liza followed suit, instantly relaxed by the punch of the vodka burning down her throat. The fertility drugs were still rampaging through her body. Sometimes the pressure on her ovaries was so intense that she felt like she might explode. The smart move would be to stay away from alcohol altogether. But Liza moderated her intake. It was either a few drinks or prescription drugs. She needed something to take the edge off.

"I know this is rude, but I have to make one call. Do you mind?" Billie's number was ringing before Tom could answer.

"Hello?" A groggy voice came on the line just as Liza was about to hang up.

"Billie?"

"Christ—what time is it?" Her voice was a thick slur.

"Around five, I guess. Are you sick?"

"No, just pissed. I was waiting for some asshole to call, and he never did, so I ended up getting drunk. What do you want?"

Liza was momentarily taken aback. "I got a text message from Kellyanne."

"Yeah, she quit that stupid show, and she's coming in tonight."

Liza heard Billie light up a cigarette and take a deep drag. "Are you smoking in the house?"

Billie sighed. "Calm down. I've got the window open."

"Go out on the deck, Billie," Liza said sharply. "And take an ashtray with you. Violating that rule could cost thousands of dollars. It's in the lease."

"Okay, okay. Shit! I still can't believe I'm paying fifty grand for this joint, yet I'm forbidden to smoke a fucking cigarette."

"How did she sound?" Liza asked.

"Who?"

"*Kellyanne.* I hope everything's okay."

"She's fine. It's not like she was in a hurricane. It was just a moronic reality series. One of the producers kept trying to fuck her. That's why she bailed. She should've just let him. She fucks for rent. Why not for a TV show?"

Liza glanced over at Tom, who was nursing his drink and patiently waiting for her attention. "I have to go. I'm with a colleague. I'll see both of you sometime tomorrow."

But Billie had already hung up.

Liza gave her BlackBerry a double take, shaking her head in disbelief.

"Problem?" Tom inquired.

"One of my summer sisters is Billie Shelton, the rock singer."

Tom's eyes widened. "I remember her from Harrison Beck's party. She was the first one to get naked and jump into the pool."

Liza managed a half smile. "That's Billie."

"Not to worry, though. As far as memorable moments go, nothing trumps Harrison whipping out his cock for your benefit."

Liza made most of her drink disappear and already felt like asking Tom to fix her another one. She was going home to Justin tonight. But what she really wanted was to join Billie and Kellyanne in the Hamptons, no matter how late.

As much as she looked forward to the reunion,

Liza had to admit that along with that came a nagging sense of irrational hope.

Maybe this time would be different.

God, she felt that way before every gathering with the girls. So much went into their escapes—meticulous planning, giddy anticipation—but the actual events never quite lived up to the hype. Liza was always left with a certain longing. The bond they shared was never quite nourishing enough. It was empty-calorie companionship. She yearned for deeper connections, more stimulating exchanges, something . . . different.

Tom seemed to pick up on her inward distraction. "Are things better at home?"

She looked at him as she sipped. "You first. How are things at your house?"

"Lonely," Tom said quietly. "I haven't had a meaningful relationship since college, and that one was just my wasting an incredible girl's time. Now I don't even have meaningless affairs. They're too risky. Nothing is worth some one night stand's snapping a cell phone picture and running off to TMZ or Perez Hilton."

For a moment, Liza said nothing. She was stunned by his raw honesty. But it also made her feel good that he trusted her so much. "It sounds awful, Tom, but maybe it could be liberating. If people found out the truth, then you'd be free to live your life."

Tom drained the last of his drink and stared plaintively into the bottom of his glass. "That's not the sort of freedom I'm looking for. I want the career Anderson Cooper has. I want that kind of money. I want that kind of promotion. I want that kind of access to big interviews. I'll never get there by becoming the *gay* face of CNBC." He winced at the word. "And that's what will happen. It'll overshadow everything I've worked for." He glanced at her near-empty glass. "Another round?"

Liza nodded somberly. "Sometimes I hate America."

Tom chuckled. "Let's keep that between us. Can you imagine the campaign Sean Hannity would wage if that got out?"

Liza scowled. "He's a partisan pig."

Tom laughed, finishing up the new drinks. "These are a bit stronger."

"Good." Liza gamely accepted hers and chased down the first swallow, which practically set her throat on fire. "You know, you could be the one," she offered optimistically. "You could be the guy who changes everything."

Tom clinked her glass in a mock toast. "Nice try. But you really don't believe that."

Liza sighed. "No, I really don't. It sounded good, though." She drank up.

Tom looked melancholy. "If I came out, there'd be the inevitable torrent of attention. But all of it would be focused on the gay angle. How long have I been gay? Who am I dating? What's my position on same-sex marriage?"

Liza groaned. "Maybe staying in the closet isn't so confining after all. How pathetic is that?"

"Very," Tom murmured, drinking deep. "I don't want to end up on the cover of *People,* like Lance Bass. Being gay isn't the most interesting thing about me. It would follow me everywhere, though. The activists would be after me to take up all the gay causes, too. But I've never really identified with the culture-at-large. Most of my friends are straight. To me it's just a matter of sexuality, and that's such a private thing."

Liza could feel a definite buzz sensation from the alcohol. "It makes me sad that you don't feel comfortable dating. You deserve someone special."

"Don't feel too sad. I'm not exactly living the life of a monk."

Liza gazed at him with keen interest.

"There's something to be said for successful married men. They're discreet, and they have a great deal to lose. Sometimes that makes for a wonderful arrangement."

"*Tom Shapiro*," Liza said in a faux scolding tone. "You're a home-wrecking slut."

He laughed sheepishly. "Actually, I've never wrecked a home . . . but I am a bit of a slut."

"Anyone I know?" Liza inquired silkily.

Tom named a major movie star, an international sex god married to a world-famous actress and humanitarian. Together they had the devotion of the media and an exotic coterie of adopted children from faraway countries.

Liza was thunderstruck. "You're joking."

Tom shook his head. "It happened at the Mercer."

"Okay, I'm no longer sad. Now I'm jealous."

"You should be," Tom said, raising his glass with a sexy grin. "That night with him was worth a lifetime of loneliness." He whistled at the memory. "So what about you? How's that fucking husband of yours?"

"He's the same," Liza said quietly. "He'll always be the same. That's the problem, I'm afraid."

"I imagine that most men would find you too intimidating. What's the joke? If a woman wants to turn a guy off completely, she just has to mention that she has an MBA from Harvard."

"Yeah." Liza laughed a little. "It's called dropping the H-bomb. Apparently, my husband's immune to its detonation."

Tom looked impressed. "That says something about him."

"What? That he's too stupid to realize?"

Tom gave her a strange look. "Man, you are brutal."

"I know," Liza sighed. She drank more and considered having a third. "Maybe I'm just frustrated. The claim to fame in our relationship had always been the sex, and now we don't have that, so . . . I'm wondering what's there."

"Do you think it could be a medical issue?" Tom asked.

Liza scoffed at the notion. "Justin treats his body like a holy temple. I don't think it's a physical problem."

"What about a porn addiction?"

Liza shook her head. "I've never seen him show an interest in anything like that. Ever."

For the next few miles, Tom just sat there in distracted silence. Finally, he spoke. "It's unlikely that he's lost interest in sex."

"So you're telling me that he's getting it somewhere else." Before Tom could answer, Liza finished her drink and passed him her empty glass. "Hit me again."

He hesitated and cocked an eyebrow, then went about the business of prepping their third round. "I just don't want you to get blind-sided. An FDNY calendar cover boy doesn't have to go looking for it. Be aware. Protect yourself."

"I don't care anymore," Liza said, only half-meaning the words. "Here I am on my last round of fertility drugs to freeze my eggs, and I'm so tender where it counts that I'd probably turn down sex with George Clooney. Maybe I should be grateful to the firefighter groupies for keeping him satisfied."

"That's certainly charitable."

"I know. Stick around. I'll probably get mean after this third drink."

Tom laughed at her and handed it over.

Suddenly, Liza gave him a penetrating gaze. "Let me ask you something, Tom. Do you think I'm a fraud?"

His answer was an expression of bewilderment.

"Harrison Beck thinks I am," Liza explained. "He says I pretend to be this power feminist, but then I run around dressing like a party girl and marrying firemen."

Tom shrugged. "How does that make you a fraud? All of those things can be true at the same time."

She nodded thoughtfully, appreciating his reasonable assessment.

"We're all hypocrites to a degree," Tom went on. "I consider my sex life a matter of absolute privacy, but *The Roundtable* dedicated significant airtime to the outing of that married senator from Louisiana. I rationalized it because he was such an aggressive opponent of gay marriage, gays in the military, and hate-crime legislation." He clinked his glass against hers and grinned. "Here's to two self-righteous frauds."

Liza laughed and raised her highballer in salute.

"It's surprising, though," Tom remarked.

Liza returned a quizzical look. "What is?"

"That Harrison Beck got to you this way. I thought you ate macho men like him for breakfast."

"I don't know. Maybe it's the extra hormones I'm

injecting into my body." She drank, contemplating the situation as the limousine coasted toward Manhattan. "Sometimes I wonder what I really believe in, though. I rail against the medical establishment for propagandizing women's health care, and here I am with a syringe in my purse, frantic to beat the biological clock. I hardly ever eat and, when I do, I feel guilty and worry about getting fat. I've actually stood naked in the bathroom mirror and considered breast implants. And I fantasize about finding a rich husband and having a baby and never working again." She stopped and took in a deep breath. "Oh, and I'm generally attracted to men who are no more evolved than an ape at the Bronx Zoo."

Tom smiled easily. "You're being too hard on yourself."

"Am I?" Liza wondered. Suddenly, an internal thunderbolt hit, sending her mind into overdrive. She recalled a popular, hard-charging song by Pink and instantly conceived the second book concept that had been eluding her for months.

Stupid Girls.

That was a perfect title for her next polemic. She could write about the dichotomous roles that women end up playing in contemporary society. It'd be a more personal book than *Whore*. This time, she'd not only write about other women's stories but about her own. She just hoped that the self-examination would be therapeutic and cathartic as opposed to painful and debilitating.

Liza dug into her Miu Miu ostrich satchel and jotted a few notes into a small leather journal, confident that the idea would hold up even under the harsh glare of sobriety.

"A writer's work is never done," Tom mused,

kicking off his shoes and slouching back against the plush seats.

"Something like that," Liza murmured. She put away the journal and slipped off her Christian Louboutin slingbacks, then tucked her feet underneath her legs and smiled tipsily at him.

Tom gestured to the privacy screen. "The driver probably thinks we're back here nailing each other."

"I bet limousine drivers gossip like sorority girls." Liza giggled. "You know what would be funny? If I left my panties behind."

Tom shook his head and pointed to her drink. "That's it," he scolded playfully. "I'm cutting you off."

She giggled again and touched his knee. "God, that sounded like something Billie Shelton would say."

"Not really," Tom countered. "When she stripped on the pool deck at Harrison's party, she wasn't wearing any underwear."

Liza busied herself with her drink to avoid comment. Sometimes it struck her . . . Billie's raunchy rock star excess . . . Kellyanne's willingness to live her life as a passive sexual vessel for a controlling rich man . . . what exactly was the common thread among them?

Tom took a break from personal confessions and brought up media gossip—the precipitous fall of the former morning show queen turned embattled evening news anchor, the surprise exit of an MSNBC star, and the rumored affair between an ABC White House correspondent and a high-ranking White House cabinet official.

When the limousine stopped in front of Liza's apartment building in TriBeCa, she was grateful for the time spent with Tom and reluctant to end it. "This was fun. We should carpool more often."

Tom smiled at her. "Anytime, my friend." Suddenly, he became distracted, shifting his gaze out the window and onto the sidewalk. "Now that's just wrong." His voice went thick with lust.

Liza turned to see Justin walking toward the building, shirtless and soaked in sweat, a small gym bag in one hand and a slim can of Red Bull in the other. His wet shorts clung to him like a second skin, and the imprint of his crotch bulge was impossible to ignore.

"That's my husband. I want you to meet him."

Justin was eyeballing the limousine just as Liza zipped down the window. "Hey, baby," he called out, strutting toward the curb and whistling at the conspicuousness of it all. "You're traveling like a star."

"Hardly!" Liza said, louder than she intended. The alcohol was really doing its number now. "I bummed this ride from a real star." She giggled longer than the joke warranted.

Justin zeroed in on her with a knowing half-smile, then bent down to peer into the cabin and make friendly eye contact with Tom. "I think my wife's hammered."

"I think you're right," Tom said, extending his hand as Liza struggled to get into her slingbacks. "Tom Shapiro."

Justin shook firm and fast. "Justin Beal."

Liza beamed at Tom. "Tom's the host of *The Roundtable*. He's a *major* rising star. I'm so proud of him." She leaned over to kiss Tom on the cheek.

Tom smiled uncomfortably.

"I should probably get you upstairs and into bed," Justin said.

"To sleep, right?" Liza asked. And then sotto voce to Tom she added, "All we do is sleep. We never fuck anymore."

Justin's jaw tightened as he opened the limousine door and pulled Liza onto the sidewalk.

She stumbled slightly, falling against his hard frame before turning back to her confidant. "Tom, I love you. Honestly, I do."

"I love you, too, Liza," Tom said, delivering the line in the patronizing tone one is forced to employ when dealing with an overly sentimental drunk. He gave Justin an apologetic look as he passed Liza's handbag through the window.

"Do you play racquetball?" Justin asked.

"Not regularly. But I can hold my own in the game. Why?"

Justin grinned. "I'll kick your ass sometime. It'll be payback for bringing my wife home wasted." His challenge was teeming with jock humor and devoid of any hostility.

"You're on." Tom laughed. "I might even let you win."

Justin shut the door and heartily slapped the roof of the limousine.

Liza watched as the gleaming black stretch weaved back into traffic and disappeared down the street. Instantly, she was overwhelmed by a sense of emptiness. The chatter with Tom had been nonstop. Now she was standing next to her husband, and they had nothing to say to each other.

Justin pitched his Red Bull into a waste bin. "Let's go upstairs." He reached for her elbow.

Liza reflexively pulled away and lost her balance, almost falling down.

Justin reacted fast to help her recover, then pulled

her inside with a firm hand. "Stop acting like a dumb bitch."

Liza's head began to spin. Maybe it was the vodka. Or maybe it was the sudden and intense anger. No matter, she knew that it was going to be a long night.

The elevator ride seemed interminable. A seething silence settled in and never broke.

When they stepped inside the loft, Justin slammed the steel door with a pent-up fury. "Don't *ever* disrespect me like that again!" he roared.

Liza betrayed no reaction and walked toward the spiral staircase that led to the master bedroom. "I'm going to take a shower."

"It's none of that faggot's business what we do in bed."

Liza spun around hotly. "Then tell me whose business it is. I'm just trying to get a man involved here. And don't call my friend a faggot. As usual, you have no idea what you're talking about."

Justin's laugh was bitter. "Maybe you were too drunk to see the way he was looking at me. Given the chance, he would've sucked my dick right there on the sidewalk."

"You're disgusting."

"Who else have you told?" Justin demanded.

"Told what?"

"That we don't fuck."

At first, Liza just stared at him. "Unlike you, I'm more concerned about the problem than about who knows."

"I don't see it as a problem," Justin said.

"So this is your idea of a good marriage?"

He answered with a shrug. "You can't have it both ways. You want to wear the pants in this relationship. You want to make the big money and bark out orders and walk around like you've got a cock between your legs. That doesn't turn me on."

Liza gave him a sharp look. "I suppose I could quit everything that I'm doing. Then we could live on your salary. Maybe poverty would get you hot."

Justin glared at her.

Liza thundered on. "And while we're on the subject of roles, you should know that sometimes I feel like I've got a fourteen-year-old roommate instead of a husband. You're not responsible for a goddamn thing around here except yourself. You go to the fire station, you hang out with your buddies, and you play sports. That's it. So you're not exactly a turn-on, either."

Justin's face was impassive. None of this seemed to reach him. Or maybe he just didn't give a fuck.

"Are you sleeping around?" Liza asked. "If so, I should probably get tested."

Justin laughed at her. "Yeah, maybe you should."

A ferocious anger erupted within Liza. Her rage was so powerful that it actually made her dizzy. She felt a sudden compulsion for violence and frantically searched the immediate area for something to throw at him.

Before she could stop herself, a beautiful blown and acid-etched glass vase by Tommie Rush was in her hands and flying through the air.

Justin dodged it with little effort, sending the two-thousand-dollar decorative piece smashing against the wall behind him. A rainbow of shattered shards skated across the stained concrete floor.

"You fucking bastard!" Liza practically screamed her throat raw.

Justin moved in fast, pushing her against the wall and putting a hand to her neck.

For a microsecond, Liza experienced a cold fear, thinking that he might strangle her. But the feeling passed, and she knew instinctively that it was merely a show of dominance.

"You want to call all the shots all the time. Don't you, baby? But then when you don't get any dick, you want to make it out like something's wrong with me. What kind of bullshit is that?"

Liza squirmed to get away as Justin pushed up her Proenza Schouler dress and cupped his hand between her legs. She winced. The hormone cocktail had made her so tender that his touch was painful.

"If you want me to fuck you, then tell me to. Bark out the order. Just like you do with everything else."

She wanted to push him away. He smelled like a locker room. But something about his attitude fascinated her. Justin's behavior was demeaning and disrespectful. In fact, it came close to promoting abuse. And yet a secret part of her was dazzled by it and found the act of surrendering strangely, blissfully erotic.

"Tell me," Justin insisted.

Liza could see and feel his erection straining against his gym shorts. And the realization hit her that she had truly missed his cock. It was an inch too big. Blow jobs were a workout. Vaginal sex was intense. "I can't," she heard herself say. "I'm too sore from the fertility drugs. You'll kill me."

He turned her around to face the wall, grabbed a fistful of hair, and snapped her head back with a brutal tug. "That's not the only hole I can use." His fingers played roughly with her ass.

No man had ever been granted access there. Liza was an anal virgin, thinking the act unhealthy and a gross example of sexual oppression and control . . .

and yet the mere suggestion of the forbidden had stirred something within her. She could only describe it as a secret yearning for rebellion. But with this realization, the desire Justin had juiced up began to cool. She felt ashamed.

All of a sudden, Liza resented his attempt at domination. She twisted out of his grasp and smoothed down her dress. The spell was broken. "You stink. I mean that literally. Get your hands off me and go take a fucking shower."

He kicked his gym bag across the floor and started off. No doubt his limited mind was churning out a plan to cheat on her again as soon as possible.

It occurred to Liza that Justin was afraid of her. Even his attempt at roughness was a reaction to his fear. She'd embarrassed him in mixed company. Now he wanted to put it to her and show her what a man he was. But masculine desperation did nothing at all for her.

Liza found herself thinking about Harrison Beck. She marveled at the fact that he wasn't afraid of her, that he wasn't desperate, either.

She dug into her Miu Miu bag and pulled out the little journal again. Turning to the page where she'd scribbled her notes on *Stupid Girls,* she began to write. *This week I met the man who will make me end my marriage . . .*

Kellyanne

9

The three-hour flight from Miami International to JFK provided Kellyanne more time to think about the mess that was her life. Nothing in *Elle*, *Vanity Fair*, or *People* could pique even casual interest. Her inward distraction was total.

The hours that followed her retreat from the *Soul Mates* set had been difficult. Consecutive days of standby had effectively killed her cell phone battery. A flirtatious guard manning a massive security gate on a nearby Star Island property had offered his own phone.

On instinct, Kellyanne had called Walter first. He was her go-to man for everything. When the initial attempt went straight to voice mail, she tried again. And then a third time.

Finally, Walter had picked up and hissed, "What is it?"

Kellyanne had been stunned, hurt, and momentarily speechless. "Walter, it's me."

"I know that. You've called three times in as

many minutes. I'm with my kids. What is it?" He'd spoken in a cold, hushed whisper.

"I just wanted you to know that I quit the reality show." She'd paused a beat. "And I'm leaving tonight for the Hamptons."

"Fine. We'll get together in New York." And then he'd hung up.

Instantly, tears had sprung to Kellyanne's eyes. Walter was somewhere with Allison, Brock, possibly even Cagle, his troubled youngest, and in that set of circumstances, she was absolutely nothing to him. Kellyanne had always known that. She knew it more now. Never in her life had she heard such dismissal in a man's voice. And that included every Hollywood casting agent who'd told her, "Hell, no!"

It was disturbing that Walter could react in such unpredictable ways. A vague conversation about Liza's East Hampton summer share invitation had ended with his scratching out a fifty-thousand-dollar check. And yet Kellyanne's frantic call to announce that she'd quit a television show had failed to conjure up even a simple question as to why.

Next, she'd reached out to Pommie, who was busy pinch-hitting as waitstaff for a caterer friend at a rich teenager's beach party. Pommie had informed her that Jab was off for the day and passed along his number.

Kellyanne's call had woken up Silk Electric's main bartender. His voice was thick and barely audible.

"Jab, it's Kellyanne. I'm stranded on Star Island."

"You poor thing," Jab had teased, showing signs of life. "That sounds like *Survivor.* I thought you were on a dating show." He'd laughed at his own joke.

Kellyanne had truly smiled for the first time in days. "More like *Fear Factor.* I'd rather eat dead bugs than stay here. Can you come get me? Are you okay to drive?"

"Yeah, I just need a Starbucks fix," Jab had said.

She could hear him yawning and stretching over the receiver. "I'm sorry to impose. I know you've got the day off, but—"

"It's no problem," Jab had assured her easily. "I need to get this skank out of my apartment anyway."

Kellyanne had shaken her head. When it came down to sex, men were such a combination of good and evil. "I'm at forty-five Star Island Drive. I'll be waiting outside the gate. Hurry, Jab." She'd hung up, her body flooding with relief as she returned the phone to the security guard.

The man, whose badge pronounced him Rockland, had continued raking her up and down with an indecent gaze.

"Thank you," Kellyanne had said earnestly, then left him there to guard his post and fantasize about what would never be. She'd taken off toward the street, located a nice spot in the sun, and sat down on her Vuitton beauty case, settling in for the wait.

When Jab had rolled up in his beaten down BMW 3-Series, it was a glorious sight for Kellyanne's eyes. She tossed her bags into the backseat and slid into the front like a teenager running away from home with a delinquent boyfriend. "Drive fast."

Jab had smiled, put the manual shift into gear, and roared off.

The jolt had slammed Kellyanne against the passenger seat. She buckled her safety belt as an afterthought, her head already splitting from the sonic blast of "Icky Thump" by the White Stripes.

"Where to, gorgeous?"

Kellyanne twisted down the stereo volume.

"You're my first damsel in distress of legal age. This is officially hot."

Kellyanne had laughed at him. Jab Hunter was the horniest guy she'd ever known. "What happened to your skank?"

"My roommate was heading out to work, so I pushed her off on him."

"You're a true romantic."

"Trust me. There was no romance involved. I picked her up at Nocturnal, brought her back to my place, and we're barely through the door when she starts yelling at me to fuck her in the ass. It was intense." He grinned and cast a sideways glance. "If you must know, I felt violated."

Kellyanne rolled her eyes. "Maybe you should file rape charges."

"Don't get me wrong. Ultimately, it was consensual." Jab hit the MacArthur Causeway and picked up speed, opening up the BMW's ancient engine to maximum revs. It barely performed. But at least they were moving away from Star Island.

"So . . . what happened back there?" Jab inquired.

Kellyanne sighed deeply. "It was awful. I'll tell you about it sometime. But right now I don't have the stomach to go into it."

"That fucker from the restaurant hit on you, didn't he?" Jab demanded, his voice filled with menace as he hit the steering wheel with a strong fist.

"Something like that," Kellyanne admitted, appreciating the fact that someone in her life actually gave a shit. "But it's over. I'm out of there." Disturbingly, a gut thing told her that it was only over for the moment. The situation would come back to haunt her. She just knew it.

Jab reached over to supportively pat Kellyanne's knee. "I knew that asshole was trouble."

In a gesture of thanks, she touched his hand. All of a sudden, she noticed the cell phone sitting in the console between them. "Do you mind?"

With Jab's sweet nod of permission, Kellyanne went to work securing a flight to New York for later that night. She'd been ferociously determined to leave Miami immediately and was lucky enough to secure a seat on Delta Airlines for less than three hundred dollars.

"Do you need a ride to the airport?" Jab offered.

Kellyanne's answer was a look of imploring gratitude. "If you could take me by the apartment to pack some things *and* do that, I'd love you forever."

"How much love?" Jab teased, winking at her.

"*Friend* love. Not skank love," Kellyanne clarified. "Are you sure that you have time for all of this?"

"My only plans for the day are to get drunk, get high, and get laid. I can fit it all in." And then Jab turned up the music volume, rocking out to Finger Eleven and Sick Puppies until they arrived at the Jade building on Brickell Bay.

When they walked through the expansive lobby, Julio, the typically warm and charming doorman, had reacted coolly toward Kellyanne and given off strong vibrations of disapproval.

It occurred to her that she never entertained company in her apartment. Now she'd suddenly turned up with Jab, who was young, blessed with a genetically perfect worked-out body, and so good looking that even in a city teeming with beautiful people, he earned whiplash-inducing double takes from women—and men—of all ages.

Kellyanne had no doubt that Walter paid Julio

something extra to keep a watchful eye on her comings and goings . . . and, more important—her visitors. For the first time, he'd actually earned his money, because she lived like a fucking recluse otherwise.

"This is sick," Jab murmured as they stepped inside the ultramod elevator that would catapult them to the forty-first floor. "I can't believe you live here." He glanced at the control panel. "Forty-eight stories!"

"I'm still getting used to being up so high," Kellyanne answered.

On the journey up, Jab had been as wide-eyed as a tourist experiencing the natural wonder of Niagara Falls for the first time. He gasped as they entered the sleek apartment. The maid service had shown up regularly during Kellyanne's absence. Everything was spotless and gleaming.

"You should see my place," Jab said, checking out the waterfront views. "It's a shit hole compared to this. And I share it with a roommate."

"At least your name's on the lease," Kellyanne pointed out. "I could be homeless at any time. That's no way to live. Believe me. It looks more glamorous than it really is."

Jab was practically salivating over the plasma television when he muttered, "Let me know if it doesn't work out with your guy. I'd gladly blow him on a regular basis for the chance to live here."

Kellyanne cut a harsh look in his direction.

"That came out wrong," Jab said. "I didn't mean it that way."

Kellyanne had no trouble letting it go. "Don't worry about it."

"I'd never allow a guy to stick his dick in my mouth. You know that, right?"

Kellyanne had given Jab an amused glare. He was just messing with her. "Shut up. You can watch TV while I pack. Help yourself to anything in the kitchen. There's beer in the refrigerator, and the bar's fully stocked, too."

She disappeared into the master bedroom, pulled three large Vuitton suitcases from the closet, and proceeded to carefully arrange all of her clothes, shoes, electronic devices, photographs, and personal papers. Kellyanne packed as if she might not ever return to Miami. She hadn't planned to do that. The impulse was pure instinct.

"So how does this man feel about your going off to the Hamptons for the summer?" Jab called out from the living room. "If I had the money to keep a woman like you, I'd never let you out of my sight."

Kellyanne stepped out of the bedroom, holding her new favorite belt—a velvet piece by Chanel with a gorgeous crystal-and-resin buckle. Walter had bought it for her in Paris last month while vacationing there with his wife, Connie. "Jab, please. You'd get bored and start looking around for the next hot girl. That's the age-old story. Men chase, they catch, and then they start all over again."

For a moment, Jab just tipped back a bottle of Blue Marlin and stared at her. "I know I'm a pussy hound. But you'd be rehab for a guy like me."

Kellyanne considered him, wondering what it might feel like to be with a man closer to her own age again, instead of one thirty-plus years older. She'd been faithful to Walter all this time, so the idea was infinitely tempting.

Jab had cut quite a swath through the waitress pool at Silk Electric, and the reviews were wildly enthusiastic. Though the consensus had always been that he was a hopeless cad, there were rarely hard feelings toward him. His ex-lovers praised his amazingly fit body, his impressive endowment, and his incredible skills in bed.

"I'd just be one more waitress for you," Kellyanne told him lightly. "And then you'd become obsessed with getting Pommie into bed."

Jab quickly rose from the sofa and moved toward her. "That's crap." He closed in, wrapping his arms around her waist and resting the Blue Marlin bottle in the crack of her ass. "The first part, I mean. I'll always want to show Pommie what she's missing. People change. But I think that girl's a hard-core lesbian for life."

Kellyanne laughed, feeling torn, half of her wanting to extricate from his embrace, the other half enjoying the closeness and the erotic energy of a possible encounter. She was barely able to look at him. "I'm a mess, Jab."

"If that's the case, you're the most beautiful mess I've ever seen. I'll take my chances."

In that moment, Walter's rude dismissal had ricocheted in Kellyanne's mind. And now the notion of a zipless fuck with Jab, the kind she had read about in Erica Jong's *Fear of Flying,* seemed inevitable.

Jab put his mouth onto hers, softly at first, then with delicious passion and insistence. "I'm going to make you come," he whispered. "But not the short little climax you feel all in one place. That's the kind you're used to, isn't it? I'm going to make you come so hard that you feel it throughout your entire body."

As a general proposal, it was difficult to turn down. But Kellyanne gently pushed him away. "I can't,

Jab . . . there's too much going on in my head. All I want to do right now is get out of Miami."

Jab grinned, shaking his head regretfully. "And I was so close."

Kellyanne laughed. "Honey, you have no idea."

Now she was storming through the Delta terminal at JFK, desperate to retrieve her checked baggage, make the trek to the Jitney airport connection, and board the night's final bus for Long Island. It was strange. But she felt like a new life was waiting for her there.

Kellyanne's recharged cell phone jingled to the music of Destiny's Child's "Independent Women," a ring tone dedicated exclusively to Liza. "I'm here! My plane just landed!"

"I'm on my way to the airport," Liza said. "Wait for me, and we'll drive in together."

"You don't have to do that!" Kellyanne wailed. "It's late. And I already made plans to take the Jitney."

"Cancel them," Liza insisted. "I pay a fortune every month to keep my car in a parking garage. I should get some use out of it. We'll be exhausted, but it'll be worth it to wake up in the Hamptons tomorrow morning."

A half hour later, Kellyanne was embracing her friend outside the ground transportation exit. Immediately, she was struck by Liza's gaunt look. Kellyanne had never seen her so thin. By comparison, Victoria Beckham was a heavy girl. And the smell of alcohol on Liza's breath concerned her.

"You look amazing, as always," Liza gushed. "You tanned, blond, fit, and flawless . . . *bitch*."

Kellyanne laughed. "You look great, too, but

you're so *skinny!* I'm going to make my mother's recipe for frozen peanut butter pie, and you're going to eat the whole thing. I insist!"

"I accept!" Liza shrieked. "As long as there's chocolate involved." She helped Kellyanne maneuver the cart that was overburdened with Vuitton cases. "My God, look at all this luggage. Are you moving here permanently?"

Kellyanne halted. "Honestly, I don't know where I'll end up after this."

Liza hooked an arm under hers. "Well, we've got the entire summer to figure that out."

They tumbled the luggage into the cargo area of Liza's black Lexus LX 470.

"Are you sure that you're okay to drive?" Kellyanne asked. "Don't take this the wrong way. But you look tired, and it's obvious that you've been drinking."

Liza's body tensed. She started to protest, then seemed to think better of it. "Follow the signs to the Long Island Expressway," she said, surrendering the keys.

Kellyanne accepted them gratefully. "Bless your heart. I've been a passenger all day. I'd *love* the chance to drive." She climbed behind the steering wheel and carefully adjusted the seat and mirrors. "It feels strange being up so high. But I kind of like it. Maybe I should trade in my little sports car for a monster SUV like this." But as she gave voice to the idea, it dawned on her that only Walter could make that decision. The Mercedes roadster was registered in his name only.

"I'm so glad that you're here," Liza trilled. "But be warned—it's going to take both of us to keep Billie in line."

Kellyanne's eyes widened. "Oh, God—how wild is she?"

"Worse than ever. Or maybe the same. Who knows? We're used to spending a long weekend together once a year. This is an entire season. I suppose it'll be a miracle if we're still friends by Labor Day. Veer to your right up ahead."

Kellyanne nodded, still trying to adjust to the road handling of the large vehicle. "Don't worry. We're going to have an amazing time. I just know it." She smiled at Liza to underscore her confidence on the matter.

Liza grinned in response, vaguely hopeful but certainly not convinced. "I got your text. What happened with the show?"

Kellyanne groaned. "I'll tell you everything—provided I'm at a pool or on a beach *and* have a drink in my hand."

"I'm sorry it was a bad experience . . . but I'm glad it got you here earlier than planned."

"Me, too," Kellyanne whispered, willing herself to banish all thoughts of Walter, Brad "Bonzi" Lucas, and Adam Griffie. She glanced over at Liza. "Am I *finally* going to meet Justin? I can't believe you've been married all this time, and I've never laid eyes on your husband."

Liza's mouth tightened. "When you finally meet him, he might be my ex-husband."

Kellyanne was stunned. "Sweetheart, I'm sorry. I didn't realize you were having problems."

Liza sighed. "We're too far apart, I guess. Intellectually . . . economically . . . it just doesn't work. And now we don't even connect sexually. I think he prefers his women dumb and poor."

"Really? Maybe *I* should marry him," Kellyanne cracked.

Liza managed a half-smile and waved her left hand. "You can have him. I'll even throw in the ring."

"Have you tried counseling?" Kellyanne asked, her tone more serious now.

"A man like Justin isn't hardwired for couples therapy. He considers psychiatry a threat to his masculinity. If the problem at home can't be solved with his dick, then it's not his problem."

"So . . . what do you do now?"

Liza gazed out at the dark road ahead. "I probably should see an attorney. I think he's cheating. He didn't admit to it outright, but he didn't deny it, either. And the truth is, I'm not sure that I even care one way or the other. Maybe I'm not cut out for marriage. Not in the traditional sense, anyway. My literary agent has been involved with the same man for twenty years. But they don't live together. And sometimes they take separate vacations. I can see myself in a relationship like that. With the right man, of course."

"But what if you wanted children?" Kellyanne wondered. "How would that arrangement work then?"

Liza's hands dropped to her lower abdomen. "Funny you should ask. I'm scheduled for my second egg retrieval next week."

Kellyanne shot her a look, a question in her eyes.

"The drugs are a real bitch," Liza confessed. "But when I do decide to get pregnant, then I'll have a greater chance of conceiving, whether that be with a man in my life or with a sperm donor."

"So you're stockpiling your eggs?" Kellyanne couldn't keep the incredulity out of her voice.

"Is something wrong with that?"

"No, of course not," Kellyanne answered quickly. "It just seems so . . . I don't know . . . calculating."

"You have to be. For the next ten years, I want to focus on my career and grab every opportunity that comes my way. I'll start thinking about a baby after I turn forty. But there's too much risk and uncertainty to rely on my body at that age. My eggs are vital now, and the freezing technology is incredibly sophisticated."

Kellyanne grew silent. It amazed her how Liza could sit there and announce what she'd be doing at forty. Meanwhile, Kellyanne was in the dark when it came down to simply predicting where her life might be after the summer. "It sounds like you have everything figured out."

"No, I'm just giving myself options," Liza said. "Believe me. I have *nothing* figured out."

"At least you have a ten-year plan," Kellyanne countered, revealing a bit of the awe that she felt toward Liza. "Plus, you have a real career and assets in your own name."

"Yeah, well, that's just a matter of being practical. Every woman in today's society should be financially independent. Otherwise, she's a fool."

Kellyanne winced at the words. They made her feel like an anachronism. Sometimes she considered herself a bimbo mistress relic from the eighties, a plaything to some money baron who kept her anxious for expensive gifts and lonely on important holidays. Girls like her never came out on top. They were usually left with nothing but the bitter regret of having wasted their most productive years.

The digital car clock tripped past midnight, and at least another ninety minutes of driving loomed ahead. Kellyanne's eyelids felt heavy. There'd be plenty of

time for Liza to weigh in on her pathetic life and deliver her feminist firebrand robo-lecture in full. So at
the moment, Kellyanne was desperate to change the
subject.

"I wonder what Billie is doing right now."

Billie

10

She was drunk dialing Todd Bana. "Answer the phone, motherfucker!" Over and over again, she punched in the number, refusing to leave a message, knowing from personal observation that his BlackBerry was attached to him like nerve fibers.

Finally, Todd picked up, only to scream, "Jesus Christ, Billie! What the fuck do you want?"

His hostility barely registered. Billie was wasted. She was pissed off, too. So shouting was her preferred method of communication anyway. "I want some goddamn progress, you son of a bitch!"

"At one o'clock in the morning?" He laughed at her. "You're a nutcase. Hey, I've got an idea. Why don't you hang up and go boil a rabbit."

In the background, a woman cackled.

Billie could hear Todd inhaling sharply. The bastard was loaded and banging some stupid bitch. And here she was sitting alone in the dark like a fat girl on prom night, living on the hope that March Donaldson might call.

"Hold on." Todd's tone was curt. A moment later, Billie heard him murmuring in a thick, sexy voice. "No, no, no . . . snort it off my cock . . . get every bit . . . don't waste it, baby . . . good girl . . . very good girl."

Billie experienced an immediate white-hot rage. "You're with some slut getting coked out of your mind!"

"What's your point?"

She fought the urge to throw the phone against the wall. "My point is that I haven't heard a fucking thing about those songs you want me to record. I'm taking a big risk by going in this new direction. I don't mind my bass player partying like a rock star, but I wish my label president would act like a real suit."

"Be careful what you wish for," Todd said ominously.

"What the fuck is that supposed to mean?" Billie demanded.

"It means that a buttoned-down exec would look at your numbers and tell you to get lost."

Even in her alcohol-soaked haze, Billie knew to fold instead of fight. A few drinks and two Ambiens ago, the idea to call Todd and raise hell had seemed like a good one. She'd only lashed out at him because March was unreachable.

"I'm scared, Todd," Billie whined. "This is a new thing for me—recording someone else's songs. Maybe I'd relax a little if I heard the demos."

Todd sighed. "Two of the tracks were on Ariel's last album. 'Submission' and 'Naked in the Rain.' Check them out on iTunes. Van can e-mail you an audio file of the third song next week."

Billie's stomach lurched as the impact of Todd's

words began to resonate. "You expect me to take sloppy seconds from *Ariel*?"

Ariel was a former Miss Teen USA who'd shot to worldwide fame after a star turn in a successful *High School Musical* rip-off called *Homecoming Dance*. But just as her first hit single was building, her career had been derailed by scandal. A DUI accident in Los Angeles had killed a pregnant woman and her two young children. Leaving an all-night party at seven in the morning, Ariel had driven the wrong way down an exit ramp, causing the head-on collision that also claimed the life of the twenty-two-year-old personal assistant traveling with her.

"White Tiger considers those tracks some of their best work," Todd assured her in a voice just patronizing enough to make her want to take a sledgehammer to his balls. "Ariel's album tanked after the accident. Nobody will identify those songs with her. Once you lay down the vocals, they'll be yours."

Billie was hardly convinced. "This is bullshit, Todd."

"I agree. Anything but sex or sleeping at this hour usually is."

"There's no way—"

"*Billie*," Todd cut in savagely. "I'm with a gorgeous piece of ass, we're both on a coke high, and it's time for me to fuck her brains out."

Click.

She started to protest, then realized that the Napoleonic shit had hung up on her. "Cocksucker!" She hoped that bitch infected him with hepatitis tonight.

Billie considered calling Todd right back. But before she could act on that impulse, a stronger one sent the cellular device sailing across the room. It smashed against an antique mirror. A sickening crack fanned out like a spider's web and threatened seven years of bad luck.

She buried her face into the tangled sheets that had gone unlaundered all week, inhaling deeply, desperate to breathe in March's scent. When would he call her again? For a long time Billie just lay there, unable to erase the mental image of March spooned against Amaryllis, sleeping and satisfied. Is that what he was doing right now? The horrible possibility consumed her until she drifted into oblivion.

"You should sue for sexual harassment," Liza said.

Billie couldn't resist a slight roll of the eyes as she tried to factor the worst-case scenario. Was it her killer hangover, Kellyanne's reality TV woes, or Liza's feminist bullshit?

"I made a mistake," Kellyanne said matter-of-factly. "Nobody forced me to sign on for that show. Now I just want to move forward. Legal action would cost too much and take too long. I'm done with it. And I want things to stay that way."

"But it's not just about you," Liza argued. "Your case could spotlight the indignities that so many women face in that industry. I think the reality genre is a form of pornography."

Billie slathered on more bronzing oil, drank deep on her Bloody Mary, and chomped down on the celery stick garnish. "Yeah, Kellyanne could stand up for all the sad, single sluts of the world and become the Norma Rae of lame dating shows."

Liza, the self-righteous skeleton, shot her a polar look.

Billie ignored the silent reprimand, her gaze falling on Kellyanne's perfect tan. It was on glorious display in her Michael Kors white bikini with gold chain insets. The girl's beauty was so exquisite that it became impossible to ignore. And how fucking unfair that she had possession of such a gift yet squandered it on a rich old man and deadend career moves.

Liza rose up from the chaise, adjusting her white floppy hat and oversized Tom Ford sunglasses.

"Careful, Liza," Billie teased. "I think you might be burning."

Kellyanne grinned.

"Instant gratification isn't my thing," Liza said. "A tan looks great in the short run, but the sun damage will haunt you for the rest of your life."

In answer to the minilecture, Kellyanne stretched languidly, letting out a faint, almost orgasmic moan of pleasure. "Nothing natural that feels this good could be bad for you."

"I'm going inside to make more Bloody Marys," Liza announced. "Anybody?"

"Oh, I'm fine, thanks," Kellyanne said.

"Don't be such a pansy girl with the vodka," Billie complained. "That last round tasted like a virgin batch."

Liza slipped into her Manolo Blahnik yellow flat thong sandals and started for the house, laughing a little. "I could leave out the tomato juice altogether and give you a glass of straight vodka. I bet the drink still wouldn't be strong enough."

Kellyanne smiled absently at the remark. She was staring down at the intricate mosaic design on the bottom of the pool, completely lost in her own reverie. "Do you think she's right, Billie?"

"About what?"

"Am I letting down other women by walking away from this?"

"It's *your* life," Billie pointed out. "Besides, if you cared about other women so much, you wouldn't be fucking someone's husband."

Kellyanne's face registered real shock.

"Why do you look so surprised?" Billie challenged. "Did I say something inaccurate?"

"The situation is complicated," Kellyanne said quietly.

"It's not like I'm moralizing," Billie assured her. "I'm just saying that you don't owe anybody any explanations." She cut a glance back toward the house. "Liza's always going off about what women need to be doing for each other. I say the bitch should practice what she preaches. I mean, come on. Why not eat a bagel for sisterhood? That might actually do something for the body image crisis. Have you noticed how fucking skinny she is?"

Kellyanne nodded uncomfortably. "Some women have trouble keeping on weight. And it could be stress-related, too. Last night she mentioned problems at home with Justin. It sounds serious. She thinks he's cheating."

Billie shrugged. "From what I've seen so far, she won't be far behind him. I wonder if she made him sign a prenup. He's not earning shit as a fireman. She could be looking at paying out major alimony. Now that would really test her equality principles."

"Look!" Kellyanne suddenly exclaimed, pointing at the pool gate.

A beautiful golden retriever was propped up on its hind legs, negotiating the latch with nimble front paws until the gate fell open. Then the dog trotted across the deck, jumped into the crystal blue water with a loud splash, and swam the entire length of the pool, exiting at the opposite end to shake off and lick the faces and feet of Billie and Kellyanne.

"That's Annie," Billie explained. "She comes by every day for a morning and afternoon swim."

"Oh, bless her heart!" Kellyanne squealed. "She's precious! I wish we could keep her for the summer."

"She belongs to some big designer who lives down the street. He's got his own show on HGTV."

Liza was stepping out of the house just as Annie flitted through the gate as stealthily as she'd arrived. "Bye-bye, Annie!"

"That is *so* adorable," Kellyanne gushed. "Oh, I miss having a dog. I wanted to get a small breed, but Walter forbade it. He's allergic."

Billie moved fast to relieve Liza of her Bloody Mary and wasted no time in sipping greedily. The extra vodka gave the drink some necessary bite. "Oh, yes. Much better."

"K.K. just called about a party tonight," Liza announced. "He's hosting a cocktail hour and dinner for close friends and realized that he needs some authentic estrogen on the guest list."

Billie pulled an ugly face. "I'm in no mood to be a fag hag tonight."

"I know," Liza agreed, a bit guiltily. "I didn't commit us to anything. I only said we'd try to stop by for a drink." She turned to Kellyanne. "This is your first weekend. What do you feel like doing?"

"I'm open to *anything*," Kellyanne answered sincerely. "Honestly. I'm just thrilled to be out of Miami. You could tell me that we're going to search for ticks on Annie tonight, and I'd be fine with it."

Billie howled with laughter.

Liza chuckled as she perched down onto the edge of her chaise. "Well, I don't think it'll come to that. I was thinking we could do some shopping together at Citarella's this afternoon. We could pick out some great wine and load up on all kinds of gourmet munchies. Then tonight we could check out Sunset Beach on Shelter Island. It's always a packed scene, and they make the best Mojitos I've ever had. March Donaldson will be there. He's the guy I spar with on *The Roundtable*."

Billie's stomach lurched at the mere mention of March's name. She hadn't heard anything from him in days, and now Liza was suddenly a fucking central intelligence agency about his social plans.

"Oh, he's hot," Kellyanne put in. "I never agree with what he has to say, but he's definitely fun to look at."

"How do you know that he'll be there?" Billie inquired, fighting to keep her tone casual. "Is that one of his regular hangouts?"

"I don't know," Liza said. "But he sent me a text this morning, so I know he'll be there." She gave Billie a wicked smile. "With Amaryllis, I'm sure."

"*Great,*" Billie managed to deadpan, still fuming internally. She checked her cell phone again to make certain she hadn't missed a call or a text. Not a goddamn thing.

"Who's Amaryllis?" Kellyanne asked.

"March's fiancée," Liza explained. "She's a Connecticut debutante."

"And we hate the bitch," Billie added.

"She works in PR for Stella McCartney," Liza continued evenly. "Her parents have a gorgeous estate in Watermill. The landscaping is immaculate. We should rev up the Vespas and ride over there for a look."

"Yeah," Billie snarled. "And maybe Amaryllis will invite us in for afternoon tea." Knowing that she was going to see March tonight had her completely fucked up. No guy had ever gotten to Billie quite like this. She downed what remained of her Bloody Mary, deciding that the only way to deal was to get fully loaded. And she had all day long to do it.

The stereo was blasting Jennifer Lopez at maximum volume. "You can turn me on, throw me off track/Boy, you do it well . . ."

Liza swiveled her hips and vamped in the mirror, whipping around her freshly blown-out hair. "How do I look?"

Billie surveyed Liza's ballerina-thin neck, her long chopstick legs, and the Diane von Furstenberg butterfly-print tank dress. "You look like a lollipop. If cock is the only meat you allow in your mouth, then you really need to start swallowing. You could use the calories."

With a measured calm, Liza sprayed her pulse points with Sarah Jessica Parker's Covet fragrance. "Billie, I think you need to see someone. A professional. I'm convinced you have some form of Tourette's."

Kellyanne appeared in the doorway of Liza's master bathroom, stunning in a Tory Burch silk tie halter top and second-skin tight jeans by a Swedish Denim company called Acne. "Don't laugh. I brought all that luggage, but I forgot to pack nipple covers."

Liza located a new strip of Nippets and handed the packet over.

"Thanks. You're a sweetheart," Kellyanne said. She seemed to speak in a perpetual breathy singsong.

It was at once soothing and annoying. "I *love* that dress. It's genius."

Liza pursed her lips in triumph, as if validated. "Billie thinks I look like a lollipop."

"Billie!" Kellyanne admonished, half-laughing and clearly trying to stop. "That's mean."

Billie shrugged, taking a swig from the Voss water bottle that now contained X-rated premium vodka. "Do we really need to bullshit each other? Isn't that what the men in our lives are for?" She adjusted the neckline of her teal-colored Betsey Johnson dotted tunic and finger-combed her hair into place. "I'll say this, though, Liza. For an anorexic bitch, you look damn good. If I had a dick, I'd fuck you."

Liza delicately smoothed over an eyebrow with the tip of her ring finger. "Forget songs. You should write greeting cards."

Kellyanne laughed, putting another coat of gloss onto seemingly liquid lips.

"Look at us," Billie marveled as she stood in front of the full-length double vanity mirror, flanked by Liza on her right and Kellyanne on her left. "We weren't this hot in our college days." Suddenly, she swayed backward on her Brian Atwood platform sandals.

Liza reacted quickly to stop her fall. "Okay, you either need flats or a pot of coffee." She paused a beat. "Or rehab."

Billie steadied herself on the Plexiglas heels. "I just lost my balance for a second. I'm fine." She took in a deep breath and gave all of them a curious assessment, wondering how this group had made a friendship sealed in the crucible of a Cancún college party last almost ten fucking years.

Everybody wanted the *Sex and the City* girl clique model—sisterly love, emotional intimacy, loyalty, and all that shit. But Billie had rarely seen it work in the real world. Sure, some women tried. They even pretended. But shine a blue light on most girl posses, and the evidence was right there—the weak bonds, the blind determination to prove to themselves—to prove to the world—that they had their own Carrie, Samantha, Miranda, and Charlotte thing going on. Maybe the delusion made them feel less lonely.

Most women hated Billie. For starters, she was too honest. If a pair of jeans made a girl's ass look big, she said so without being asked. And no longtime crush, boyfriend, or husband was ever off limits. When Billie wanted to bang a guy, it was game on. Most women hated Kellyanne, too. She was too fucking beautiful. What other reason did they need? As for Liza, she was nobody's dream sorority sister—too intelligent, too ambitious, too opinionated. It was no wonder the three of them had glommed together over the years. They were settling for whatever was there.

Billie gave everyone a final once over in the mirror. "Bitches, I think we're ready."

Shelter Island was a remote and secluded jewel on the eastern end of Long Island. Part of its charm was the quaint isolation. The island was only accessible by an open-decked ferry that shuttled back and forth between the North and South forks. Throwback touches to an earlier, more innocent age were everywhere. Billie's favorite was a hand-stenciled sign nailed to a tree. It warned drivers of crossing turtles.

As Liza gunned the Lexus down Route 114, Billie lay slumped in the backseat, more than living up to her goal of being properly smashed in advance of the night's event. Her new plan was to pretend that March Donaldson didn't exist. Even if he walked up and slapped his dick across her face, she'd still ignore him. The asshole could rot in hell with that slab of dry ice from Connecticut. Billie didn't care anymore.

She listened with vague interest as Liza and Kellyanne blathered on about how beautiful everything was in the Hamptons. Billie's thoughts drifted to how nice it would be to have a second home in one of the hamlets, a peaceful place to escape from the city. Of course, Amy would tell her that she couldn't afford it. But if Todd's relaunch idea worked, then she'd be swimming in cash.

West Neck Road became Shore Road. Liza followed it to the beach and turned left into a parking lot. Billie swung out first, spotted a dingy waterfront restaurant, and murmured, "What's the big fucking deal?"

Venturing closer, it became clear. The sunset and harbor views were spectacular. Billie climbed the stairs to discover three outside decks, each one at full capacity and overflowing with kinetic social energy. The decor was simple—rattan chairs, benches, and strings of little white lights. Kat DeLuna's melodic Caribbean jam "Am I Dreaming?" percolated in the background.

The atmosphere made Billie ravenous for a cigarette. She dug into the crocodile hobo bag that had set her back two grand. Something to tell her kids if she ever had any: Never shop online late at night when you're drunk. "Fuck!"

"What's wrong?" Kellyanne asked.

Billie continued digging, even though she knew it was a futile effort. "I left my goddamn cigarettes back at the house." She spotted a hunky guy smoking in the sand and made an instant beeline for him. "Hey, can I bum one of those? I'm about to die."

He smiled at her with perfect teeth and tapped out a Parliament. "Do you need a light?"

Billie shook her head, whipped out a vintage Cartier lighter, dragged deep, and filled her lungs with the sweet poison. "Thanks."

"My pleasure." His hair was styled in a severe buzz cut, his body was lean and lanky, and he dressed down in a gray tank, camo cargo pants, and an orange cotton hoodie. The sum of it all was a poor girl's Justin Timberlake. He studied her for a moment. "You look familiar."

"That's because I'm a fucking rock star."

He laughed. "That's a good one. Do you mind if I steal that sometime?"

"Why? Do you think it'll get you laid?" She started off to catch up with Liza and Kellyanne.

"Maybe," he called out. "It'd sure work for you if you came back to my room tonight!"

Grinning, she took another drag and waved him off, trudging through the sand in her Brian Atwoods. Christ! She'd paid nine hundred bucks for these shoes. Did a girl have to be in fucking Cirque du Soleil to walk sexy in them?

She nearly tripped over a fat chocolate Labrador that was sacked out in the sand, no cares in the world. "Oops," she giggled, bending over to stroke the pooch's adorable face. "Sorry, sweetie."

The dog licked her hand and went back to sleep.

Billie glanced up at the obvious owners, an attractive older couple holding court just a few feet away. She smiled at them. "I'll have what he's having."

The husband laughed uproariously; the wife managed a tight smile and glared at Billie behind Fendi sunglasses.

The bistro's uncovered deck was packed. Liza and Kellyanne had secured what appeared to be the last table on earth. A first round of drinks had already been ordered, and a fresh Mojito sat waiting.

Billie gulped down the concoction of rum, sugar, lime, and mint as if it were Gatorade. The drink was beyond delicious. Instantly, she wanted another. She stopped a fast-moving waitress and pushed the empty glass into her hand. "Bring me two of these as soon as humanly possible and keep them coming after that."

Liza laughed. "I could have a word with management. Maybe they'll set up an IV drip."

Billie thrust out a forearm and made a fist. "I'm game for that." Anxiously, she scanned the crowd. March could be on one of the other decks. He could be inside the restaurant, too. She wanted the chance to ignore him. In fact, her body was burning for the opportunity.

"Kellyanne, I think you have some admirers," Liza observed, discreetly gesturing to a rowdy trio of twenty-something guys.

To say they were hammered would be the understatement of the night. The three stooges were laughing, gawking, and adjusting themselves over the sight of the blond goddess from Alabama. And in true testosterone posse fashion, there appeared to be a sexually confident leader, a funny dork, and a financially successful asshole.

Kellyanne rolled her eyes skyward as the ringleader approached, leaving his idiot friends behind to sort out the cash for whatever bet had been wagered.

He walked right up to Kellyanne and politely asked, "Do you clean houses?"

Kellyanne's model-perfect face became a master-piece of bored disbelief. "Excuse me?"

"I'm looking for a housekeeper."

Kellyanne tossed an annoyed look to Billie and Liza, as if questioning her hearing. "Sorry. I guess your search continues."

He reached into his back pocket. "Let me give you one of my business cards just in case you change your mind."

"Don't bother. I won't." Kellyanne spun around, ignoring the lame offering.

Billie watched the interloper glance back at his buddies and shoot them a self-satisfied asshole grin. Actually, she thought the guy was sort of hot. His who-gives-a-fuck attitude gave him a certain sex appeal. But the smug shit needed to be schooled on the fact that all the gym work he put into his Vin Diesel arms would never compensate for the Stein Mart wardrobe, gay-porn-star goatee, and Johnny Knoxville idol worship.

"Oh, now I'm *really* going to need a drink." The voice booming behind her belonged to March Donaldson.

Billie experienced a powerful thump in her gut. It was fucking ridiculous. The bastard had her at "Oh." She turned slowly, intending to look fast, then look away. But she ended up just standing there, robbed of all breath, drinking in every detail and finding herself thirsting for more. Her desire for him seemed unquenchable.

She watched him play primarily to Liza while Billie got a casual, "Hello, nice to see you again." March was social maestro as introductions went back and forth with Kellyanne and Amaryllis. Another attractive couple entered the mix—Jay and Gopa Dobson.

March announced that he and Amaryllis had flown in from Manhattan on Jay's helicopter. Billie had taken the goddamn Jitney bus. She was slowly boiling with fury now.

The loser who tried to hit on Kellyanne was still standing on the periphery, wondering what to do with the business card nobody wanted. He was five foot ten. He was only mildly handsome. It was so unfortunate. But when a March Donaldson entered the room, men of this caliber were rendered as meaningless as bugs on a windshield.

Billie knocked back Mojito after Mojito, her frustration building as the party mushroomed. MSNBC's Dan Abrams turned up with a pretty blonde, but his eyes tracked Kellyanne like heat-seeking lasers. The interior designers Jamie Drake and Peter Falk made their way over with shrewd housing investors Audrey and Phillip Davis. As Amaryllis glowered off to the side, Audrey openly swooned over March. The woman with the gorgeous turquoise choker was thrilled to encounter a fellow Republican who—like her—was proud to say so.

The more the evening progressed, the easier it was for March to ignore Billie. She left to bum another cigarette, finding her Timberlake clone in the same spot. His name was Shayne Cutter. He announced that he was staying on Shelter Island for the summer to finish a screenplay. The name Billie Shelton rang no bells for him. Without apology, he admitted to listening to only hip-hop since the age of twelve. She entertained the idea of fucking him later that night and wandered back to the group.

"Billie, where have you been?" Liza asked. "We ordered some food!"

She surveyed the crisp french fries, steamed

mussels, shrimp rolls, and fried calamari. It looked delicious. It smelled divine. But all she wanted was another Mojito.

Amaryllis was engaged in a serious conference with Jamie and Peter. "If you saw what she did to my parents' pool house, then you would understand why I sent her a new set of cards with the title *inferior desecrator* under her name."

Casually, March sidled up to Billie, sipped his drink, and took in the scene. "Are we having fun yet?" He spoke in a deliberately low voice.

Billie's spirits were instantly buoyed by his acknowledgment. Her desperation was total. She hated him for that. And she would make him pay for it, too. "I'm not wearing any underwear."

March swallowed hard. "Don't tell me that. It's not fair."

"It's not supposed to be. But I did it for you."

He seemed to be concentrating on the situation as if it were hard science. "Go to the bathroom. I'll count to sixty and follow you there."

Billie liked his plan. It was hot and dangerous and risky. She had the son of a bitch exactly where she wanted him—horny enough to choose her even with his fiancée standing three feet away. A man's cock truly had a will all its own.

She walked inside the ladies room, only to find a trashy blonde in front of the mirror, touching up a makeup job that had been botched from the start. Billie checked the stalls. They were empty. Now she just needed this imitation Tara Reid to beat it.

"*Billie Shelton*? Oh, my God! I, like, love, love, *love* your music!"

Christ. Of all things to contend with at the moment—a fucking fan.

"I saw your concert at Jones Beach last year! It was awesome! Nobody's going to believe this! You've got to take a picture with me!" She rushed Billie, pressed against her cheek to cheek, and thrust out her right hand to frame them inside her cell phone camera's tiny lens. When she inspected the captured image, she beamed, displaying it with pride. "This rocks!"

Billie smiled weakly, growing increasingly anxious. Fans like this were usually good nourishment for the ego. But she had half a mind to flush this bitch down the toilet. March was probably loitering outside by now, feeling conspicuous and ready to bolt.

Thinking fast, Billie clutched her stomach with both hands. "Ugh . . . I think I'm going to be sick." She tilted her head toward the exit. "Do you mind?"

"Oh, God! No! Is there anything I can do?"

Billie shook her head. "I'll be fine. I just need a few minutes."

Finally, the girl got the hint and took off.

Billie paused for a count of ten before flinging open the door and pulling March inside with a degree of strength and power that surprised her.

He was caught off guard, too, losing his balance and bracing the sink to steady himself. He laughed and groped for her, kissing her neck, his fingers, lips, and tongue practically searing into her. "We should lock the door."

"Then we'll *definitely* get caught." Billie pushed him inside the last stall, shoved him onto the commode, and latched the door.

March flattened his feet against it, helping Billie climb onto the toilet and holding her legs as she struggled for traction.

"These goddamn shoes! I should take them off."

"No," March said quickly. "They're fucking hot.

Keep them on." He worked harder to steady her body, the proof of his effort in the corded veins popping out of his forearms. "Do you have any coke?"

She shook her head.

He groaned. "Fuck, I'd kill for a line right now."

Billie hiked up her Betsey Johnson dress and squatted over him. "I made a special trip into the city this week. I went to J. Sisters just like you said. Do you like it?"

March arched his back to inspect the work, then dipped two fingers into his mouth to moisten them before slowly tracing the outline of his meticulously sculpted initials, moaning his appreciation. "MDD . . . this is definitely my pussy now." He slid a finger inside, teasing her. "How'd you know my middle name was Douglas?"

"I Googled you."

He chuckled slightly, angling his neck to taste her.

Billie waited until his mouth was almost there. And then she unleashed a slap across his face with such force that she had to grab the top of the stall's side panel to keep from falling down.

March reeled from the impact, then rose up, grabbing her firmly by both arms and shoving her against the door. He was close enough to breathe her breath. He was red-faced and angry. He was still turned on. "What the fuck? Do you like to play rough? Is that it?"

Billie gave him a placid little smile. "That's not it at all. Do you actually think I'm going to let you treat me like some throwaway piece of ass?" She didn't wait for his answer. "You suck. And I can't wait to shave tonight."

March dropped a hand down and rested it between her thighs. "You don't mean that."

"Oh, yes I do." It took nearly everything that she had to ignore the exquisite heat of his palm as it inched upward.

"Liar." He smiled like the cocky bastard he was.

Billie reached up to touch March's cheek. For a half movement, she caressed it, but then she dug her freshly manicured nails into that gorgeous face that had been bronzed by a thousand Texas suns.

March froze. His eyes went wide with fear.

All of a sudden, Billie halted. Her claws were deeply imbedded but not ripping skin . . . *yet*. She had the entire left side of his face in play. Her arm was perfectly angled, the tension in it as tight as a drum. All she had to do was work her way down. "I could fuck you up so bad that you wouldn't be able to go on television for a month."

"You're crazy." He didn't mean it in a good way.

Billie smiled at him. "I know." With her free hand she reached down to stroke the crotch of his Rock & Republic jeans, finding him hard—and getting harder. "Nine out of ten men surveyed will say that the best sex they ever had was with a girl who was just a little bit psycho."

March took in a deep breath, stifling a moan.

"I want you to think about that when you're in bed with your frigid fiancée tonight." And then Billie pushed him onto the toilet, unlatched the stall door, and stalked out to search for Shayne Cutter.

She found him smoking on the beach. Where else? He was talking on his cell phone but ended the call when he saw the sexual determination in Billie's hooded eyes.

Shayne took her by the hand and led her to his room at Sunset Beach. They shared a cigarette on the way. Not a single word was spoken. His suite was warm, cozy, and inviting—white walls, a carpeted floor, a minibar, and a large private balcony with a beautiful view of the water.

Billie noticed an Apple laptop on the desk. Several red-lined script pages were scattered around it. He really was working on a screenplay. She ventured over to have a look, picking up one of the more marked-up sheets of paper. From what she could tell, his project was some kind of vampire movie called *Not Enough Blood*.

Shayne stepped over, removed the page from her hand, and kissed her with an insistent passion. He tasted of Parliaments and Mojitos. "Is there anything I should know?"

Billie just looked at him.

His hands found their way to her ass, cupping her cheeks and giving them a delicious little squeeze. "What you like . . . what you don't like . . ."

"You can put it anywhere," Billie said.

Liza

||

The cramping had been intense. In fact, a day after Liza had been administered the HCG drug to promote egg release, she'd nearly doubled over in agony. The pressure on her ovaries had been unreal. But that was last night. This morning she was recovering nicely, having undergone her second egg retrieval at Reproductive Medicine Associates of New York, an approved partner center of the Boston-based Extend Fertility.

"Things couldn't have gone better," Dr. Allan Copperman said. "We have thirty-two eggs from this cycle." He patted her forearm. "Still a little groggy from the sedation?"

Liza nodded.

Dr. Copperman had harvested fluid from her ovaries using an ultrasound-guided needle. The eggs had been identified under a microscope. They would soon be flash-frozen and secured in a liquid-nitrogen storage tank. Recent advancements in cryopreservation—one being a technique to avoid the formation of ice crystals during the freezing and thawing processes—had greatly improved the success rate of pregnancies.

The procedure was high-tech baby insurance. Liza knew that her decision to go through with it was the right one. The prospect of motherhood no longer seemed like a fatalistic deadline. Now it was a personal reality *whenever* she wanted to choose it—ten years into the future, perhaps even later. From her vantage point, the biological clock was still running, but it had stopped ticking like a time bomb. The attendant sense of freedom was empowering.

"We're going to have you rest for another hour," Dr. Copperman said. "Then you'll be free to go. Do you have any questions?"

"You probably won't see me again for ten years," Liza said wryly. "Take good care of my eggs."

Dr. Copperman smiled. He was a kind man with thick dark hair, a big smile, and a comforting bedside manner. "They're in capable hands. I assure you."

Extend Fertility's storage facility was state-of-the-art and protected by a fail-safe backup system, round-the-clock security, and a triple-checked client identification procedure. Liza had once joked to Christy Jones, the company's founder and CEO, that she should consider heading up Homeland Security. On Christy's watch, the domestic threat of al Qaeda would probably disappear overnight.

Liza rested peacefully, taking in the antiseptic surroundings, realizing that the next time she passed through these doors, it'd be for ICSI. An embryologist would fertilize one of her eggs with the injection of a single sperm in preparation for transfer to her uterus. But whose sperm? That'd be the real question facing her.

Since she returned home from the most recent weekend in the Hamptons, Liza and Justin had barely spoken. It amazed her how disengaged she could feel from a man who slept in the same bed with her. Night after night, Justin simply rolled over to one side, tucked his body into the fetal position, and snoozed like a satisfied baby.

It was over with him. Intellectually, Liza knew that. But emotionally, no matter how dysfunctional the situation, she felt a strange reluctance about taking the necessary measures to put an official break into motion. Part of her still loved him. And another part of her wasn't quite ready to be alone again. She wondered how long she could endure this state of limbo.

She took a deep breath and pushed Justin out of her thoughts, firing up her MacBook Pro and accessing the clinic's Wi-Fi network. She could make better use of the downtime by checking her public e-mail account and updating her blog.

Scrolling through the new messages, Liza noticed the usual assortment. There were scores of reader comments on *Whore*. The trade paperback release had triggered a new wave of passionate interest. There were also requests for speaking engagements, which she automatically forwarded to her lecture agent, plus the odd marriage proposal.

Of course, the most disturbing aspect of having a Web presence—and a high-profile media one— was exposure to the vicious attacks that came with it. Within her first few weeks of appearing as a regular pundit on *The Roundtable,* a doctored photo of Liza with a noose around her neck and a muzzle over her mouth had turned up on various blogging sites. And just days after launching her own blog, someone had posted a comment detailing his fantasy of ejaculating into her face and then slitting her throat.

Liza tried to be philosophical about the issue. The anonymity of online posts allowed dark prejudices and sick anger to surface, particularly toward women. And it was not merely an appalling lack of civility. It was genuine harassment. As a result, she knew women who only blogged under a gender-neutral pseudonym. She also knew of colleagues who'd simply abandoned the practice altogether.

Liza refused to be silenced or sidelined by what she considered to be lowest-common-denominator intimidation. She was determined to gut it out. Besides, the worst offenders were no doubt cowardly creeps posting in their stained bathrobes. So it was her custom to give these messages no more time than it took to click the DELETE button. But this morning, one missive in particular captured her attention.

From: travisowen@yahoo.com
To: liza@lizapike.com

Subject: Watch Her Bleed

  Shut up, bitch. Or you will be next.

  Travis Owen

A palpable unease swept over Liza as she read the words once, twice, three times. It was the subtext—not the vague threat—that bothered her. *Watch Her Bleed* was the title of Harrison Beck's slasher movie. Travis Owen was the name of its psychopathic character who goes on a murder binge targeting powerful and influential women. And at the end of the film, he escapes from an asylum for the criminally insane and lives to kill again, ostensibly in the inevitable sequel.

Something about the message left a distinct chill. Perhaps it was the idea that someone had actually taken the deliberate measure to not only create an e-mail account under the name of a fictional character but to write a message from that character's point of view as well. That degree of intent made Liza uncomfortable, though she ultimately trashed the e-mail.

The incident triggered a recall of one of her peers, Tuesday Kent. They'd met while in graduate school at Brandeis University. Both Liza and Tuesday had earned the wrath of other would-be feminist scholars on campus. With their stunning looks, interest in and acceptance of fashion, and appreciation for relationships with men, they were openly disdained, considered dubious torchbearers for the cause, and dismissively chided as "lipstick feminists."

They were also fiercely competitive with each other. Liza and Tuesday had dueling columns in *The Justice,* the independent weekly student newspaper. When Liza upstaged Tuesday by securing a call-in radio show on the university station WBRS-FM, the race was on to become the next Naomi

Wolf. Postgraduation, Tuesday had crossed the ticker tape first. She landed a big publishing deal for *The Baby Girl Diaries,* a personal manifesto about growing up in the confines of a strict, patriarchal, upper-class suburban household. It became a phenomenally successful bestseller.

Tuesday had been shrewd in using the Web to marshal a community of dedicated followers, building a network of like-minded Baby Girls all across the country with her online message board and sophisticated electronic newsletters. But then came the trouble.

What Tuesday had thought was the occasional random comment suddenly hardened into a sinister trend of violent threats and character-assassinating taunts. Posts began popping up online with increasing frequency, everything from the prediction that Tuesday would die from a chainsaw rape to the outrageous charge that her Baby Girl nickname stemmed from a long-term sexual relationship with her father. Law enforcement officials laughed it off, telling her that it was just harmless online talk.

Eventually, the Web-based terrorism pushed Tuesday over the edge. She cancelled public speaking engagements. She stopped writing. She developed agoraphobia. And the saddest irony of all was that, in the end, she returned home to Highland Park in Dallas, where she moved back in with her parents and once again became the Baby Girl that she'd made a career out of disavowing with such ferocious aplomb.

Curiously, Liza logged onto Tuesday's official Web site. With the exception of a few stray message board comments wishing her well and calling for her return, the site hadn't been updated in over two years. Tuesday Kent remained underground. It was such a sad and wasteful turn of events. Liza remembered her as being so vital.

A thought lanced her brain about the e-mail she'd received from this Travis Owen. It occurred to Liza that Harrison Beck could be the culprit. Perhaps his idea of an inside joke? Her suspicions began to mount. If it was his attempt at humor, then it was a thoroughly tasteless effort. But then again, this was the same man responsible for bringing *Watch Her Bleed* to the screen. What else could she possibly expect from him?

The hour passed quickly and, along with it, the lingering effects of the anesthesia. Liza checked out of the clinic and slowly negotiated her body into a cab. The tenderness would remain for the next few days. After taking a deep breath, she announced her address to the driver.

She switched her BlackBerry from silent mode and checked for missed calls. There were four—one from her literary agent, one from Tom Shapiro, and two from Kellyanne.

The device vibrated in Liza's hand. She smiled and answered the call before it had a chance to ring. "Third time's the charm. I just walked out."

"How did everything go?" Kellyanne asked.

"Thirty-two eggs," Liza said, groaning slightly.

"*Thirty-two?*" Kellyanne exclaimed. "In your itty-bitty body? I can't believe it."

Liza laughed. "They're not goose eggs. You can't even see them without a microscope."

"I know, but still. Was Justin with you?"

"No." She paused a beat. "He's at the fire station."

"So you were there all by yourself? Bless your

heart! I knew that I should've insisted on coming with you."

"I'm fine," Liza assured her. "I was in and out within two hours. I don't even have an incision."

"Well, I didn't know what to do with myself, so I made my mother's frozen peanut butter pie. Part of your recovery is going to be eating the whole damn thing."

Liza grinned. "What are your plans for the rest of the day?"

"I'll probably go to the beach. And then I might do some shopping."

"I have a few calls to return. I'll check in with you later, okay?" Liza signed off and rang Tom Shapiro.

"You're a lightweight," Tom said right away. "I haven't seen a girl that drunk in a limousine since my junior prom."

"Well, I hope she got more action than I did."

He chuckled. "Actually, she cut my dick with her braces while attempting a blow job and threw up at the sight of the blood."

Liza laughed. "I assume that's the defining moment when you gave up on women."

"Yeah—that and Don Johnson. When I was ten years old, I liked *Miami Vice* way too much."

"Such a sweet, confused boy."

"Did you know that your husband challenged me to a racquetball game the other night?" Tom asked.

"That doesn't surprise me. He's always up for a game. Are you any good?"

"I can hold my own."

Liza smiled at the cocky edge in his voice. "Justin's an athletic cyborg, Tom. Even with a sport

he's never played before. He could take up windsurf-
ing tomorrow and make lifers look like first-timers.
You'll be totally annihilated."

"Care to put some money down on that?" Tom
challenged.

"That would be stealing," Liza teased. "I like you
too much for that."

"You know, you really are a bitch. I'm going to
stop defending you to other people."

Liza laughed again. "Before I forget—I've got a
topic idea for the next show."

"Hold the thought," Tom said. "We're dark for the
next three weeks."

"Oh, that's right," Liza murmured, recalling the
on-and-off summer schedule. She felt an immediate
sense of relief. This would allow her the flexibility to
spend more time in the Hamptons. "Are you going
anywhere fun?"

"To the West Coast for a few days. But it's work.
We're shooting a Hollywood red and blue version of
The Roundtable. Mel Gibson, Alec Baldwin, Susan
Sarandon, and Bo Derek are already booked."

"That should be interesting. I hope Alec hasn't
left you any voice mail messages. And don't let Mel
drive."

"Yeah," Tom remarked wearily. "So far it's been a
scheduling nightmare. Their publicists are making us
crazy, too. They want all the questions in advance,
and every day we get a new list of no-fly-zone topics.
No one wants to come off looking like a dumb actor."

"That'll be the ultimate test of their thespian
skills," Liza put in dryly. She sighed. "Well, I'm going to take a break from politics and relax. When

you get back, you should come to East Hampton for a few days."

"Sounds like fun. And I've already seen Billie naked, so that awkwardness is out of the way."

Liza smiled. "Now, *she* could match you drink for drink. In a whiskey shot contest, I bet Billie could outlast a gunslinger from the Old West."

The cab jerked to a stop in front of Liza's building.

She pushed some cash into the driver's hand and swung out. "I just got home, Tom, and I always lose reception in the elevator. Call me when you're free. We'll set up a plan for East Hampton. I really want you to come."

Liza breezed past the doorman on her way to retrieve the mail. She bumped into a neighbor, Teddy Easton, at the boxes. "So make me feel like a slug. Tell me how far you rode this morning."

He smiled shyly, glancing down at the Cat Cheetah handmade carbon fiber bike that was easily ten thousand dollars. "Sixty miles."

"Only sixty? You're going to get *fat*." She delivered the last bit in a singsong voice.

Teddy grinned. "Hey, you're one to talk, Mary-Kate."

He was a print and runway model, primarily for European fashion houses where the new hot look was stick-thin, tall, and gaunt. A Dior Homme representative had discovered him on a street-search talent mission called Boy Safari. The quarry that day happened to be a pedigreed male waif.

Teddy was a nineteen-year-old heir to the Easton Oil fortune. Money would never be an issue, and the idea of college bored him, so modeling seemed like a cool way to garner attention and make himself the It Boy among his friends. He hoped that it would lead to acting, too. With his extreme slenderness and androgynous features, Teddy rivaled many women, even with his severe buzz cut. A recent denim campaign that cast him in the role of faux concentration camp survivor had received a torrent of media outrage. But the jeans were still flying off the shelves.

As they walked toward the elevator, Liza regarded Teddy's physique with something close to envy. He was six foot two with a twenty-nine-inch waist. She guessed his body mass index to be eighteen or lower. "What's your exercise routine?"

"I get up, cycle anywhere between twenty and sixty miles, take a coffee break, run five miles, take another coffee break, swim half a mile, and then I try to get in a yoga class by the end of the day."

"I don't think I could get through one of those things," Liza grumbled.

"It's my job." He shrugged, then navigated his bike through the open elevator doors.

Liza followed him inside. "I didn't hear anything about food in your routine."

"Food? What's that?"

She grinned knowingly. This boy was skin and bones, and he didn't eat. They had more in common than she wanted to admit. "Eat a pizza, Teddy. I beg you."

He raised a thin eyebrow. "I will if you will. Let's share one."

They disembarked on the same floor. Teddy lived two apartments over in a smaller unit.

Liza waved him off and ventured inside the loft, surprised to hear the television blaring from the living room. She stepped closer and discovered Justin sprawled on the sofa, wearing nothing but boxer briefs and watching *Jackass Number Two*. Again. "I thought you were at the station."

Justin let out a deep belly laugh as someone's finger-puppet-covered penis got bitten by a snake. He didn't bother looking away from the giant screen. "Nope. I'm here."

Liza experienced a familiar firestorm of anger and resentment. She vaulted upstairs without a word and proceeded to pace the area like a panther in a cage, debating whether to throw the stupid bastard out on his ass. In the end, she decided to pack her things and take an extended break to sort through her true feelings.

She sank down onto the unmade bed and started to cry. Tears of frustration, regret, and uncertainty rained down her cheeks. A strong part of her yearned to engage him, to get a good fight started. But Justin had an infuriating ability to opt out of arguments and treat her like the most insignificant person on earth. It was a tactic that stirred her most violent impulses. In the right circumstances, Liza could envision herself actually hurting him, or at least attempting to. The thought frightened her.

She pulled herself together, retrieved two Prada wheel-away trolleys from the closet, and methodically gathered everything she'd need for the next three weeks. The focused nature of the task had a necessary calming effect.

Justin made no move to assist her as she brought the luggage pieces downstairs one at a time. His interest remained glued to the disgusting *Jackass* antics.

Liza set down the second and final bag with a

loud thud, then stood directly in front of the television until Justin acknowledged her.

"What?"

"We need some space," Liza said evenly. "I'm going to stay in the Hamptons for the next three weeks."

"This is a funny part. Do you mind?"

She spun around and switched off the power. "*This* is not the funny part. This is the part where you act like you care even a little bit about us. Otherwise, it's over, Justin. We can end it. Right here, right now. And you can take the next three weeks to find a new place to live. One that you can actually afford. And I promise you that won't be in a Manhattan zip code."

Justin scratched his balls, kicked back, and cradled his head in his hands. "I'm not going anywhere."

Liza merely stared at him, amazed that she was in this kind of situation . . . with this kind of man. A surreal feeling swept over her. How could this be her existence? It should be some other woman's life. But right now it was hers.

Justin extended his right arm and aimed the remote control between her legs, zapping *Jackass Number Two* back into obstructed view.

Without a word, Liza rolled her luggage into the corridor and closed the door, her mind in tumult over what move to make next.

Teddy Easton appeared again and politely relieved her of one of the bags. He was suited up in a sleeveless tank and tiny running shorts, a black iPod strapped to his bony arm. "Escaping?"

"Only to the Hamptons," she replied quietly. "Not far enough, I'm afraid."

They rode the elevator in easy silence.

Liza could hear the music buzzing from Teddy's headphones. Fergie was singing, "It's time to be a big girl now/And big girls don't cry . . ."

Kellyanne

12

She was sunbathing on Georgica Beach when the call came through from Adam Griffie.

At first, Kellyanne hesitated to answer, fearing that Brad "Bonzi" Lucas had complained to the William Morris Agency about her abrupt exit. But something compelled her to pick up, if only to get the unpleasantness over with. Walter Isherwood's girl or not, she felt certain that Adam was striking her off his client list.

But his tone was uncharacteristically warm. In fact, Adam was downright chatty before delivering the bottom line. "I think I might have an acting job for you. A real one."

Kellyanne was stunned. Her mind took off in at least a dozen directions, all of them variations of her secret dream that this day might come. *The* call from out of the blue. An offer to play the ingenue in a big-budget action thriller starring Clive Owen. A character part in a Paul Haggis–scripted ensemble piece such as *Crash*. A plum new role on a megahit such as *Grey's Anatomy* or *Twenty-Four*. And so on.

"*As the World Turns* is hiring a new contract player," Adam explained. "They're looking for a beautiful blonde with an authentic Southern accent."

It sounded too good to be true. Kellyanne's stomach did a complete revolution.

"The character's an abstinence counselor with a dark past," Adam went on. "It's a great role that intersects with most of the main story arcs. Soap work is a grind, but this is a great opportunity for some major exposure."

"I . . . I don't . . . know what to say," Kellyanne stammered.

"Say you're interested."

She gripped the phone tighter. "I am!"

"The writers have worked up a full treatment for this Anna-Claire character. She's going to be revealed in layers, peeled away like an onion. If you nail it, this is the stuff of Daytime Emmys."

Kellyanne had never heard Adam sound so upbeat. It was a complete about-face. Maybe he'd believed in her talent all along. Everyone said the big break was always connected to the perfect role that allowed an actor to shine. And in more cases than not, it was a great agent who found it.

Adam cleared his throat. "Listen, Kellyanne, I don't know what your . . . *arrangement* is with Walter, but the show shoots in New York. It'll mean relocating from Miami."

"That's not a problem," she said quickly.

"Good to hear." He laughed a little. "Walter might stonewall me from getting that apartment I want at Indian Creek. But who gives a shit? I'd rather have a new star on my roster."

"I believe Walter will be happy for me. I truly do."

"Let's hope so," Adam murmured. His tone was skeptical. "Most men like him are only interested in their own dreams."

Kellyanne fell silent. Deep down, she knew Adam was right.

"Now this isn't exactly a done deal," Adam cautioned. "You still have to read for the part. But they went nuts over your head shots and reel, and I know that once they hear that sweet Southern twang in your voice, they won't be able to sign Kellyanne Downey fast enough."

"This is *amazing!*" she screamed, leaping to her feet and running toward the surf to kick around in the water.

The sky was a perfect periwinkle blue. The sun was a bright orange ball of rejuvenating heat. The beach was sparkling clean. And just beyond the dunes was a gorgeous backdrop of magnificent estates and fairy-tale mansions. This was a glorious moment that Kellyanne wanted to seal in her memory forever—the day she got *the* call . . . where she was . . . what she was thinking . . . how she was feeling.

"I'll be in touch as soon as I have details about the reading. Have a bag packed and your car gassed up for the airport."

"Actually, I'm in New York," Kellyanne said. "Well, East Hampton, to be exact. I'm here for the summer."

"Perfect. Be ready to move fast." He started to sign off.

"Adam!" Kellyanne blurted. "I almost forgot. Technically, I'm supposed to be in Miami shooting that reality show, *Soul Mates.*"

"Oh, yeah, I forgot about that. What happened?"

His interest in this new subject was so marginal that he sounded like the old Adam.

"I had a bad experience with the producer, and I quit," Kellyanne explained matter-of-factly. "He threatened to—"

"Summer reality shows are a joke," Adam cut in. There was a faraway quality to his voice and the distinct clacking of fingertips on a keyboard in the background. He had officially checked out. "The networks throw a bunch of shit on the schedule and hope some of it sticks. Most of those shows get yanked after a few airings. You probably won't get paid for whatever you did there. But who cares? We're moving on."

"Thank you, Adam," Kellyanne gushed, appreciating the inclusive pronoun. It closed out the conversation that made her feel like a real actress for the first time in her life.

She raced back to her spot on the sand, feeling as if she were floating on a cloud. Her heart was positively soaring. This was real happiness. And it belonged to her exclusively.

Desperate to share the news, she started to call her parents. But then she stopped herself. It was too soon. Better to wait until the role had been officially offered and accepted. Spreading the word prematurely could jinx the situation. Kellyanne was superstitious that way.

Of course, she could tell her summer roommates. Liza and Billie understood the nuances of the business. They'd instantly realize what this call from her agent represented and how incredible a juicy role on *As the World Turns* could be for her career.

She dialed Billie first. When it went straight to voice mail, she hung up and tried Liza, who answered on the second ring in a voice only half its full compass. "Liza?"

"Hi, Kellyanne." Her tone was somber. "I'm sorry about not calling you back."

"No, it's okay. Where are you?"

"Somewhere on the Long Island Expressway. It turns out *The Roundtable* will be dark for the next few weeks, so I hired a car service to bring me back. I should be there in about two hours."

Kellyanne's excitement about Liza's early return was tempered by the depressive quality in her voice. "How are you feeling?"

"Good. Still a little sore, but . . ."

Kellyanne was hardly convinced. "You sound down, sweetheart. Talk to me."

Liza sighed deeply. "It's just my fucking husband. And he's not worth the airtime."

"Honey, there's no man issue that two pretty girls and a bottle of Pinot can't fix," Kellyanne said.

"Is that so?" Even through the phone, it was clear that Liza was almost smiling.

"Absolutely. It's obvious to me that if Justin isn't counting his blessings every day for you, then he's a complete idiot. I know the boy can put out a fire, but he probably couldn't pour rain out of his boot with a hole in the toe and directions on the heel."

Liza laughed. "What is this? Am I driving into *Petticoat Junction*?"

Kellyanne stretched her body in a show of worship to the relentless sun. "You're talking to an Alabama girl who's celebrating her roots today. They just might do me some good after all. I'll explain later. But here's the plan. I'm going to call my Uncle Kirby and get his recipe for shrimp and cheese grits. He owns a waterfront restaurant in Mobile, and people come from all over for that one dish. I'm cooking dinner for us tonight, and you're going to eat even if I have to tie you to a fence post and spoon-feed you like a fussy baby. Then we're going to drink a few bottles of wine and solve all the world's problems. Any questions?"

"No, ma'am."

"Good. Dinner's at six." Feeling infinitely competent and useful, Kellyanne hung up and tried to call Billie again. Once more, it rang directly into voice mail. But this time she left a message. "Hey, sweetheart, it's Kellyanne. Just wondering what your plans are for tonight. I'm making a big dinner. Let me hear from you."

She had a strong feeling that Billie would be MIA. There'd been a hushed phone call earlier that morning, and then Billie had rushed out of the house as if a three-alarm fire were blazing.

Kellyanne's cellular jingled to the music of Dr. Dre's hip-hop classic "Nuthin' but a 'G' Thang." It was Walter's dedicated ring tone and so ridiculously incongruous that she almost laughed every time it played. But today she was stone faced. "Hello?"

"How's my girl?" Walter asked.

Kellyanne bristled at his patronization. "Fine, thanks." She paused a beat. "How are your kids?"

"Doing *fantastic*. All of them. Just *fantastic*." He was trying too hard. There was obvious tension in his voice.

Kellyanne wanted to ask about Cagle, Walter's youngest son—a twenty-two-year-old college dropout. His transcript was checkered with false starts from at least half a dozen top schools all across the country. And as Jab had filled her in on the way to the airport, Cagle was recently arrested for drug possession and sexual assault.

"I'll be in New York for a few days starting tomorrow," Walter announced.

"That's great," Kellyanne lied, struggling to sound even mildly enthusiastic. Because inside she was thoroughly deflated. Her weekend with the girls would be ruined.

"I'm staying at the St. Regis. My schedule's crazy with back-to-back meetings and dinners, but I'll be able to break away here and there for some fun. My plane lands at eleven. Be at the hotel by noon. I'll want to put your special de-stressing talents to work before my first appointment. How does that sound?"

Worse than Abu Ghraib. That's the way Kellyanne longed to answer him, but she just held the line as a miserable feeling of dread spread over her. Finally, she spoke. "I heard from Adam today. I'm up for a role on a soap. It's a great part. But they want me to read, so I might be—"

"Tell Adam to put it off until next week," Walter cut in brusquely. "I'm paying a lot of money to let you play for the summer, so when I'm there I want you available."

Kellyanne experienced a wave of revulsion. He made her sound like some kind of sex slave. She fought the urge to slam the phone shut. In the end, she tried to reason with him. "Chances are I will be. It's just—"

"Why is Adam sending you out for that kind of work anyway?" Walter interrupted. "I'm not going to miss a good blow job just so you can audition for some crappy soap opera."

Kellyanne resigned herself to being at his beck

and call. Fighting too hard against it might provoke him to seek out Adam and cause trouble. For once, her agent was regarding her as a marketable actress, as opposed to some old bastard's bored mistress. And she wanted to keep it that way. If the reading conflicted with Walter's visit, then she'd somehow figure out a way to make it work. The most important goal was landing the role of Anna-Claire. After that, everything would be on Kellyanne's terms.

In the meantime, she shut her eyes and prayed for Walter to be stricken with a bout of impotence that would resist every erectile dysfunction drug on the market. And then she prayed for world peace.

The engine's running but nobody's driving.

The voice of Kellyanne's father boomeranged in her mind. He was a man who never got lost and displayed little patience for people who did. Joe Downey could probably sniff out the right direction in a pitch black jungle. But this particular trait had skipped Kellyanne's genetic makeup.

For the last hour, she'd been driving up and down East Hampton streets and residential roads, trying to get her bearings for the area but coming up frustratingly short. Somewhere in between, she'd pulled over so that Uncle Kirby could dictate his recipe for shrimp and cheese grits. Now she was navigating Liza's Lexus down Jericho Road, eventually coasting onto Montauk Highway.

Kellyanne started to relax. These were familiar surroundings. She could easily find her way back to the house from here. Coming up on her right was a quaint white clapboard storefront called McGraw's Fish Market. Smiling at the country blue awning and the handmade sign advertising four lobsters for thirty-eight dollars, she made the split-second decision to turn into the white gravel drive.

It seemed like the logical thing to do. After all, she still needed shrimp for tonight's dinner, and the customer promise of this little place was, "The Finest Fish, The Freshest Choice." How could she possibly go wrong?

As Kellyanne pushed open the door, the jangle of a bell attached to it announced her arrival. The fishy odor practically knocked her over, but the shop was clean, tidy, and possessed an old-time charm.

A well-heeled woman in her mid-to-late sixties stood at the counter, breathlessly reciting an order to the man behind it. "Tucker, I need eight more lobsters. I just had an additional six people announce that they were coming for dinner, and I'm taking home two extra for good measure. Nobody RSVP's anymore. They just *assume*."

"I've got you covered, Mrs. Gold. You must be having a big summer party. This morning you took home a ten-pack of these bad boys."

Kellyanne smiled to herself, finding the man's Long Island accent amusing. It was all twanging nasals, diphthong drawls, *er*'s coming out as *ah*'s, and *w*'s larding onto *a*'s. She absolutely adored it.

"Don't remind me," Mrs. Gold snarled good naturedly. "Half the people I'm feeding tonight, I don't even like."

He laughed gently. "Then I'm no longer offended about not being invited. I packed these in seawater-soaked newspaper. Remember to keep the cartons upright and put them in the refrigerator as soon as you get home."

"You already told me that this morning, Tucker. I'm not senile yet!" The woman spun around and gave Kellyanne a disapproving glance before stalking out.

Kellyanne got a better look at Tucker as he emerged from behind the counter. His deeply tanned muscular arms were loaded down with Mrs. Gold's lobsters, and he wore a smudged white apron, red T-shirt, khaki cargo shorts, and black Croc sandals.

He was thirty-something, six foot one, and ruggedly handsome with thick dirty blond hair, soulful green eyes, and a sexy two-day stubble. Rushing by her to keep up with his demanding customer, he grinned and rolled his eyes skyward in a way that communicated a certain joy in his beleaguered situation. "I'll be right with you."

Kellyanne watched him leave, observing as he carefully packed the trunk of Mrs. Gold's vintage Jaguar XJ6. She was struck by his intoxicating vibrations of strength, sweetness, virility . . . and decency. That was the quality that really killed her.

Tucker stepped back inside, smoothing his apron as he made his way around to the iced-down fish that was his livelihood. "Sorry about that. What can I get for you?" He rested his impressive forearms on the countertop, dangling hands that were large and wonderfully masculine. His fingernails were clean, short and square cut.

That's when Kellyanne noticed the simple white gold wedding ring. A tiny part of her was crestfallen. All the good ones—and the bad ones—were usually taken. And so went the story of her life. She took a deep breath. "I need some big-ass shrimp."

Tucker smiled at her with perfect teeth. "I've got plenty of big-ass shrimp. How much do you need?"

Kellyanne stared through the glass, considering the question as she noticed an owner's special on striped sea bass. "It's just dinner for me and a friend. I don't know. Maybe a dozen?"

He nodded in agreement and grabbed two handfuls from the jumbo shrimp pile.

"Oh," Kellyanne began helplessly. "Could you also cut off the heads and peel them and clean out the yucky stuff?"

"*Clean out the yucky stuff?*" he repeated, his tone teasing. "We call that deveining."

Kellyanne made a face. "Ugh—that sounds even worse." The bell jangled in perfect synchronization with a gorgeous little boy's exploding through the door. He had flowing blond surfer locks, the deep brown tan of a lifeguard, and the same green eyes as the man he was running toward. "Daddy, Daddy!" he called, racing around the counter to embrace his father's leg.

Tucker wiped his hands with a well-worn rag and bent down to kiss the top of his son's head. "Parks! What's going on, son?"

"I missed you, Daddy. You're my best friend."

"And you're my best friend. How cool is that?"

Kellyanne's hand covered her heart. She'd always thought that a father's devotion to a child was incredibly sexy. She thought even more so now. In fact, observing this rapport was devastating—in the very best way. "He's precious. How old is he?"

Tucker beamed with pride. "Almost four."

"Bless his heart."

"Parks, would you like to help me get this pretty lady's shrimp ready?"

In answer, Parks jumped up and down with delight.

Tucker quickly positioned a metal folding chair beside him and lifted Parks on top of it so that he could reach the counter. "Why don't you peel that pile right there, son. Help out your dad. I need a strong first mate to get this work done."

Kellyanne watched in wonder as the boy's tiny fingers removed the scales with expert precision, his face a masterpiece of pride, determination, and desire to please. It was the sweetest scene she'd ever witnessed.

Tucker shot a glance toward the door. "Where's your Aunt Rae?"

Parks remained focused on his task. "She's sitting in the car on her cell phone yelling at Uncle Scott."

Tucker laughed and stroked the boy's hair. He glanced back at Kellyanne and winked. "One thing about kids—they tell it like it is."

Kellyanne smiled warmly. A few minutes later her order was cleaned, packed, and ready. She paid in cash.

Parks bagged the purchase and presented it to her with a flourish.

"Tell the pretty lady what we tell all our customers," Tucker prompted.

"Thank you for shopping at McGraw's Fish Market! We hope to see you tomorrow!"

Tucker bit down on his lower lip, stifling a laugh. "That's a little pushy, son." He grinned at Kellyanne. "We hope to see you again."

Over the years, Kellyanne had heard some superlative lines from powerful and prominent men. The U.S. senator who told her she was the most beautiful woman he'd ever seen. The highest paid actor on television who told her she was the hottest girl in Hollywood. The Academy Award–winning producer who told her she was too gorgeous for celluloid.

So the simple irony wasn't lost on her. She'd stumbled across a fish market. An unassuming man—who was not trying to hit on her—had indirectly told her she was pretty. And yet it was the greatest flattery of all.

She extended a hand to Parks. "Thank you, kind sir. I'll definitely be back."

Billie

13

He slapped her ass so hard that the palm-to-cheek impact popped like a gunshot. "You like that, don't you, bitch?"

Billie managed to moan out a yes.

March relentlessly tore into her from behind, gripping her arms for balance as he increased his amperage with a selfishness that bordered on brutality. "What are you?"

"I'm your dirty little whore."

"And you like it when I fuck you this way, don't you?"

"Yes!"

Cocaine turned March into an animal. His stamina became almost more than she could endure, and the coke rush made him exponentially aggressive. He was demanding, firm handed, ruthless, and vulgar.

Billie's cock-tease act at Sunset Beach had done a real number on him. So had seeing her disappear with Shayne Cutter. She left the next move up to March, and he played it sooner than she ever expected.

He called three times on Monday. She refused to answer. He called five times on Tuesday. She ignored him. By the time Billie picked up his first call on Wednesday morning, March was in such a state that an elopement to Las Vegas could've been negotiated. He wanted her that bad. And when he finally got her, he was a bastard possessed.

"I want to come all over your face."

Of course, he did. Didn't they all?

One hand surfed down the slope of her back while the other pulled Billie up by her hair. He crushed his mouth onto hers. "Are you my slut?" His hips were thrusting at jackhammer speed, plowing so deep that he was bottoming out and bumping up against her cervix.

Billie nodded her answer, unable to speak as she climaxed and grimaced simultaneously, an exquisite duet of pleasure and pain.

March pushed Billie onto her knees and stood over her while he finished himself off, his breathing and moaning on a steady rise until he cried out with a wall-rattling, "Fuck!"

Billie closed her eyes as his warm semen splattered all over her forehead, nose, cheeks, mouth, and neck. The explosion seemed to go on and on.

When it was over, March cradled her face in his hands, admiring his pretty mess. "Jesus Christ. That's fucking beautiful."

"Would Focus on the Family agree?" Billie asked. But before he could answer, she was sucking him clean of every last drop.

March laughed the laugh of the satisfied, shuddering slightly, as he was sensitive to postorgasm ministrations. Still, he appreciated and expected such dedication to his cock.

Billie had seen bigger. In fact, March's dick was average. But at the end of the day, attitude trumped size, and he carried himself in a manner that added two inches, if not more. He loved his cock. He was tyrannical with it. He knew what it could do. Some men might be bigger, but they were almost always smug about the fact that they were packing more than the next guy. March didn't care about other men. He only cared about women. And there was the difference.

They were in a small room at the Hotel Elysée on East Fifty-fourth Street, a hideaway eclipsed between two huge office buildings.

Billie wiped her face with a towel and lit a cigarette. She loved fucking in hotels. Somehow the sex was always better.

With no offer to share, March snorted the last bit of cocaine and flung himself onto the bed, landing stomach first.

Billie blew smoke rings and stared at his amazing, muscular ass. "When are we going to be together again?"

"We're together now."

"I know, but . . . I'm just wondering. That's all."

"I'll be back on Friday. Maybe over the weekend."

Billie felt anxious. This wasn't enough. She wanted a firm plan about the next time.

He rolled over onto his back. "We'll see what happens."

Cigarette still in hand, she climbed on top of the bed and straddled his washboard abs.

March grinned lazily. "This is a nonsmoking room."

"So I'm a bad girl."

"A nasty girl." He took possession of her Marlboro Light, dragged deep, and returned it. "I want to fuck you again, but I have a flight to catch."

He was flying to Colorado Springs to speak at a dinner being hosted by Focus on the Family.

Billie shook her head. "That blows my mind."

"What?"

"That you're showing up to give some speech about conservative Christian values. It's like your navy suit is a costume." She laughed out loud. "Hey, you're Batman!"

"Just because I like to have a little fun doesn't mean I don't believe in my work."

"Oh, please. That crowd's idea of fun is a church picnic. You're cheating on your fiancée, snorting coke, and fucking like a porn star. Don't tell me there's not a difference."

March stole her cigarette again. "Maybe we're all hypocrites."

"Speak for yourself," Billie scoffed.

His eyes flashed irritation, and he blew smoke directly into her face. "Right now I'm speaking for you and me."

"How am *I* a hypocrite?" Billie demanded. "I'm the grand fucking marshal of the live-and-let-live parade! You go out there stumping to ban gay marriage. That's telling people how to live. Why should I care if a couple of fags want to get hitched? Hey, I'm no Diane Sawyer, but as I understand it, you Republican types are supposed to be probusiness. Well, shit! What's better for the economy than a bunch of gay weddings?"

March's jaw was clenched tight. "You're out of your element, Billie. You sound much more intelligent with my dick in your mouth." He pushed her off his body and over to the side of the bed. "I need to take a shower."

"Fuck you!" she screamed.

March stood up. "Most of my life is spent talking political shit. That's not why I called you. I thought you'd be a fun escape."

Billie was torn. She was alarmed by his sudden use of the past tense. But she was still pissed off about his insult. "I'm not some idiot slut! I've got a degree from goddamn Dartmouth!"

"Congratulations," March said. "But my point is that you don't read or keep up with any of the issues. If I wanted a debate, then I'd call your Hamptons roommate. Liza's my current events foil. You're my fuck toy."

She stared daggers at him. It always came down to the same slights. Men respected Liza for her intellect. They admired Kellyanne for her beauty. But they just used Billie and left her to rot on the side of the road.

March snatched her iPod from the nightstand and fingered the smudged video screen. "And back to the subject that got us here. You want to project yourself as a wild, edgy rocker chick, but you're heading into the studio to record Ariel covers." He paused a beat. "Welcome to the hypocrisy club." And then he tossed the device onto the bed, walked into the bathroom, and shut the door.

Billie waited until she heard the shower running. That's when she started to cry. Rivulets of angry, bitter, frustrated tears rolled down her cheeks as her mind raced with dark plots to make the son of a bitch pay for treating her this way.

She dressed quickly, then gathered up the clothes

March had arrived in—shoes included—and stuffed them inside his wheeled Tumi travel case. With cold water cool, she rolled it into the hallway, onto the elevator, and out of the hotel.

A silver-haired executive type darted out of a cab, holding the hand of a girl young enough to be his granddaughter. They rushed inside the Hotel Elysée. Apparently, it was all the rage for secret trysts.

Billie shoved the Tumi into the backseat of the vacated cab. Then she tumbled in and told the driver to take her to Central Park. On the way, she removed March's identification tag from the luggage, laughing wickedly.

How did a good Christian man end up at a hotel in the middle of the day without any clothes? Hmm. Maybe March could explain that little riddle to all the assholes at the Focus on the Family dinner tonight. *If* he made it there.

Her cell phone vibrated to life. She checked the screen. Guess who? A glorious wave of comeuppance coursed through her. She let it ring a few times before picking up.

"Where the hell's my luggage?" March roared. "You crazy bitch! I'm going to miss my flight!"

She answered him in a calm, pleasant, almost detached voice. "You must have me confused with your travel assistant. I'm just your fuck toy." And then she hung up.

Billie left his Tumi in the cab and found herself strolling aimlessly through Central Park, falling deeper and deeper into a place where she simply wanted to forget who she was.

The password to such blissful ignorance was in the medicine cabinet at her apartment. She found her way there, peeled off her clothes, and stepped into a

cold shower. It was a scorching June afternoon, and
the window unit air conditioner could only do so
much. She slammed back a few vodka drinks and
swallowed a handful of Ambien. Those beautiful
white babies always knocked her out. And this afternoon she took a few extra to countervail any discomfort from the heat. She just longed to be completely
out of it . . .

"Billie! Billie!"

Somewhere in the deepest recesses of her mind
she could hear the sound of Amy Dando's voice. She
could also feel the pinch of long nails digging into her
exposed shoulders as someone shook her violently.

Billie managed to flutter her eyes open.

"What the fuck is wrong with you?" It *was* Amy.
The perfect eye makeup distracted Billie from the
blazing anger in her manager's gaze.

Oh, God, she was *so* tired. All Billie wanted to do
was sleep. Just holding up her eyelids was an exhausting effort. She started to fall back into the silky
folds of oblivion.

"Wake up, Billie!" Amy shrieked. "Wake up, or
I'm calling 911 and having you taken to the goddamn emergency room!"

Billie groaned faintly in protest. Not the hospital.
She didn't want to go there. Why had she ever given
Amy the key to her apartment? Right now that seemed
like the worst decision she'd ever made in her whole
fucking life. "Stop yelling," she pleaded in a faint
whisper, forcing her eyes open.

"How long have you been here like this?"

Billie just stared back at her blankly. She had no
idea what time it was . . . or even what day it was. "I
don't know."

"*You don't know.*" Amy shook her head in disgust.

"But I'm okay," Billie insisted weakly. "You can go."

"There's nothing I'd love more than to take you up on that offer," Amy hissed. And then she ferociously pulled Billie forward and up, yanking with great force until the object of her rage was standing on two feet.

Billie's body felt as limp as a rag doll. All she wanted was to be left alone. The Ambien daze was one stubborn bitch. Her head bobbed to one side. Maybe she could sleep this way . . .

"Goddamn you, Billie!" Amy screamed.

And then she felt herself being pushed . . . out of the living room . . . into the bathroom . . . the light was so bright . . . somebody turn off the fucking light . . . oh, shit . . . her head hit a hard surface . . . jets of freezing water began to soak her . . . it was a shock to the system.

"Are you awake now?" The tiled acoustics gave Amy's voice some added boom.

Billie kept her eyes open and met the lesbian bitch's gaze, holding up an arm in a silent plea for mercy from the water.

Amy cut off the shower. "I'm going downstairs to get you some coffee. There's nothing in this fucking apartment but liquor and cigarettes."

"By the way, I sure could use one," Billie croaked.

Amy disappeared, then returned a few moments later to throw a pack of Marlboro Lights and a matchbook from Butter in Billie's general direction. "Don't set yourself on fire." She left again.

Billie heard the slam of the apartment door and fumbled for the cigarettes in a near-catatonic daze. She lit one and brought it to her dry lips. The relief was sort of like heaven. Every drag seemed to slowly wake her up. She lay slumped in the tub, cold and soaking wet, fascinated by the subtle texture changes in the filter as she smoked it down.

Amy stormed back inside and pushed a tall Starbucks into her hand. "You're a goddamn mess."

Billie sipped gingerly on the hot liquid. Fuck. It was black. She hated it black. She liked it loaded with sugar and cream. First Amy ruins her nice long sleep, and then she brings her bad coffee. What the hell kind of management was that? "This tastes like shit."

"Then you must be drinking your career. That's the closest thing to total shit I can think of."

Billie fired up another cigarette.

"I got an earful from Todd Bana last night."

"Oh, yeah? What did that prick want?"

"You missed the first recording session with White Tiger."

Billie puffed away, nonplussed by the news. Those lazy motherfuckers had only written one new song for her. They deserved to wait. "What day is this?"

"It's Friday morning."

Christ! Had she been sleeping for a day and a half? If Amy had left her alone, she probably could've gone a solid two days. "Oh, well. Tell Todd to reschedule."

"You tell him. I'm done." There was an ominous ring of finality in Amy's voice.

Billie looked at her with a wounded expression.

"I can't do this anymore. I've got clients who need my attention. Clients who actually care about the future of their career. You know, Billie, at first I didn't agree with this new direction that Todd suggested, but the more I thought about it, the more I came to believe that he was probably right. You're not a disciplined songwriter, and it's been a fast downhill slope since *Dick Magnet*. You have the rare opportunity to work with one of the hottest production teams in the business while you're at a low point, and you fucking blow them off."

"They expect me to sing backwash tracks from Ariel's last record," Billie spat. "I don't do retreads. And if you were any kind of manager, you wouldn't want me to."

"That CD dropped a few days after her DUI arrest, and it was dead on arrival. But it's still considered one of this industry's bigger could-have-beens. It was at least seven tracks deep with hit singles. Two of them could be yours. And the new White Tiger track is a radio-ready smash."

"Whatever." Billie rolled her eyes and blew smoke up toward the ceiling. "Who Is She?" was infectious, sure, but it was also repetitive. A hard-core Alzheimer's case could probably commit the lyrics to memory after one listen. And it was hardly an original. For the main hook, those White Tiger hacks had sampled the guitar riff from Rick Springfield's "Jessie's Girl."

"Whatever?" Amy repeated, leveling a look of disgust. "There are artists far more successful than you who'd kill for that track right now. Ashlee Simpson wants it. So do Rihanna and Kylie Minogue. But Todd convinced White Tiger to save it for your project."

Billie stubbed out her cigarette in the sink. "Big fucking deal." She peeled off her wet cotton tank and Hanky Panky underwear, then slipped on her robe.

"I wouldn't knock it," Amy warned her. "It's the best thing you've got going at the moment. Everyone thinks you're over, Billie. Some of your newer songs have leaked onto the Internet, and bloggers are ripping them to shreds. I don't think I could book a tour for you right now, even a short one. A twenty-five-hundred-seat theater would be too big. I'd be lucky to get interest from casinos in second- and third-tier markets." She shook her head regretfully. "It didn't have to be this way. But you're the architect of this train wreck, and this is where we part ways. I wish you luck. I really do." She started for the door.

"Amy!" Billie shrieked, her heart lurching with fear. "You can't be serious!"

"Oh, I'm very serious. You're the one who's fucking around. I'll put an official letter in the mail this afternoon."

"You can't cut me loose! I'm Billie Fucking Shelton!"

Amy looked at her with genuine sadness. "A few years ago that name actually meant something."

At first Billie couldn't believe it. But then Amy Dando walked out of her life.

Liza

14

She looked like hell—no makeup, unwashed hair stuffed into an old Brandeis baseball cap, battered Levi's, and a distressed SuperEXcellent yellow cotton tee emblazoned with the phrase YOU LOST ME AT HELLO in faded pink letters.

It was Liza's ritualistic writing costume. She'd been working like a demon for the last few days, trying to shape her *Stupid Girls* proposal into a presentable product. The intense focus on her new book helped to purge Justin from her mind, and it was a necessary emotional break. When she finally resurfaced, she knew that a clearer head would prevail.

Liza dashed into Citarella on Pantigo Road. Long writing hours always left her fatigued and hungry. Cravings for sweets were particularly insane. But rather than give in to the temptations of candy and chocolate, Liza chose the healthier path of natural sugar. She loaded up on strawberries, blackberries, raspberries, star fruit, mango, cantaloupe, honeydew, kiwi, pineapple, grapes, peaches, guava, and papaya.

"You have to stop doing this."

Startled by the voice, Liza spun around.

Harrison Beck stood behind her, holding a coffee in one hand and stuffing one of Citarella's famous doughnuts into his mouth with the other. "You show up at my party uninvited. Now you're stalking me in the market. It's ridiculous." He licked a tiny dust storm of powdered sugar from his lips and smiled.

Against every impulse to do otherwise, Liza found herself smiling back at him. "I don't know which is worse—your movies or your attempt at flirting."

"Definitely my flirting," Harrison said easily. "I should note, however, that so far in my lifetime two women have agreed to marry me."

"They've also agreed to divorce you," Liza pointed out.

Harrison shrugged. "That just means I'm road tested. At least I'm capable of commitment. And, obviously, I'm worthy of it. I've got the alimony expenses to prove it." He glanced down into her shopping cart. "Where's the real food?"

Liza gestured to the last bit of doughnut between Harrison's fingers. "Apparently, at the pastry counter."

Without warning, he pushed what remained of the treat into Liza's mouth, immediately laughing at his successful effort.

At first, she staged a shocked miniprotest, then simply gave in and enjoyed the small bite of sweet warm cake. It was delicious. She grinned at him. "You son of a bitch."

"That good, huh?"

"Better."

"Have a cup of coffee with me."

Liza hesitated. "I can't. I'm on deadline. I just ran

in here for some sustenance. Maybe when I get out from under."

"How about dinner tonight?"

Even though Liza appreciated his persistence, she demurred. "I really need to work. I have an angry agent and a frustrated editor regularly checking in on my progress."

"Come on," Harrison said, swatting away her excuse like a gnat. "I'm a writer, too. I know how it works. There are only so many good pages you can produce in a day, then it becomes diminishing returns. A nice meal will rejuvenate you. The Palm at eight o'clock. Consider it a working dinner. You can tell me all about your new book."

Liza regarded him carefully. If nothing else, the man had presented a slam-dunk case. There was every reason to say yes to his invitation. "Eight-thirty," she said. "I'll meet you there."

"And you'll pick up the check, too."

She gave him an incredulous look.

"You owe me at least that much for the crack about my dick."

"Fine," Liza agreed with faux exasperation. "As long as you promise not to whip it out in public again, I'll pay for your dinner."

"Deal." Harrison extended his hand.

Liza shook firm and fast.

He held the grip longer than the moment called for, and there was undeniable poetry in the pressure. "I'll be sitting at the bar around eight . . . should you decide to come early to join me for a drink."

The hours that followed were a total waste. Instead of sitting in front of her computer, she was standing in her bedroom, wishing that the Yves Saint Laurent hand-painted silk voile strapless number wasn't hanging in her closet back in Manhattan.

God, it was so critical that Liza be working, but her ass simply would *not* stay in the chair. She needed bum glue. That's what the Australian writer Bryce Courtenay called it. If only Liza could purchase such stuff by the ten-gallon drum.

Her BlackBerry vibrated, and she peered down to discover that—as expected—her agent was dialing in with a midafternoon call. "Hello, Linda."

"What are you answering the phone for? You should be writing," Linda Konner barked.

"I don't screen your calls. You could be ringing me up to extend my deadline."

"Dream on," Linda huffed. She was a great literary agent—a tough negotiator, a no-nonsense operator, and a shrewd mover in all areas of nonfiction. "How's the writing coming along?"

"Very well," Liza answered truthfully. She paused a beat. "And very slowly."

Linda sighed. "Speed it up. Kate's getting nervous. I want to show her something soon."

Kate Goodman was Liza's editor at New Woman Press, the first publishing imprint from mogul Toni Valentine, who was quickly rising among the corporate titan ranks to earn her media nickname as the female Rupert Murdoch. *Whore* had been the house's phenomenally successful launch title and solidified Toni Valentine's reputation as a Midas-touch cultural prognosticator. She'd conquered film, television, the Web, and now publishing.

"I don't want to stress you out," Linda continued. "But this needs to be your number one priority."

"I know, I know," Liza said quickly, feeling anxious.

"Everything else that you're doing is exciting, but those opportunities only happened because you wrote a bestseller. That's your product. That's also where the real money is. Don't lose sight of that. Your second book has been bumped from this fall to next spring to next summer, and now we're probably looking at next fall. It's time to go to contract again, and I don't want an unreliable delivery history to get in my way when it's time to talk numbers. We're going for a *major* deal. You put Toni in the publishing business, and it's time for her to pay up."

"This book is going to be *good,* Linda," Liza said passionately. "It's different than *Whore.* It's more personal. Women are going to relate. I'm calling it *Stupid Girls.*"

"I love the title," Linda praised. "It's provocative. I'll call Kate and let her know that you're on the right track. Keep writing." And then Linda hung up.

The conversation kicked Liza into proper gear. She worked nonstop for the next several hours, breaking only to scoop up an occasional bowl of the colorful fruit medley she'd assembled from her earlier run to Citarella and speed surf her favorite Web sites for breaking news.

She checked her recent column on *The Huffington Post,* the left-leaning digital newspaper conceived by Arianna Huffington that had recently become the fifth-most-linked-to blog on the Internet. Liza had fired off a rant on right-wing female blowhards called "Conservative Women in the Media: The New Old White Guys." Periodically, she surveyed her entries

for comment posts. Scrolling down, Liza scanned the
feedback quickly, then stopped.

> **travisowen**
> This phony bitch needs to shut up. She's a lying
> whore. Her real name is Liza Beal. She married a
> fireman but won't take his last name. I guess
> she thinks no man's name is good enough. If she
> were my woman, I'd brand OWEN onto her ass
> like she was a head of cattle. The director Har-
> rison Beck made a brilliant film with WATCH HER
> BLEED, and this slut trashed the movie and him
> on national television. She's a know-it-all cunt.
> I'd love to watch HER bleed.
> posted 02:17 pm

The comment had already been flagged as abu-
sive. In short order, it would be removed from the
site. Liza zeroed in on the words. There was a disturbing quality to online attacks. They could easily
give her the feeling of being stalked. But in reality, it
was some bored asshole clicking the mouse and going from site to site, trying to come off sinister in
their anonymity. They were just cyberspace punks.
Nothing more.

She went back to work in earnest, framing the entire book, determining chapter subjects, drafting
chapter titles, and making a list of essential interview subjects and research priorities. But the most
satisfying task came from free-writing the sample
chapter, "Will You Marry Me, Boy?"

Liza dug deep. She pushed past the denial and
through the discomfort as she examined her relationship with Justin with brutal honesty. What had
drawn her to him? What did that reveal about her?

And why did the public perception of a divorce loom darker than the private unhappiness of a dead marriage? In unflinching prose, she put everything on the page. It read like the literary equivalent of an exposed nerve.

She also wrote about the disappearance of feminism from the public consciousness. The cause was no longer an organized social movement. Today it was being played out within personal relationships, a place where many women had put down their swords and abandoned the fight altogether. Liza admitted that in some ways she was one of them.

It was after seven o'clock when she stopped writing. She rushed into the shower, put the dryer to her hair, applied her makeup, threw on a Yohji Yamamoto silk-and-cotton sailor blouse over Odyn jeans, slipped a few Van Cleef & Arpels diamond bracelets over both wrists, stepped into a pair of spike-heeled Gucci white leather pumps, and raced out the door, spraying Viktor & Rolf's Flowerbomb into the air as she walked through the mist.

At eight o'clock sharp, Liza arrived at the Palm at the Huntting Inn. She encountered Sarah Jessica Parker, Matthew Broderick, and Jessica and Jerry Seinfeld leaving as she entered. Taking in the dark paneled decor, she smiled at the caricatures of local notables and international stars that lined the walls. Billy Joel was up there. So was Steven Spielberg.

She spotted Harrison at the bar. He looked hot-summer-night handsome in beige linen pants and a white embroidered camp shirt unbuttoned to reveal a thick mane of tangled chest hair.

Liza eased onto the stool next to him as he finished the last swallow of a deep amber liquid on the rocks. "You started early."

Harrison grinned. "It's called bracing myself." He signaled to the bartender. "What are you drinking?"

"A glass of the Marquis Phillips Shiraz would be perfect."

Harrison ordered another Scotch for himself. "Our table should be ready in a few minutes." He gave her an admiring glance. "You look beautiful tonight. You smell beautiful, too."

She smiled her thanks, relieved to see the wine arrive with such fast efficiency.

Harrison raised his short highballer. "To your new book."

"I can drink to that." She gently clinked her glass against his, appreciating the sentiment.

"Did you have a productive writing day?"

Liza could feel her own eyes shining. "One of my best ever. It all came together. Everything clicked."

He gave her a knowing nod. "There's no better feeling."

Almost instantly, she felt overwhelmed by his attentiveness—the compliments, the genuine interest in her work. It amplified the emptiness she felt with Justin in a way that made her feel unbearably lonely, even as she sat here with Harrison.

"Tell me about your new book."

"For starters, it's called *Stupid Girls.*"

He smiled. "I've been with my fair share of those. Let me know if you need insight from the male perspective."

Liza gave him a quick roll of the eyes and practiced a cold run of an elevator speech that encapsulated the main premise of her project. Upon finishing, she was pleased with her delivery.

Harrison seemed visibly impressed. "It sounds very personal."

"It is," Liza agreed. "But it's also very universal. The most personal things almost always are." She sipped on her wine. "And what about you? Can I look forward to seeing *Watch Her Bleed Two*?" Her voice carried a tone of playful menace.

Guiltily, Harrison cast his eyes downward into his Scotch.

"Oh, God!" Liza exclaimed, punching his thickly muscled upper arm. "You're actually doing a sequel?"

"It's not official," Harrison said sheepishly. "But I gave my agent a magic number, and the studio's offer is getting close. Believe me, I tried to price myself out of it. Now I'm in a position where I won't be able to say no to that kind of money. I'd be a fool."

Suddenly, Liza remembered the creepy online messages that had been sent to her from Travis Owen, the movie's misogynistic psycho killer. "Did you send me an e-mail through my Web site recently?"

Harrison gave her a curious look, shaking his head. "No, why do you ask?"

Liza shrugged. "Never mind. It must've been a prank."

He opened his mouth to inquire further.

Liza cut him off. "Don't ever make a creative decision based solely on money. You'll always regret it."

"How about basing my decision on the fact that I have three children?" Harrison countered. "This deal could secure their futures for life. If the price for that is being called a sellout or taking some critical jabs when the sequel's released, then I'll pay it. The freedom and peace of mind will be worth that."

Liza fell silent. She could hardly judge him for putting his children's best interests first on his agenda.

"You can relax, though. It'll be at least a few years before a sequel hits theaters."

Liza breathed an exaggerated sigh of relief.

Harrison laughed, tipping back his glass. "I think you might actually like my next film. I just finished the script. It's a true story about a New Orleans doctor who was falsely accused of murdering patients in the aftermath of Hurricane Katrina." He crossed his fingers. "Jodie Foster is considering it."

"I've never read a screenplay before," Liza said.

"I'd love for you to take a look at it." His tone was earnest. "I mean that. You might have some notes on the female point of view. If Jodie passes, it's going out to Reese Witherspoon next, then Jennifer Connelly. The role is tough. I want an A-list actress in the part."

"Jodie Foster would be amazing. I haven't read it, of course, but she brings so much integrity to every role."

"I know. I'm having trouble with financing at the moment, and a marquee name like that would green light this picture in a heartbeat."

A host interrupted to inform them that their table was ready. Liza and Harrison were escorted to a cozy booth in the corner of the restaurant and seated directly behind a glowing Gwyneth Paltrow and her husband, Chris Martin of Coldplay.

Harrison selected a bottle of wine—a South American red—and proceeded to order up a feast that included oysters on the half shell, sesame seared ahi tuna, Caesar salad, steamed Nova Scotia lobsters, creamed spinach, sautéed wild mushrooms, and three-cheese potatoes au gratin.

Liza ate more than she could believe without even the faintest degree of reluctance or shame. The intense afternoon writing hours had left her positively ravenous.

It was a blissful evening—delectable food, fantastic wine, and animated conversation that flowed effortlessly. They talked more about her new book and his new screenplay, then moved on to discuss their favorite visual artists, all the exotic places they wanted to travel, and their eclectic tastes in music.

Harrison's eyes sparkled when he told her about his children. Cassandra was eighteen and starting her first year at Smith College in the fall. Mariah was sixteen and captain of her high school swim team. Alexis was four and obsessed with all things Hello Kitty.

As a busboy cleared the table, the white-jacketed waiter appeared to lobby them for dessert, but the idea of so much as a morsel more of food seemed impossible to comprehend. They declined the offer of an after-dinner drink as well and requested the check.

"I'm a terrible husband but a good father," Harrison announced with philosophical directness. "I love my girls. I love my ex-wives who gave them to me, too." He sighed heavily, pouring the last of the second bottle of the 1995 Faustino. "Divorce sucks. But sometimes it's the only way to keep your dignity and preserve what was good about things."

"Didn't it give you a crushing sense of failure?" Liza asked.

Harrison considered the question. "I wouldn't say that. There were elements of success in both of my marriages. I try to remember those aspects and fake amnesia to all the rest." He stared at her thoughtfully. "You haven't mentioned your husband all night."

Liza averted eye contact and busied herself with her napkin. "Is it that obvious?"

"Believe me, I hate to bring it up. I wish you didn't have one. But yes, it is."

She looked at him. "It's complicated."

"It always is." Harrison tilted his head, pursing his lips sympathetically as the waiter swooped in and discreetly left the check. He pushed the bill to her side of the table. "I believe we have a deal."

Liza reached into her red satin Zac Posen clutch and slapped her American Express Black on top of the leather guest check presenter.

He gave her a mischievous smile. "And just because you paid for dinner, don't expect to get laid tonight."

"You're enjoying this, aren't you?"

"I feel like the girl. I'm probably going to wait by the phone all day tomorrow, too. You know, hoping you'll call to ask me out again."

She laughed at him. Harrison was smart, funny, and sweet. Frankly, it amazed her that this was the same man who'd created the ugly gore on display in *Watch Her Bleed*.

Liza signed over a generous 30 percent tip, and they ventured out into the cool night. A galaxy of stars gleamed in the dark sky. There was a whipping breeze and a sharp tang in the air. It smelled like a beach town. She closed her eyes and took everything in. "I love it here. I should buy instead of rent."

All of a sudden, Harrison's hands were on her hips. He stood behind her, nuzzling her neck. "Come back to my house for a drink."

His cologne was strong in her nostrils—Tobacco Flower by Fresh. She breathed in the heady, masculine hints of eucalyptus, mint, sun-kissed vines, and ripening olives. The fragrance was made for him. She reached back to stroke his cheek. "I can't."

He kissed her shoulder. "It's a beautiful night. We could sit out by the pool."

Liza hated the idea of going back to an empty house. Kellyanne was in the city with Walter, and Billie was God knows where. No one had heard from her in days. She found herself weakening to the idea of going home with him. But she knew where the night would inevitably lead. And she wasn't ready for it to go there.

"We could take a walk on the beach," Harrison murmured, continuing the hard sell.

"I had a wonderful evening, but it's time to say good night." Liza turned around, kissed his cheek, and walked to her car, fighting temptation the whole way. It dawned on her that she wasn't the kind of woman who could cheat on her husband, even one who'd cheated on her.

Stupid girl, Liza thought. And then she drove away.

"You've got to stop," Teddy Easton pleaded. "I can't take anymore."

Reluctantly, Justin pulled out. He could easily hold this pretty male model down and make him take it, but he was tired of the little bitch's whining.

Teddy rolled over onto his back. "Sorry. You're just too big. It hurts. I usually only have sex with Asian guys." He took a swig from the giant Dasani water bottle on the nightstand and raised a perfectly waxed eyebrow. "I couldn't turn you down, though. I had to try."

Mildly annoyed, Justin stripped off the condom and reached for his True Religion jeans. Being with Teddy was like fucking a skeleton. In fact, he was bonier than Liza. Still, Justin could've plowed his tight boy pussy for hours. All those cycling miles had built up a tiny ass of pure muscle. What a waste.

He checked the clock on his cell—just a few minutes past midnight. There was plenty of time to find a willing hole to take the pounding he wanted to give.

"I'd pop a few Vicodin and suffer through it if I didn't have to leave for the airport at four-thirty in the morning," Teddy said. "Can you imagine?" He laughed a little. "I'd be too fucked up to find my gate."

Justin managed a weak grin and slipped on his paint-splattered Salvage T-shirt. "Maybe next time." He stepped into his Cole Haan sandals and started for the door.

"Hey!" Teddy called, tossing something into the air. "A little happy for your trouble."

Justin caught the object with his right hand. It was a small, expensive looking scrap of burnt-orange leather. He gave Teddy a quizzical look.

"It's an Hermès condom holder. Very posh." He giggled. "A booker in Paris gave it to me."

"Thanks," Justin muttered. He transferred three Magnum XL rubbers from his front pocket into the sleek new case before walking out to hunt down his next prey.

He hit a Chelsea nightspot called the Secret Lounge and gave the stone-faced doorman a cool nod as he breezed past the industrial entryway into the dark-walled, dimly lit club.

The crowd was gay, good looking, and upscale. A glinting chandelier illuminated two velvet-bolted circular sofas. European house music pumped from the sound system. It was a million miles from Engine 40, Ladder 35 on Amsterdam and Sixty-sixth.

Justin headed straight for the bar and slid onto one of the few remaining pink-cushioned stools.

The bartender approached right away, giving him *that look* as he took note of his wedding ring. Without preamble, he set down a caipirinha with a splash of Red Bull. "This is our claim-to-fame *cock*tail. If you don't like it, you don't have to pay for it."

Justin sampled the offering and pushed it back. "I'll have a beer."

The bartender looked thunderstruck. "Really?"

Justin laughed and repossessed the drink. "No, I'm joking. It's good. Thanks."

The bartender winked and breathed a sigh of relief before moving on to an impatient Wall Street type.

"*Justin?*"

He turned to face the source of the surprised voice and couldn't believe his luck as he stared into the HDTV-perfect face of Tom Shapiro.

"What are you doing here?"

Justin shrugged easily. "I'm having a drink."

"Oh, well, that's . . . uh . . . great. I—I was just hanging out with one of my producers from the show. She likes the music here."

Justin glanced around. "Where is she?"

"She left," Tom answered, struggling to sustain direct eye contact. "She wasn't feeling that good."

"That's too bad," Justin said in a dull voice. And then he slipped off the barstool and strode over to an unoccupied black banquette in the corner. He looked up to see Tom staring at him with confused interest, wondering if the invitation to follow was there. In answer, Justin allowed his legs to fall open and dropped a hand to his inner thigh.

Tom hesitated, the moral debate all over his face.

Justin stroked a thumb across his denim crotch.

Tom swallowed hard and stepped over to join him. "I want to take you up on that racquetball game you mentioned."

Justin nodded vaguely, grooving to the ambient beat of the music that throbbed like a pulse, watching the flickering light of the votive candles that tossed shadows onto Tom's face.

"I should leave," Tom whispered. "Liza's a good friend."

Justin inched closer. "Liza's in the Hamptons."

Tom shook his head. There was a lustful longing in his eyes. But the loyal part of him still seemed to be winning the private war. "It doesn't feel right."

Justin leaned in to kiss Tom on the mouth. His lips were hard and unyielding, his tongue aggressive and probing, and nanosecond by nanosecond, Justin could feel all of Tom's reasons why not melting away. Suddenly, Justin drew back. "Trust me. When I'm fucking you over and over again in her bed, it's going to feel right."

Kellyanne

15

"I've been cheated/Been mistreated/When will I be loved?" The old country-rock nugget blared from the tinny speakers of the CD player as Linda Ronstadt belted out precisely what Kellyanne was feeling.

Bundled up in a terry-cloth robe, she sat miserably in the Astor Suite of the St. Regis Hotel, waiting for Walter to put in a cameo appearance between meetings.

Kellyanne had never resented him more. In fact, the change in area code had unleashed a hostility that she found impossible to contain. She responded to his selfish expectations by acting out in passive-aggressive ways.

She hit below the belt by not swallowing his cum. That was his favorite part of oral sex, too. When she took him out of her mouth and jerked him to a climax with her hand, forcing him to shoot all over his stomach, the disappointed look on Walter's face had been priceless. To add insult to injury, Kellyanne explained that his ejaculate had developed a horrible taste, then went on to speculate aloud whether his age might have something to do with it. Every day she prayed that he'd trade Levitra for Prozac and go back home to Miami.

But more disturbing than Walter's presence was the fact that Adam Griffie hadn't called. The waiting was slowly killing her. She even began to question her own sanity. Had Adam really talked to her about the perfect role of a Southerner on *As the World Turns,* or was that notion just the manifestation of a dream?

Being stuck in the city was wrecking her mood as well. Walter's visit for a few days had stretched into a full week. In any other circumstances, Kellyanne would've appreciated her surroundings. Though small at six hundred square feet, the Astor Suite was beautifully appointed with silk wall coverings, antiques, deeply carved crown moldings, and a full bathroom of Italian marble. There were French sliding doors between the bedroom and living area, plus a separate powder room. No matter the opulence, she was sick of the goddamn hotel and desperately longed for the Hamptons.

She gazed out the window at the bumper-to-bumper traffic on Fifty-fifth Street and finally noticed that the CD player had advanced to the next track. "Poor, poor pitiful me/Oh, these boys won't let me be." Once again, Linda Ronstadt was providing the soundtrack to her fucking life.

Kellyanne cut off the music and switched on the plasma television, clicking through the channels at breakneck speed. It was the same bullshit on every news network—the presidential election, the endless war in Iraq, the shaky economy, the gossip of another idiot star rushing off to rehab.

Suddenly, a promo captured her attention. She turned up the volume, and that generic male announcer voice—so ubiquitous and so familiar—filled the room.

"It's the hottest reality series of the summer . . . and it's only on Fox!" Images of Vlad Branigan canoodling with bikini-clad contestants—in the hot tub, on a boat, at the beach—filled the screen in a barrage of quick-cut edits. "Can one man find true love in the city of lust?"

Now Vlad was addressing the camera. "Miami is wild. I've never seen so many gorgeous women in one place. And they're willing to do *anything* for love."

Kellyanne watched with a surreal sense of detachment as her own likeness appeared—an excerpt from one of her video confessionals. "He's close enough to Brad Pitt for me. I'll get him. Just watch." A split-second night-cam vision scene hinted at a man and woman engaged in sex.

Her stomach dropped fast, and a sick feeling spread across her abdomen. She'd never spoken those words. Well, she'd said them, yes, but not in that particular order or context. A sense of helplessness swept over Kellyanne. This was the editing hatchet job that Bonzi had threatened her with.

The announcer was back, speaking over a montage of romantic interludes, cat fights, and emotional breakdowns. "For the most eligible bachelor in the country, bed buddies come and go, friends with benefits fade in and out . . . but *Soul Mates* are forever. Watch him make the biggest decision of his life, and brace yourself for the last minute surprise that will rock his world. *Soul Mates*. This summer. Only on Fox."

The hotel phone jangled, startling her and ringing several times before she had the presence of mind to answer. It was Walter. He was downstairs with an hour to kill. At the moment, Kellyanne preferred jumping out the window to entertaining him.

He crashed through the door a few minutes later, jerking off his tie and bitching at her for not having a drink ready.

Like a zombie, she poured his favorite—Dalwhinnie—over some half-melted ice and offered it to him.

Walter's face was splotched with red, and he was breathing hard as he drank deep on the Scotch. He untied Kellyanne's robe and pawed roughly at her breasts, kneading them like baker's dough.

She winced as he pinched a nipple.

He grinned with satisfaction, thinking she liked it.

What would the old bastard do if she told him the truth? And the truth was that she was no more aroused right now than she would be for a root canal. All she wanted to do was blow him fast and send him on his way. But Walter had other plans.

He put down his glass and unhooked his belt. "Bend over the sofa."

This encounter was more tedious than most. He was only semierect and had difficulty staying inside her. His cock flopped out like a wet noodle at least a dozen times.

Kellyanne submitted her body to his incompetent desire and teleported her mind to a different place. She thought about Tucker McGraw, the handsome fish market proprietor, and his precious mini-me,

Parks. She found herself smiling as she pictured them—big man and little man in their matching Croc sandals—prepping her jumbo shrimp with old-fashioned masculine pride and purpose. The image was a sweet escape.

Finally, Walter climaxed with a grunt, then pulled up his pants and collapsed into an armchair. He was sweating profusely.

"You don't look well."

His rheumy eyes flashed irritation. "Just get me a towel and another drink."

Kellyanne slipped on her robe before freshening his Scotch and grabbing a hand towel from the powder room. "Maybe you should see a doctor."

"Why? Isn't going out with a bang the best way to expire?"

She thought about him dying in the middle of the act. It simultaneously frightened and disgusted her. "Don't talk like that."

He sipped his drink and blotted his face with the towel, indulging in an inward distraction that appeared more troubling than usual. Business issues could always trigger a foul mood, but this was the worst shape Kellyanne had ever seen him in.

She'd picked up on the basics just from overhearing a few cell phone conversations. After several booming years, real estate was in crisis, and now the ax was falling on condominiums—Walter's primary vehicle. Miami, in particular, was taking quite a beating. Within the next few years, over twenty-four thousand new condo units would be flooding an inventory-heavy market. Falling prices were forcing appraisals down, and scores of presale buyers were suing Walter to get out of contracts.

"Things will turn around," Kellyanne told him. She squeezed his shoulder for emphasis.

He clasped her fingers, holding her there. "That fucking Arab got six hundred million in loans for more than twenty properties, and every single one is in foreclosure. Nobody seemed to notice that he didn't know shit about real estate. But they didn't know shit, either. So there you have it."

Kellyanne waited quietly for the moment to pass.

He could easily build to a boil on the subject of amateurs and the investors who poured money into their projects. Not long ago, there were limited sources for equity debt financing. But then hedge funds, special real estate funds, and community banks all jumped into the race, betting on unproven developers to win. Some did. Most didn't. And now it was a bloodbath. Though Walter knew that he'd be among the strong players who survived, he also realized that it might take years to dig out from the rubble.

"All these meetings are a pain in the ass," he said, still holding her hand. "It helps to have you waiting for me. I need the stress release."

"I'm shocked that you're still here," Kellyanne replied evenly. "It's been a whole week."

"I hope I can wrap this up in the next few days. I need to get home." He let go of her fingers. "And you probably want to get back to your girlfriends in the Hamptons, right?" There was a hint of derision in his delivery of *girlfriends*.

She said nothing.

Walter stood up to tuck in his still-crisp shirt and reknot his Mimi Fong tie. "I met an investor last night who just sent his girl in for anal bleaching. He says she's got the prettiest asshole he's ever seen. Why don't you check into that?"

Kellyanne turned on him hotly. She already spent enough time with two-blade razors and baby powder, dry shaving her bush into the perfect isosceles triangle that was his preference. But bleaching her anus was out of the question. "Get serious."

Walter narrowed his gaze. "I am. If you're not going to swallow, blow jobs aren't fun anymore. I need something to keep me interested. Giving it to you in the ass sounds like the ticket."

Kellyanne just stared back at him in disbelief.

"Don't look so surprised." His smile was nasty. "And don't let that Gloria Steinem wannabe fill your pretty little head with girl-power shit, either."

Kellyanne gave him a confused look. "What are you talking about?"

"I'm talking about your loudmouth feminist friend. Whenever that bitch comes on television, I scramble for the remote to press the MUTE button." He scoffed. "Don't listen to her. You've developed an attitude and a smart-ass mouth since you've been here. I don't like it. Remember—I put in fifty grand for this summer vacation. If that doesn't deserve an all-access pass to that body of yours, then what does?"

That night, she started swallowing again. And the son of a bitch stayed in New York for five more days.

When he left, Walter insisted that she accompany him to the airport. Just before boarding his flight, he announced that he'd be back in two weeks, possibly for another ten-day stay. If Kellyanne had been given a guarantee that Walter Isherwood would die from his

next sex act, then she would've stripped down to
nothing and fucked him right there in the Delta terminal at LaGuardia.

The days that followed brought the worst of all possible outcomes. *Soul Mates* launched to incredible
ratings, demolishing its time slot's competition. The
show's success drew headlines for a socko five-
point rating with adults eighteen to forty-nine and
13 million viewers overall.

Fox marketing went into hyperdrive, declaring it
the summer's first network megahit, scheduling an
encore airing, and announcing one-week delay repur-
posing on sister channels Fox Reality and MyNet-
workTV. Rabid fans flooded YouTube with clips of
the show's saucier bits. TMZ broke the story that an
ex-girlfriend was accusing Vlad Branigan of infect-
ing her with herpes. *Soul Mates* was officially a phe-
nomenon. And the hysteria continued to build. Episode
two pulled in 14 million viewers, improving on the
debut by an astonishing 1 million.

If the portrayal of Kellyanne had been damaging
in the first hour, then it was totally devastating by
the end of the second show. Slick-trick editing had
managed to depict her fed-up exit midway into film-
ing as petulant outrage over being told that sneaking
into Vlad Branigan's bedroom after hours was forbidden. Footage of her yelling, "I quit the goddamn
show!" was looped over and over again.

Reaction interviews with her former castmates
only dug the knives in deeper. The most vicious of all
came from Dee Lonergan, the proudly self-described
bitch whom Kellyanne had barely tolerated during
that miserable week on Star Island. "She found out
that acting like a complete slut was against the rules,

so she quit," Dee summarized for the camera, clearly relishing every syllable. "That's rich. If you ask me, this show was never a good fit for Kellyanne. When do they start shooting *Who Wants to Marry an Alabama Skank?*" I think she could actually do much better on something like that."

The campaign of personal destruction didn't end there. Throughout the program, viewers were prompted by the show's smarmy host—a cringeinducing ex-NFL quarterback sporting new porcelain veneers too big for his mouth—to log onto the *Soul Mates* Web site and cast their votes in the "Slut-O-Meter" poll, which pitted Kellyanne against Hooters waitress Bunny Corvette. Results were updated live and scrolled onto the bottom of the screen. There was no contest. By an extreme margin, Kellyanne earned top honors.

She was devastated. Her cell phone exploded with calls—Pommie, Jab, her father, her mother, and Uncle Kirby, among others. But she let them all go to voice mail. Right now there was only one person she wanted to hear from—Adam Griffie.

Finally, he called. "I thought this *Soul Mates* shit would die quickly. But *everybody's* talking about it."

Kellyanne groaned her displeasure as she entertained the idea of asking Walter to pay for a lawyer. There had to be a legal recourse for this kind of malicious deception. When Liza had suggested it weeks ago, Kellyanne refused to consider the idea, going on the long-held Downey principle that you don't pour gas onto a fire. But things were different now. She felt under attack more than ever. "What if I sued?"

"Sued who?" Adam balked.

"I don't know . . . Three Kegs Entertainment. That's Bonzi's production company. He threatened to humiliate me like this if I didn't sleep with him. That's sexual harassment."

"You signed a contract," Adam reminded her. "Those reality boilerplates waive any and all rights to legal action based on the outcome of the show."

"But it's all a lie!" Kellyanne cried. "This is my reputation!"

"Yeah, well, most people concerned about their reputations don't sign up for these shows. Exhibitionists who want attention do."

Kellyanne mentioned Gloria Allred, the high-profile superattorney who took on sensational victim's rights cases.

"You might get a press conference out of that," Adam surmised with little encouragement. "And the talk shows would pursue you for a day or two. But Bonzi and the network won't budge an inch. Besides, it'll be tough to cry sexual harassment when the die has already been cast with the actual show. He's putting you out there as a drunk slut. Whether that's true or not is irrelevant. Images are damning, and perception is reality. If you take them on, your relationship with Walter will become fair game, too. That's not an arrangement most people would find noble or sympathetic. My advice—just hope this goes away soon."

Kellyanne thought about fighting back. It'd take a will of iron, impossibly thick skin, deep financial resources, and a plan to win. At the moment, she had none of those things. She unleashed a dramatic sigh of defeat. "Have you heard anything from *As the World Turns*?"

"They want you in for a reading next week."

Her mood instantly brightened . . . but then it was darkened again by a subterranean uncertainty she picked up in Adam's voice. "Is something wrong?"

"This *Soul Mates* business makes me nervous," Adam admitted. "My gut tells me that all of the attention is going to be a liability. This isn't stunt casting. It's a legitimate role. They want a serious actress. Let's see what happens." His tone lacked even cautious optimism.

Kellyanne was crushed. Doomsday thoughts flooded her mind as angry tears watered her eyes. She wanted this part so bad that her body ached for it. Why not her? Goddammit! Why not? Considering all the users and humiliations over the years, she deserved this break.

Adam promised to e-mail details about the reading, then signed off.

Kellyanne barely said good-bye. She just tucked her legs underneath her chin and sat there on the bed, disturbed and distracted, her mind burning with regret for all the bad choices, missed chances, and crushed dreams. And, as it always did whenever she had the temerity to look back, there was one memory that scorched the most. Los Angeles, 2004 . . .

"Everyone's a whore in this town," Michelle Estes said. "The city is full of them. Studio execs, stars, producers, agents—everybody." She stabbed at the avocado in her Greek Californian Salad. "It's not just the call girls. It's a way of life here."

Kellyanne merely nodded as she sipped more kouros, a light Greek white wine.

"Do you see that guy in the white Prada shirt two tables to your right?" Michelle asked.

Kellyanne spotted him without appearing too obvious.

Michelle leaned in conspiratorially. "That's Robert Bradley. He's a plastic surgeon in Century City. Loves blondes. For a few fucks and a couple of blow jobs, he'll give you a new pair of tits. And he's the best in town." She smirked. "At breast augmentation. The man's a lousy lay. His dick is too small, and he sweats too much." Michelle made an ugly face. "He should really throw in some liposculpting to make it a fair deal."

Kellyanne found herself staring at Michelle's enhanced cleavage.

"Perfect Bs."

They were lunching on the sprawling patio of Taverna Tony's at the Malibu Country Mart, a casual yet chic outdoor shopping center situated with the roaring Pacific on one side and the scenic Santa Monica mountains and canyons on the other.

Kellyanne spread some hummus onto a small piece of grilled pita bread as she sorted out the new facts.

Michelle Estes, her friend from method class, was less struggling actress and more working high-class prostitute. And the half-truths didn't end there. The multimillion-dollar sand castle they were living in on Broad Beach was hardly an incredible sublease deal. It was an act of generosity from one of Michelle's regular johns, a top-tier actor currently on location in Australia.

Kellyanne had also discovered that Michelle worked for Judith Love, a discreet madam who managed a small group of meticulously selected, exceptional girls. For every appointment, Michelle easily made a few thousand dollars. Her nickname was Elvira, given not for anything to do with the Mistress of the Dark, but in tribute to her uncanny resemblance to Michelle Pfeiffer's character in the film *Scarface*. Michelle Estes had the same drop-dead ice blond looks and the same superior blond attitude. *I'm hot, and everybody wants to fuck me. What else is new?*

Kellyanne sipped more wine and regarded Michelle with on-the-sleeve resentment. She felt played. The lattes and girl talk after method class, the shopping excursions, the dinners out, the club adventures, the invitation to leave her dodgy apartment in a not-so-great neighborhood for a three-month free ride in a beachfront Malibu mansion—all of it had been part of a strategic campaign to recruit her.

Michelle's real agenda had started to spill last night. More details followed the next morning while they drank coffee on the waterfront deck. And the entire charade was on the table at the popular Greek restaurant where they sat now.

"You'd be a natural," Michelle insisted.

Kellyanne narrowed her gaze. "A natural hooker? You're such an angel to say that. Bless your heart."

"It's not a stigma," Michelle maintained. "It's a solution." She recited two famous names—an actress starring on a new hit television series about suburban housewives and the eco-friendly wife of a movie director. "Both of them used to work for Judith."

"That doesn't mean I'm willing to."

Michelle pushed her half-eaten salad over to the side. "You're practically doing what I'm doing already. You just haven't made it official yet. And you're not getting properly compensated."

Kellyanne started to protest.

"Come on, girl. Get real. You're a hurricane hooker, just like me. I'm from Florida. You're from Alabama. The wind blew us west, because we wanted to make it in Hollywood. How many horny producers and bullshit actors have you gone to dinner with—and slept with—in hopes of getting a part?"

Kellyanne just looked at her.

"Judith's a boutique madam for the power elite. You'll make top dollar *and* make some important introductions. This is how I landed that speaking part on *CSI* during February sweeps. If they pay to fuck you, they're more inclined to help you career-wise. It sounds weird, but it's true. Judith says it's because a successful business transaction has already taken place." Michelle laughed a little. "Personally? I think these men love the idea of getting pussy for nothing and fucking over naive girls. If they didn't pay for it on the front end, then they don't want to pay for it on the back end. But I'm in a different league. I get paid to get them off. But more important, I get paid to leave. So they're not on guard about my wanting more than what they intend to give. This relaxes them. And when these guys are relaxed and feeling like a stud, a real career boost has a better chance of coming my way. It's a win-win."

What frightened Kellyanne the most was that this was all starting to make sense to her. The fear triggered an impulse to bolt. "I'll be out of the house by midafternoon."

Michelle shook her head regretfully. "No one's asking you to move out."

"But that was part of the sweetener package for this pitch, right?" Kellyanne accused. "If I'm not going along, I should take off. You and Judith probably have another mark picked out."

"It's not like that," Michelle said quietly. "I consider you a real friend. We've talked for hours. I know about all the disappointments you've had to deal with since moving here. It's been one jerk off guy after another." She paused a beat. "And if you think that's going to change . . ."

"For me, the answer isn't—"

"Michael Zanker," Michelle cut in.

Kellyanne fell silent. She read *Variety* and *The Hollywood Reporter* to keep up with cocktail party conversation. Michael Zanker was a prolific producer and part of the town's unofficial yet prestigious Billionaire Boys Club. His recent string of high-octane blockbusters—a remake of *The Towering Inferno* set in Las Vegas, the vigilante drama *Bulletproof*, its sequel *Still Bulletproof*, and the terrorist thriller *Blast Point* had collectively racked up a cool billion in domestic box office receipts alone.

Michelle fingered the stem of her wineglass. "If you wanted to give this a try, you could see him tonight."

There was industry talk percolating about Michael Zanker's plans for a big-budget film based on the DC Comics heroine Batgirl. The word was out that he wanted an unknown to fill the spandex.

As if reading her mind, Michelle said, "By the way, all this talk about a Batgirl movie is bullshit." She rolled her eyes. "It's Zanker's cocaine project."

Kellyanne gave her a puzzled look.

"He only talks about it when he's high. Action

movies with female leads rarely work, and he's already snorted the idea that the budget needs to be one hundred million. Don't believe anything he says about it. It'll never get out of development. Trust me." She laughed. "I can name three girls off the top of my head who are walking around telling everyone they're going to be the next Batgirl. I used to be the fourth. *Don't* fall for it. The real movie on his schedule is *Trigger Finger.* Matt Damon's already attached. It's about a bad cop. I've got the script at the house. There's a great innocent-girlfriend part that you'd be perfect for."

Kellyanne was instantly wary. "If it's such a great part, why aren't you going after it?"

Michelle smiled wryly. "I can't do innocent. I'm not that good an actress. Besides, Zanker has this thing about casting new talent. And by 'new talent' I mean girls he's recently *conditioned.* I saw him a few years ago. He ended up giving me the philandering bitch–wife role to Colin Farrell's demolition expert in *Blast Point,* but all of the domestic scenes ended up on the cutting-room floor. They eventually turned up in the special-features section of the deluxe DVD. But nobody has time to watch all of those extras." She shrugged helplessly. "What's a call girl to do?"

Kellyanne was up to speed on *Trigger Finger.* It'd been a buzz project in the trades for weeks. Michael Mann had just signed on to direct. And Denzel Washington was rumored to be in negotiations to play a tough police captain. In the general sense, Kellyanne had to admit that she'd easily sleep with a producer if it meant joining Damon, Washington, and Mann on a film project. So what was stopping her now?

Michelle seemed to pick up on the fact that Kellyanne was slowly warming to the idea. "Just think of tonight as a trial run. If you decide it's not for you, so be it. But you'll still make some good money and meet one of the most successful producers in the business."

Kellyanne could feel anxiety building. That she was actually considering this seemed crazy. Just recently she'd turned down an offer to pose for *Playboy*. And yet here she was close to saying yes to prostitution.

"It's not a dark path," Michelle said. "*If* you stay away from drugs. Judith says that's where most girls go wrong. They get stuck doing it for the cocaine and needing the cocaine to do it." She reached out to squeeze Kellyanne's hand. "Don't overthink this. It's not an indictment on your morals. It's a strategic move. And working for Judith, you'll only go out on dates with the upper echelon. I'm talking about the men who make it onto those annual Hollywood power lists in magazines."

Kellyanne took a deep breath. She swallowed hard. She swore to herself that, in a town full of users, this was nothing more than a shrewd way for someone like her to operate. "What's the split?"

Michelle smiled triumphantly. "Judith gets thirty percent."

Michael Zanker lived in a gorgeous home on Stone Canyon in Bel Air. When he opened the door, Kellyanne was surprised to see how short he was—five foot six.

He raked her up and down with obvious appreciation. "Judith said she was sending over a knockout. You're much more than that."

Kellyanne smiled her thanks, nervously taking in the minimalist Japanese-inspired decor.

"May I offer you a drink?"

She politely declined, wondering how one thing would lead to another. Michelle had told her that Zanker was a time management obsessive. He wanted his girls to arrive and depart in punctual two-hour blocks.

He was in his midthirties, physically fit, and handsome in that effective sales representative sort of way—attractive, sexually appealing, but ultimately unmemorable.

"I want to show you something." His voice was tender. He took her by the hand and led her through the impeccable house and into a dedicated screening room.

At first, Kellyanne assumed that he wanted to show off a rough cut of a new film. But the entertainment was something else entirely. What filled the massive screen was crude hidden-camera footage of Zanker interviewing a young actress for a role in one of his movies. It ended with her taking off her clothes and performing fellatio on him. And then another one played—same story, same setup.

Kellyanne sat through at least half a dozen of these clips, betraying no reaction even as Zanker closely monitored her for one.

Mercifully, the screen went blank.

"What do you think?" he asked.

She looked at him. "I think after the second interview, it all became rather predictable."

He grinned. "Those are utility girls. I just use them for pleasure. They aren't worthy of a part in one of my movies. Only the women I choose to condition are elevated to that status."

Kellyanne recalled Michelle using the term *condition,* too. "What does that mean exactly?"

"Come with me." He took her hand again and this time ushered her into a small guest room that contained little more than a low platform bed. "Take off your clothes."

Kellyanne braced herself. She'd slept with worse. And for less. If Michelle was right about his time issues, then she only had about an hour left. *Yes.* She could do this. Slowly, she untied the Diane von Furstenberg wrap dress, let it fall to the floor, and stood there in her La Perla best.

Zanker took Kellyanne's face in his hands, gazing at her in a state of absolute marvel. "You are truly exquisite. The word *beautiful* is almost too ordinary to describe you."

She hoped he'd remember that speech when the studio wanted a name actress for the part of Matt Damon's girlfriend in *Trigger Finger.*

Suddenly, Zanker reached down to grab something on the edge of the bed. "I want you to wear this." He presented her with a black hood fitted with breathing holes around the nose and mouth.

Kellyanne looked at him in disbelief.

"This is part of your conditioning." Zanker's smile was as cold as his voice. He slipped the hood over her head.

Kellyanne experienced a mounting panic as everything turned pitch black. She could breathe, but the instant blindness scared the hell out of her. "No! I can't—"

Zanker shoved a rubber ball into her mouth and strapped it tightly around the hood.

Kellyanne tried to stop him, but he grabbed her by both wrists and pushed her down onto the bed.

She could hear the crinkling of a Mylar-wrapped condom being ripped open.

"Stop fighting me," Zanker hissed. "I'm not going to hurt you. This is *conditioning*."

Kellyanne's fear intensified. And she felt played all over again. Michelle had given her no hint as to this rich asshole's perversions.

"Your beauty makes no difference right now. You can't be seen. You can't be heard. You're just a receptacle." He pushed himself inside her. "I hate actresses. You're all selfish, greedy bitches who want something for nothing."

Unable to scream or beg him to stop, Kellyanne just laid there motionless, counting the seconds, counting the minutes . . . until the hour was up.

Zanker used her sexually, violating her with his body and various toys as he taunted her with the constant refrain, "Do you feel beautiful?" When it was over, he told her that she had three minutes to get dressed and leave.

The moment she heard him exit the room, Kellyanne yanked the rubber ball out of her mouth and tore off the black hood, crying hysterically as she scrambled for her dress and shoes.

There was an envelope of cash on the pillow. She counted three thousand dollars in crisp hundred-dollar bills. But that wasn't nearly enough for what she'd just been through.

Kellyanne made her way to the front of the house. She found Zanker kicked back on the sleek living room sofa, drinking a beer and talking on his cell phone.

For a moment, she stood there, staring daggers at him.

Casually, he dropped the mobile to his side. "I'll set up a screen test with Matt. Leave me your number."

The rage that coursed through her rattled her bones. "Rot in hell, you sick fuck!"

Zanker was unfazed and returned to his conversation.

She stormed out and raced back to Malibu. The house was empty. Michelle had left a note on the counter, promising to be back at midnight. Below the clumsily drawn heart that closed the message, Kellyanne scribbled "Judith's share" and dropped nine hundred dollars. She owed them nothing. It was a clean break.

By the time midnight ticked around, she was already on a red-eye flight to New York, desperate to leave behind the Hollywood meatgrinder, Michelle Estes, and the horrific memory that she knew would last forever . . .

And so far it had. She wiped away a tear. The emotional wounds remained raw. Years later, the episode still represented Kellyanne's lowest point in life. The reality-show fiasco paled in comparison. Part of her had been permanently damaged that night in Bel Air. There was a crack in her soul. And this had set her up as perfect prey for a controlling man like Walter Isherwood. She'd been weak, she'd been broken, and she'd wanted so desperately to believe that being taken care of was the answer.

Do you feel beautiful?

She could still hear Zanker's voice inside her head. Or was it Walter's now? Did it even matter anymore? Sometimes Kellyanne wondered what her life might've been today if she'd stayed in Los Angeles, if she'd left her number with that sick bastard, if she'd done the screen test with Matt Damon, if she'd never met Walter.

Oh, God, if only . . .

Billie

16

"I missed my flight because of that crap you pulled at the Hotel . . . Elysée! Do you realize I lost . . . a twenty-five-thousand-dollar . . . speaking fee?" March's breathing was labored, and his hazel eyes blazed with renewed rage.

Billie smiled. She could feel his hands tighten around her throat. The sensation was thrilling. March might be pissed off and twenty-five grand poorer, but he was back where he belonged—deep inside her. And anger meant that he actually felt something. Love could come later.

For now, it was pure, hot, jackhammer sex.

Billie put her strongly responsive vaginal muscles to effective use. Without warning, she contracted them, squeezing March's cock like a Venus flytrap.

He cried out in astonished pleasure. And his amazing hands—that only moments before had hinted at killing—were now caressing as he collapsed on top of her in an exhausted, satisfied, sweat-slicked heap.

Billie played with March's dirty blond hair, bliss-fully content to have him all to herself again. She wanted to bask in the sensual nirvana. He was still inside her. They were skin on skin, body on body. His intoxicating, manly scent was potent in her nostrils.

Oh, God, she tried to just enjoy the moment. In fact, she gave it her goddamn best effort. But the familiar anxieties began to build. How long would this moment last? When would she see him again? Why did he want to marry that bitch Amaryllis?

Rolling over and onto his back, March moaned with erotic contentment, placing a proprietary hand on the inside of Billie's thigh. "It's hard to stay mad at a woman with a trick pussy." He sighed. "Do you have any coke?"

"I wish."

With his free hand, March reached for a silver case on the nightstand. "Then this will have to do." He tapped out a fresh joint, fired it up, and inhaled deeply, displaying more ganja know-how than a lifetime subscriber to *High Times*.

They were at the Hudson on West Fifty-eighth. Mr. Political Superstar had gone all out, splurging on a standard room just shy of 150 square feet. The matchbox was only big enough for a double bed and a stainless-steel desk and chair.

Billie took a hit of the weed and stared at the dark-paneled African wood walls. "You really know how to impress a girl."

"What?"

"I've stayed at Comfort Inns that had bigger rooms."

March repossessed the joint. "This is a hot hotel. It's got style."

"Whatever."

"Does it matter? We just needed a clean bed for a few hours."

"Yeah, God forbid you treat me to a meal before or after. I might get confused and think you want to start picking out china patterns."

"Call room service."

"It's not the same."

He passed the joint. "Here. You obviously need this more than I do."

Billie didn't refuse. She sucked the magic smoke straight into her lungs. "Would it kill you to take me out to dinner sometime?"

March laughed and snatched back his herb. "Where's this shit coming from? We just fucked our brains out, and now you're making noises like a nagging housewife."

"So I'm not supposed to want anything more? Being treated like a slut is all I should aspire to when it comes to the fabulous March Donaldson?"

"You're ruining my high." He took another deep drag and closed his eyes.

"Go to hell." She rose up to bolt from the bed.

But March grabbed her arm. "Billie, come on, what's wrong with you?"

"Quite a bit, obviously." She twisted free of his grasp. "I bet you wouldn't think twice about taking Liza out for dinner."

"You're right," he said simply. "I wouldn't. But we work together. There's a difference."

Billie fought the urge to spit in his face. "You suck."

He laughed at her in frustration. "You know what my situation is. I'm engaged. I've got a politically sensitive career. Nothing's changed for me."

"But what about *me*?" Billie cried. "I'm supposed

to just wait around and jump whenever you throw a scrap of time my way?"

"Well, shit, Billie. You're a rock star. Call up Nickelback. Ask them to take you to lunch. I can't be everything for you."

Now it was Billie's turn to laugh. "Oh, please, get over yourself. I don't want you to be my everything. But you could be *something*."

March smiled and shook his head, then pulled her down to kiss her on the mouth and wrestle playfully. "This bitch drives me crazy!" he yelled out. It was exasperation. It was admiration. It was something else, too . . . affection. Real, unguarded affection.

Billie saw an opening and went for it. "I was watching you and Amaryllis at Sunset Beach," she began quietly. "She doesn't excite you."

"Billie . . ."

"I've never had sex like this before. Have you?" She didn't wait for him to answer. "It surprises me every time. We're electric together. You can't deny that."

"I don't. And it works." He patted the mattress. "But right here. Nowhere else." His tone was absolute.

Billie tried to conceal her disappointment but couldn't help the hurt being telegraphed all over her face.

March sighed. "Don't look at me that way."

She felt the tears building in her eyes. Only her anger kept her from breaking down. "You're such a bastard."

He smiled, almost as if it was a private joke. "I'll write you a poem. Will that help?"

Before Billie realized it, her hand lashed out against his face. "Don't mock me!"

March barely reacted. He just smoothed the point

of impact with his palm and looked at her. "I can't keep up, Billie. One minute you're the good-time hookup, and the next minute you're this lovesick schoolgirl. What the hell do you want from me?"

"I want some goddamn honesty."

"Okay, I'll start. You're taking the fun out of this. And when it stops being fun, I'm gone." He paused a beat. "Your turn."

His answer crushed her. Billie got the strong sense that his coldness ran deeper than she could imagine. A part of him was so unreachable. But still, she wanted to try. "I wish you'd treat me like you treat Liza. She's a real person to you. You respect her. I want that."

March's smile was almost sad. "You want a relationship."

Billie just stared at him.

His eyes were candid. "I can't offer that. I can't offer you anything other than . . . *this*."

She shook her head mutely.

March grinned at Billie for a long moment before finally pulling her down into his arms for a tender embrace.

She thought about resisting him, if only because she didn't want to know what it felt like to be held this way. But she succumbed to her naked need and allowed it to happen. Right away, she regretted the indulgence. It felt too damn good. And Billie knew that she'd never stop wanting more of it.

He kissed her shoulder, and almost against his will, he said, "I think about you, too. The other night I was with a group of people, and I was bored out of my mind. I wanted you there. Sometimes I wish . . ."

Billie held her breath for the rest.

But March's voice just trailed off into silence. He traced her torso with his fingertips.

"What do you wish?" Billie prompted.

He hesitated. "I wish you were my type."

"Judging by Amaryllis, your type is frigid and dull."

He smiled wanly. "I run a conservative think tank. There are certain expectations that go along with that. And if I ever run for public office, I'll need the right partner."

"So marrying her is a business arrangement."

March winced at the crude assessment. "I wouldn't put it that way."

"How would you put it?"

"We complement each other."

"I guess Tina Turner was right all along. 'What's Love Got to Do with It?'"

March nuzzled her neck. "Maybe you should do a remake. You could sing the hell out of that song. When was that a hit—eighty-four, eighty-five? It's time for a new version."

Billie tangled her leg around his, loving the intimacy, hating herself even more for allowing it, but still wishing it could linger for hours, for days, for weeks . . . forever. "Oh, so you're giving me career advice now? Maybe you should be my manager. I'm in the market for one."

"Clean up your act. I can guarantee you a gig singing 'God Bless America' at the next Republican convention."

"I'll keep looking," Billie deadpanned.

March laughed. "Hey, I almost forgot. Kip mentioned that you owe him some money. He says you've been dodging his calls, too."

Billie tensed immediately. Kip was the dealer with the Wall Street vibe that March had referred her to during their first rendezvous. "I'm not dodging him. He called once. I was in the shower. Right now I'm trying to sort out my money situation. My ex-manager used to handle all of that. He'll get the cash."

"Make sure that he does. Kip may look clean cut and wear expensive suits, but he's still a fucking drug dealer. Don't forget that."

"Is that a warning?" she trilled lightly.

"No, Billie, that's good advice." His tone was serious.

The truth was, Billie had started using a new dealer, because it was either pay Kip what she owed him or get more drugs from another source. Now she just wanted to change the subject. "I went to your Web site."

March's eyes widened. "OurAmerica.com?"

Billie nodded. "The extreme right side of things must be a lucrative racket. You can't really believe most of that shit."

"I'll admit there's a certain business advantage to courting the values crowd. But I'm also a white guy from Texas. At the end of the day, it's not such a stretch."

"I guess it's sort of like me going pop," Billie reasoned philosophically. "I have a certain contempt for it, but at the same time, I need to make real money. Maybe we're not hypocrites after all, you and I. Maybe we're just pragmatists."

March smiled. "Yeah, well, don't be offended if I decline to make that one of the talking points in my next Rotary Club speech." He checked the clock on his iPhone and groaned. A hot second later, he was on his feet, shoving peppermint into his mouth and throwing on his clothes. "Are you really sure about this?"

"About what?"

"Going Celine." He grinned. "I think I might miss my raunchy rocker bitch."

Billie shrugged. "I need a radio hit. When I hear Alicia Keys singing 'No One,' that works for me. Doing what I've been doing has put me in a spot where I can't pay my dealer on time. Fuck that."

"I hear you. That's why I'm about to go tell a group of rich evangelicals that prayer in school is the most important issue facing our country today."

He rolled his eyes and slipped on a diamond-striped Stefano Ricci dress shirt, working the buttons with lightning speed. "You know, I just read that Madonna dumped her record label to sign with Live Nation, the concert promoters. And Apple's starting up a music division. Everything's changing. I think it's a smart move to widen your audience."

March stepped into his pants and fastened his belt, then leaned down to kiss her on the mouth. "But when I come to see your next concert, you have to do 'Make Me Laugh and Make Me Come and I'll Fucking Marry You,' even if the audience is full of teenagers." He scanned the room quickly for any leave-behinds.

Billie reached for his hand as he started for the door. March could make her laugh. He could make her come, too. So why wouldn't he fucking marry her? "Don't rush off like this." Her voice was almost pleading.

He gave her a strange look.

"I've heard some great things about the food at Cafeteria downstairs. I thought we could—"

"Billie, didn't we just go through this?" His voice was annoyed and impatient. "I can't be seen with someone like you."

The words sliced into her and cut deep.

March sighed his regret, ostensibly for the insensitive phrasing. "You know what I mean. How would I explain being spotted with a wild music scene chick like you? Unless you plan to announce that you're switching over to Christian rock. Then maybe we could make a go of it." He smiled at his own joke.

She glared at him with fresh tears in her eyes. "Take off then, you son of a bitch. I'll even give you a thirty-minute head start. That way we won't be on the sidewalk at the same time. I wouldn't want you to risk staining that squeaky clean reputation of yours."

March stepped toward the door and suddenly turned back to face her. "Listen, Billie, this is what it is. I've been clear about that from the beginning. But if we have to constantly redefine things every time we get together, then I think we should just end it."

Something in his voice told her that he already had. But she wanted to be sure. "When will I see you again?"

"I don't know." March opened the door. "I'll call you." And then he walked out for good.

Liza

17

Liza observed Kellyanne stretched out by the pool, sacrificing her body to the sun in a gold-foil Norma Kamali bikini.

Having just completed her morning swim, Annie the golden retriever lumbered over to lick Kellyanne's face and feet.

"Hello, sweetheart," Kellyanne gushed in an uninspired happy-talk voice that unsuccessfully disguised the darkness of her true mood. But she seemed genuinely grateful for the animal distraction.

As Annie trotted away, Liza stepped onto the deck in a white cut-out swimsuit by Dolce and Gabbana that emphasized her thin body, protected from those aging UV rays by a wide-brimmed white floppy hat and loads of SPF 45. Behind the giant Dior rimless shield sunglasses, there was deep concern in her eyes. She offered up a tall glass loaded with crushed ice and filled to the top with Bolthouse Farms Prickly Pear Cactus Lemonade.

"Bless your heart," Kellyanne murmured.

"This morning marks a brand-new day," Liza announced with her best Zen-like spin, settling into the chair next to Kellyanne.

"Any word from Billie?"

Liza shook her head. "And I'm done leaving messages. She has our numbers. She knows where the house is."

Kellyanne made a helpless gesture.

Where once Liza had been preoccupied with worry, she was now annoyed and insulted. Billie had been MIA for weeks, refusing to return calls and answer texts. Even urgent messages imploring her to get in touch were ignored.

"I think she's shacked up with some guy."

"Probably," Liza agreed. "But it's not the boy from Sunset Beach. Like an idiot, I drove to Shelter Island last week to see if he was still hanging around."

"And?"

"He was. But he hasn't seen or heard from Billie since that night."

"I just hope it's not drug related," Kellyanne said. "If so, a disappearing act like this is a bad sign. She could be on a bender. Walter's youngest son has a problem. For the most part, he's functional with it. But when he falls out of contact, everyone in the family starts to worry." She paused a beat. "Of course, Billie could also be off recording or performing somewhere. It'd be just like her not to mention that and make us feel like fools for worrying."

Liza shrugged. "Maybe. I did call Amy Dando— her manager . . . or more accurately, *ex*-manager."

Kellyanne looked up in surprise. "*Really?*"

Liza nodded. "You know, I'm not sure how accurate it would be to refer to Billie as a rock star in the present tense."

Kellyanne sighed. "Well, I'll still trade places with her. Better a career on the skids than no career at all."

"You're going to be a soap star," Liza declared with upbeat cheer. "That part on *As the World Turns* is yours. I can feel it."

Kellyanne made a show out of covering her ears.

"You can't let your mind be poisoned by what's going on," Liza said fiercely. "Just go in there and *knock them out*. You know that you can."

Somewhere in Kellyanne's eyes was a sign of confidence regenerating.

Liza tilted down her sunglasses and gave her a determined look. "I can't imagine how excruciating it must be to see yourself being exploited this way. This *Soul Mates* business is disgusting. But it's a temporary storm. You just have to ride it out. I see this in politics all the time. A scandal hits and there's an intense focus, a relentless piling on. Then the interest shifts to something else, and everything becomes quiet again. Don't lose sight of the fact that memories are short, either. This will pass."

"God, I hope you're right," Kellyanne whispered. "I want that job. I *need* that job. It could really mean a fresh start for me . . . without Walter."

Liza gave her a probing ray-gun gaze. "Run for your life. I think you could be happier in a rathole apartment living off cash advances from credit cards. At least you'd have your freedom."

Kellyanne brought a hand to her mouth, then seemed to think better of it. Her nails were down to the quick and cracked with dried blood from her nervous biting. *Soul Mates* had her fraying at the edges.

For several long seconds, Kellyanne just lay there.

But finally, she began to speak. "Sometimes I wonder how I got here. I'm almost thirty. And I'm living this *dumb* life. It's hard to look back, because it's so pathetic. I haven't accomplished anything."

"That's not true," Liza said. "You went to college. You have your de—"

"Oh, big deal," Kellyanne cut in. "So I went to college. I got my diploma." She twirled a hand in the air. "Whoop-dee-fucking-do. What can I do with a degree in *theater*?"

"What do you want to do?" Liza challenged.

"I want to act!" Kellyanne shrieked.

"Then *do it*. But nothing's going to happen for you in Miami. Move back to Los Angeles."

Kellyanne winced at the suggestion.

"Or move here to New York again," Liza suggested. "Just don't give up until you're making a living at it."

Kellyanne stared at the sun. "Cue the theme from *Rocky*."

"Maybe I'm oversimplifying the idea," Liza admitted. "But people have landed in both places with less than thirty dollars in their pocket and made it work. Talent and looks have always been there for you. It's the focus and drive that you're missing. And if you could only break this habit of getting steered off course by men who are completely unworthy . . . my God, you'd probably have a fucking Oscar by now."

Kellyanne smiled wanly. "That's so true."

"But you've been this way ever since I can remember," Liza went on. "Who was that asshole you were dating when we met in Cancún for the first time?"

Liza sat there as Kellyanne put her sex memory chip to work, rewinding past Walter to name the manic-depressive musician in New York, certain jerky actors, egocentric producers, and high-strung directors in Hollywood, then on to her college lovers. And there'd been a reasonable number—the Crimson Tide's quarterback, an assistant football coach, a delicious tennis player on scholarship from South Africa, a hot fraternity guy, later his hotter older brother . . .

"Okay, slut, enough already!" Liza cut in with exasperated good humor. "It was March of 1999!"

Kellyanne laughed, covering her face in her hands.

All of a sudden, the name seemed to come to her. She grabbed Liza's wrist and squealed, "*Heath Warren!*"

"That's him!"

"Oh, God, I haven't thought about him in ages. He was one of my English professors. I thought he was *so* hot!"

Liza stole a look to the heavens, as if pleading for divine mercy. "I hated that pompous prick. You were a college girl on spring break in Cancún, and he wanted you to stay cooped up in the hotel room with him while he wrote his *literary novel.*"

Kellyanne giggled. "He said I was his inspiration. He couldn't write unless I was around."

"Oh, please. That bullshit was all about control. By the way, I don't think his book was ever published."

"I don't think he ever finished it. I broke up with him that summer, and he still had at least one hundred pages to go." Kellyanne gasped. "Do you remember that dinner all of us had at La Madonna? I thought the two of you were going to kill each other!"

Liza traveled back. "Ugh! I wanted to stab him in the head with a fork! Monica Lewinsky's book had just been released, and Heath said something so unbelievably sexist."

Kellyanne laughed at the memory. "You really got the best of him that night. The entire table was speechless. I think he was pissed off for the rest of the trip."

Liza shook her head in disbelief. "What did you ever see in that guy? He was so full of himself."

"I know," Kellyanne murmured. "Heath thought the sun came up just to hear him crow." She finished the Prickly Pear Lemonade as they enjoyed the glorious sunshine in easy silence. "God, that seems like so long ago. And yet here we are . . . still friends." She turned to make eye contact. "Thank you."

Liza met her gaze with curiosity.

"For sticking with me all these years," Kellyanne clarified softly. "I've been on such a dead-end path, and you've been on such an ambitious one. You could've dumped me a long time ago. I wouldn't have blamed you. And watching your success has been inspiring. It's made me think about my own life, my own choices." Her smile was shy. "I guess you're my hero."

Liza glanced down. It was so true. They were worlds apart. Kellyanne believed it was Liza's loyalty that kept their relationship intact. But shamefully, Liza wondered if it might be something else entirely—a chance to feel superior . . . smarter, stronger, more successful. She never threw that back in Kellyanne's face—or Billie's, for that matter—but there was a certain lazy comfort in being around them. Liza didn't have to compete.

This realization stung. It was a quality she didn't like about herself. And Kellyanne, in particular, deserved better. She was kind, thoughtful, consistent, caring, a good listener, and more intelligent than she gave herself credit for. If Liza took months to return a call, Kellyanne never took it as a personal affront. She was always just happy to hear from her, and they picked right back up without a beat of awkwardness, as if no time had passed between them.

"I don't mean to embarrass you," Kellyanne said.

"I'm not embarrassed," Liza replied quietly. "I'm just not quite worthy." She looked at her. "I might seem like I have it all together, but you're a better person than I am. And frankly, I'm lucky to have you as a friend."

Kellyanne reached out to squeeze her hand. "Enough of that. It doesn't take much to have me bawling my eyes out. And enough about *me*. Let's move on to you. Have you talked to Justin?"

"Not about anything significant. I'm not sure there will be a *talk* per se. I'll probably just serve him with papers after Labor Day."

"Billie says he could get alimony."

Liza shook her head. "Over my dead body."

"And what about Harrison?" Kellyanne inquired. "How are things there?"

"We're . . . *friends*," Liza replied pointedly. "And we'll remain that way until I finalize the situation with Justin."

Suddenly, Liza rose up and dipped feet first into the pool, shivering instantly. "Oh, my God! The water's *freezing*!"

Kellyanne grinned from the chaise like the bathing beauty she was.

"Harrison and I are going out to dinner one night

this week. Probably Nick and Toni's. You should join us. It'd be good for you to get out."

Kellyanne's reluctance was transparent. It was clear that the idea of company appealed to her. But it was also clear that the idea of being in public after last night's *Soul Mates* did not. "What if I made dinner for us here?" she suggested. "I could do shrimp and grits again."

Liza nodded enthusiastically. "I think Harrison would love that. We're meeting for lunch later on. I'll tell him to plan on it." And then she carefully placed her Dior shades onto the deck and submerged herself into the water with a graceful half-dive.

Cittanuova was the next best thing to a sidewalk café in Rome . . . or Hollywood.

Liza and Harrison were on the outdoor terrace at the contemporary trattoria, dining al fresco on the De Padova table and chairs. The Italian restaurant was in the heart of East Hampton village on Newtown Lane, and the atmosphere was casual, animated, celebratory, and *rich*.

An ultratan and ultratoned Kelly Ripa sat at the next table, laughing infectiously as she twirled pasta on her fork. Nearby was Renée Zellweger, eating alone and deeply engrossed in a book—David Halberstam's *The Coldest Winter: America and the Korean War*.

Harrison had insisted that they try a bottle of wine from the Long Island–based Channing Daughters Winery, a 2006 Vino Bianco with delicious aromatic notes of white peaches, honey, and vanilla.

Having just finished the last of a roasted chicken panini, Harrison sat there, drinking his wine and smiling as if he had a secret to tell.

"What?" Liza wanted to know as she pushed aside her Insalata Cesare.

"Nothing," Harrison murmured, still grinning. But it was so clearly *something*. "I like this. I like you. I like . . . *us*."

She was affected by the sexy gleam in his eyes. Cittanuova scene seekers were humming all around them but, at the same time, the strangers were all invisible. Liza and Harrison were tucked away in a private world. A realization began to spread through Liza that something big—and something she couldn't deal with—would happen very soon. She gave him a cautious look.

"Don't get uptight. I'm not going to ask you to wear my class ring . . . *yet*."

Liza smiled.

"I'm just letting you know that I'm not going anywhere." His hand found hers across the table.

Something in her quickened as she sipped her wine and gazed back at him. It was the most unexpected of alliances. Liza Pike and Harrison Beck. And yet here they were. The mere idea of them scared her. But she was determined to feel the fear and move forward nonetheless.

"I know your situation is complicated. But I'm a patient man."

Liza took a deep breath. "I made a commitment to myself to table the divorce until after Labor Day. This has nothing to do with any second thoughts and everything to do with my book. I have to finish it." She gave him a faux glare. "In fact, I should be working on it right now instead of having this three-hour lunch with you."

Harrison smiled. "If you need to take off, go.

Don't stay on my account." He chose that moment to flag down the waiter and order the house gelato.

"Well, I'm not going to leave now," Liza huffed. And she meant it. Her relationship with Harrison had changed her relationship with food. Sharing meals with him had become an indulgent, enjoyable ritual. And he was quite decadent about it, perfectly content to linger at a restaurant for hours.

This was so different from her experience with Justin, who ran out of conversational energy before the first course arrived, ate fast, and then gave off anxious signals that he was ready to leave.

What you don't know will end up hurting you.

That was so true in life. And especially true in love. The next time around, if there was a next time, Liza would *know* the man she was going to marry. Every critical question would be asked, too—about children, financial goals, family history, spirituality, commitment to fidelity, sexual needs, the whole gamut. Leaping in was no longer an option when it came to husbands.

Harrison stared at her with a certain lustful longing. For several seconds, he seemed to vibrate with it.

His look was so steady and sure that it practically engulfed Liza. Pure desire swept through her, almost forcing her out of her chair and onto his lap. But the moment thankfully passed.

"Harrison, I can't be starting up with the next to come while I'm waiting to finish up with the last to go. That's not how I want to live my life. And that's not how I want to start over. So until I'm *legally* a single woman, I think we should just . . . enjoy each other as friends."

"Do you mind if I sleep with other women?"

The question stunned Liza into silence.

Harrison held a straight face for as long as he could before breaking into a laugh. "Gotcha!"

She shook her head in exasperation just as her BlackBerry vibrated and chimed to announce a new e-mail message. Instinctively, Liza reached for it.

"I hate those things," Harrison complained. "I check e-mail once a day. That's enough."

But she could no longer hear him. Liza's distraction was total as she scanned the new message.

From: travisowen@yahoo.com
To: lizapike@mac.com

Subject: WHORE

> I read your book, WHORE. I guess it was an au-
> tobiography? Ha! Stop trying to protect the fu-
> ture sluts of America. Just let the little bitches
> dress like prostitutes and grow up too fast. Ask
> any guy. Baby pussy is a good thing. So shut
> the fuck up. You don't want me to get pissed
> off.

> Travis Owen

The communication was all too familiar now. The threats had been showing up with disturbing regularity on her Web site, and in the comment section of her blogs on *The Huffington Post*. But this was the first one to hit her personal e-mail address, which was known only to key business associates and close friends.

"Everything okay?" Harrison asked.

"Oh, it's nothing," Liza murmured. "Just some meaningless propaganda." And then she prayed that it was.

Kellyanne

18

Kellyanne returned to McGraw's Fish Market with a certain girlish anticipation. There was no denying it. She had an innocent crush—on the shop's owner *and* his son.

Stepping inside to the chime of the bell on the door, she waited patiently for Tucker to finish up with a chatty grandmother type. The woman reeked of old money and lovingly clutched an impeccably groomed Maltese accessorized with bright pink bows and a flashy jeweled collar.

"Give me a pound of your crab salad, too. I served that at my last garden club meeting, and everybody thought it was delicious."

"Happy to hear that." As Tucker turned around to flash his customer a quick smile, he noticed Kellyanne for the first time and acknowledged her with a sly wink.

A flurry of butterflies went loose in her stomach. His on-the-sleeve kindness and integrity put her in a state of awe. There was no trace of a come-on in his gesture. The man positively oozed goodness.

"I ran into your sister and that darling boy of yours at Scoop du Jour," the woman said. "He's a fine young man. Excellent manners."

Tucker beamed as he reached for a plastic container. "He's been after me all summer to let him learn how to surf. The kid's got no fear of the water at all."

"You're doing an amazing job with him. But I know how difficult it must be for you. Holly was dearly loved by so many here."

Tucker nodded somberly and scooped the crab salad into the container.

"Parks is so happy and well adjusted, though," the woman went on. "That's a blessing to see."

Tucker went through the process of bagging and ringing up, then insisted on taking the small package out to the woman's car.

He stepped back inside and halted, grinning and shaking an accusing finger at Kellyanne. "You're the lady who likes the big-ass shrimp."

She laughed. "Guilty as charged."

"Another dozen for you?" He took long strides to return behind the counter.

"Eighteen this time, and—"

"Clean out the yucky stuff?" Tucker finished. "I got it covered." He grinned and went to work.

Even in his bulky cargo shorts, Kellyanne could tell that Tucker had the most amazing ass she'd ever seen on a man. "Where's your little helper today?"

"You just missed him. He usually pops in around lunch. My sister keeps him during the day. They're off to a birthday party that'll have a space jump. So he's stoked." Tucker turned back and smiled.

"Forgive me for prying, but I . . . I couldn't help overhearing . . ."

He stopped working. "Yeah, I, uh, lost my wife about two years ago. A drunk driver smashed her head-on, right out there on Montauk Highway."

Kellyanne could feel the blood drain from her face. "I'm so sorry."

"Day by day. You know?"

She nodded, completely at a loss for words.

Tucker returned to the business of the shrimp.

A thought occurred to her. She knew it was too forward and grossly presumptuous, but she gave voice to it anyway. "I have an embarrassingly flexible schedule. If your sister ever needs a break or has a conflict . . . I'd adore the chance to look after Parks."

He spun around, regarding her with an amused curiosity.

Suddenly, she felt supremely foolish and extended her hand. "By the way, I'm Kellyanne Downey. I probably should've introduced myself *before* offering to assume responsibility for your child."

He laughed, wiped his hands, and shook gently. "Tucker McGraw. I appreciate it, but I can't just hand off my son to the big-ass shrimp lady. We'll have to get to know you a little better first."

It was a no. Yet Kellyanne felt not even the slightest hint of a rebuke. There was a soothing quality to Tucker's voice and a soulful sensitivity in his eyes. He treated her with a quiet dignity and respect, a circumstance so alien coming from a man that she briefly wondered whether she deserved it.

"I don't open the shop until noon on Mondays. Parks and I usually hit Flying Point in the morning and check out the surfers. Maybe you could join us next time."

Kellyanne smiled. This was the first time a man had ever asked for the privilege of her company without the implication or expectation of sex being part of the equation. It was the most wonderful feeling. "I'd love to."

Adam rang just as she was starting the car. "You have two hours to get to Brooklyn for the reading," he announced without preamble.

Kellyanne's heartbeat surged. "You've *got* to be kidding me."

"I don't know what happened. I've been trading voice mails with the casting director for weeks to stay current on this, but I just got a call from an assistant. They've broadened the search. Readings are going on right now."

A hopeless feeling shot through Kellyanne's solar plexus, and she let out a defeated sigh.

"Just go. They want a real beauty. I think you still have a good shot. Who knows? The *Soul Mates* baggage could work in your favor. Notoriety might be an asset, especially since you'll be playing against type. That's a good publicity angle."

"You say that as if slut is my default position," Kellyanne shot back. She glanced down at her vintage Bruce Springsteen T-shirt and cut-off denim shorts. "Adam, I'm not even properly dressed."

"Don't worry about it," Adam barked. "You barely have enough time to just get there and be seen." He gave her the Brooklyn address for JC Studios, then hung up.

Kellyanne programmed the destination into the GPS system of Liza's Lexus. As she gunned it down Montauk Highway, waves of alarm coursed through her.

Nothing about this felt like the beginning stages of a career break. Instead, it smelled suspiciously like more desperation all over again.

Kellyanne called Liza to explain about taking off with the car and bailing on dinner. She signed off and glanced over to notice the McGraw's Fish Market bag on the passenger seat.

The shrimp would spoil without a cooler, and letting it go to waste struck her as disrespectful to Tucker, so she stopped at the next available gas station for a quick Styrofoam and ice fix to rescue the seafood he'd prepared with his own hands.

For the rest of the way, Kellyanne fought hard to reinforce the situation with positive energy. *As the World Turns* was the second-longest-running soap opera in history and had churned out such stars as Meg Ryan, Julianne Moore, Courteney Cox-Arquette, and Dana Delany. Landing a contract player role would mean a grueling twelve-hour schedule and twenty to forty script pages to memorize for a single day's shooting. But it would also mean claiming a professional stake of her own. At last!

Upon reaching JC Studios, Kellyanne felt suddenly emboldened. It could happen. It *would* happen. She had to believe that more than anyone.

She dashed inside, slightly feverish and scarcely aware of anything beyond her own success-oriented agenda. But her optimism was put to the test when she discovered a room spilling over with blondes almost like herself—thirty years old (or close to it on either side), attractive, and fit. The only upside was that many of them had a brittle East Coast look about them. And as for the few Southern transplants in the running, none of them were a match for the Alabama goddess of sun and sand.

A ripple of awareness seemed to roll over several of the assembled soap dreamers. There were rude double takes and bitchy whispers all around.

"Are you *that girl* from *Soul Mates*?" one out-of-work actress asked.

"You do know you're auditioning to play an abstinence counselor, right?" another inquired.

As she sweated out the humiliation, Kellyanne delivered a silent stream of vile imprecations to Brad "Bonzi" Lucas.

Suddenly, a pretty, obese, apple-cheeked woman in her midthirties approached, clipboard in hand. "I did something awful. I hope you'll forgive me." She had an eager-to-please, rapid-fire delivery. "One of the supervising producers canceled you off the reading list, but I *had* to meet you. I'm *so* obsessed with *Soul Mates*. That's why I called Adam at the last minute. Is Dee really an evil bitch?"

A certain panic surged into Kellyanne's brain. "Do you mean I'm not even supposed to be here?"

"That's right, honey," an actress with pock-marked skin called out. "They cast for *Law and Order* hookers on the other side of the bridge."

The cacophony of laughter that came next instantly flushed Kellyanne's face. She knew it was scarlet. If the opportunity to exit the room via astral projection had been available, she would've jumped at the chance.

The heavy girl just stared back guiltily. "I can still get you in," she said in a hushed whisper. "I'll just say I never connected with your agent. You should totally read for this part. You're prettier than anyone else here."

Kellyanne cut a glance to the other actresses. They were dressed in character for Anna-Claire. She was dressed for a barbecue. Her heart drummed away. But what the fuck did she have to lose? If nothing else, she'd stand out from this gaggle of blond she-beasts.

"Yes, Dee really is an evil bitch," Kellyanne answered finally, taking pity on the TV junkie. "And Vlad is a total pig, not to mention a complete bore. If you have a crush, you can dream much better."

The woman seemed lit from within after receiving this nugget of inside reality wisdom. She pressed a script page into Kellyanne's hand and pointed to the door. "They still have your résumé and head shot."

She could feel an uptick of adrenaline as she entered the audition room to find three men and one woman seated behind a long rectangular table.

The hawk-faced man whose name plate pronounced him the head writer scowled at her attire right away. He looked impossible to charm or amuse.

Kellyanne's mind spun with positive computations. She'd read countless stories about seemingly disastrous auditions that resulted in actors actually getting the role. And that knowledge kept her planted in the room.

"Good afternoon, y'all. I'm Kellyanne Downey." She poured on the accent a bit thickly. But it was authentic.

"*Kellyanne Downey,*" the supervising producer repeated, and not in a way that made anyone think he was happy to hear the name again.

He staged a hushed miniconference with the casting director and executive producer, both of whom lobbed back unencouraging looks.

"We tried to get word to your agent," the supervising producer said. "But since you're already here. Go ahead and read."

Kellyanne glanced at the first line of dialogue.

"Just because you're physically ready for sex doesn't necessarily mean that you're emotionally ready." Her delivery was warm and earnest, as if talking to a niece.

"Okay, thank you," he called out, dismissively.

For one second, Kellyanne just closed her eyes and listened to her heartbeat and sweated and congratulated herself on having the temerity to walk into that room in the first place. It was a familiar place in her head. She'd been there far too many times.

And now it was over . . . so, so *over*.

Billie

19

Billie had never been so fucked up. There was a little bit of everything in her system—alcohol, cocaine, crystal meth, Ambien, Vicodin, even a handful of over-the-counter diet pills. Amazingly, she could still function.

"Play it back," Babydoll commanded from the studio.

The engineer in the control room obeyed the rude order. Within seconds, an urgent rock beat exploded through the monitors.

Babydoll and Tigger were the freakishly goth twenty-something fraternal twins who made up the production team known as White Tiger. While the music blared, their darkly painted eyes remained tightly closed, and their black-clad bodies swayed in a spastic, rhythm-obsessed groove. They were in some kind of hypnotic trance, at once listening for what they loved and hated about the track. It was creepy.

With fingernails that looked like they'd been pol-
ished with a nail color called Crude Oil, Tigger pan-
tomimed slicing his neck.

The engineer killed the playback.

"You caught a decent mood on that, but the vocal's
not quite there," Babydoll said. "Try it again."

Simultaneously pissed off and insecure, Billie
waited for the engineer to restart the prerecorded
backup.

Once again, high-energy bubblegum rock—remi-
niscent of Rick Springfield's 1981 hit "Jessie's
Girl"—blared from the monitors.

Billie gripped the RE-20 mic as if her life de-
pended on it, ripping into another vocal pass.

Does she know that I'm your lover?
Or do you keep that undercover?
Why don't you tell her I'm your side thing?
Your after-midnight nasty plaything
I know why you want me, I know why you
need me
Cuz she's not sleazy, Cuz she's not easy
Princess likes it sweet, Princess likes it nice
But I like it rough, and I let you do it twice
Who is she?
I bet she's asking
Who is she?
What do you tell her?
Who is she?
I'm the bitch from your honeymoon
Who is she?
I did your husband in the very next room
Who is she?
Just me

Babydoll signaled for the engineer to stop recording, then conferred with her brother and Todd Bana for a long exchange that Billie couldn't hear.

Finally, Tigger's voice crackled through the monitors. "You're not living it yet. Take a break. Get inspired. We'll try again."

Billie shot a look of dismay to the engineer. "What the fuck? That was a good vocal, right?"

The handsome, easygoing black man with one-carat diamonds gleaming from each ear merely grinned. "I've worked with them before. This could go all night."

Christ! It was nine o'clock in the evening. She was at Monster Island Recording Studio on West Twenty-first Street. And she was about to fall over. "Do *you* think my vocal was off?" Billie asked the engineer again.

He gave her a diffident shrug.

"Maybe it's their bullshit song!" She stalked out of the control room, meandering around until she found a bathroom.

There was a nice hit of coke in the pocket of her Rich & Skinny high-waist jeans. Yes! She needed something to get through the session. She snorted the powder off her long pinkie nail, lit a cigarette, and slid down the wall until she was sitting straight-legged on the floor. God, she wanted to sleep. But the cocaine would kick in any minute. It had to. Otherwise, she was fucked.

Todd Bana pushed open the door and stepped inside, closing it behind him. "You look like shit. And you sound like shit."

Billie struggled to glance upward.

Todd's face was dark, his eyes blazing. "You're fucking loaded."

"So?" Billie shot back, blowing smoke in his direction. "Is that only allowed when Mr. President is shooting it up my ass? You're the one who got me into meth."

He gave her a disgusted look. "It's supposed to be an *occasional* tool. I didn't realize you were an addict. I thought you had some backbone."

"Oh, I've got plenty of backbone," Billie snarled, feeling some definite oomph from the coke. "How else could I stand in that control room and sing that crap?"

His smile was cruel. "Is that your idea of singing these days? We thought you were vomiting."

"Fuck you!"

Todd snatched her Fendi bag.

"Hey, give that back!" She lunged for him, losing her cigarette in the process.

But he moved too fast, sidestepping her, rifling through the satchel, finding her pills, and one by one, throwing the plastic bottles onto the floor with an echoing clatter. "What the fuck, Billie? Look at all this shit!"

"It's from a doctor! I had a toothache! I needed something for the pain! And sometimes I have trouble getting to sleep!" She grabbed her purse from his hands and crawled around, desperately reclaiming her medicine.

"Go home," Todd said acidly. "You're in no shape to record. You're in no shape to do anything."

Billie stood up defiantly. "I'm fine! It's not me! It's them!" She pointed at the door. "It's those fucking freaks! This isn't how I record! I usually lay down vocals live with my musicians! This is fucked up! What kind of producers are they, anyway? They don't even work the boards! They just sit there looking like

Marilyn Manson groupies! I bet they're fucking each other! Two sick incestuous Satan worshipers! That's what they are!"

Todd laughed at her. "It's no wonder Amy dumped you. You're out of your goddamn mind."

"That dyke didn't cut me loose! I fired her!"

"Sure, baby, sure." He sighed impatiently. "Just get yourself cleaned up, okay? They'll be in town over the next several days to work with Gwen Stefani. We can reschedule the session."

"I said I'm fine!" Billie insisted. "Let's just nail this fucking track down!"

Todd held up his hands in mock surrender. "Okay, bitch. If you think you can. Don't let me stand in your way."

Billie studied him for a long moment.

Todd was such an arrogant bastard. And sexy in the way that only certain asshole guys could be. March Donaldson might be light years ahead of him sexually, but Todd still packed a big cock, and he knew how to use it. In the area of consolation lovers, a girl could do worse.

Billie pressed up against him and slipped a hand underneath the waistband of his jeans, pouting the luscious lips that had sucked him all the way to heaven and back on more than one sober and drugged out occasion. "Tigger told me to get inspired," she whispered. "I have a delicious idea on how to do that . . ."

Todd attempted to extricate himself.

But Billie clung to him with an almost savage intensity. The rush-rush of the coke was peaking. Oh, God, she felt as if she were the queen of the universe, or at the very least, the only bona fide rock goddess who could resuscitate Olympic Records from an industry-wide slump.

She toyed with the button and zipper on Todd's fly. "Fuck my throat. Come on. I want the taste of your cock in my mouth when I lay down this track." Slowly, she sank to her knees and peered up at him with hungry, determined eyes.

Todd groaned helplessly, pushing down his jeans and freeing his erection through the slit of his Thomas Pink boxers. His voice was thick with lust. "I am here to serve the artist." And then he shoved her head down with both hands . . .

A short time later Billie was back in the control room. There was a strange motor inside her, and it was running completely separate from her free will. She belted out the lyrics with a coke-fueled ferocity that bordered on the certifiable.

Does she know I keep you up every night?
Thinking 'bout our next time, you know that ain't right
What would happen if she read your e-mails?
All those dirty things you write to me without fail
I know why you call me, I know why you text me
Cuz she's not horny, Cuz she's not sexy
Princess likes romance, Princess likes to make love
But I don't need flowers, I just want to fu—
Who is she?
I bet she wonders
Who is she?
I think she knows
Who is she?
I'm the one who gets his booty calls
Who is she?
I'm the reason why he climbs the walls

Who is she?
Just me

Billie sang to that right-wing bastard March Don-aldson. She sang to his blue-blood bitch fiancée Amaryllis Hartman, too. Line by line, she inhabited the lyrics, every note bubbling over with gut-filled rage. Her vocals were raw, impassioned, and better than any singer had a right to be. If ever there was a second coming of Janis Joplin, then it was Billie Shelton at Monster Island on this track.

When she finished, Babydoll and Tigger were staring at her in slack-jawed amazement.

Todd Bana gave her a self-satisfied smile. No doubt he thought his impressive anatomy had some-thing to do with the talent she'd just displayed.

Even the engineer was blown away. "Damn, girl, where'd you get those pipes?"

Billie popped her hips and cooed, "I got it from my mama," coyly aping the smash hit by will.i.am.

The engineer cackled. "Miss Thang!"

Billie grinned before turning to address the studio with a newfound smug confidence. "That was just a scratch vocal, but I think you can use it as a final take."

Babydoll nodded. "It doesn't get any better than that, Billie. You rock."

"Yeah, that's what they tell me." She stepped out-side to get some fresh air and smoke a cigarette. Her nose was runny, and there was drainage going down the back of her throat like a goddamn faucet. Sud-denly, a wave of sickness overwhelmed her. She wretched on the sidewalk, gagging violently as she puked up what felt like the entire contents of her stomach. An instant film of sweat prickled her face and body. But she was better.

Part of the vomit had dribbled onto her AC/DC cap-sleeved vintage Trunk tee and stained the LOCK on the LOCK UP YOUR DAUGHTER banner. Billie smeared the mess with her palm and wiped her hand clean on her jeans. Shit. This crash was going to be one mean bitch. She fired up a Marlboro Light, pacing the sidewalk as her mind raced on all cylinders.

It was time to get her shit together career-wise. No more fucking around. But everything appeared to be falling into place. After all, she'd just recorded her first number one record. "Who Is She?" possessed the same quality as Avril Lavigne's "Girlfriend." Love it or hate it, the hook dug into the brain and stuck there like Krazy Glue.

Her mind shifted. She stewed about Todd Bana. Sometimes that five-foot-five fuck came off short-sighted and desperate. It was always White Tiger this and White Tiger that. Could Olympic really take her all the way? Billie began to wonder.

There used to be a proven system. A single got pushed to radio. Tower Records sold it. MTV played the video. The cover of *Rolling Stone* actually mattered. But everything was different now. Nobody listened to the radio anymore. Tower had gone bankrupt. MTV showed reality crap in 24-hour blocks. And a plug from that piggy pink-haired faggot Perez Hilton could do more for an artist than a dinosaur rag like *Rolling Stone*.

She tossed her cigarette stub into the gutter and lit another one, still ruminating. It was a brand-new world. Companies like Olympic were no longer the gatekeepers. They'd lost control. Todd could be on his way out, too. Sure, he was young. But he was also old school. Christ, Todd talked about MySpace as if it were a hot new thing. Even Billie realized that the social network site had lost its cool factor.

When her cell phone rang, she knew it was him.

"White Tiger is going fucking crazy!" Todd gushed. "They want to write more songs for you."

"You make it sound like such an honor. Maybe those freak twins are the lucky ones. Have you ever thought about that? Billie Shelton is singing *their* songs."

"It's a win-win," Todd said.

"Don't talk like a schmuck. I can hear that kind of shit in a one-day business seminar at the Learning Annex. Think big, motherfucker. Find a way to get my music in a movie or on a TV show like *Grey's Anatomy*. Or maybe you should slap your big cock across Ryan Seacrest's face until he says yes to a guest spot on *Idol*. And I want to record a remake of 'What's Love Got to Do with It?' Ask those freaks to produce. Call me when there's real news to report. I'll be in the Hamptons."

She hung up and flagged down a cab. There was still time to catch the Jitney at Lexington. The last connection left around eleven. Billie hopped on bus number seventy-three with minutes to spare and settled in for the three-hour ride.

Trying to sleep proved futile, even after swallowing two Ambien pills. Some kook in the row ahead was playing a vampire movie on a Sony VAIO. It was the 1922 silent classic *Nosferatu*. Billie pressed her face between the space in the cushions and watched the entire film, thinking about Shayne Cutter and wondering if he'd finished his screenplay.

The bus was half-empty. Billie stretched out on her row of three seats and gave napping another shot. She was just drifting off when a stupid bitch across the aisle distracted her.

"I want to do the show," the girl said loudly into her cell phone. "I know another girl who's interested, too. She's about five-ten, really hot, looks like me . . . The thing is, I can't get off work until four-thirty, and I can't, like, not work. I would really love to do it. I mean, it sounds awesome. A shoot for *Hamptons* magazine? I want to be in that magazine! Oh, my God . . . Oh, my God . . . Okay, so I'll be in touch. Ciao."

She hung up and made another call. And then another one after that. It was the same shit over and over again about some two-bit modeling gig that she was obviously not getting paid for.

Finally, the Jitney driver made an announcement. "The rule is one phone call—no more than three minutes. We have one passenger who's been on three calls lasting at least five minutes each."

"The phone is off!" the girl screamed. "Okay? So let's chill out."

Billie glared at her, making a quick assessment. The girl was an unremarkable beauty of indeterminate origin and no discernable talent—a total waste of human matter. "Fucking bitch," she muttered.

"Excuse me?" the twit challenged. "I don't appreciate that. I was on a *business* call."

"It sounded like volunteer work to me," Billie fired back. "Real models don't have to beg for gigs after midnight. They have agents."

The few passengers within earshot broke up into fits of laughter.

Humiliated, the girl covered her face with a pageboy cap and pretended to fall asleep for the remainder of the journey.

A short time later, the driver began to make all the tedious stops—Manorville, Southampton, Water Mill, Bridgehampton, Wainscott, and, finally, East Hampton.

Billie stepped off the bus and called Liza right away.

She answered with a groggy, "Hello?"

"I'm back!"

"Billie?"

"Which one of you lazy bitches is going to come pick me up? I'm at the Jitney stop."

"It's two o'clock in the morning," Liza croaked.

"Then you should get here in a flash. There's no traffic to fight."

Liza sighed. "Where have you been? We've tried calling you a million times. Is everything okay?"

Billie laughed. "Why wouldn't it be? I'm a rock star."

Liza

20

"Where's your sense of romance?" March challenged. "This is a fairy tale—a rich prince, a glass slipper. Maybe it's been updated to conflate with some of the raunchier elements of today's culture, but it's a classic setup. That's the reason for its success."

The Roundtable was back. *Soul Mates* was Topic A. And the gloves were off. This was bare-knuckled political debate, a verbal blood sport that took no prisoners.

Liza lunged forward. If she could've choked March with his own Armani tie and not been arrested for it, she would have. "What little girl dreams about a herpes-infected jerk sticking his tongue in twenty other women's mouths while she sits around and waits on him to decide whether he's interested—*or not*?"

Tom Shapiro raised a cautious hand. "Hold on, Liza. There's no medical confirmation regarding Vlad Branigan and any STD. At this point, it's only being reported as an accusation."

"I didn't mention anyone by name. I was speaking figuratively."

Tom remained firm. "We're talking about *Soul Mates*. He's the star of the show. And this allegation is in the headlines. Your implication is transparent. I have to insist that this program be fair and responsible."

Liza was shocked. Tom had never road-blocked her with such stridency. In fact, his treatment toward her bordered on hostile. But she charged forward anyway. "March, when you have children, is this the sick fairy tale you have in mind for your own daughter?"

March disarmed the masses with his trademark sexy grin. "What I have in mind for my own daughter is no dating until she's thirty. By then, I figure she'll be too old for a reality show like this."

The crew erupted with laughter, followed by Tom, and finally, even Liza herself.

If she could say nothing else for him, March Donaldson was a charming son of a bitch. Liza imagined that one day he'd run for high public office—and win.

"In the interest of full disclosure, I should say that I'm close friends with one of the show's cast members. She's been treated horribly by the producers and network involved, so my opinions on this subject might be stronger than usual. But I think most people who know me would agree that, personal connection or not, *Soul Mates* is a show that I'd find repugnant on even my most generous day."

March tilted his head and opened up his hands. "I just don't see the overarching danger here. It's a dumb reality show. To hold it up as a window into society is ridiculous."

Liza saw a chance to knock him down. "That's a lame cop-out, March. Even for you. Popular programs *are* a window into society. That's why we're here every week to provide commentary. It's not just an excuse to get your teeth whitened."

March's jaw went tight as he absorbed the vanity dig.

Liza thundered on. "My concern is the larger message that gets floated with crap like *Soul Mates.* There are millions of young women watching this show with uncritical eyes, and what seeps into their psyches is this notion that the brass ring for them is male validation. Don't sit here and tell me that's not dangerous for certain viewers. And I shudder to factor the impact on the women who actually participate in this contrived sexist garbage."

Tom interjected. "Let's bring in one of the show's behind-the-scenes consultants. If you've been watching *Soul Mates,* you'll recognize her as Dr. Deb, but in her professional civilian capacity she's Dr. Debra Brunman, now joining us via satellite from Culver City, California. Dr. Brunman, do shows like this dangerously reinforce female insecurities?"

"Tom, I'm a mental health professional, and there is nothing remotely dangerous about this program, whether participating as a viewer at home or as a contestant on the actual show." Bleached and Botoxed to the nth degree, the good doctor spoke in a gratingly robotic Elizabeth Dole–like cadence. "In my experience, it's the viewpoint of feminists like Liza who inflict the most harm on our young women. She makes them feel like less for wanting to fall in love, get married, and raise a family. It's my position that we need to support *all* of girls' dreams and aspirations."

Liza launched into full attack mode. "I'm curious about your credentials, *Dr. Deb.* Where did you attend medical school?"

"I have a PhD in counseling," she replied crisply.

"From what school?" Liza demanded.

"West Coast College of Art and Science."

"And is that an *accredited* institution?"

Dr. Brunman hesitated. "Yes, I believe that it is."

Tom started to protest Liza's line of questioning.

She cut him off with a polar look. "Actually, you're wrong about that, *Dr. Deb*. The West Coast College of Art and Science is an *unaccredited* diploma mill that requires no academic study at all for its degrees. So in light of your inadequate educational platform, I'll excuse your ignorance on today's subject."

Dr. Brunman's face turned scarlet.

Tom jumped in. "And that's it for our Culture Wars segment. We'll be back next week with more fireworks, I'm sure." He nodded intimately to the camera. "This is Tom Shapiro. Please join us again."

"And we're out!" the producer shouted.

March laughed uproariously. "Please—somebody put the last guest on suicide watch!"

Crew members chuckled at the suggestion.

"Damn!" March went on. "And here I thought the first ten minutes of *Saving Private Ryan* were tough to sit through." He turned to Liza. "Does the military know about you?"

Tom lashed out. "What the hell was that? This isn't your show. You can't just take down one of my guests."

Once again, his behavior mystified her. "Tom, when people attack me, I shut them down. That's how I operate. You know this. The real concern is the person who booked that idiot. Last night it took me thirty seconds on Google to find out she was a fraud."

"She's got you there, buddy," March chimed in.

"Let's face it. This is Liza's world, and we're just visiting."

Tom stormed off without a word.

Liza and March shared a dismayed look.

"Do gay men have a menstrual cycle?" March whispered.

Against all impulses of political correctness and good taste, Liza laughed. "You are *so* annoying."

"Thank you. I try."

She rolled her eyes and started walking out.

March fell into step beside her. "Maybe the ratings are slipping. I do a lot of these shows, and that can make a host pretty uptight."

"It's not that," Liza said. "The numbers are up. Tom has improved on year-ago averages by over thirty percent."

"What do you do—subscribe to Nielsen?"

"No, I just happen to expand my reading beyond *The Weekly Standard* and *Sports Illustrated*."

"Don't forget *Maxim*. I need something for the bathroom."

Liza put her hand on the exit door, then suddenly halted, the bizarre situation with Tom heavy on her mind. She looked back in the direction of the studio. "I don't want to leave like this. I should go talk to him."

"Maybe you should ask Dr. Deb for advice on how to handle it."

Liza tugged playfully at the Armani tie she'd pondered as an instrument of death just minutes before. "One day I think I might actually kill you." She smiled with exaggerated sweetness and started off.

March held out a hand to stop her. "Can I ask you

something?" He cleared his throat. "About a friend of yours?"

Liza gave him a curious look. She had a feeling . . .

"What's the deal with Billie?"

And the feeling was spot on. "In what context?"

"Is she crazy?"

"She's a rock star. She has to be a little bit crazy. Otherwise, what's the point?"

March shrugged in tacit agreement and glanced down at his Gucci loafers. He laughed to himself and shook his head as if to say, "What the fuck am I thinking?"

If Liza wasn't exactly sure a moment ago, then she was now. "You're having an affair with her."

March returned a guilty look. "You're trying to class it up."

"I was giving you the benefit of the doubt. My mistake."

"A few weeks ago she got pissed off and stole my luggage. I missed a flight to Colorado Springs and had to bail out on a speech that night. It cost me twenty-five thousand dollars."

Liza smiled wryly. "That sounds like Billie. So was it worth it?"

"I'm still thinking about her."

"Why are you telling me this?"

"I don't know. It's not a confessional . . . I just wanted some insight, I guess. There's a danger to her that I find . . . that I *found* appealing."

"In other words, you were addicted to the sex."

He smiled at her and nodded. "You see, this is why I like feminists. At times like these, it's almost the same as having a beer with a guy."

"Billie needs to be loved," Liza said earnestly.

"Okay, now you've ruined it. You sound like a chick again."

She leveled a serious look.

"At first, I thought she was just a wild time. I mean, come on, she's a rock singer. But she's just so needy."

"You're talking about a girl who lost both of her parents—one of them to suicide—before she got out of high school."

March blanched, every flippant instinct flash-frozen on his tanned and handsome face. "I didn't know that."

"There are obviously some substance abuse issues, too," Liza continued. "It's strange. I think she craves and despises the love of an audience at the same time, which would explain the hot and cold nature of her career. That kind of acceptance must be intoxicating, but after a concert, when no one's around . . . I can't imagine a lonelier feeling. So if you're just looking to get in the occasional grudge fuck for that twenty-five grand, show a little humanity and leave her alone." She observed him for a moment, picking up on his discomfort. "I take it this is more than you wanted to know."

"Yeah," he admitted quietly. "You could say that."

"Every girl has a story, March. That's Billie's. I'm sure you have no plans to break off your engagement with Amaryllis and appear in public with someone like her. That would be a disconnect to your family values image." Liza's eyes hardened.

He smiled without showing his teeth.

For the first time, Liza stared back at March . . . and didn't like him. "It's sad. Billie probably thinks that she's not good enough for you. But the real truth is, you're not good enough for her."

March looked exposed.

What an asshole. Choking him was too kind. He should be pushed cock-first through the wood chipper on George W.'s ranch in Crawford, Texas. But by next week, Liza would no doubt be laughing at March's dumb jokes again.

She left to seek out Tom Shapiro, scrolling her BlackBerry for new e-mails on the way. The most recent message brought her to a halt.

From: travisowen@yahoo.com

To: lizapike@mac.com

Subject: Favorite Song.

> I've been playing that old song by Blondie over and over again. Do you remember how it goes? "I will drive past your house. One way or another I'm gonna find ya."

Thinking of you, Travis Owen

"Sick fuck!" Liza hissed under her breath, giving serious thought to changing her e-mail address as she deleted the message.

The door to Tom's dressing room hung open, and he sat on a small sofa, desperately texting on his BlackBerry.

Liza pushed the e-mail terrorist out of mind and knocked twice to announce herself. "I think we were all much better off before we had those things."

Startled, Tom glanced up with a jolt. He seemed nervous, almost guilty, but not angry.

She stepped inside his sanctuary. "Are we okay? I tried calling you over the hiatus. I thought we had a plan for the Hamptons."

"Yeah . . . I meant to call you back, but . . . things got crazy." He glanced at his watch and avoided eye contact, as if already anxious for her to leave.

"Tom, it's been weeks since we've talked. That's unheard of for us. And you singled me out on today's show. What's going on?"

"Nothing," he answered. "I'm just in the middle of some . . . personal stuff. You're catching shrapnel. But it's not just you. Everyone around here is."

"Well, I'm a good listener," Liza said, easing down beside him. "And not a bad problem solver for life issues that aren't my own. Maybe we should take advantage of that limousine bar again."

Tom gave up a weak smile. His BlackBerry vibrated. Stealthily, he turned the device facedown.

In the corner, Liza noticed a gym bag half open and spilling over with racquetball gear. "Did you ever take on my jockstrap husband?"

"No, I've been playing with Jim Cramer, the *Mad Money* guy. He's an animal on the court."

Liza grinned. "Let me know if you want Justin's number. He could definitely give you a workout."

"He's probably too much for me," Tom murmured. His BlackBerry vibrated again. This time he stood up. "Listen, I'm in a text war with one of my producers over this immigration special we're trying to set up."

She took the cue. "The invitation to the Hamptons still stands. I'll be there through Labor Day, working on my new book. You're welcome anytime."

Tom nodded noncommittally.

Liza left feeling confused, sad, and unsettled. The

relationship dynamic she shared with Tom had shifted
on a dime. Something—or someone—had come between them.

Justin lived for action. The hotter it was, the better it
was. When the three-tone alarm sounded, he knew
he was going to get some good stuff. Oh, baby. He
loved a triple.

The fire burned out of control—orange flames,
black smoke, poison gas. And somewhere in this
apartment was an eight-year-old girl named Addison.

Her stupid cunt of a mother—the one who'd fallen
asleep smoking a cigarette and caused this shit—was
downstairs on the sidewalk losing her mind.

Justin moved on one knee, shuffling one boot
ahead, feeling his way through the dark, staying low.
Above the floor, the difference between two and five
feet could be four hundred fucking degrees.

"Hot enough, Calvin Klein?" It was Dick Flick,
his rescue partner. Everybody called him that because his favorite movie of all time was *My Big Fat
Greek Wedding*.

Justin whacked the bedroom door with a Haligan
until it burst open. The heat was more intense, the
smoke thicker. He heard a choking, sobbing shriek.
"Addison?"

No one answered.

Justin moved along the wall, crawled to another
closed door, and attacked it. Once inside, he found
his reason for being there screaming in the bathtub.
"I've got her!"

Fearfully, the girl shrunk away.

"It's okay," Justin said soothingly, scooping her
up in one quick sweep. "Your mom's waiting for
you downstairs. Let's go see her."

One little hand dug into his Nomex coat, the other grabbed the harness of his air tank and tripped the panic button on his PASS alarm.

Justin quickly reset it. His gut twitched. He could hear the fire eating through the ceiling, melting the staples and joists of the electrical system. "Let's go, DF. Get down first and tell the news crew to shoot my best side."

"That'd be your ass, right?"

Justin laughed and moved quickly, following his partner out along the same path that they used coming in.

Two men—nicknamed Pit Bull and Indiana Jones—were on the scene, working water lines that could spit two hundred and fifty gallons a minute. They sprayed defiantly into the flames, creating a steaming mist.

"Who's cooking back at the house, boys?" Justin asked. "I'm starving!"

"Hey, Mrs. Pike!" Indiana Jones called out. "You owe me five bucks from last week! Pay up!"

"Yeah, what's the problem?" Pit Bull put in. "Don't your TV star husband give you milk money no more?"

Justin shook his head. All the guys gave him hell, either for his underwear-model looks or for his liberated wife. Sometimes he hated them for it. But he'd still die for them . . . any fucking minute, any fucking day, any fucking fire.

There was enough smoke to lure WNBC, WCBS, plus a photographer from the *New York Post.* Channel Four's news chopper hovered over the blaze. Channel Five's film crew shot the happy ending. And the tabloid's lensman framed Justin and Addison in his best shot. Tomorrow's headline would scream HOT

RESCUE and feature that picture, along with a beef-cake inset of Justin's FDNY calendar cover.

Oh, man, it felt awesome to get up close and personal with a big fire again. For weeks, Justin had been stuck doing glorified milk runs like stabilizing car accident victims and breaking dogs out of locked-up cars. But this call had provided real action without serious injuries. And that was a damn good day at the office.

"Is your photo shoot over, Calvin Klein?" Dick Flick asked with a snort.

"Shut up and get on the fucking rig," Justin shouted. "You're just jealous because nobody wants to see your ugly mug in the papers!"

He smiled. It was nice to have that retard back on the job. Dick Flick had been recently forced off duty to deal with a breathing ailment after flunking the department's lung exam.

Justin loved him like an uncle. Even when Dick Flick dumped his wife and two kids to take up with the newly rich 9/11 widow of one of their own brethren, Justin stuck by him. He and Dick Flick had almost died together while buddy-breathing and awaiting rescue themselves during a hellacious sky-scraper fire. As far as Justin was concerned, the man could do no wrong.

When Justin and the rest of the engine and ladder crews stormed the firehouse kitchen, Danny Boy was busy chopping beef for cheese steaks. "How was the fire?"

Justin grabbed a handful of meat and stuffed it into his mouth. "Hot and smoky, you stupid twat. So we put it out."

The burst of macho laughter that came next shook the wood paneling on the cheap rec-room walls.

"Get fucked," Danny Boy shot back.

"He already did," Dick Flick put in. "On the way back. By the way, your sister says hello."

Everybody howled.

Danny Boy raised his carving knife in a mock threat.

They ate like pigs and complained like bitches. Pissed off at the union. Pissed off at the city. Pissed off at Rudy Giuliani. They'd forever be pissed off at that money-grubbing motherfucker.

Talk turned to sex—a wish list of the five celebrities they wanted to bang. Somebody joked that Scarlett Johansson would need a scheduling secretary to deal with all of them. It was the same conversation at the end of every meal. But Justin never tired of the banter. He loved the camaraderie. He loved these guys. He loved this life.

There was something soul-affirming about saving people. And he also appreciated the finality of a firefighter's community work. A cop could arrest a thug but see him out on the streets a few days later. But once Justin and his brothers put out a fire, it stopped burning.

He slipped out of the room to check his cell phone, grinning as he read the text from Tom Shapiro.

Anytime, anyplace. It's yours. Call me.

Justin tapped out a reply.

I might use you later tonight.

He waited. One thousand one . . . one thousand two.

What time???

The desperation revealed in the speed of the reply—not to mention the extra question marks—made him smile. His thumbs moved over the keyboard to answer.

Not sure. Just be ready.

It was amazing how much power Justin wielded over Tom Shapiro. He lorded over him. He fucking *owned* him. God, the feeling was fantastic.

This didn't mean that Justin was queer, though, or even bi. He still considered himself very hetero. Gay sex was just a hobby. Some men played golf. Some men watched NASCAR. Justin fucked guys into total submission.

The first incident happened a few years after he married Liza. He was helping the new engineman—a battalion chief's handsome nephew they'd nicknamed Hollywood—move into his first hole-in-the-wall apartment in Queens.

Justin joked about not getting any head at home and advised the young guy to stay single as long as possible. And then Hollywood offered to give him a blow job. Justin laughed it off. But a few minutes later, the determined dude was sucking his cock like a champ, better than any woman ever had. When it was over, they stepped out for chili and beer. Not much was said about what happened. But they expanded on the sessions until Hollywood died in the same skyscraper blaze that had almost killed Justin and Dick Flick.

In the beginning, he loved Liza. September 11 had done a number on both of them. She wanted a hero. He needed a damsel in distress. But how could a man stay in love with a woman who wanted him to be someone else? It's not as if he tricked her to the altar. From the jump, he was a fireman making a shit salary. But one day, Liza just decided that he was no longer good enough. Suddenly, she wanted him to make more, say more, do more, feel more. And the bitch had a subtle way of showing contempt that made him want to punish her in secret.

So Justin did. By neglecting her sexually and choosing to satisfy his own needs with other men, he was playing out the ultimate rejection. Liza had no clue, not even the slightest suspicion. That's what thrilled him the most. She walked around—so superior, so intelligent—yet all of this was happening right under her nose . . . with her neighbor Teddy Easton a few doors down, with her good friend Tom Shapiro at CNBC, and with others, too—the fitness trainer at Equinox, the famous New York Yankee, the divorce attorney who billed at a thousand bucks an hour. Yet she still thought he was the dumb fuck in the marriage. Fancy that.

His Nokia sang to life with Elton John's "The Bitch Is Back," a ring tone dedicated exclusively to her. "Hey."

"This won't take long," Liza began. "I'm on my way to the apartment to pick up some things. I've decided to stay in the Hamptons until Labor Day."

"Okay."

"That should give you plenty of time."

"For what?"

She sighed. "*Justin.*"

"What does that give me time for? I'm stupid, remember?"

"It gives you time to move out," Liza said firmly.

"Mature relationships require effort. They also require mature people who are willing to try. I can't do this anymore. I don't want to do it anymore."

Justin thought about Harper Ward, the divorce attorney. He had a socialite wife, four perfect children, and a weekly addiction to Justin in full firefighter gear, pillaging his ass.

"If you ever split up, I'll represent you as counsel," Harper had promised recently, after a particularly intense session. "I'll get you this loft. I'll get you alimony. I'll get you everything . . ."

Evenings on the beach had become Liza and Harrison's ritual. Sunsets and Merlot. That was their thing. Physically, it got no more intimate than him threading his hand through hers at some point as they walked. But emotionally, she was already a goner.

Liza could relax with Harrison in a way that she never had been able to with any other man. To make other relationships with men work—and this went as far back as college—there had always been an instinctive impulse to reduce her own stature to accommodate them in some way. But Harrison never transmitted the implicit signals that triggered those feelings. He was openly proud of her accomplishments, keenly interested in her work, and infinitely curious about the way that her mind went about its many calculations on issues of the day.

Liza had thought such a creature didn't exist. But, in fact, there *was* a straight, successful man who wanted a fiercely opinionated, highly principled woman, even a woman who cared as deeply about her career as he did about his.

Liza knew that she was strong and viable on her

own. But with Harrison by her side, she already felt as if her world were expanding. And she knew with absolute certainty that she could do more with him than she could ever do on her own. It was a strange, new, yet wonderful feeling.

She shivered slightly. The breeze off the Atlantic was whipping up her pleated shimmer dress by 3.1 Phillip Lim.

"Are you cold?" Harrison asked. But before she could answer, he stopped in the sand, pulling her close and wrapping his arms around her.

Liza experienced an instant warmth.

"I want you to meet my girls." His whisper was in her ear. "And they want to meet you, too. Especially Cassandra, my oldest. She's a little feminist. She's read *Whore* cover to cover at least twice. I'm supposed to visit her at Smith College this fall, and I've been informed that if you don't arrive with me, then there's no reason for me to come."

Liza drew back a little. "I like her already."

"Yeah, I'm not so sure I want the two of you to get together, though. It could spell doom for me at the dinner table. I think Cassandra hated *Watch Her Bleed* more than you did." He kissed her forehead.

As her mind shifted to the most recent e-mail from Travis Owen, Liza managed a distant smile. She'd shielded Harrison from the disturbing messages, knowing that his natural instinct would be to worry, overreact, and smother her with manly protection. Even though part of her longed for that, Liza resisted, hoping the creep would grow bored with his own antics and just recede from memory. But if the pattern continued, she would tell Harrison.

He was regarding her with concern. "What's wrong? You seem distracted."

"I'm just worried about Billie," Liza murmured. It was the truth . . . just not the whole truth.

Kellyanne

21

Parks McGraw bobbed in the swell of the Atlantic surf, riding a wave on his boogie board. It might've been a mere ankle-buster for a hot pro like Kelly Slater but, for the little boy, it was a tidal surge of big-man magnitude.

"Daddy, that wave was *epic*!" he shouted from the beach. He was clad in ultra-rad Quicksilver swim trunks, his shaggy blond hair was slick with salt water, and a messy triangle of zinc oxide was smeared across the nose of his sun-blasted face.

Kellyanne had never seen a happier, more gorgeous child. "Bless his heart. He's starting to sound like them, too."

Tucker laughed.

Parks idolized the Flying Point Crew, a group of guys in their midteens to late twenties who ran the Flying Point Summer School Surf Camp in Southampton. He made every attempt to look, talk, and dress just like them.

"And here comes the million-dollar question," Tucker predicted.

Parks ran over to them. "Daddy, how many summers before I do the surf camp?"

"You have to be seven years old, son. That's about three summers away."

Parks accepted the answer with a serious, upbeat nod, just as he had every other Monday morning for the last six weeks. Then he raced back to attack the waves again.

Kellyanne observed him with unabashed adoration. Her heart swelled as she fought the impulse to grab him, squeeze him, and smother him with kisses. "Look at that little butt!" she squealed in delight as Parks lost his board at the water's edge and bent over to retrieve it. "He's got your butt!"

Tucker smiled. "Leave my butt out of this."

"But he does," Kellyanne insisted lightly. "He's got your butt, your eyes, your hands, your walk. That boy's the spitting image of you."

"He's got his mother's mouth," Tucker said. "Holly had lips just like his."

Kellyanne fell silent.

And then Tucker did something that literally took her breath away . . . he slipped his hand into hers. It was such a simple, innocent display of affection. But tears still sprang to Kellyanne's eyes. The gesture meant more to her than she wanted to admit.

Oh, God, she'd been craving this for weeks. A touch, a kiss, a look—any sign at all that Tucker thought of her as more than the big-ass shrimp lady who tagged along on his Monday morning ritual with Parks. And the fact that he'd made such a move within the same breath of mentioning his late wife wasn't lost on her.

Kellyanne squeezed Tucker's hand, and they stood there on the beach, on this sparkling August day, watching Parks mimic the paddle movements of the older surfers surrounding him.

Ford Stewart, the member of the Flying Point Crew whom Parks regarded as nothing less than a superhero, swam over to give his board an encouraging little push.

"Take it away, Oakley!" Ford bellowed. He'd given him the insider nickname because Parks drooled over the display of Oakley sunglasses whenever he ventured inside the Flying Point Surf and Sport Shop.

Ford was nineteen, the son of two schoolteachers, and a popular, swoon-inducing instructor for the young girl campers, not to mention the mothers, nannies, and au pairs who dropped them off. With his laid-back stoner charm, surfer dude hair, and tattooed torso, he was beach stud personified.

Parks roared with excitement, beaming from the Ford Stewart assist as he rode the crest of the wave, having the time of his life.

Tucker smiled broadly as the scene unfolded. With an enviable masculine cool that came naturally to both of them, he traded long-distance air knuckles with Ford, then pointed at Parks. "Look at him go!"

She watched him watch his son. If ever there was any greater joy on a man's face, then Kellyanne had yet to witness it. The moment was glorious.

Parks wiped out on the wet sand, recovered in a flash, and dashed toward them. "Daddy, did you see me? That ride was *ill*!"

"It sure was," Tucker said, laughing gently.

"You were awesome!" Kellyanne praised.

Parks moved in close, wrapping one arm around Tucker's knee and his other arm around Kellyanne's thigh, squeezing them all together in a group hug. He gazed up. "Watch me again!" And he took off toward the water.

"One more time!" Tucker called out. "And then we've got to go!" He shook his head in bemused wonder, releasing Kellyanne's hand and looping an arm around her waist as his father's proud gaze stayed locked onto Parks like a tractor beam. "That boy."

She leaned into Tucker. This was the closest they'd ever been, and the proximity nourished her in the most profound way. It was like nothing she'd ever felt before. It was love. Deep love. The kind of love that filled every sense of emptiness she'd ever known.

"Thank you," Kellyanne whispered. She clutched both hands around his muscular arm and pressed her cheek against his broad shoulder.

He glanced at her curiously. "What are you thanking me for?"

"For letting me share this time with you and Parks. It makes me happy. I don't think I've ever been so content."

"This is the real Hamptons. There's a slogan around here—'Your vacation is our life.'"

"I could get used to this life," Kellyanne murmured.

Tucker chuckled. "A glamour girl like you? I can't see it. You'd get bored here after the summer."

"That's not true!" she protested, stomping a foot in the sand to drive her point home.

Now he was laughing. "What would you do? You

couldn't work at the fish market. I'd end up firing you."

Kellyanne was instantly offended. "Why?"

There was a flirtatious gleam in Tucker's eyes. "I don't know. Probably for sexual harassment."

Kellyanne could hardly believe it. The man was *finally* making his move. "Oh, so you think *I'd* be harassing *you*?"

He opened up his hands in a smug I'm-God's-gift gesture. "Obviously."

"Maybe you'd be the one harassing me."

He shook his head, and a sly grin spread across his face. "I'd keep you in the back cleaning fish. That way you'd smell too bad to fool around with." But all of a sudden, Tucker's expression turned serious. He licked his bottom lip and brushed a windblown strand of hair away from her eyes. "God, you're beautiful."

Kellyanne could hardly look at him. She wanted him so badly that she feared all her desire might be telegraphed in her eyes . . . and possibly scare him away. There'd been no woman in his life since Holly. She'd be the first. And instinct told her that it was important to let Tucker set the pace for everything. Unfortunately, the man moved slower than cold molasses running uphill in the wintertime.

He held her face in both hands, running sandy thumbs across her cheeks. "They say it doesn't matter how long it's been . . . that it's kind of like riding a bike." And then his mouth closed over hers.

Kellyanne shut her eyes. For the first time in her life, she imagined herself as a heroine in a romantic epic. It felt that spectacular to be in his arms.

Tucker's kiss plundered on, and she yielded to

him with complete and total abandon. He was so good, so pure, so decent. No better man could be out there. She felt certain of that. This guy was gold.

His approach to life was amazingly simple. He loved Long Island and had grown up in Hampton Bays, mowing lawns and building roofs on the mansions of Gin Lane until he saved enough money to start his own business. McGraw's Fish Market was a modest success, and Tucker lived with frugal discipline. He paid cash for everything, refused to own a credit card, and believed that the only loan a man should ever take on was for a home mortgage. His small cottage in Sag Harbor suited him fine.

The only TV program he watched regularly was *The Suite Life of Zack and Cody* on the Disney Channel, because it was Parks's favorite show, and he loved the sound of his son's laugh. Tucker owned a computer but rarely turned it on, thinking the Internet overrated and preferring the grit of newsprint between his fingertips when he read the paper with his morning coffee.

He thought politicians were in it for themselves, that paying a star 20 million a picture was obscene, that music got no better than the Eagles in perfect harmony, and that gossip was a waste of time.

Kellyanne stayed lost in the best kiss she could ever imagine, with the best man she would ever know. She felt truly, divinely, exquisitely . . . blessed.

If only to breathe, Tucker drew back, pecking the tip of her nose and tracing the outline of her upper lip with his index finger. "Have dinner with us tonight. At the house. I'll throw something on the grill."

Kellyanne nodded yes. It was easy. Because she would've said yes to anything he asked.

"If you feel like it . . . maybe you could stay over."

Her heart soared. "That sounds nice."

Tucker grinned and threaded his hand through hers, leading her down the beach toward Parks, who was listening with rapt attention to the surfing wisdom of Ford Stewart.

"Daddy!" Parks shouted. "Ford says I don't have to wait three more summers to do camp!"

Tucker and Ford engaged in a cool handshake, then bumped shoulders in a macho man-hug.

"I think we can relax that age rule for Oakley," Ford said. "He might be ready next summer. But if not then, *definitely* the summer after that."

Parks twirled around with his boogie board and started to sing. "I'm so happy, I'm so happy, I'm so happy."

Ford grinned. "This little dude's a trip. I could give him a private lesson in the afternoon. Nothing major. Just show him a few tricks."

"Daddy! Private lessons are the best!"

Tucker looked at Ford. "I know you get a hundred bucks an hour from the rich kids. How much for a fellow townie?"

Ford considered the question, scratching the faint stubble on his chin. "Hook me up with four lobsters. I need to impress my girlfriend's parents."

Tucker put out a deal-closing hand. "Done."

"*Sweet.*" Ford shook hard and fast and gave the whooping Parks an energetic high-five. He shot Tucker a teasing glance and zeroed in on Kellyanne. "Your lessons are free, by the way."

Tucker laughed. "It's bad enough you're corrupting my son. I can't have you doing the same to my girl."

The two little words thrilled her. *My girl.* Kelly-anne experienced a weightless sensation. And when Tucker's warmly possessive hand claimed her lower back, and his calloused fingertips skated down to the top of her Juicy Couture terry eyelet string bikini bottom, she was flying above the clouds.

They managed to nudge Parks toward the beach-front lot, where luxury vehicles like Liza's Lexus LX 470 were parked alongside the beaten-down vans and pickups driven by the surfers.

Parks bobbed his head up and down. The Flying Point Surf and Sport Shop was ready for business, and the music of Linkin Park was rocking from inside. The little boy stared longingly at the open door.

"Let's move, Parks," Tucker said sternly. "We have to get you over to Aunt Rae's, so I can get to work."

"Why not let me take him for the day?" Kelly-anne suggested quietly. "I'll let him hang out here for a little while and then take him back to the house."

Tucker appeared uncertain. "Rae has him on a schedule."

"I'll make sure he has a good lunch and gets in a nap," Kellyanne promised. "And later tonight we'll both drive over."

He still hesitated. "Are you sure about this?"

"*Yes.* Besides, your sister could use the break. And I could use the company. Liza works on her book all day, and Billie usually sleeps in the afternoon." She gave Tucker an imploring look.

"Okay." He shared the new plan with Parks.

The boy pumped his fist in the air with a loud hoot and grabbed Kellyanne's hand to pull her inside the shop.

Tucker grinned and started for his Jeep Wrangler, then turned back to yell, "Don't let him talk you into buying him anything in that store!"

But Kellyanne couldn't resist. If Parks coveted something, she added it to the pile, which now included patchwork Billabong shorts, a Quicksilver tee, Reef sandals, a dive watch, and even a new style of Oakley sunglasses called Monster Dog. They were too big for his little face—ridiculously so—but Parks thought they were the coolest shades in the world.

Tucker would be furious. But Kellyanne decided to deal with that later. Spoiling Parks gave her such a wonderful feeling inside. The damage came to over four hundred dollars. Out of sheer habit, she put down the credit card that billed directly to Walter's corporate office. Suddenly, she snatched it back and wrote out a personal check drawn on the bank account that stashed her Silk Electric earnings and paltry commercial residuals.

Head to toe, Parks wore everything out of the store and insisted that they find Ford to show him the new sunglasses. "Now I'm *really* Oakley!"

"You sure are, dude." Ford tried on the Monster Dogs and struck a cool pose. "Nah. They look better on you."

Parks slipped them back on, glowing with pride.

Kellyanne was helpless again when he led her to the Fudge Company next door for ice cream. Over an enormous scoop of chocolate chip cookie dough, he talked nonstop about his upcoming private lesson with Ford, his desire for a puppy, and his wish that everyone start calling him Oakley instead of Parks.

Several times, Kellyanne had to stop from laughing at the way he went on and on about himself. It was hilarious. Only on the edge of four and already just like a man. As soon as they arrived at the summer share, Parks discovered the pool. She helped him change back into his swim trunks, and he jumped in with his boogie board, splashing with wild glee.

A few minutes later, Billie shuffled out, looking terminally hungover. She scowled at Parks. "What the fuck is that?"

Kellyanne glared at her. "A child."

"What's it doing here?"

"*He* is Tucker's son, Parks."

Billie covered her bloodshot eyes with jumbo Chanels. "I take it the fisherman's too poor to afford day care." And then she flopped down onto a chaise, fiddled with her iPod, and began flipping through *Us Weekly*, muttering curses about Lindsay Lohan.

Kellyanne gave full consideration to pushing Billie into the pool. But in the end, she told herself that all the alcohol toxins still lurking in Billie's skin pores might upset the water's sensitive chemical balance. With a positive psychology mind-set, Kellyanne focused every bit of her attention on Parks.

Until her cell phone began to play Dr. Dre's "Nuthin' but a 'G' Thang." Oh, God, she hated that song. It was Walter.

Kellyanne hadn't seen him for more than six weeks. For her, the hiatus had been paradise found. But for Walter, it was only a series of calamitous events that kept him away. The storm of lawsuits from presale buyers looking to get out of their contracts had intensified, forcing one of his condo projects into foreclosure. His wife, Connie, had fallen off the ladder in the library of their Key Biscayne home and broken her hip. And Cagle, his youngest son, had been despondent over a breakup with a girlfriend and nearly overdosed on liquid heroin; now he was recovering in a Malibu rehab facility that would cost Walter eighty thousand dollars a month.

The absence was heaven, but enduring regular phone calls had become an underestimated chore. Walter droned on endlessly about his problems—the relentless real estate lawyers, Connie's constant bitching about pain, Cagle's rehab bills, even his own back trouble. Kellyanne forced herself to listen with vague interest, offering occasional platitudes of encouragement. Her plan was to enjoy the summer and make a clean break from Walter after Labor Day.

"How's my girl?"

The question sickened her. Walter Isherwood could go to hell. She was Tucker McGraw's girl now.

"I just passed the Jade building on my way to a meeting, and I thought, 'I can't wait until my girl's back in that swanky pussy palace where she belongs.' "

Kellyanne fought the urge to vomit.

"I'll be in New York . . . where the hell are you?"

She made a half-hearted attempt to hush Parks. "I'm babysitting for a friend."

"It sounds like you're at a Chuck E. Cheese's. Go someplace where you can talk."

"Hold on," Kellyanne said acidly, hating it when he snapped out orders. She covered the phone with her hand. "Parks, I have to take this call inside. Don't go near the deep end, okay? Stay right where you are."

He nodded obediently, then paddled away on his boogie board.

Kellyanne stalked over to tap Billie on the shoulder.

The perpetual party casualty looked up with an annoyed expression, making a show out of removing the earpods that were booming Kanye West's "Stronger" at deafening volume. "What do you want? You know I'm a total bitch until at least three in the afternoon."

"It's five, actually," Kellyanne corrected. "I need you to watch Parks for a few minutes. Make sure he doesn't go into the deep end."

"What am I? Super Nanny?"

"Billie, *please*. I'll be right back." She dashed inside and padded into her bedroom, praying desperately that a minute ago she had *not* heard Walter utter the words *I'll be in New York.* "Okay. It's quiet here."

"As I was saying, I'll be in New York at the end of the week."

Shit. Kellyanne closed her eyes.

"I booked the same suite at the St. Regis. I'm just there for one night, but I'll be making up for lost time with you. Count on that."

The mere thought repulsed her. His life had been in such continual discord that she never expected this to happen. Kellyanne honestly believed that she'd get through the remainder of the summer without being beckoned to the city and forced to serve out another term as Walter's hotel sex prisoner.

"You must be hungry," Walter said thickly. "I bet you've missed daddy's big dick."

Kellyanne recoiled. "Please don't talk dirty over the phone, Walter. You know how much I hate that. It's disgusting."

"You spoiled little bitch!" Walter exploded. "I've been going without it for six weeks! You'd be *here* to get me off if I hadn't been so fucking gullible as to bankroll this summer escape of yours! Show some goddamn appreciation!"

Kellyanne could visualize the fat vein that throbbed on Walter's forehead whenever he got angry. She knew it was being put through a serious workout right now. "Calm down."

"*Calm down?*" His voice was seething. "No, you *get down* . . . on your knees and suck my dick! That's how I expect to be thanked for all the things I do for you. And if you don't want to do it, I can find a replacement *like that.*" He snapped his fingers. "Don't think that being branded this summer's most famous reality TV whore makes you special. I could pop a Levitra and find ten girls just like you before my cock gets hard. But *me*? I'm one in a goddamn million. There's not another sucker in the world who'd pay fifty grand to let his mistress play Barbie's beach house for three fucking months. Believe that."

There was a beat of silence.

"Are you finished?" Kellyanne asked coldly.

"No, I'm not finished. In fact, I haven't even started yet." His voice painted a dark threat. "Your feminist friend can pull off that empowerment bullshit, but you can't, baby. My flight lands at eleven on Friday. Be at the hotel by noon." And then Walter hung up.

Kellyanne's eyes welled up with tears as the anger, bitterness, and resentment crystallized in a torrent of emotion. All these wasted years with him . . . and for what? To be regarded like a street hooker. And to hate the bastard so much that she secretly wanted him to die.

The *Soul Mates* insult was the lowest blow. Walter knew firsthand how excruciating those few weeks had been for her. Not to mention for her parents. But just as Liza had predicted, the storm winds eventually shifted as other scandals rose up to assume media domination. Thank God for the conservative senator's airport bathroom gay sex frolic. His personal Waterloo had eclipsed everything for days. After that came the comedy superstar's suicide attempt, then the leaked hotel security video of the trashy pop star physically abusing her children.

The relief was also aided by the fact that the success of *Soul Mates* had been short-lived. It burned hot and fast, like a hot pink meteorite flashing through the night sky and extinguishing before hitting the ground. In fact, ratings erosion had been so severe that Fox yanked the show off the schedule and posted the last few episodes online to placate the few remaining die-hard viewers. Bonzi's next effort, *America's Hottest Bartenders,* had suffered a worse fate—premiering to abysmal numbers and getting the official ax the very next day.

So just as quickly as she'd become a scandal culture icon, Kellyanne was dismissed as a forgotten footnote of tabloid excess. In the weeks that followed, she'd fashioned her own spiritual retreat. She took long walks on the beach. She read self-help books like *Happier: Learn the Secrets to Greater Joy and Lasting Fulfillment.* She sipped coffee by the pool with Liza every morning. She made a regular Vespa ride to Wainscott to shop at Lisa and Bill's produce stand and indulge in the cheese Danish at Breadzilla. She joined Liza and Harrison for regular dinners at Nichols for seafood pie, never once feeling like the proverbial fifth wheel. And she made the magical discovery that was Tucker and Parks Mc-Graw. The sum of it all sealed off the hurt of being rejected by *As the World Turns*.

My flight lands at eleven on Friday.

So fucking what? She no longer had any use for that information. Her disconnection to Walter—to everything and everyone in Miami—was total. He could burn the contents of her apartment. He could drive her Mercedes into Biscayne Bay. Kellyanne would start over with nothing. Correction. She would start over with *everything*. Because all she needed was her self-respect.

Be at the hotel by noon.

"Never again, you son of a bitch," she whispered. "You better hope that the St. Regis butler gives good head."

She blotted her eyes with a tissue and dashed back to relieve Billie. With every step, she felt the most delicious sense of freedom. From now on, it'd be a whole new way of living, dreaming, and loving.

Kellyanne stopped. Her heart lurched. Her stomach twisted. Her mouth gaped open. She took in all the scenes at once.

Billie sunbathing in complete oblivion as she lay flat out on the chaise, her eyes shielded by gigantic pitch black plastic lenses, her ears plugged tight by bud headphones.

Parks facedown near the bottom of the pool's deep end, his Sunkist orange boogie board drifting on the surface, in the corner, so far from his reach.

Kellyanne fell to her knees. Because she knew. And the agony of the reality took her down. The sound that came next was primal. It was her heart shattering into a million pieces. She screamed louder than she ever thought humanly possible.

Billie never heard a thing.

And Parks never moved. He was motionless. He was lifeless. He was already dead.

Billie

22

Billie was lost in the lazy Dirty South hip-hop of Kanye West's "Can't Tell Me Nothing," her head bobbing to the beat as her mind related to the lyrics.

"I feel the pressure, under more scrutiny," Kanye rapped. "And what I do? Act more stupidly."

She grooved to the music. Fuck, yeah. Billie was into this shit. Suddenly, an idea dawned on her. Maybe she should take her sound in a more rhythmic direction. A sexy urban vibe could generate real career heat. Nelly Furtado had glommed onto Timbaland, and the rest of that story was platinum.

Billie grimaced. Why hadn't Todd suggested this? Did she have to think of every fucking thing? Sure, the White Tiger session had produced a solid winner. "Who Is She?" was a hot-ass track. But the rest of their songs were so *craptacular* that Billie had refused to show up to record them.

Internet freaks were still pissing on the tunes from her third—and permanently shelved—CD that had leaked online. It was the same old shit. Everybody

accusing her of phoning it in since *Dick Magnet*.
Everybody grousing about "Make Me Laugh and
Make Me Come and I'll Fucking Marry You" being
her only great song. Whatever. Those screen suckers
didn't pay for music anyway. They stole it through il-
legal downloads. And why record substandard White
Tiger drivel and give those cheap fucks more grist
for the bad-buzz mill?

Billie thought about calling Todd Bana and telling
him to get his goddamn head in the game. She'd put
her future in his hands. And so far, all she had to
show for it was one single in the vault. Better material existed out there for her. Did she have to find it,
sing it, *and* promote it? Screw Todd Bana!

Maybe she should start her own fucking record
label. Plenty of independent acts were doing it. But
the thought instantly exhausted her. Billie was an
artist, not an entrepreneur. Plus, there were certain
things that only a major label could make happen.
When all was said and done, the big corporate giant
had her in a sling. Christ!

She tapped her iPod, killing Kanye West and giving life to 50 Cent. The mogul thug's swaggering,
filthy slab of sultry beats called "Ayo Technology"
blasted loud enough to cause brain damage. When
Justin Timberlake started cooing the hook, Billie
was in hip-hop heaven. She dreamed a little. It'd be
an awesome coup if JT produced a cut for her. Any
linkage to that sexy motherfucker was hotness guaranteed.

Billie jolted violently as the music stopped cold.

Liza had ripped the headphones from her ears
and slung the iPod across the deck. "Call 911!" she
shouted, then raced to the pool's edge and dove in
with her clothes on.

Kellyanne was collapsed on the other side, screaming her vocal chords to shreds.

What the fuck was happening?

Billie saw the little boy sunken at the bottom . . .
like a pebble. Why were they freaking out? He had
to be playing dead. Kids pulled that kind of shit all
the time.

Liza pulled him out of the water, gingerly placing
him face up on the concrete. She glanced at Billie.
"Call the fucking ambulance!"

Billie fumbled for her cell phone and dialed. The
emergency bitch seemed to have a million dumb
questions. "Where the hell are we?" Billie shrieked.

Liza yelled out the North Bay Lane address as
she tilted back the boy's head and lifted his jaw to
open his airway.

Billie relayed the information and tossed down
the phone. She stood up, not sure of what to do,
feeling useless.

Liza seemed to be examining the child for any
sign of life, first with her ear to his mouth, then with
just her hand. "He's not breathing."

Kellyanne's screams turned to eerie silence. As
tears rolled down her cheeks, she stared with the
blankest eyes Billie had ever seen.

Liza pinched the boy's nose, closed her lips around
his mouth, and breathed in two slow breaths. She
placed her hand on the inside of his wrist. And then
she waited. "There's no pulse. I'm starting CPR."

Oh, shit. Billie clutched her stomach.

Liza placed the heel of her hand between the boy's
nipples, compressed his chest at least thirty times,
and again gave him two breaths, this time more significant ones.

Nothing happened.

Billie blanched. If the kid died, everybody would blame her. She knew that. Well, fuck. How was this *her* fault? If the little brat couldn't swim, then he shouldn't have been in the goddamn pool.

Liza started to repeat the CPR pattern. Suddenly, she halted. "He's breathing!"

Billie experienced a wave of relief.

Kellyanne shut her eyes, pressed her hands together in prayer, and thanked God over and over again.

Billie thought it was *Liza's* rescue. Southerners! They loved to cook the books and give Jesus credit for just about everything.

The boy opened his eyes and coughed up water. He appeared weak and disoriented . . . but he was alive.

Liza maintained a steady hand on his pulse.

From a distance came the sound of an advancing siren.

"*Kellyanne,*" Liza said firmly, "Parks is shivering. Go inside and get him a blanket from the linen closet."

Kellyanne broke out of her trance. She disappeared into the house, returning with a cream-colored fleece throw just seconds later.

The ambulance arrived, and paramedics rushed the scene in full emergency response mode. The boy was lifted onto a stretcher. When someone announced that he'd be taken to Southampton Hospital, Kellyanne insisted on riding with him.

"I'll call his father," Liza said. "We'll meet you at the hospital."

Kellyanne mouthed a silent, desperately grateful, "Thank you."

Billie watched them go. It was crazy. Just a few

minutes earlier, everything was fine. But now that
annoying kid had almost drowned, and Kellyanne
had suffered some kind of psychotic break.

She braced herself for the blame game. It was
coming. Billie could feel it. As soon as the initial
shock and drama subsided, everybody would start in
with the finger-pointing. Liza's Wonder Woman act
made her bulletproof. And Kellyanne was too beautiful and too damaged to attack. So the default maneuver would be to bash Billie. What fucking bullshit!

Now Billie found herself in the passenger seat of
the Lexus. She was still in her Michael Kors chain
lace-up one-piece. Liza was still in her lived-in
jeans and L.A.M.B. tee, soaking wet.

They drove in hot pursuit of the ambulance. Liza
had one white-knuckled hand on the steering wheel,
the other on BlackBerry duty. She dialed Information for the number to McGraw's Fish Market, then
followed up with a call to the boy's father, breaking
the news in a calm, measured tone.

Billie wished she'd stayed back at the house. All
the hullabaloo had her itching for a couple of drinks
and some pills. The kid was going to be just fine.
Why did they all have to do the hospital vigil bit?

Liza was speeding. She veered slightly to the right
as Old Northwest Road became Stephen Hands Path.
"What happened back there?"

"I was watching him," Billie lied. God, she needed
a cigarette. "He was fine. I just closed my eyes for a
minute, and then . . ."

"*A minute?*"

Billie said nothing.

"You were *completely* out of it. The entire population of East Hampton could've been drowning in
that pool, and you wouldn't have known it."

"Oh, come on!" Billie raged. "Don't try to put this shit all on me! What about Kellyanne? She shows up with this kid who can't swim, and the first thing she does is turn him loose in the pool! Then she pulls a disappearing act like fucking Criss Angel!"

It was a silent ride for the next ten minutes.

When they arrived at Southampton Hospital, Liza parked illegally and rushed inside the emergency room entrance.

Billie noticed an older woman smoking outside and stopped to bum a cigarette.

The woman quietly obliged.

"We smoke the same brand," Billie observed. She put the Marlboro Light between her lips and allowed her new best friend to fire it up. "This is better medicine than anything they've got inside."

The woman grinned, appearing tense but still grateful for the company and the distraction. "I've always hated hospitals," she said.

Billie took a meaningful drag. "Yeah, they suck."

The woman was attractive, probably in her mid-fifties, and sporting the largest solitaire diamond on her left hand that Billie had ever seen. No doubt she lived in one of those massive estates hidden behind twelve-foot privet hedges.

The woman's husband was having heart surgery—a triple bypass. The doctors said he'd die if he didn't quit smoking. But he couldn't kick the habit. Neither could she.

Billie told her about the near drowning.

The woman took a long drag, shaking her head. "There was an angel looking out for that child today. Last summer, my daughter's best friend lost her seven-year-old in a pool accident. It's not like on television where there's screaming and splashing.

Drowning is a silent killer. A child can slip under-water and sink straight to the bottom. Only takes a minute."

Billie felt emboldened. None of this was her fault. The woman's story proved that. She walked inside to find Liza, Kellyanne, and Tucker in close conference with a young female doctor wearing green scrubs. From a distance, the news looked good. There were thankful smiles, sighs of relief, and warm, celebra-tory embraces.

But when Kellyanne saw Billie, the expression on her face turned to ice. She fought Liza's attempt to hold her back and came vaulting toward Billie, eyes blazing. "I'll never forgive you for this! Never! You make me sick!"

Liza moved fast to intercede. "Kellyanne, this isn't the time or the place."

Billie glared at both of them. "And there won't ever be a time or a place. Nobody's going to blame me. This shit happens all the time. It was an *accident*."

"God!" Kellyanne cried. "You're the most selfish person I've ever met in my life! I asked you to watch him for a few minutes! Just a few minutes! But you can't be bothered to do anything for anyone but your-self! And you don't even care! A precious little boy almost died, and you don't even care! What kind of monster are you?"

"Maybe you're the monster," Billie shot back. "Stop trying to pass the buck and think about that for a minute. If the brat couldn't swim, then at the very least he should've been wearing a pair of those float-ies. Seems to me like five bucks and a trip to Target would've kept him out of this hospital. But what do I know?"

Liza attempted to pull Kellyanne away.

But Billie bulldozed on. "And why did you push him off on me anyway? Why was that phone call so fucking important? Who was it?"

Kellyanne didn't respond. She didn't have to. The ugly answer was all over her beautiful face.

"It was him," Billie said. "Your rich old married sugar daddy from Miami called, and you couldn't get rid of that kid fast enough. That's the reason he almost died."

Kellyanne turned ghostly white. She seemed fatally stricken by the accusation. Glancing over her shoulder, she froze.

Tucker was staring, his granite face immobile. He'd heard every single word. And he looked impaled by them. "Is this true?" His voice was equal parts surprise and disgust. "I trusted you with my boy, and as soon as the telephone rings, you hand him over to *this woman*?" He pointed at her as if she were some kind of degenerate.

Billie wanted to kick him in the balls. No way was a fucking fisherman going to pass judgment on her. She opened her mouth to protest.

But Tucker waved all of them off and stalked down the corridor, shaking his head with self-loathing. He stopped suddenly and punched a wall with a balled-up fist. "I should've known!"

Shamefully, Kellyanne buried her face in her hands.

Billie didn't stick around to survey the rest of the damage. She found Liza's keys in one of the waiting room chairs and took off with the Lexus, driving aimlessly as the deeper truths presented themselves.

A little boy had come close to dying. Because of her. And Kellyanne's future with a decent guy was shot to hell. Because of her.

Billie tried to reach March. His phone rang straight to voice mail. He never answered her calls. She knew that contact was on his terms only, and ever since their last encounter at the Hudson, he'd cut it off entirely. But she dialed back several times anyway, just to hear him recite the outgoing message.

Tears rained down Billie's cheeks as she pulled into a gas station to buy cigarettes and whatever alcohol she could find.

That night she hit Stereo by the Shore, the former Tavern space along Tuckahoe Road. It was the beach sister to Stereo NYC and the hottest dance club in the Hamptons.

Billie needed to party. But more important, she needed to forget. And it had nothing to do with the almost-drowning. That episode was already a distant memory. Right now what she wanted to crash out of her mind was anything associated with Todd Bana.

His call had come through just a few hours ago. "Billie, it's over. White Tiger's sick of your bullshit. They're done."

"What do you mean *done*?"

"They want out of the Billie Shelton business."

Billie had snorted. WHITE TIGER SCRATCHES OFF SHELTON! DROWNING KID SAVED IN THE NICK OF TIME! Even with those dopey headlines, it was still a slow news day. "Who cares? I'm better off without those goth freaks. They only gave me one decent song anyway."

"Which is no longer yours," Todd had announced. "'Who Is She?' went to Ashlee Simpson."

That little slam had truly enraged Billie. "They can't give my fucking song to that lip-synching bitch!"

"It's not *your* song. It's theirs. And now it's hers."

"Whose side are you on?" Billie had demanded. "This is bullshit!"

"*Was* bullshit." Todd's tone had been flat, the words hitting with frigid finality. "I want out of the Billie Shelton business, too. You're off the Olympic roster."

And before she could launch into a spew of venomous curses, the line had gone dead. It was over. She was out. The motherfucker had actually dropped her from the label.

Billie tried not to think about it as she held court in one of the freestanding pagodas in the VIP area. She was downing Dom Perignon and snorting strawberry cocaine, courtesy of a brilliant thug known as Domestic Violence.

She was crushed up against his two-man posse—one an ugly errand boy called Sea Biscuit on account of his twelve-inch dick, the other a statuesque bodyguard and near clone to actor Djimon Hounsou. They called him Big Smurf because his skin was so black it looked blue.

Stereo by the Shore was full, frantic, and loud. The party carnage could only be described as heavy-duty. And Billie was right in the middle of the so-hot-it-must-be-lethal riot, sex-scamping her way to career resurrection.

Big Smurf's big hands were working their way up her Derek Lam silk camisole dress. And she let them. There was no Amy Dando to clean up after her this time. Billie had to find a new way to make the deal happen.

"I sound like Joplin!" she shouted over the stripped-down beat of Lil Mama's "Lip Gloss."

Domestic Violence chugged the Dom straight from the bottle. "Who?"

"Janis Joplin!"

"Never heard of that bitch." He glanced at Sea Biscuit and Big Smurf, who offered clueless shrugs.

Billie could hardly believe their ignorance. Hip-hop was a whole new world. Obviously, she'd have to adjust. "I guess you could say I sort of sound like Amy Winehouse!"

Domestic Violence perked up. "Oh, damn, so you got some bluesy shit going on! That's hot!"

"Real hot," Big Smurf echoed.

The only reason the ex-cons had ever heard the name Amy Winehouse at all was because Jay-Z provided the guest rap on her "Rehab" remix.

Domestic Violence was nodding. "I could work with some shit like that."

He was a second-tier artist/producer, nowhere close to the level of a Timbaland, Pharrell, Swizz Beatz, or Danja, but still considered a name. His biggest success to date had been his own hit, "Yeah, I Did That," which offered the backstory for his stage name in graphic detail—the girlfriend he pushed out of a moving car, the girlfriend he sent to the emergency room twice in one night, the girl-friend he put in a wheelchair. And that was just the first verse.

Since the age of eighteen, Rikers Island had been his home away from home. The essence of *authentic thug* emanated from Domestic Violence like kettle steam. His tattoos had been carved in with straight razors, his muscles built up in the prison yard. He was the kind of man who made people instinctively power-lock their car doors, even if he was on the other side of the street. And all of that could only do Billie good.

She grinned. Running into this walking rap sheet outside the club had been deliciously serendipitous. She had no intention of placing drummer ads in music papers and tacking BASS PLAYER WANTED flyers in guitar shop windows. That was the old rock direction. She was taking a new street path. Because a white hip-hop bitch *always* got attention. That was provocative, rebellious, printworthy, *forbidden.* And Billie needed to stand out like neon to get a major label's attention.

Right now the business was tense, reactionary, and in constant panic mode about a feared free fall. Execs were signing and cutting artists for the wrong reasons. The music was secondary. Selling it was all the suits cared about—having it out by a certain release date, getting it in a movie or on a TV show. She included White Tiger in that group. Babydoll and Tigger might wear makeup and dress like morticians on acid, but they still had the musical souls of McDonald's CEOs.

Billie went back and forth constantly, embracing the idea of selling out one minute, then reacting against it the very next. Was she a musical purist? Was it the drugs? Who knew? And who fucking cared? If she wanted to make a decent living in this business, she would have to bend over. Literally, no doubt. That much was obvious. And to make some real money, she'd probably have to launch one of those cheap fashion lines.

Christ! Did raw talent even matter anymore? And goddamn the iPod! The concept of buying an album was on the way out thanks to that fucking device. People just wanted to download a few good tracks, if that many. All of this made the portals of the major league music industry practically impenetrable. But Billie would find a way back in. She had to.

Sea Biscuit was pouring Dom straight down her throat as Billie lay flat-out on the VIP table with her head hanging over the edge. Big Smurf had her dress pulled up to her waist and was giving her a gynecological exam. Domestic Violence was probing her mouth with his fingers. She could taste the metal of his bling jewelry.

DJ AM did his thing. At Sea Biscuit's persistent request, the mix-master was finally blasting Domestic Violence's trademark smash and claim to fame. The music beat its way into Billie's coked out skull. Upside down, she watched Amaryllis Hartman make her way to a pagoda nearby with an armada of doe-eyed, waiflike, size zero-to-two shop girls in close pursuit.

"Hey, bitch!" Billie called out. "I fucked your fiancé."

Amaryllis flashed Billie a look that translated to seeing garbage on the side of the road. "Maybe you did," she said. "But he would never admit to it." Before disappearing into the crowd, Amaryllis held up the hand that sparkled three-carat proof of March Donaldson's commitment to her.

The confrontation wrecked Billie into a night of excess that would become her all-time personal best—or worst—depending on the view. She went back to being a human Dom Perignon funnel. She inhaled more strawberry coke. She popped Ecstasy. She mixed in some marijuana.

While Sea Biscuit drove and Big Smurf captured grainy stills of the action on his cell phone camera, Billie sucked Domestic Violence in the backseat of his Bentley.

They rode to Gerard Point, a secluded bayside spot that separated Accabonic Harbor from Gardiners Bay. Billie's new hip-hop Svengali carved an old-school prison-style tattoo with the initials FTW between her shoulder blades. It stood for FUCK THE WORLD. She didn't feel a thing. Even when she took off her dress and let all three of them have their kicks with her on the deserted pebble and rock beach.

Everybody had left her—Amy, Todd, March, Liza, Kellyanne. But everybody always did. From high school on, it'd been Billie and Billie alone. It was still that way. She'd show them, though. Hell yeah. She'd show them good. After all, she was Billie Fucking Shelton . . .

Kellyanne

23

When Tucker calmed down, she told him everything.

And in keeping with the kind of man that he was, Tucker wasn't interested in the details. He didn't blame her for the accident. He didn't judge her morals. He didn't lob intrusive questions. It was enough for him that the relationship with Walter Isherwood was behind her.

He only asked Kellyanne to promise that she'd never see Walter again. And if there was any business left to be done in Miami regarding her personal things, Tucker wanted to be the one to handle that.

Kellyanne had never seen him drink before, but tonight he'd consumed three Corona Lights. Meanwhile, she'd sloshed back an entire bottle of Merlot to wine up the courage to tell him about her sordid past. And then he hadn't even blinked once about any of it. Honesty was his steadfast rule. "I don't like secrets," he'd told her.

Now Tucker was turning the 2004 Cosentino bottle upside down and pulling a funny, shocked face on the fact that it was empty. He smiled easily. "Don't get smashed. I've got plans for you later on."

Kellyanne felt exhilarated. Luck was raining down and positively soaking her. Tomorrow she'd be waking up in the arms of Tucker McGraw for the very first time. Because she was here, at Tucker's cozy house in Sag Harbor, watching him shovel in his third piece of the frozen peanut butter pie she'd made. "You're going to get sick!"

"I don't care." He ate some more.

She laughed. They'd enjoyed a wonderful dinner— grilled steaks and salad for them, a hot dog and Tater Tots for Parks, who had fallen asleep earlier watching a Disney Channel marathon of *The Suite Life of Zack and Cody*.

Parks was home now. Safe and sound. He'd been kept over for observation at Southampton Hospital. Though he'd been alert and in typically ebullient spirits just hours after being revived, the doctor had warned of a secondary drowning syndrome that could occur after a submersion accident—as late as seventy-two hours later. And there were other complications to fear—acute respiratory distress, neurological impairment, pneumonia, and bronchospasms.

Beyond the initial ET intubation, the battery of tests on Parks had been frighteningly extensive—an arterial blood gas analysis, chest radiograph, urinalysis, electrolyte-level readings, coagulation profile, a rapid glucose determination, and hypoxia concerns.

Thankfully, every report had been relayed with superlative news. But it never left Kellyanne's awareness that the situation so easily could've gone the other way. Had she been one minute or even thirty seconds later in making that horrible discovery in the pool, had Liza not responded with such immediate competence . . . God, she couldn't bear to think of it.

None of the circumstances had brooked any lingering hostility or resentment from Tucker. He'd been up front about his own relaxed ways with Parks around water—Rae's, too—admitting that the boy's fearless approach to swimming made it easy for them to forget how young he was and how closely he must be watched.

But Kellyanne would never forgive herself for letting Parks out of her sight for those critical minutes. It was the single most shameful mistake she'd ever made in her life. That Tucker had forgiven her almost seemed impossible. And sometimes she wondered if she deserved a man so good.

The Eagles were singing about "Life in the Fast Lane."

Tucker gave her what he called a "ten-cent tour" of the house. They crept into Parks's bedroom and spoke in hushed whispers, giggling like coconspirators as Tucker gingerly removed the Oakley Monster Dogs from the boy's face and returned them to their case on the nightstand.

"He'll wake up and put these on again," Tucker whispered. "But if I hide them, he'll come wake *me* up." He pointed an accusing finger at her. "This is all your fault."

She covered her mouth to muzzle her laughter.

"And how much did those cost anyway?" Tucker asked. "They look expensive."

"Oh, they were only ten dollars," Kellyanne lied.

"*Ten dollars?* That's too much. You're spoiling him. He's only four." Tucker held up three fingers.

"I'd never spend any more than two ninety-nine for something like that."

She prayed he'd never find out that the sunglasses actually cost one hundred dollars.

Tucker showed her the bathroom he intended to remodel, the kitchen that he already had, and the sketches for a wall unit he had in mind for the living room.

It was so easy just being with him. Kellyanne imagined that days, weeks, even months could stretch on in total bliss—with Tucker as her only company. She clung to him as he closed his eyes and listened to Timothy B. Schmit croon "I Can't Tell You Why."

When the ballad ended, he took her hand and led her into the bedroom. A framed portrait from his wedding sat on top of the dresser. He was younger, thinner, with shorter hair. And Holly was beautiful— a stunning brunette in the league of a young Teri Hatcher. They looked happy and hopelessly in love. Kellyanne couldn't stop staring at the photograph.

"You two would've gotten on like a house on fire," Tucker said, wrapping his arms around her from behind.

Kellyanne turned to face him and stroked his cheek, smiling. It was the sweetest sentiment . . . from the sweetest man. She wondered how she'd lived all these years without him in her life.

That night Tucker made love to her four times.

During his first attempt, he came faster than a teenage boy on prom night. For a moment, she worried that he might be upset or embarrassed. But he cracked an easy self-deprecating joke and just held her in his arms until he was ready again.

On the second try, Tucker revealed an amazing

stamina. His skills as a lover were unmatched. He played her body like a flamenco guitar, going back and forth between softly tender and passionately insistent. He whispered sweet endearments, marveling at her beauty and how good she made him feel.

It was as if Kellyanne were a virgin. And maybe she was. Because this had been the first time a man truly communicated love for her in a sexual way. She fell asleep in rapturous exhaustion.

Tucker gently woke her twice in the night to ravish her again, and Kellyanne eagerly indulged his every desire, thrilled to discover that all the pleasure she gave to him came right back to her, only stronger. It was a physical, emotional, and spiritual miracle.

When she opened her eyes the next morning, the first thing she saw was the impossibly tan sole of Parks's little foot. Sometime in the early morning he'd slipped into the bed and found a place between them in the twisted sheets, upside down. One arm was slung over Tucker's leg, the other resting against Kellyanne's calf. He was zonked out on his stomach, exactly like his father.

Tucker stirred and reached out to thread a hand through hers, grinning the grin of a truly satisfied man. He raised his head slightly and glanced back at Parks. "That sneaky rascal. Where'd he come from?"

Kellyanne just smiled and patted the boy's butt.

Parks shifted restlessly in his sleep, nearly kicking both of them in the face.

They laughed together, joking about their narrow escape of two matching black eyes.

He yawned and reached down to stroke his son's back. "That stinker won't stay in his own bed for anything. You better get used to this."

Kellyanne gazed into Tucker's gorgeous eyes. She saw love in them. And she knew the same thing was shining from her own. "Believe me. I want to."

Rae Danes was already apologizing for running late as she entered through the front door. She started a loud rant that began in the living room. "Scott misplaced my keys *again*! I don't know how he stays organized at work. At home he can't put anything back where he found it." When she reached the kitchen, the spiel ended.

Kellyanne and Parks were sitting at the small table, poring over action photographs of Ford Stewart in the September issue of *Eastern Surf* magazine.

"Oh." Tucker's sister looked surprised. And then again, she didn't look surprised at all.

Parks jumped up to embrace her.

Kellyanne smiled. "Tucker just left five minutes ago. Would you like some coffee?"

Rae shook her head. She was four years younger than Tucker, married to a contractor, and lived ten minutes away in an identically framed house with no children and three cats. They were trying for a baby. Six months ago she'd suffered her second miscarriage. She enjoyed a growing business making jewelry with crystals, minerals, and semiprecious stones. Kellyanne was wearing one of her necklaces—a gorgeous sterling piece with glass beads. In look and manner, Rae reminded her of Calista Flockhart.

Kellyanne sat there in an old McGraw's Fish Market T-shirt and a pair of Tucker's boxer shorts, not quite knowing what to say.

Rae dispatched Parks to seek out his backpack and gather the things that he wanted to take with him for the day. "I assume my brother left with a smile on his face this morning."

Kellyanne shrugged sheepishly.

"Good for him. Two years is a long time." Rae glanced at the refrigerator door that was covered with Parks's artwork, then stepped over to straighten out a crooked ocean drawing that depicted three people on the beach—a man, a woman, and a child. She pointed to the scribble of yellow hair on the female figure. "This is you."

As Kellyanne took in the full import of the meaning, an immediate knot of emotion formed in her throat. "Bless his heart." It came out as a whisper. She put both hands to her chest, and a single tear rolled down her cheek.

"Listen," Rae began cautiously, "I don't know what your intentions are, but I do know that this is very sensitive ground you're walking on."

Kellyanne nodded mutely.

"This isn't a summer reality show that you can quit. We're talking about a single father and a little boy here. If you decide to just take off after Labor Day and leave my brother with a stack of medical bills he can't afford and my nephew wondering where the hell you are . . . well, that wouldn't be fair."

"I love them, Rae. And I'm staying. I'm staying for good."

"That's all I need to know, I guess . . . I just had to get that on the table."

Kellyanne absently toyed with the glass beads of the Rae Danes original looped around her neck.

"I have a bracelet that goes with that," Rae said casually. "If you're interested."

"Yes, I am. In fact, I'd love it." The offer touched her. But Kellyanne's thoughts were preoccupied by something else. "What medical bills are you talking about?"

"From the accident," Rae explained. She shook her head, as if embroiled in an internal debate. "Tucker would never mention this. He's too proud. He considers the responsibility completely his own. And he doesn't want you to feel any worse about what happened than you already do."

"Tell me, Rae," Kellyanne insisted.

She bit down on her lower lip and sighed. "Tucker's got medical insurance, but the coverage isn't great. He talked to a friend of mine who works in the hospital's administration office. There could be a bill coming as high as twenty thousand dollars."

Kellyanne could never allow him to absorb that. Not for an accident that happened on her watch. A heartbeat later, she came up with a plan. It'd mean breaking her promise to Tucker. It'd mean doing something she swore she'd never do again. It'd mean beginning the big lies as soon as the morning after.

She arrived at the St. Regis a few minutes past eleven. Check-in time was three, but Walter always booked a day before and after his main itinerary to avoid the hotel clock.

The Astor Suite was the same as she remembered it—small but sumptuous. She loaded a CD into the stereo and played a dulcet, lilting Ingrid Michaelson track over and over again. "All that I know is I'm breathing/All I can do is keep breathing . . ."

When Walter walked through the door, he looked old. Maybe it was the cumulative effects of his sickly wife, addicted son, and stressful career. Or maybe it was the initial juxtapositional shock of see-

ing the sixty-four-year-old after so many uninter-
rupted weeks with the younger, more vital Tucker.

Kellyanne poured him a Dalwhinnie over fresh
ice while he went about the business of putting aside
his luggage, removing his jacket, and loosening his
Hugo Boss tie.

Walter accepted the drink, embraced her, and
kissed her on the mouth.

Instinctively, Kellyanne resisted him. His lips
were fleshy, his breath stale, and his body felt alien
to her.

Walter drew back. "It's been a long time. And after our last conversation, I wasn't sure if you'd be
here or not."

She grinned coyly. "You know what they say
about long-distance relationships."

He took her in appreciatively. "You look beautiful,
as always." Then he fingered the purple silk faille of
her Oscar de la Renta dress. "This is nice." He let a
beat pass as he searched her eyes for something.
"Take it off." His fingers started undoing his belt.

Kellyanne couldn't edit the reluctance on her
face.

"That dress makes you look too much like a lady.
I've got a lady at home. I want to see a naked whore
sucking my cock." Curling his lips into a supercil-
ious smile, he pushed down his pants.

She stripped as if the purpose for doing so were a
clinical one. Off went the de la Renta, the Chantelle
bra, the lacy La Perla boy shorts. But rolling around
in her mind as each piece went down was her reason
for being there. The ultimate goal. She experienced
a flashback to Michael Zanker. But she pushed it out
of mind.

Kellyanne dredged all of her available resources for a final gust of control. It was no wonder they referred to the act as a job. She approached the task as if it were housework—mopping the kitchen floor, scrubbing the toilet, vacuuming the rug. And like those dreary chores, the shit got done if a girl just kept at it.

"Oh, baby, I've missed this!" Walter cried out, climaxing a moment later. He seemed more than satisfied as he murmured breathless praises and finished his Scotch.

She stepped into the powder room and emerged wearing one of the plush terry cloth robes that the hotel provided.

"What'd you do that for?" Walter complained. "I haven't seen you in six weeks. I don't want to look at you all bunched up in a robe. Strut around here bare-ass like God intended."

Kellyanne didn't argue.

"Good girl. No reason to cover up your tits and ass while I'm around." He gave her a scrutinizing gaze. "Have you put on weight?"

She thought about all those seafood pie nights at Nichols with Liza and Harrison. She thought about all the sinful ice cream at the Fudge Company with Parks. "Maybe a little."

He nodded approvingly. "It looks good on you. Come over here."

Thinking fiercely about the larger purpose, she obliged.

Walter began to paw at her, grabbing her buttocks and popping her cheeks until they splotched red. "I see some jiggle. And I think it's all going right here." He laughed.

Kellyanne wanted so badly to slap him across the

face. So it required the full engagement of every cell in her body for her to mollify him with a faint smile and an affectionate hand through his thin silver hair.

He tweaked a nipple. *Hard.*

She winced, giving him a harsh, reproachful look. "Sensitive?"

"You know that hurts."

"It hurts, huh? That's too bad. I wouldn't want to hurt you. Would you want to hurt me?"

Kellyanne felt certain that the question was loaded. She wondered what he knew. Or what he thought he knew. "Why would I want to hurt you, Walter?" Her tone was dull. It was simply the best that she could do. "You take care of me. When I need you, you're there."

"That's right." He pulled her down onto his lap and began stroking the inside of her thigh. "I've always taken good care of you, haven't I?" His tone was softer, bordering on the indulgent.

Kellyanne relaxed a little. Maybe the underlying tension was just the awkwardness of being apart for so long.

Walter played gently with her breast now, circling her areola with his finger. "Have you missed me?"

"Of course." She hooked her arms around his neck and stared plaintively out the window. Miserably, it dawned on her. She couldn't have felt more like a whore if she'd been parading around Hunts Point in fishnets and stilettos. "I have to ask you something . . . a favor."

"What kind of favor?"

She drew back and caressed his cheek as she looked at him, really looked at him, in a way that she probably hadn't since the blush of their first few months together. It was the best fucking acting job she'd ever done in her life. "I feel bad about asking. You've already been so generous to me this summer."

Walter ran a hand across her hip and gave her a comforting smile.

Kellyanne experienced a sweeping sense of shame. There was a wounded tenderness in his eyes, and for a moment, she saw the man who'd endeared himself to her a million years ago, when she'd been schlepping lattes at the Coffee Shop on Union Square.

"I'll give you whatever it is that you need. You know that, right?"

She nodded gratefully, placing a hand on his chest.

He ran his fingers over hers. "You stopped biting your nails." It was strange. There was almost a hint of sadness in his voice.

Kellyanne grinned, admiring them herself. For the first time since grade school, she had significant nail growth. They were short and neat now, but she planned to have a real manicured look one day—something pretty, perhaps a soft pink polish, or maybe even the French style with white tips. Tucker had instilled the will for her to kick the nasty lifetime habit. He made her want every part of herself to be as beautiful as possible.

Thinking of him gave her the courage to make the ask. "I need money, Walter . . . but maybe you can't help me right now. I'm sure with the foreclosure—"

"I'm not strapped for cash."

Kellyanne smiled inwardly. She'd expected him to react that way. There was only one thing left to do—announce how much. Then he'd scratch out a check just to prove that Walter Isherwood, Master of the Universe, was still that, even while facing a brutal downturn in the market. "I need twenty thousand dollars."

Wordlessly, he reached for his jacket. A loose check and a Mont Blanc pen were in the inside pocket. He scribbled out the request, using her slim thigh as an impromptu writing surface. "I assume this is for that widowed fish shack owner you're fucking." His voice was casual.

Kellyanne froze.

Walter signed his name with a bitter flourish, piercing the paper with the pen's sharp point, staining her leg with ink. He pushed her onto the couch and stood up. His hand gripped the check tightly as he waved it in front of her shocked face. "Nothing's free, you manipulative little bitch. If you really want this, you're going to have to earn it. Just like any other whore would."

Everything around her blistered and burned.

"You must think I'm a senile old fart."

"Walter . . . I—"

"Shut the fuck up." He crossed over to the telephone and called the front desk. "Steve Bell's room . . . Thank you . . . Steve, it's Walter . . . I'm staring at her right now . . . Let's have some fun." The receiver went down with a bang. He turned on her viciously.

Kellyanne felt a frisson of absolute fear.

"Did you really think that I'd front the bills for your summer getaway and not keep an eye on you?" He ripped a manila envelope from the side pocket of his luggage and tossed out several long-lens surveillance photographs of Tucker kissing her on the beach.

She looked back at Walter in complete astonishment.

"So what's the money for?" he sneered. "Does this guy need a new fishing boat? Or is he one of these sad-sack Americans without health insurance? I know his kid got waterlogged this week. That must've cost a small fortune at the emergency room."

Kellyanne hated that Walter knew anything at all about Tucker and Parks. They were too good. And he was too full of ugliness.

"You won't last with that loser. A spoiled whore like you? No way. I thought your feminazi friend was teaching you how to live a life on your own. But you can't last ten minutes without a man—a rich one or a poor one."

Kellyanne picked up the de la Renta and covered herself with the dress. It had a high neckline, cap sleeves, and cinched waist. Tucker had seen her wearing it once and told her that she "looked like that lady from the *Breakfast at Tiffany's* movie." At the time, the comparison had thrilled her. But she didn't feel like Audrey Hepburn right now.

Walter waved the check again, taunting her. "I bet another one of these that you'll be back in Miami before Thanksgiving."

She stared at him defiantly. "I'm never coming back. I never was."

His smile was nasty. "That's good. Because I've already got another girl living in the condo. She's driving the same car, too."

"What's her name? I should send her a sympathy card."

He snatched the dress and threw it down onto the floor, leaving her exposed. "I paid for that. I think I'll have it cleaned and take it home to her."

"I don't mind walking out of here naked. As long as I know that I'll never have to see you again." The room was suddenly cold.

"You can still walk out wearing this." He dropped the check onto the cocktail table.

Kellyanne glanced down at it. *Twenty thousand dollars.* She could make all the arrangements with Southampton Hospital's finance department. Tucker would never even have to see the bills.

Three quiet knocks rapped the door.

Walter stepped over to answer it. He put his hand on the latch, then hesitated, turning back. "I think I'm just going to watch. I've never had a front-row seat to see a real whore in action." And then he opened the door.

Steve Bell ran a New York–based real estate group that had invested heavily in two of Walter's Miami developments. He was in his midfifties, thirty pounds overweight, and wore his hair in a stubborn comb-over similar to Donald Trump's.

With him was Vanessa Bradley, a twenty-three-year-old massage therapist who'd recently been voted off the VH-1 reality dating series *Rock of Love,* featuring Bret Michaels of the rock group Poison. She had that porn star chic look—bleached hair, wet lips, and a tanning bed pallor.

"She's the girl I was telling you about," Walter said.

"Show us, baby," Steve prompted.

Vanessa beamed proudly, then bent over to spread her ass cheeks and display her freshly bleached pucker.

Walter poured himself a Scotch and settled back to enjoy the entertainment.

Kellyanne kept telling herself that she was doing it

for Tucker. The constant reminder was the only thing that got her through the ordeal. And somehow she still felt faithful to him because her body never responded to the worshipful and relentless attentions of Steve and Vanessa. It was as if Kellyanne's sexual nerve endings had shut down. Only Tucker could activate that part of her now.

I don't like secrets.

Her heart broke a little bit as the voice of the man she loved so dearly played in her mind. Oh, God! If only they could've started their new life together with nothing but the truth between them.

Everyone had their secrets, though. For Kellyanne, there was the encounter with Michael Zanker and now this last freak show involving Walter. She planned on taking both of them to her grave . . .

Liza

24

Harrison couldn't stop reading the most recent one.

From: travisowen@yahoo.com
To: lizapike@mac.com

Subject: Watch YOU Bleed.

> Shut up, bitch. If I've told you once, I've told
> you a thousand times. But you just won't listen.
> Now it's official. YOU are next.
>
> Travis Owen

Liza regretted ever telling him about the e-mails.
"I think you should have a gun."
At first, she just looked at him. "Harrison, I've
never even held a can of pepper spray. What am I
going to do with a gun?"
"That's what classes are for. And I could show you,
too."

Liza shut off the MacBook Pro and folded down the screen. "If I armed myself every time an angry man with a computer and too much time on his hands sent a hostile message over the Internet, I'd be a one-woman militia."

He nodded with sarcastic enthusiasm and took a frustrated bite out of his Dreesen's doughnut. "I like the sound of that!" He yelled this with his mouth full.

She rolled her eyes and continued to work around him, gathering up her things for the drive into the city.

He watched her while he finished his doughnut, then said, "When are you going to start taking these threats seriously?"

Liza looked at him evenly. "Honestly? Never."

He held her eyes for a moment. His expression was worried.

But she began ticking off an obscene greatest hits list in a tone that conveyed her tedium for the subject. "Let's see . . . in the past, there have been pictures posted of me with a noose around my neck and a muzzle over my mouth. Oh, and there was the lovely gentleman who fantasized about jacking off in my face and then cutting my throat. That's a personal favorite. Apparently, he didn't like my review of *The Passion of the Christ*. Go figure." She rolled her eyes. "I've been lucky enough to achieve a degree of prominence. Add the fact that I'm a woman. Now throw in that I happen to be very opinionated. What do you have? A perfect recipe for moronic and misogynistic vitriol." She moved closer to him and touched his knee for emphasis. "You know this. That's what your film was about."

He groaned at the reference to *Watch Her Bleed*. "I'll never live down that fucking movie where you're concerned."

Liza squeezed his kneecap. "This isn't as sinister as it appears. In some ways, today's Internet is yesterday's bathroom wall." She shrugged. "It's an ugly part of society we just have to deal with."

Harrison still looked worried and refused to relent. "I might buy that if we were talking about some asshole in a chat room. But this guy has your *personal* e-mail address."

"So does a Nigerian who needs my urgent help transferring overseas funds."

He managed a faint smile at her crack about the ubiquitous e-mail scam.

"On the surface, this is disturbing. I'll give you that. The first time one of those e-mails appeared on my BlackBerry . . . it really got to me. But what am I supposed to do? Stop writing? Stop talking?"

There was a stubborn look in his eyes. "*Get a gun.*"

"Oh, God! We're back to that?" Liza walked away from him to fill a glass with ice and pour a Diet Coke. "You're driving me crazy." She said it through gritted teeth, but she kept her tone affectionate. There was a brief silence as she waited for the fizz to die down. "There's no way to police something like this. It's not like I can narrow down the list of possible suspects. Conservatives hate me. Christians hate me. I realize that's oxymoronic, but it's the truth. I mean, aren't they supposed to have love in their hearts for all of God's creatures?" She paused to drink some soda. "Muslims aren't too thrilled with me after my last column. And speaking of guns, the NRA wouldn't mind using me for target practice. Everyone in the adult video industry would cheer if I perished in a tragic dildo accident. Am I leaving anyone out? Oh, yes—Opie and Anthony, the idiot shock jocks. They call their fans '*Pests.*' And they live up to the name. A few months ago, I had to disengage the comment section on my Web site for two weeks because of those fuckers." She sighed. "And did I mention Tom De-Lay?"

His expression remained grim. "It only takes *one* wacko."

Liza gave him a pointed look. "Yes . . . that's becoming abundantly clear."

Harrison was *not* amused.

"*So* protective," she teased. "And we're not even sleeping together yet."

"Yeah, well, whose fault is that?"

She smiled, leaning into the counter in her tight Nudie jeans, setting the angle of her denim butt with perfect precision.

He noticed.

She knew that he would. More Diet Coke went down the hatch. Liza had every intention of doing this relationship right. They'd become friends first. Done. She'd get divorced. Coming soon. They'd start officially dating. After the third dinner, she'd break down and have sex with him. And then she'd probably end up becoming his third wife. God. A man's *third* wife. She never would've imagined that for herself.

Harrison tossed a resentful glance to her bulging Jean Paul Gaultier white leather tote. "I still don't understand why you have to go in to the city."

"I have to print out my book. I can't proofread on the screen. I need the actual pages in my hands for that."

"Use my printer. I've got a brand new HP at the house."

"Not the same," Liza insisted. "I want to use the printer that spit out *Whore,* which is my old clunker at the loft. It's superstitious, I know. But writers have weird little rituals. You know that."

"It's Labor Day," Harrison complained.

"And I'll be back in time for dinner at Della Femina. What time is our reservation again?"

"Eight." His voice was a grumble. He slurped his coffee and gazed out at the pool.

"You know, I should've done this yesterday, but instead I let you drag me to that *awful* party."

Harrison looked put upon. "I'm never going to live that down, either."

"No, you're not. But if it's any consolation, I think I had a better time watching your horrible movie."

Harrison had convinced her to attend P. Diddy's annual White Party at his East Hampton palace. The Labor Day bash was famous for its fall-in-line or hit-the-road fashion edict: ALL WHITE AND ONLY WHITE. From headwear to footwear and everything in between—including jewelry—monochromatic ensembles ruled. Violators were asked to leave by thick-muscled security guards.

Yesterday Billie had been part of this unfortunate group. She'd shown up in a shade of cream and been denied entry. Her escort, Domestic Violence, had gone in without her and latched onto Mariah Carey, who was half dressed and probably exhausted this morning from sucking in her stomach for so long.

Everything had been beautifully decorated and lavishly appointed with food and liquor, but the overall affair was a total ratfuck—shoulder to shoulder with the likes of Tommy Lee, Bruce Willis, Pamela Anderson, and *The View* cast-off Star Jones alongside her is-he-or-isn't-he husband, Al Reynolds.

Harrison had cajoled her into going by talking up what was supposed to have been an incredible fireworks display of white-only explosions. But the East Hampton Town Council had squashed that, citing safety concerns about the light show's potentially drawing too many boats and ships to the rocky waters in the Hedges Bank area.

They'd ended up leaving early and found themselves in the cramped living room of Tucker's house in Sag Harbor. Until his bedtime, Parks had entertained them, parading around in his Oakley Monster Dogs and rhapsodizing about his private surfing lesson from Ford Stewart. And then there'd been too much wine and a spirited couple-against-couple game of Trivial Pursuit.

"I still can't believe we lost that game last night," Harrison said.

Liza smirked as she sipped her Diet Coke. "That's the third time you've mentioned this since showing up here." She checked her watch. "An hour or so ago. Get over it!"

He shook his head. "I can't. We're two smart people. We went to Eastern schools. I'm a filmmaker. You're a writer. And we got our asses handed to us by a girl from Alabama and a guy who rings up dead fish all day. I can't get it out of my mind."

Liza laughed at him. "You're such an intellectual snob. This is not an attractive quality."

"I want a rematch," he said, not hearing her. "I wonder if they're up for it tonight." His face was determined. "Call—"

"I'm not calling anyone. Anyway, I think Kellyanne mentioned something about going to his sister's for a big barbecue."

But Harrison continued to stew. "I'm pissed at myself for missing that baseball question. I *knew* Hank Aaron's final game was with the Milwaukee Brewers. Why'd I say Braves?"

Liza gave him a look. "Don't you have a script to rewrite?"

Jodie Foster had said yes to star in *Mercy Killer,* Harrison's new movie about the New Orleans doctor accused of murdering her patients. Foster wanted a major rewrite to punch up the film's female point of view. Liza's publisher, media mogul Toni Valentine, had put the project on the fast track at Valentine Features after the two-time Academy Award–winner signed on.

In *Watch Her Bleed,* Harrison had depicted strong, accomplished, ambitious, and opinionated women as murder victims in scenes of brutal, almost orgiastic violence. Now he was—sort of—dating one in Liza. He'd be directing one in Jodie Foster. And he'd also be answering to one in Toni Valentine. The irony made Liza smile to herself.

"I should go." She kissed him on the cheek and slung the heavy Gaultier tote over her shoulder.

"Think about the gun." He was serious.

"No." And so was she. "Besides, if I had one, I'd probably shoot *you* with it right now. And that's not the point, is it?" Liza started for the door. "I'll meet you at the restaurant."

"Call from the road to let me know that you're okay."

She smiled at him. "Get some work done."

There was a glint in his eyes as she mentioned this.

Liza hesitated. She became suspicious. "What's going on?"

"I got an e-mail from Toni Valentine early this morning."

"On Labor Day? Does she ever *not* work?"

He shrugged. "I guess there's a reason why some people become moguls." He gestured toward her.

Liza scoffed at the implication. "Please. Compared to Toni I'm just a girl with a few part-time jobs. What'd she say?"

"She suggested you as a script doctor for *Mercy Killer*." The look on his face told her that he liked the idea.

Liza was shocked. "*Me?* What do I know about scripts? I've never written a screenplay!"

Harrison waved off the concern. "Doesn't matter. You have a strong female voice. Toni thinks that bringing you on board will make Jodie happy, too." He paused a beat. "And I really like the idea of us working together to create something." His excitement was real.

"Let me think about it." But in her mind Liza already knew that the answer would be yes. The movie would film on location in New Orleans. With preproduction, production, and post, that'd mean several months there. It'd also mean quitting *The Roundtable*. But it was time. Her relationship with Tom Shapiro had deteriorated for inexplicable reasons. And frankly, the he said/she said routine with March Donaldson had grown tiresome.

Harrison followed her out to the Lexus. "I don't like it that you're driving back and forth alone. I could ride along and keep—"

"Harrison, you have to stop. If I do it your way, I'll end up like Tuesday Kent."

His face was blank.

"The Baby Girl Diaries."

The light of recognition sparkled in his eyes. "Yeah, of course. Whatever happened to her?"

"She let Internet threats get to her to such a degree that she had a breakdown. Her career disappeared overnight. And she ended up moving back in with her parents. Is that what you want for me? Because I'd rather take my chances with a mystery psycho than live with two known crazies."

He stepped away from the SUV, shaking his head and smiling as she drove away.

Before she reached Montauk Highway, Liza was cell-to-cell with Kellyanne. "Harrison is *wrecked* about losing Trivial Pursuit last night."

"Oh, my God," Kellyanne replied. "Are you serious? Bless his heart. Tucker's acting just as stupid, though. He's strutting around like he's the new Super Bowl champ."

"Harrison's a bigger idiot. He wanted a rematch tonight."

"Well, I think they're even. Tucker wants to win again just to prove it wasn't a fluke. Men!"

"Correction—*boys*!"

Liza and Kellyanne laughed, then glossed over the subject of Billie, whom they both considered a lost cause. She'd moved out of the summer share and cut off both of them after the confrontation in the hospital. Now she was shacking up with Domestic Violence at his New Jersey compound. Her lifestyle had become anathema to them. Perhaps it always had been.

Liza hung up and drove the rest of the way in indulgent silence, basking in the euphoria that was the relief of knowing her book was *done*. What a fantastic feeling!

She was ferociously proud of the manuscript, too. The contents were certain to stir controversy. Liza anticipated that many women would take umbrage at the notion of her calling out all of them as stupid girls. But she included herself in that group. Liza owned the label for some of her more fucked-up choices in life. And any woman out there who couldn't do the same was just floating down a river called Denial.

As she turned the key to let herself into the loft, Liza heard the throbbing pulse of a dance beat. Instantly, she bristled with anger. If her fucking husband was having some kind of party . . .

But the downstairs living and kitchen areas were empty. Accepting reality but feeling nothing, she rolled her eyes. So the party was going on upstairs. Big shock.

Liza hadn't spoken to Justin in almost a month. There was nothing to say. Her focus had been finishing her book by Labor Day. And her next goal would be finishing this marriage by Christmas.

She glowered at the spiral staircase. Her office was upstairs. And she'd have to walk through the bedroom to get there. Putting her things down on the console table, she decided to have a drink and wait. But after a moment of smoldering rage, she reconsidered. This was her goddamn apartment! Justin and his groupie whore could go somewhere else.

She snatched her tote and started up, determined to print her manuscript and get the hell out. The Euro disco music boomed louder and louder.

And then Liza saw them . . . in her bedroom . . . on her bed. The shock knocked the breath from her body. For long seconds, she couldn't look away.

"Say it!" Justin panted. "I want to hear you say it!"

"You wear the ring, but he fucks me," Tom Shapiro grunted.

"Louder!" Justin demanded, tearing into him as he pinned down Tom's arms. "Louder, or I'll stop!"

"You wear the ring, but he fucks me!" Tom cried out.

"That's what you should tell the bitch next time you see her," Justin growled.

And by then Liza was quietly descending the stairs. They never even knew she was there.

She made it back to East Hampton in record time, driving like a demon and blasting Marie Digby's acoustic version of Rihanna's "Umbrella" like a broken record. As the betrayal and her own ignorance burned deeper and deeper into her brain, a strange kind of madness began to set in.

Marie's luminous voice and the trite-but-true lyric had saved her from insanity. "Know that we still have each other/You can stand under my umbrella . . ."

All she could think about was Harrison—getting back to him in the Hamptons, working with him on *Mercy Killer,* and one day . . . *marrying* him on her second try. He was her best friend. And she was his. The first time around, Liza had missed looking for that essential ingredient. *Stupid girl.*

Her stomach tightened with anxiety. Almost three hours without her BlackBerry. That was a lifetime record. But in her agitated haste to leave the TriBeCa loft, Liza had left it on the console table of the entryway, only to discover her mistake more than halfway to Long Island. No doubt Harrison had been trying to reach her numerous times.

Liza dashed inside through the front door to call

him from the landline and put his worried mind at ease. She stopped suddenly. Her heart bolted in her chest.

There was a stranger in the living room. A thin, handsome, college-age boy with sandy-colored hair. He wore jeans and a Hunter College Hawks T-shirt. His blue-green eyes zeroed in on her with a disturbing intensity. "I'm Travis Owen." The voice was flat.

Everything that happened next was like a reenactment from the movie she hated . . . by the man she loved. And like she always did whenever under attack, she fought back. Because when they found her dead, as she knew that they would, she wanted them to know . . .

Liza Pike was a fighter . . .

Epilogue

Faye Hudson was startled by the sound of a splash as she prepared to read Page Six. Rising with a start, she peered out at the pool.

The sight provided instant calm and momentary comfort. It was Annie, the golden retriever, dog paddling away on her regular morning swim. Some things *were* the same at this house on North Bay Lane.

"Excuse me, Miss Hudson?"

She turned expectantly on Scott Danes, the contractor leading the retinue of workers rebuilding the living room. His brother-in-law was the future husband of Kellyanne Downey, the woman who had discovered the body of Liza Pike. It was a small world in the Hamptons.

"I just want to be clear. You want *all* of the living room furniture taken away?"

She nodded. Symbolically, it was important to her that everything be stripped—the floors, the walls, even the vents and fixtures. Would it make a difference? Could this place ever feel like home again? Or was it destined to always give off these horrible crime-scene vibrations?

Scott gestured to the *New York Post* that lay open at the foot of Faye's tufted recamier. "I picked up that newspaper this morning and found myself reading about my future sister-in-law." He grinned ironically. "Kind of strange."

Faye sighed deeply, bracing herself to read the same column. Back when the boldfaced names had been just that—only boldfaced names—her Page Six ritual was innocent fun, like eating candy in the morning.

But now there were real people behind the gossip tidbits. Liza Pike, Kellyanne Downey, and Billie Shelton. Faye had met them. Those girls had called her house home. They had *lived* here . . . in every sense of the word.

Memorial Day to Labor Day. It was roughly just three months. It marked only one season. And yet so much had changed for all of them in that time. She found it nearly impossible to fathom.

Faye Hudson no longer relished Page Six. In fact, right now she positively dreaded it. But people said that the worst aspects of a day were the ones to get rid of first. So Faye took that wisdom to heart, picked up the *New York Post,* and began to read . . .

The Killing Kind

The gory details continue to pile up in the bizarre Labor Day stalking/murder of feminist firebrand and media supergirl **Liza Pike.** In a sick twist on art imitating life, Hunter College film major Leonard Tidwell, 21, took his cues from a popular horror film and stabbed Pike to death in her East Hampton summer share. This followed months of cyber-threats delivered under the moniker Travis Owen, also the character name of the psychotic killer who targets outspoken and accomplished women for murder in *Watch Her Bleed,* last year's $113 million blockbuster from writer/director **Harrison Beck.** A Hunter College classmate of Tidwell's gave one of our reporters this nugget: "He was totally obsessed with that movie and saw it, like, at least a hundred times. I thought he was weird, but I never thought he'd go out and kill somebody." Pike's final book, *Stupid Girls*—completed shortly before her death—is set for release this fall.

No more Drama for this Baby Mama

Fifteen-minute scandal queen **Kellyanne Downey** (of last summer's reality bomb *Soul Mates*) is now proud mommy to Holly Elizabeth McGraw. The teeny-tot arrived two months early, but mother and daughter are doing fine at Southampton Hospital. Downey will marry Long Island native **Tucker McGraw** later this summer. The baby is lovingly named after McGraw's deceased first wife and Downey's close friend, the late feminist author **Liza Pike.** Also on the horizon for Downey is a new weekly talk show on Hamptons Plum TV. *Coffee on the Beach* will pair the Southern beauty with young surfer **Ford Stewart** for a laid-back gabfest on the sand.

My crazy Ex-Rock Star

Webster's should declare **Billie Shelton** the new synonym for *over.* She's fresh off an embarrassing showcase at Lotus, where the troubled label-less rock singer sleepwalked to crowd jeers through a lame hip-hop set alongside rapper/producer/ex-con

Domestic Violence. Now comes word of her arrest for assaulting former manager **Amy Dando** with a liquor bottle in the lobby of Dando's office building on lower Broadway. Shelton was released after posting $55,000 bail. Cocaine and opiates were found in Shelton's system after her arrest.

We Hear

That **Ashlee Simpson**'s fire-breathing **White Tiger**–produced single "Who Is She?" is a lock to top the charts . . . That **Tom Shapiro,** host of CNBC's *The Roundtable,* just inked a book deal with media mogul **Toni Valentine** to answer all those curious questions about his personal life . . . That last week's death of Miami real estate developer **Walter Isherwood** at the St. Regis was discreetly handled by hotel management so as not to add to his wife's grief . . . That the engagement between political talking stud **March Donaldson** and Stella McCartney PR priestess **Amaryllis Hartman** is officially kaput . . . That FDNY hunk and young widower **Justin Beal** is shopping for rings and close to popping the question to *The Sex Factor* authoress **Pila Anderson** . . . That **Jodie Foster** dropping out of the Hurricane Katrina medical drama *Mercy Killer* has put the troubled Valentine Features film out of its misery and permanently shut down production.

Sightings

Reality TV producer **Brad "Bonzi" Lucas** complaining to others on line for the loo at Bungalow 8 about his ouster from Fox . . . Manorexic male model and oil heir **Teddy Easton** cycling on the George Washington Bridge . . . Jewelry designer **Rae Danes** launching her exclusive line of crystal charm bracelets at Henri Bendel . . . Fashion stylist **K.K. Vermorel** huddling with **Jenny Barlow** at Bette to strategize the star's look for Cannes . . . New Hollywood scribe **Shayne Cutter** celebrating his first two-film pact with the Weinstein Company at Sunset Beach on Shelter Island . . . Olympic Records honcho **Todd Bana** leaving Whiskey Blue with a gorgeous blonde on each arm . . . Film director **Harrison Beck** knocking back Scotch after Scotch alone at Murf's Backstreet Tavern in Sag Harbor until closing time.

Read on for an exclusive excerpt
from J. J. Salem's next book

The Strip

Coming soon in hardcover

from St. Martin's Press

Prologue

There were definite upsides to fucking a married man. After the act, he didn't roll over and go to sleep. He didn't reach for the remote to zone out on ESPN. And he was usually gone before unsexy concerns—his laundry, his dinner, his latest golf score—rose up to kill the mood. Yes, an *unavailable* man could be very hot indeed.

"Looking for these?"

Gucci Marlowe glanced up.

Mike Burke was twirling her Cosabella thong around his index finger and flashing a dimpled smile that made her want to forget the dead body she was leaving him for.

"Keep them as a souvenir." She scooted on her skin-tight True Religion jeans, stepped into her Taryn Rose snake-embossed booties, and slipped a vintage Peter Frampton rock tee over her head.

Mike made a show out of bringing her panties to his nostrils and inhaling them like an addictive drug.

Gucci laughed as she vaulted into the bathroom to

swipe on some lip gloss and finger-comb her hair into place. To be fair, a woman running on almost no sleep and wearing yesterday's clothes should not look so goddamn good. Memo to the women queued up for the next round of Botox: The real secret was in multiple orgasms.

All of a sudden, Gucci's gaze fell on a loose photograph propped up against the mirror. Mike's kids—two boys, both under ten. They looked just like their cheating bastard father. She wondered if they would grow up to do the same thing one day.

Gucci had met Mike while playing a game of craps at Caesar's Palace. He flirted. She flirted back. The action moved to the bar at Pure and an hour after that, upstairs to his room. A year later, they were still meeting whenever business brought him to Las Vegas, which was every four to six weeks. The fact that their encounters seemed to grow more passionate and satisfying made it difficult to stop.

"You don't play fair," Mike called out.

Gucci finished a quick Listerine rinse before answering. "How's that?"

"You insist that I turn my phone off, but yours stays on."

She strutted back to retrieve her Kooba bag and gave him a withering look as she slung it over her shoulder. "The day I have to sit around like a little mouse while you lie to your wife is the last day you'll ever see me naked."

He let out a sigh and gave her a sexy, irresistible smile. "Can't we at least have breakfast? I feel so used."

"There's a corpse at the Wynn. Probably a murder victim. I don't have time for pancakes." She started for the door.

"What am I supposed to do about this?" He pointed to the impressive hard-on tenting the top sheet that was loosely draped over his lean and tan body.

Gucci's eyes skated from Mike's face to his crotch and back again. "Not my pig, not my farm." And then she winked and walked out.

She was stalking through the Wynn lobby on her way to the Resort building elevators when Jagger Smith fell into step beside her. His shit-eating grin triggered an instant of pure irritation. "Don't start."

"That outfit looks familiar." One beat. "Wait. Now I remember where I've seen it. On you. *Yesterday*."

Gucci mock-laughed. "God, you kill me. I should put in a word to Steve Wynn. Maybe he'll cancel Danny Gans and set you up as the comedy headliner."

Jagger laughed. "Well, at least one of us got lucky last night. David twisted his knee. He ended up popping an Oxy and going straight to bed."

"Is he okay?"

Jagger shrugged. "Good enough to dance tonight. Nobody puts Baby in a corner."

Gucci gave him a wry glance. "Such dedication."

Jagger was young, black, and so ridiculously good-looking that Blair Underwood could be his ugly brother. He reached the first available elevator and gallantly gestured for Gucci to step inside first. "Which floor?"

"Thirty-six-forty-one."

"I think it's more fear than dedication," Jagger said. "The Strip's new diva goes through dancers like Douglas goes through wives. Last week she fired a guy for missing a step in a run-through."

Gucci sighed. "The life of a showgirl."

"It's not all bright lights and sequins," Jagger put in.

She laughed a little as the elevator continued its ascent. Jagger had been her partner for just over a year, and their bond was already sealed in the crucible of annoying department bullshit. Being a woman. Being attractive. Being black. Being gay. Together they covered almost every boneheaded -ism and intolerance. But they were a stronger team for it.

A thick uniformed patrol officer stood guard at the entrance to the suite and wordlessly handed Gucci a clipboard that held the crime-scene log.

She scribbled her initials and badge number on the second line. The first name on the sheet belonged to Kirby Douglas, the coroner.

Jagger signed in next, took note of the first to arrive, and grinned. "Play nice, Detective. He's going through a divorce."

"Yeah, well, until the asshole stops getting married, he'll always be going through one," Gucci cracked as she ducked under the crime-scene barricade tape and ventured inside the room.

A moment later, a torrent of sensations hit her, and they were all so disgustingly familiar . . . the loud silence, the acrid death smell that reeked of corroded copper and cheap quick-sale hamburger, the faint whiff of gunpowder.

Gucci could hear her own heart beating as she surveyed the carnage on the bed. The victim was a white twenty-something male—six-foot-four, gorgeous, chiseled-bodied, and naked.

Kirby stepped toward the body and pointed to the forehead. "See the stellate pattern? Muzzle was held against the skin. Single shot. No exit wound. Dude's got a thick skull."

When Jagger spoke, it was a whisper. "That's Cam Lawford."

"Never heard of him," Kirby said dismissively. "Let me guess—you recognize him from gay porn."

Jagger turned to address Gucci. "He was a football star at Penn State. Lasted half a season with the Dolphins before a career-ending injury."

Kirby gestured to the semen stains on the sheets. "He went out with a bang in more ways than one. And with a cock that size, who wouldn't?"

"Interesting observation," Jagger teased. "Is there something you need to tell us?"

"I'm just saying." An instant splotch of red stained Kirby's cheeks. He possessed a supreme arrogance out of variance with his modest height, receding hairline, and admitted emotional/intellectual limitations.

Gucci ignored him as she surveyed the scene. The comforter and blanket were slung onto the floor. The sheets were twisted into a passionate mess. A half-burned lime-basil-and-mandarin Jo Malone candle sat on the nightstand, along with an iPod stereo paused on Diana Krall's "Peel Me a Grape," an empty bottle of Ferrari-Carano Chardonnay, and next to that, a single wine glass.

She left to check the bathroom and closet, discovering an elaborate male toiletries kit and an expensive set of street clothes—black Armani slacks and an abstract print Etro shirt.

"He was a gigolo," Gucci said matter-of-factly.

Jagger raised an eyebrow.

Kirby laughed to himself. "Well, if he ended up like this, I guess she didn't come."

Gucci just stared impassively at the Andy Warhol

Flowers print that adorned the salmon-colored wall. "No cell phone?"

Kirby shrugged. "I just got here myself."

Gucci reached into her bag and fished out a pair of latex gloves. "This is a seduction setting. The cell is out of sight and on silent." She stepped back into the bathroom and carefully retrieved an iPhone from the side pocket of the toiletries case.

Jagger suited up with latex gloves, too, then splayed out his hand.

Gucci turned the device over. "You're faster with these fucking things."

Jagger worked the touch screen with expert, nimble fingers. "There was one missed call from a Jennifer Payne. Let me check out his calendar . . . three appointments in the last two days—Jennifer, Billie, and Kristin . . . I'm in the contact links now . . . mobile numbers, e-mail addresses, lists of their favorite things . . . Jennifer likes to be dominated, for example . . . Billie's into erotic massage . . . Kristin loves anal."

Gucci took in a deep breath. "He was a smart man-whore. At the end of the day, it's all about customer service." She stepped back into the main part of the suite.

"*Jesus Christ*," Jagger hissed, following her.

"He was a client, too?" Kirby cracked. "This guy really was good in bed."

Jagger continued working the iPhone obsessively. "No, when I say Billie and Kristin, I mean *Billie Shelton* and *Kristin Fox*."

"Speak of the devil," Gucci said, gazing out the floor-to-ceiling window to see a mega-sized billboard advertising Billie Shelton's wildly successful *Rebirth* show at the London Hotel.

"Who the hell is Kristin Fox?" Kirby asked, unaware of anyone who didn't scream back from a headline on the front page of his daily sixty-second peek at *The Drudge Report*.

"She's a bestselling novelist," Jagger offered. "That HBO show *Come to Bed* is based on her book."

"The one about all the suburbanites fucking each other?" Kirby asked.

Jagger nodded.

Gucci stepped closer to the bed and stared at the face of Cam Lawford. His eyes were open, seemingly looking through her and on into infinity. She did not look away. A powerful feeling seized her gut. It was the kind of instinct that never let her down.

"I know that look," Jagger said.

Gucci continued staring into Cam Lawford's shocked and dead eyes. What happened here was an intimate murder. There was no struggle. He was at his most vulnerable. And he never saw it coming. "One of those bitches killed this man."